Dear Reader:

I don't have hobbies. I have passions. Gardening is one of my passions, and spring—when it's time to get out there and dig in the dirt—is my favorite season.

I live in the woods, in the foothills of the Blue Ridge Mountains, and my land is rough and rocky. A tough field for a passionate gardener to play in. I've solved part of the problem with many raised beds, but the rocks still find a way. Every spring, it's a battle—me against rock, and most years I win.

I'm fortunate to be married to a man who enjoys yard work. Because if I want to plant a daffodil bulb in the stony ground, I've got to call my guy with the pick. But it's worth it. Every spring when I see my daffodils popping, watch my willows greening, see the perennials I've planted in place of rock spearing up, I'm happy. Just as I'm happy to get out there with my spade and cultivator to start prepping the soil for what I might plant this season.

It's hard, sweaty, dirty work, and it pleases me to do it, year after year. For me, a garden is always a work in progress, never quite finished, and always a delight to the eye. Nearly twenty years ago, my guy planted a tulip magnolia in front of our house. Now, every spring, my bedroom windows are full of those gorgeous pink blooms. And when they fade and drop, something else will flower to make me smile.

At the end of a long day, whether it's writing or gardening, or just dealing with the dozens of chores life hands out, there's nothing quite like a walk in the garden to soothe the mind and heart.

So plant some flowers, watch them grow. The rewards far outreach the toil.

NORA ROBERTS

From #1 *New York Times* bestselling author Nora Roberts comes the first novel in the new In the Garden trilogy. Against the backdrop of a house steeped in history and a thriving new gardening business, three women unearth the memories of the past and uncover a dangerous secret.

A Harper has always lived at Harper House, the centuries-old mansion just outside of Memphis. And for as long as anyone alive remembers, the ghostly Harper Bride has walked the halls, singing lullabies at night. . . .

Trying to escape the ghosts of the past, young widow Stella Rothchild, along with her two energetic little boys, has moved back to her roots in southern Tennessee—and into her new life at Harper House and the In the Garden nursery. She isn't intimidated by the house—nor its mistress, local legend Roz Harper. Despite a reputation for being difficult, Roz has been nothing but kind to Stella, offering her a comfortable new place to live and a challenging new job as manager of the flourishing nursery. As Stella settles comfortably into her new life, she finds a nurturing friendship with Roz and with expectant mother Hayley. And she discovers a fierce attraction with ruggedly handsome landscaper Logan Kitridge.

But someone isn't happy about the budding romance . . . the Harper Bride. As the women dig into the history of Harper House, they discover that grief and rage have kept the Bride's spirit alive long past her death. And now, she will do anything to destroy the passion that Logan and Stella share. . . .

> **"Nora Roberts . . . knows exactly what to write to please her legion of fans."**
> —*Fort Worth Star Telegram*

Turn the page for a complete list of titles by Nora Roberts and J. D. Robb from The Berkley Publishing Group. . . .

continued . . .

NORA ROBERTS

BLUE DAHLIA

JOVE BOOKS, NEW YORK

THE BERKLEY PUBLISHING GROUP
Published by the Penguin Group
Penguin Group (USA) Inc.
375 Hudson Street, New York, New York 10014, USA
Penguin Group (Canada), 10 Alcorn Avenue, Toronto, Ontario M4V 3B2, Canada
(a division of Pearson Penguin Canada Inc.)
Penguin Books Ltd., 80 Strand, London WC2R 0RL, England
Penguin Group Ireland, 25 St. Stephen's Green, Dublin 2, Ireland
(a division of Penguin Books Ltd.)
Penguin Group (Australia), 250 Camberwell Road, Camberwell, Victoria 3124, Australia
(a division of Pearson Australia Group Pty. Ltd.)
Penguin Books India Pvt. Ltd., 11 Community Centre, Panchsheel Park, New Delhi—110 017,
India
Penguin Group (NZ), Cnr. Airborne and Rosedale Roads, Albany, Auckland 1310, New Zealand
(a division of Pearson New Zealand Ltd.)
Penguin Books (South Africa) (Pty.) Ltd., 24 Sturdee Avenue, Rosebank, Johannesburg 2196,
South Africa

Penguin Books Ltd., Registered Offices: 80 Strand, London WC2R 0RL, England

This is a work of fiction. Names, characters, places, and incidents either are the product of the author's imagination or are used fictitiously, and any resemblance to actual persons, living or dead, business establishments, events, or locales is entirely coincidental.

BLUE DAHLIA

A Jove Book / published by arrangement with the author.

PRINTING HISTORY
Jove edition / November 2004

ISBN: 0-515-13855-X

JOVE®
Jove Books are published by The Berkley Publishing Group,
a division of Penguin Group (USA) Inc.,
375 Hudson Street, New York, New York 10014.
JOVE is a registered trademark of Penguin Group (USA) Inc.
The "J" design is a trademark belonging to Penguin Group (USA) Inc.

PRINTED IN THE UNITED STATES OF AMERICA

10 9 8 7 6 5 4 3 2 1

For Dan and Jason.
You may be men, but you'll always be my boys.

If the plant root ball is tightly packed with roots,
these should be gently loosened.
They need to spread out after planting,
rather than continue to grow in a tight mass.

—From the *Treasury of Gardening*,
on transplanting potted plants

And 'tis my faith that every flower
Enjoys the air it breathes.

—Wordsworth

PROLOGUE

❧

Memphis, Tennessee
August 1892

BIRTHING A BASTARD WASN'T IN THE PLANS. WHEN she'd learned she was carrying her lover's child, the shock and panic turned quickly to anger.

There were ways of dealing with it, of course. A woman in her position had contacts, had avenues. But she was afraid of them, nearly as afraid of the abortionists as she was of what was growing, unwanted, inside her.

The mistress of a man like Reginald Harper couldn't afford pregnancy.

He'd kept her for nearly two years now, and kept her well. Oh, she knew he kept others—including his wife—but they didn't concern her.

She was still young, and she was beautiful. Youth and beauty were products that could be marketed. She'd done so, for nearly a decade, with steely mind and heart. And she'd profited by them, polished them with the grace and charm she'd learned by watching and emulating the fine ladies who'd visited the grand house on the river where her mother had worked.

She'd been educated—a bit. But more than books and music, she'd learned the arts of flirtation.

She'd sold herself for the first time at fifteen and had pocketed knowledge along with the coin. But prostitution wasn't her goal, any more than domestic work or trudging off to the factory day after day. She knew the difference between whore and mistress. A whore traded quick and cold sex for pennies and was forgotten before the man's fly was buttoned again.

But a mistress—a clever and successful mistress—offered romance, sophistication, conversation, gaiety along with the commodity between her legs. She was a companion, a wailing wall, a sexual fantasy. An ambitious mistress knew to demand nothing and gain much.

Amelia Ellen Conner had ambitions.

And she'd achieved them. Or most of them.

She'd selected Reginald quite carefully. He wasn't handsome or brilliant of mind. But he was, as her research had assured her, very rich and very unfaithful to the thin and proper wife who presided over Harper House.

He had a woman in Natchez, and it was said he kept another in New Orleans. He could afford another, so Amelia set her sights on him. Wooed and won him.

At twenty-four, she lived in a pretty house on South Main and had three servants of her own. Her wardrobe was full of beautiful clothes, and her jewelry case sparkled.

It was true she wasn't received by the fine ladies she'd once envied, but there was a fashionable half world where a woman of her station was welcome. Where *she* was envied.

She threw lavish parties. She traveled. She *lived.*

Then, hardly more than a year after Reginald had tucked her into that pretty house, her clever, craftily designed world crashed.

She would have hidden it from him until she'd gathered the courage to visit the red-light district and end the thing. But he'd caught her when she was violently ill, and he'd studied her face with those dark, shrewd eyes.

And he'd known.

He'd not only been pleased but had forbidden her to end

the pregnancy. To her shock, he'd bought her a sapphire bracelet to celebrate her situation.

She hadn't wanted the child, but he had.

So she began to see how the child could work for her. As the mother of Reginald Harper's child—bastard or no— she would be cared for in perpetuity. He might lose interest in coming to her bed as she lost the bloom of youth, as beauty faded, but he would support her, and the child.

His wife hadn't given him a son. But she might. She *would.*

Through the last chills of winter and into the spring, she carried the child and planned for her future.

Then something strange happened. It moved inside her. Flutters and stretches, playful kicks. The child she hadn't wanted became her child.

It grew inside her like a flower that only she could see, could feel, could know. And so did a strong and terrible love.

Through the sweltering, sticky heat of the summer she bloomed, and for the first time in her life she knew a passion for something other than herself and her own comfort.

The child, her son, needed her. She would protect it with all she had.

With her hands resting on her great belly, she supervised the decorating of the nursery. Pale green walls and white lace curtains. A rocking horse imported from Paris, a crib handmade in Italy.

She tucked tiny clothes into the miniature wardrobe. Irish and Breton lace, French silks. All were monogrammed with exquisite embroidery with the baby's initials. He would be James Reginald Conner.

She would have a son. Something at last of her own. Someone, at last, to love. They would travel together, she and her beautiful boy. She would show him the world. He would go to the best schools. He was her pride, her joy, and her heart. And if through that steamy summer, Reginald came to the house on South Main less and less, it was just as well.

He was only a man. What grew inside her was a son.

She would never be alone again.

When she felt the pangs of labor, she had no fear. Through the sweaty hours of pain, she held one thing in the front of her mind. Her James. Her son. Her child.

Her eyes blurred with exhaustion, and the heat, a living, breathing monster, was somehow worse than the pain.

She could see the doctor and the midwife exchange looks. Grim, frowning looks. But she was young, she was healthy, and she *would* do this thing.

There was no time; hour bled into hour with gaslight shooting flickering shadows around the room. She heard, through the waves of exhaustion, a thin cry.

"My son." Tears slid down her cheeks. "My son."

The midwife held her down, murmuring, murmuring, "Lie still now. Drink a bit. Rest now."

She sipped to soothe her fiery throat, tasted laudanum. Before she could object, she was drifting off, deep down. Far away.

When she woke, the room was dim, the draperies pulled tight over the windows. When she stirred, the doctor rose from his chair, came close to lift her hand, to check her pulse.

"My son. My baby. I want to see my baby."

"I'll send for some broth. You slept a long time."

"My son. He'll be hungry. Have him brought to me."

"Madam." The doctor sat on the side of the bed. His eyes seemed very pale, very troubled. "I'm sorry. The child was stillborn."

What clutched her heart was monstrous, vicious, rending her with burning talons of grief and fear. "I heard him cry. This is a lie! Why are you saying such an awful thing to me?"

"She never cried." Gently, he took her hands. "Your labor was long and difficult. You were delirious at the end of it. Madam, I'm sorry. You delivered a girl, stillborn."

She wouldn't believe it. She screamed and raged and

wept, and was sedated only to wake to scream and rage and weep again.

She hadn't wanted the child. And then she'd wanted nothing else.

Her grief was beyond name, beyond reason.

Grief drove her mad.

ONE

Southfield, Michigan
September 2001

SHE BURNED THE CREAM SAUCE. STELLA WOULD always remember that small, irritating detail, as she would remember the roll and boom of thunder from the late-summer storm and the sound of her children squabbling in the living room.

She would remember the harsh smell, the sudden scream of the smoke alarms, and the way she'd mechanically taken the pan off the burner and dumped it in the sink.

She wasn't much of a cook, but she was—in general—a *precise* cook. For this welcome-home meal, she'd planned to prepare the chicken Alfredo, one of Kevin's favorites, from scratch and match it with a nice field greens salad and some fresh, crusty bread with pesto dipping sauce.

In her tidy kitchen in her pretty suburban house she had all the ingredients lined up, her cookbook propped on its stand with the plastic protector over the pages.

She wore a navy-blue bib apron over her fresh pants and shirt and had her mass of curling red hair bundled up on top of her head, out of her way.

She was getting started later than she'd hoped, but work had been a madhouse all day. All the fall flowers at the garden center were on sale, and the warm weather brought customers out in droves.

Not that she minded. She loved the work, absolutely loved her job as manager of the nursery. It felt good to be back in the thick of it, full-time now that Gavin was in school and Luke old enough for a play group. How in the world had her baby grown up enough for first grade?

And before she knew it, Luke would be ready for kindergarten.

She and Kevin should start getting a little more proactive about making that third child. Maybe tonight, she thought with a smile. When she got into *that* final and very personal stage of her welcome-home plans.

As she measured ingredients, she heard the crash and wail from the next room. Glutton for punishment, she thought as she dropped what she was doing to rush in. Thinking about having another baby when the two she had were driving her crazy.

She stepped into the room, and there they were. Her little angels. Gavin, sunny blond with the devil in his eyes, sat innocently bumping two Matchbox cars into each other while Luke, his bright red hair a dead ringer for hers, screamed over his scattered wooden blocks.

She didn't have to witness the event to *know*. Luke had built; Gavin had destroyed.

In their house it was the law of the land.

"Gavin. Why?" She scooped up Luke, patted his back. "It's okay, baby. You can build another."

"My house! My house!"

"It was an accident," Gavin claimed, and that wicked twinkle that made a bubble of laughter rise to her throat remained. "The car wrecked it."

"I bet the car did—after you aimed it at his house. Why can't you play nice? He wasn't bothering you."

"I was playing. He's just a baby."

"That's right." And it was the look that came into her eyes that had Gavin dropping his. "And if you're going to be a baby, too, you can be a baby in your room. Alone."

"It was a stupid house."

"Nuh-uh! Mom." Luke took Stella's face in both his hands, looked at her with those avid, swimming eyes. "It was good."

"You can build an even better one. Okay? Gavin, leave him alone. I'm not kidding. I'm busy in the kitchen, and Daddy's going to be home soon. Do you want to be punished for his welcome home?"

"No. I can't do *anything*."

"That's too bad. It's really a shame you don't have any toys." She set Luke down. "Build your house, Luke. Leave his blocks alone, Gavin. If I have to come in here again, you're not going to like it."

"I want to go *outside*!" Gavin mourned at her retreating back.

"Well, it's raining, so you can't. We're all stuck in here, so behave."

Flustered, she went back to the cookbook, tried to clear her head. In an irritated move, she snapped on the kitchen TV. God, she missed Kevin. The boys had been cranky all afternoon, and she felt rushed and harried and overwhelmed. With Kevin out of town these last four days she'd been scrambling around like a maniac. Dealing with the house, the boys, her job, all the errands alone.

Why was it that the household appliances waited, just waited, to go on strike when Kevin left town? Yesterday the washer had gone buns up, and just that morning the toaster oven had fried itself.

They had such a nice rhythm when they were together, dividing up the chores, sharing the discipline and the pleasure in their sons. If he'd been home, he could have sat down to play with—and referee—the boys while she cooked.

Or better, he'd have cooked and she'd have played with the boys.

She missed the smell of him when he came up behind her to lean down and rub his cheek over hers. She missed curling up to him in bed at night, and the way they'd talk in the dark about their plans, or laugh at something the boys had done that day.

For God's sake, you'd think the man had been gone four months instead of four days, she told herself.

She listened with half an ear to Gavin trying to talk Luke into building a skyscraper that they could both wreck as she stirred her cream sauce and watched the wind swirl leaves outside the window.

He wouldn't be traveling so much after he got his promotion. Soon, she reminded herself. He'd been working so hard, and he was right on the verge of it. The extra money would be handy, too, especially when they had another child—maybe a girl this time.

With the promotion, and her working full-time again, they could afford to take the kids somewhere next summer. Disney World, maybe. They'd love that. Even if she were pregnant, they could manage it. She'd been squirreling away some money in the vacation fund—and the new-car fund.

Having to buy a new washing machine was going to seriously damage the emergency fund, but they'd be all right.

When she heard the boys laugh, her shoulders relaxed again. Really, life was good. It was perfect, just the way she'd always imagined it. She was married to a wonderful man, one she'd fallen for the minute she'd set eyes on him. Kevin Rothchild, with his slow, sweet smile.

They had two beautiful sons, a pretty house in a good neighborhood, jobs they both loved, and plans for the future they both agreed on. And when they made love, bells still rang.

Thinking of that, she imagined his reaction when, with the kids tucked in for the night, she slipped into the sexy new lingerie she'd splurged on in his absence.

A little wine, a few candles, and . . .

The next, bigger crash had her eyes rolling toward the ceiling. At least this time there were cheers instead of wails.

"Mom! Mom!" Face alive with glee, Luke rushed in. "We wrecked the *whole* building. Can we have a cookie?"

"Not this close to dinner."

"Please, please, please, *please*!"

He was pulling on her pants now, doing his best to climb up her leg. Stella set the spoon down, nudged him away from the stove. "No cookies before dinner, Luke."

"We're starving." Gavin piled in, slamming his cars together. "How come we can't eat something when we're hungry? Why do we have to eat the stupid fredo anyway?"

"Because." She'd always hated that answer as a child, but it seemed all-purpose to her now.

"We're all eating together when your father gets home." But she glanced out the window and worried that his plane would be delayed. "Here, you can split an apple."

She took one out of the bowl on the counter and grabbed a knife.

"I don't like the peel," Gavin complained.

"I don't have time to peel it." She gave the sauce a couple of quick stirs. "The peel's good for you." Wasn't it?

"Can I have a drink? Can I have a drink, too?" Luke tugged and tugged. "I'm thirsty."

"God. Give me five minutes, will you? Five minutes. Go, go *build* something. Then you can have some apple slices and juice."

Thunder boomed, and Gavin responded to it by jumping up and down and shouting, "Earthquake!"

"It's not an earthquake."

But his face was bright with excitement as he spun in circles, then ran from the room. "Earthquake! Earthquake!"

Getting into the spirit, Luke ran after him, screaming.

Stella pressed a hand to her pounding head. The noise was insane, but maybe it would keep them busy until she got the meal under control.

She turned back to the stove, and heard, without much interest, the announcement for a news bulletin.

It filtered through the headache, and she turned toward the set like an automaton.

Commuter plane crash. En route to Detroit Metro from Lansing. Ten passengers on board.

The spoon dropped out of her hand. The heart dropped out of her body.

Kevin. Kevin.

Her children screamed in delighted fear, and thunder rolled and burst overhead. In the kitchen, Stella slid to the floor as her world fractured.

THEY CAME TO TELL HER KEVIN WAS DEAD. STRANGERS at her door with solemn faces. She couldn't take it in, couldn't believe it. Though she'd known. She'd known the minute she heard the reporter's voice on her little kitchen television.

Kevin couldn't be dead. He was young and healthy. He was coming home, and they were having chicken Alfredo for dinner.

But she'd burned the sauce. The smoke had set off the alarms, and there was nothing but madness in her pretty house.

She had to send her children to her neighbor's so it could be explained to her.

But how could the impossible, the unthinkable ever be explained?

A mistake. The storm, a strike of lightning, and everything changed forever. One instant of time, and the man she loved, the father of her children, no longer lived.

Is there anyone you'd like to call?

Who would she call but Kevin? He was her family, her friend, her life.

They spoke of details that were like a buzz in her brain, of arrangements, of counseling. They were sorry for her loss.

They were gone, and she was alone in the house she and Kevin had bought when she'd been pregnant with Luke. The house they'd saved for, and painted, and decorated together. The house with the gardens she'd designed herself.

The storm was over, and it was quiet. Had it ever been so quiet? She could hear her own heartbeat, the hum of the heater as it kicked on, the drip of rain from the gutters.

Then she could hear her own keening as she collapsed on the floor by her front door. Lying on her side, she gathered herself into a ball in defense, in denial. There weren't tears, not yet. They were massed into some kind of hard, hot knot inside her. The grief was so deep, tears couldn't reach it. She could only lie curled up there, with those wounded-animal sounds pouring out of her throat.

It was dark when she pushed herself to her feet, swaying, light-headed and ill. Kevin. Somewhere in her brain his name still, over and over and over.

She had to get her children, she had to bring her children home. She had to tell her babies.

Oh, God. Oh, God, how could she tell them?

She groped for the door, stepped out into the chilly dark, her mind blessedly blank. She left the door open at her back, walked down between the heavy-headed mums and asters, past the glossy green leaves of the azaleas she and Kevin had planted one blue spring day.

She crossed the street like a blind woman, walking through puddles that soaked her shoes, over damp grass, toward her neighbor's porch light.

What was her neighbor's name? Funny, she'd known her for four years. They carpooled, and sometimes shopped together. But she couldn't quite remember. . . .

Oh, yes, of course. Diane. Diane and Adam Perkins, and their children, Jessie and Wyatt. Nice family, she thought dully. Nice, normal family. They'd had a barbecue together just a couple weeks ago. Kevin had grilled chicken.

He loved to grill. They'd had some good wine, some good laughs, and the kids had played. Wyatt had fallen and scraped his knee.

Of course she remembered.

But she stood in front of the door not quite sure what she was doing there.

Her children. Of course. She'd come for her children. She had to tell them. . . .

Don't think. She held herself hard, rocked, held in. Don't think yet. If you think, you'll break apart. A million pieces you can never put together again.

Her babies needed her. Needed her now. Only had her now.

She bore down on that hot, hard knot and rang the bell.

She saw Diane as if she were looking at her through a thin sheen of water. Rippling, and not quite there. She heard her dimly. Felt the arms that came around her in support and sympathy.

But your husband's alive, you see, Stella thought. Your life isn't over. Your world's the same as it was five minutes ago. So you can't know. You can't.

When she felt herself begin to shake, she pulled back. "Not now, please. I can't now. I have to take the boys home."

"I can come with you." There were tears on Diane's cheeks as she reached out, touched Stella's hair. "Would you like me to come, to stay with you?"

"No. Not now. I need . . . the boys."

"I'll get them. Come inside, Stella."

But she only shook her head.

"All right. They're in the family room. I'll bring them. Stella, if there's anything, anything at all. You've only to call. I'm sorry. I'm so sorry."

She stood in the dark, looking in at the light, and waited.

She heard the protests, the complaints, then the scrambling of feet. And there were her boys—Gavin with his father's sunny hair, Luke with his father's mouth.

"We don't want to go yet," Gavin told her. "We're playing a game. Can't we finish?"

"Not now. We have to go home now."

"But I'm winning. It's not fair, and—"

"Gavin. We have to go."

"Is Daddy home?"

She looked down at Luke, his happy, innocent face, and nearly broke. "No." Reaching down, she picked him up, touched her lips to the mouth that was so like Kevin's. "Let's go home."

She took Gavin's hand and began the walk back to her empty house.

"If Daddy was home, he'd let me finish." Cranky tears smeared Gavin's voice. "I want Daddy."

"I know. I do too."

"Can we have a dog?" Luke wanted to know, and turned her face to his with his hands. "Can we ask Daddy? Can we have a dog like Jessie and Wyatt?"

"We'll talk about it later."

"I want Daddy," Gavin said again, with a rising pitch in his voice.

He knows, Stella thought. He knows something is wrong, something's terribly wrong. I have to do this. I have to do it now.

"We need to sit down." Carefully, very carefully, she closed the door behind her, carried Luke to the couch. She sat with him in her lap and laid her arm over Gavin's shoulder.

"If I had a dog," Luke told her soberly, "I'd take care of him. When's Daddy coming?"

"He can't come."

"'Cause of the busy trip?"

"He . . ." Help me. God, help me do this. "There was an accident. Daddy was in an accident."

"Like when the cars smash?" Luke asked, and Gavin said nothing, nothing at all as his eyes burned into her face.

"It was a very bad accident. Daddy had to go to heaven."

"But he has to come home after."

"He can't. He can't come home anymore. He has to stay in heaven now."

"I don't want him there." Gavin tried to wrench away, but she held him tightly. "I want him to come home *now*."

"I don't want him there either, baby. But he can't come back anymore, no matter how much we want it."

Luke's lips trembled. "Is he mad at us?"

"No. No, no, no, baby. No." She pressed her face to his hair as her stomach pitched and what was left of her heart throbbed like a wound. "He's not mad at us. He loves us. He'll always love us."

"He's dead." There was fury in Gavin's voice, rage on his face. Then it crumpled, and he was just a little boy, weeping in his mother's arms.

She held them until they slept, then carried them to her bed so none of them would wake alone. As she had countless times before, she slipped off their shoes, tucked blankets around them.

She left a light burning while she walked—it felt like floating—through the house, locking doors, checking windows. When she knew everything was safe, she closed herself into the bathroom. She ran a bath so hot the steam rose off the water and misted the room.

Only when she slipped into the tub, submerged herself in the steaming water, did she allow that knot to snap. With her boys sleeping, and her body shivering in the hot water, she wept and wept and wept.

SHE GOT THROUGH IT. A FEW FRIENDS SUGGESTED SHE might take a tranquilizer, but she didn't want to block the feelings. Nor did she want to have a muzzy head when she had her children to think of.

She kept it simple. Kevin would have wanted simple. She chose every detail—the music, the flowers, the photographs—of his memorial service. She selected a silver box for his ashes and planned to scatter them on the lake. He'd proposed to her on the lake, in a rented boat on a summer afternoon.

She wore black for the service, a widow of thirty-one, with two young boys and a mortgage, and a heart so broken she wondered if she would feel pieces of it piercing her soul for the rest of her life.

She kept her children close, and made appointments with a grief counselor for all of them.

Details. She could handle the details. As long as there was something to do, something definite, she could hold on. She could be strong.

Friends came, with their sympathy and covered dishes and teary eyes. She was grateful to them more for the distraction than the condolences. There was no condolence for her.

Her father and his wife flew up from Memphis, and them she leaned on. She let Jolene, her father's wife, fuss over her, and soothe and cuddle the children, while her own mother complained about having to be in the same room as *that woman*.

When the service was over, after the friends drifted away, after she clung to her father and Jolene before their flight home, she made herself take off the black dress.

She shoved it into a bag to send to a shelter. She never wanted to see it again.

Her mother stayed. Stella had asked her to stay a few days. Surely under such circumstances she was entitled to her mother. Whatever friction was, and always had been, between them was nothing compared with death.

When she went into the kitchen, her mother was brewing coffee. Stella was so grateful not to have to think of such a minor task, she crossed over and kissed Carla's cheek.

"Thanks. I'm so sick of tea."

"Every time I turned around that woman was making more damn tea."

"She was trying to help, and I'm not sure I could've handled coffee until now."

Carla turned. She was a slim woman with short blond hair. Over the years, she'd battled time with regular trips to the surgeon. Nips, tucks, lifts, injections had wiped away some of the years. And left her looking whittled and hard, Stella thought.

She might pass for forty, but she'd never look happy about it.

"You always take up for her."

"I'm not taking up for Jolene, Mom." Wearily, Stella sat. No more details, she realized. No more something that has to be done.

How would she get through the night?

"I don't see why I had to tolerate her."

"I'm sorry you were uncomfortable. But she was very kind. She and Dad have been married for, what, twenty-five years or so now. You ought to be used to it."

"I don't like having her in my face, her and that twangy voice. Trailer trash."

Stella opened her mouth, closed it again. Jolene hadn't come from a trailer park and was certainly not trash. But what good would it do to say so? Or to remind her mother that she'd been the one who'd wanted a divorce, the one to leave the marriage. Just as it wouldn't do any good to point out that Carla had been married twice since.

"Well, she's gone now."

"Good riddance."

Stella took a deep breath. No arguments, she thought, as her stomach clenched and unclenched like a fist. Too tired to argue.

"The kids are sleeping. They're just worn out. Tomorrow . . . we'll just deal with tomorrow. I guess that's the way it's going to be." She let her head fall back, closed her eyes. "I keep thinking this is a horrible dream, and I'll wake up any second. Kevin will be here. I don't . . . I can't imagine life without him. I can't stand to imagine it."

The tears started again. "Mom, I don't know what I'm going to do."

"Had insurance, didn't he?"

Stella blinked, stared as Carla set a cup of coffee in front of her. "What?"

"Life insurance. He was covered?"

"Yes, but—"

"You ought to talk to a lawyer about suing the airline. Better start thinking of practicalities." She sat with her own coffee. "It's what you're best at, anyway."

"Mom"—she spoke slowly as if translating a strange foreign language—"Kevin's dead."

"I know that, Stella, and I'm sorry." Reaching over, Carla gave Stella's hand a pat. "I dropped everything to come here and give you a hand, didn't I?"

"Yes." She had to remember that. Appreciate that.

"It's a damn fucked-up world when a man of his age dies for no good reason. Useless waste. I'll never understand it."

"No." Pulling a tissue out of her pocket, Stella rubbed the tears away. "Neither will I."

"I liked him. But the fact is, you're in a fix now. Bills, kids to support. Widowed with two growing boys. Not many men want to take on ready-made families, let me tell you."

"I don't want a man to take us on. God, Mom."

"You will," Carla said with a nod. "Take my advice and make sure the next one's got money. Don't make my mistakes. You lost your husband, and that's hard. It's really hard. But women lose husbands every day. It's better to lose one this way than to go through a divorce."

The pain in Stella's stomach was too sharp for grief, too cold for rage. "Mom. We had Kevin's memorial service today. I have his ashes in a goddamn box in my bedroom."

"You want my help." She waggled the spoon. "I'm trying to give it to you. You sue the pants off the airline, get yourself a solid nest egg. And don't hook yourself up with some loser like I always do. You don't think divorce is a hard knock, too? Haven't been through one, have you? Well, I have. Twice. And I might as well tell you it's coming up on three. I'm done with that stupid son of a bitch.

You've got no idea what he's put me through. Not only is he an inconsiderate, loudmouthed asshole, but I think he's been cheating on me."

She pushed away from the table, rummaged around, then cut herself a piece of cake. "He thinks I'm going to tolerate that, he's mistaken. I'd just love to see his face when he gets served with the papers. Today."

"I'm sorry your third marriage isn't working out," Stella said stiffly. "But it's a little hard for me to be sympathetic, since both the third marriage and the third divorce were your choice. Kevin's dead. My husband is dead, and that sure as hell wasn't my choice."

"You think I want to go through this again? You think I want to come here to help you out, then have your father's bimbo shoved in my face?"

"She's his wife, who has never been anything but decent to you and who has always treated me kindly."

"To your face." Carla stuffed a bite of cake into her mouth. "You think you're the only one with problems? With heartache? You won't be so quick to shrug it off when you're pushing fifty and facing life alone."

"You're pushing fifty from the back end, Mom, and being alone is, again, your choice."

Temper turned Carla's eyes dark and sharp. "I don't appreciate that tone, Stella. I don't have to put up with it."

"No, you don't. You certainly don't. In fact, it would probably be best for both of us if you left. Right now. This was a bad idea. I don't know what I was thinking."

"You want me gone, fine." Carla shoved up from the table. "I'd just as soon get back to my own life. You never had any gratitude in you, and if you couldn't be on my back about something you weren't happy. Next time you want to cry on somebody's shoulder, call your country bumpkin stepmother."

"Oh, I will," Stella murmured as Carla sailed out of the room. "Believe me."

She rose to carry her cup to the sink, then gave in to the petty urge and smashed it. She wanted to break everything as she'd been broken. She wanted to wreak havoc on the world as it had been on her.

Instead she stood gripping the edge of the sink and praying that her mother would pack and leave quickly. She wanted her out. Why had she ever thought she wanted her to stay? It was always the same between them. Abrasive, combative. No connection, no common ground.

But God, she'd wanted that shoulder. Needed it so much, just for one night. Tomorrow she would do whatever came next. But she'd wanted to be held and stroked and comforted tonight.

With trembling fingers she cleaned the broken shards out of the sink, wept over them a little as she poured them into the trash. Then she walked to the phone and called a cab for her mother.

They didn't speak again, and Stella decided that was for the best. She closed the door, listened to the cab drive away.

Alone now, she checked on her sons, tucked blankets over them, laid her lips gently on their heads.

They were all she had now. And she was all they had.

She would be a better mother. She swore it. More patient. She would never, never let them down. She would never walk away when they needed her.

And when they needed her shoulder, by God, she would give it. No matter what. No matter when.

"You're first for me," she whispered. "You'll always be first for me."

In her own room, she undressed again, then took Kevin's old flannel robe out of the closet. She wrapped herself in it, in the familiar, heartbreaking smell of him.

Curling up on the bed, she hugged the robe close, shut her eyes, and prayed for morning. For what happened next.

two

Harper House
January 2004

SHE COULDN'T AFFORD TO BE INTIMIDATED BY THE house, or by its mistress. They both had reputations.

The house was said to be elegant and old, with gardens that rivaled Eden. She'd just confirmed that for herself.

The woman was said to be interesting, somewhat solitary, and perhaps a bit "difficult." A word, Stella knew, that could mean anything from strong-willed to stone bitch.

Either way, she could handle it, she reminded herself as she fought the need to get up and pace. She'd handled worse.

She needed this job. Not just for the salary—and it was generous—but for the structure, for the challenge, for the doing. Doing more, she knew, than circling the wheel she'd fallen into back home.

She needed a life, something more than clocking time, drawing a paycheck that would be soaked up by bills. She needed, however self-help-book it sounded, something that fulfilled and challenged her.

Rosalind Harper was fulfilled, Stella was sure. A beautiful ancestral home, a thriving business. What was it like, she wondered, to wake up every morning knowing exactly where you belonged and where you were going?

If she could earn one thing for herself, and give that gift to her children, it would be the sense of knowing. She was afraid she'd lost any clear sight of that with Kevin's death. The sense of doing, no problem. Give her a task or a challenge and the room to accomplish or solve it, she was your girl.

But the sense of knowing who she was, in the heart of herself, had been mangled that day in September of 2001 and had never fully healed.

This was her start, this move back to Tennessee. This final and face-to-face interview with Rosalind Harper. If she didn't get the job—well, she'd get another. No one could accuse her of not knowing how to work or how to provide a living for herself and her kids.

But, God, she wanted *this* job.

She straightened her shoulders and tried to ignore all the whispers of doubt muttering inside her head. She'd *get* this one.

She'd dressed carefully for this meeting. Businesslike but not fussy, in a navy suit and starched white blouse. Good shoes, good bag, she thought. Simple jewelry. Nothing flashy. Subtle makeup, to bring out the blue of her eyes. She'd fought her hair into a clip at the nape of her neck. If she was lucky, the curling mass of it wouldn't spring out until the interview was over.

Rosalind was keeping her waiting. It was probably a mind game, Stella decided as her fingers twisted, untwisted her watchband. Letting her sit and stew in the gorgeous parlor, letting her take in the lovely antiques and paintings, the sumptuous view from the front windows.

All in that dreamy and gracious southern style that reminded her she was a Yankee fish out of water.

Things moved slower down here, she reminded herself. She would have to remember that this was a different pace from the one she was used to, and a different culture.

The fireplace was probably an Adams, she decided. That lamp was certainly an original Tiffany. Would they call those drapes portieres down here, or was that too Scarlett O'Hara? Were the lace panels under the drapes heirlooms?

God, had she ever been more out of her element? What was a middle-class widow from Michigan doing in all this southern splendor?

She steadied herself, fixed a neutral expression on her face, when she heard footsteps coming down the hall.

"Brought coffee." It wasn't Rosalind, but the cheerful man who'd answered the door and escorted Stella to the parlor.

He was about thirty, she judged, average height, very slim. He wore his glossy brown hair waved around a movie-poster face set off by sparkling blue eyes. Though he wore black, Stella found nothing butlerlike about it. Much too artsy, too stylish. He'd said his name was David.

He set the tray with its china pot and cups, the little linen napkins, the sugar and cream, and the tiny vase with its clutch of violets on the coffee table.

"Roz got a bit hung up, but she'll be right along, so you just relax and enjoy your coffee. You comfortable in here?"

"Yes, very."

"Anything else I can get you while you're waiting on her?"

"No. Thanks."

"You just settle on in, then," he ordered, and poured coffee into a cup. "Nothing like a fire in January, is there? Makes you forget that a few months ago it was hot enough to melt the skin off your bones. What do you take in your coffee, honey?"

She wasn't used to being called "honey" by strange men who served her coffee in magnificent parlors. Especially since she suspected he was a few years her junior.

"Just a little cream." She had to order herself not to stare at his face—it was, well, delicious, with that full mouth, those sapphire eyes, the strong cheekbones, the sexy little dent in the chin. "Have you worked for Ms. Harper long?"

"Forever." He smiled charmingly and handed her the coffee. "Or it seems like it, in the best of all possible ways. Give her a straight answer to a straight question, and don't take any bullshit." His grin widened. "She *hates* it when people kowtow. You know, honey, I love your hair."

"Oh." Automatically, she lifted a hand to it. "Thanks."

"Titian knew what he was doing when he painted that color. Good luck with Roz," he said as he started out. "Great shoes, by the way."

She sighed into her coffee. He'd noticed her hair *and* her shoes, complimented her on both. Gay. Too bad for her side.

It was good coffee, and David was right. It was nice having a fire in January. Outside, the air was moist and raw, with a broody sky overhead. A woman could get used to a winter hour by the fire drinking good coffee out of— what was it? Meissen, Wedgwood? Curious, she held the cup up to read the maker's mark.

"It's Staffordshire, brought over by one of the Harper brides from England in the mid-nineteenth century."

No point in cursing herself, Stella thought. No point in cringing about the fact that her redhead's complexion would be flushed with embarrassment. She simply lowered the cup and looked Rosalind Harper straight in the eye.

"It's beautiful."

"I've always thought so." She came in, plopped down in the chair beside Stella's, and poured herself a cup.

One of them, Stella realized, had miscalculated the dress code for the interview.

Rosalind had dressed her tall, willowy form in a baggy olive sweater and mud-colored work pants that were frayed at the cuffs. She was shoeless, with a pair of thick brown socks covering long, narrow feet. Which accounted, Stella supposed, for her silent entry into the room.

Her hair was short, straight, and black.

Though to date all their communications had been via phone, fax, or e-mail, Stella had Googled her. She'd wanted background on her potential employer—and a look at the woman.

Newspaper and magazine clippings had been plentiful. She'd studied Rosalind as a child, through her youth. She'd marveled over the file photos of the stunning and delicate bride of eighteen and sympathized with the pale, stoic-looking widow of twenty-five.

There had been more, of course. Society-page stuff, gossipy speculation on when and if the widow would marry again. Then quite a bit of press surrounding the forging of the nursery business, her gardens, her love life. Her brief second marriage and divorce.

Stella's image had been of a strong-minded, shrewd woman. But she'd attributed those stunning looks to camera angles, lighting, makeup.

She'd been wrong.

At forty-six, Rosalind Harper was a rose in full bloom. Not the hothouse sort, Stella mused, but one that weathered the elements, season after season, and came back, year after year, stronger and more beautiful.

She had a narrow face angled with strong bones and deep, long eyes the color of single-malt scotch. Her mouth, full, strongly sculpted lips, was unpainted—as, to Stella's expert eye, was the rest of that lovely face.

There were lines, those thin grooves that the god of time reveled in stamping, fanning out from the corners of the dark eyes, but they didn't detract.

All Stella could think was, Could I be you, please, when I grow up? Only I'd like to dress better, if you don't mind.

"Kept you waiting, didn't I?"

Straight answers, Stella reminded herself. "A little, but it's not much of a hardship to sit in this room and drink good coffee out of Staffordshire."

"David likes to fuss. I was in the propagation house, got caught up."

Her voice, Stella thought, was brisk. Not clipped—you

just couldn't clip Tennessee—but it was to the point and full of energy. "You look younger than I expected. You're what, thirty-three?"

"Yes."

"And your sons are . . . six and eight?"

"That's right."

"You didn't bring them with you?"

"No. They're with my father and his wife right now."

"I'm very fond of Will and Jolene. How are they?"

"They're good. They're enjoying having their grand-children around."

"I imagine so. Your daddy shows off pictures of them from time to time and just about bursts with pride."

"One of my reasons for relocating here is so they can have more time together."

"It's a good reason. I like young boys myself. Miss having them around. The fact that you come with two played in your favor. Your résumé, your father's recommendation, the letter from your former employer—well, none of that hurt."

She picked up a cookie from the tray, bit in, without her eyes ever leaving Stella's face. "I need an organizer, some-one creative and hardworking, personable and basically tireless. I like people who work for me to keep up with me, and I set a strong pace."

"So I've been told." Okay, Stella thought, brisk and to the point in return. "I have a degree in nursery manage-ment. With the exception of three years when I stayed home to have my children—and during which time I land-scaped my own yard and two neighbors'—I've worked in that capacity. For more than two years now, since my hus-band's death, I've raised my sons and worked outside the home in my field. I've done a good job with both. I can keep up with you, Ms. Harper. I can keep up with anyone."

Maybe, Roz thought. Just maybe. "Let me see your hands."

A little irked, Stella held them out. Roz set down her

coffee, took them in hers. She turned them palms up, ran her thumbs over them. "You know how to work."

"Yes, I do."

"Banker suit threw me off. Not that it isn't a lovely suit." Roz smiled, then polished off the cookie. "It's been damp the last couple of days. Let's see if we can put you in some boots so you don't ruin those very pretty shoes. I'll show you around."

THE BOOTS WERE TOO BIG, AND THE ARMY-GREEN rubber hardly flattering, but the damp ground and crushed gravel would have been cruel to her new shoes.

Her own appearance hardly mattered when compared with the operation Rosalind Harper had built.

In the Garden spread over the west side of the estate. The garden center faced the road, and the grounds at its entrance and running along the sides of its parking area were beautifully landscaped. Even in January, Stella could see the care and creativity put into the presentation with the selection and placement of evergreens and ornamental trees, the mulched rises where she assumed there would be color from bulbs and perennials, from splashy annuals through the spring and summer and into fall.

After one look she didn't want the job. She was desperate for it. The lust tied knots of nerves and desire in her belly, the kinds that were usually reserved for a lover.

"I didn't want the retail end of this near the house," Roz said as she parked the truck. "I didn't want to see commerce out my parlor window. Harpers are, and always have been, business-minded. Even back when some of the land around here was planted with cotton instead of houses."

Because Stella's mouth was too dry to speak, she only nodded. The main house wasn't visible from here. A wedge of natural woods shielded it from view and kept the long, low outbuildings, the center itself, and, she imagined, most of the greenhouses from intruding on any view from Harper House.

And just look at that gorgeous old ruby horse chestnut!

"This section's open to the public twelve months a year," Roz continued. "We carry all the sidelines you'd expect, along with houseplants and a selection of gardening books. My oldest son's helping me manage this section, though he's happier in the greenhouses or out in the field. We've got two part-time clerks right now. We'll need more in a few weeks."

Get your head in the game, Stella ordered herself. "Your busy season would start in March in this zone."

"That's right." Roz led the way to the low-slung white building, up an asphalt ramp, across a spotlessly clean porch, and inside.

Two long, wide counters on either side of the door, Stella noted. Plenty of light to keep it cheerful. There were shelves stocked with soil additives, plant foods, pesticides, spin racks of seeds. More shelves held books or colorful pots suitable for herbs or windowsill plants. There were displays of wind chimes, garden plaques, and other accessories.

A woman with snowy white hair dusted a display of sun catchers. She wore a pale blue cardigan with roses embroidered down the front over a white shirt that looked to have been starched stiff as iron.

"Ruby, this is Stella Rothchild. I'm showing her around."

"Pleased to meet you."

The calculating look told Stella the woman knew she was in about the job opening, but the smile was perfectly cordial. "You're Will Dooley's daughter, aren't you?"

"Yes, that's right."

"From . . . up north."

She said it, to Stella's amusement, as if it were a Third World country of dubious repute. "From Michigan, yes. But I was born in Memphis."

"Is that so?" The smile warmed, fractionally. "Well,

that's something, isn't it? Moved away when you were a little girl, didn't you?"

"Yes, with my mother."

"Thinking about moving back now, are you?"

"I have moved back," Stella corrected.

"Well." The one word said they'd see what they'd see. "It's a raw one out there today," Ruby continued. "Good day to be inside. You just look around all you want."

"Thanks. There's hardly anywhere I'd rather be than inside a nursery."

"You picked a winner here. Roz, Marilee Booker was in and bought the dendrobium. I just couldn't talk her out of it."

"Well, *shit*. It'll be dead in a week."

"Dendrobiums are fairly easy care," Stella pointed out.

"Not for Marilee. She doesn't have a black thumb. Her whole arm's black to the elbow. That woman should be barred by law from having anything living within ten feet of her."

"I'm sorry, Roz. But I did make her promise to bring it back if it starts to look sickly."

"Not your fault." Roz waved it away, then moved through a wide opening. Here were the houseplants, from the exotic to the classic, and pots from thimble size to those with a girth as wide as a manhole cover. There were more accessories, too, like stepping-stones, trellises, arbor kits, garden fountains, and benches.

"I expect my staff to know a little bit about everything," Roz said as they walked through. "And if they don't know the answer, they need to know how to find it. We're not big, not compared to some of the wholesale nurseries or the landscaping outfits. We're not priced like the garden centers at the discount stores. So we concentrate on offering the unusual plants along with the basic, and customer service. We make house calls."

"Do you have someone specific on staff who'll go do an on-site consult?"

"Either Harper or I might go if you're talking about a

customer who's having trouble with something bought
here. Or if they just want some casual, personal advice."

She slid her hands into her pockets, rocked back and
forth on the heels of her muddy boots. "Other than that,
I've got a landscape designer. Had to pay him a fortune to
steal him away from a competitor. Had to give him damn
near free rein, too. But he's the best. I want to expand that
end of the business."

"What's your mission statement?"

Roz turned, her eyebrows lifted high. There was a quick
twinkle of amusement in those shrewd eyes. "Now, there
you are—that's just why I need someone like you. Someone who can say 'mission statement' with a straight face.
Let me think."

With her hands on her hips now, she looked around the
stocked area, then opened wide glass doors into the adjoining greenhouse. "I guess it's two-pronged—this is where
we stock most of our annuals and hanging baskets starting
in March, by the way. First prong would be to serve the
home gardener. From the fledgling who's just dipping a toe
in to the more experienced who knows what he or she
wants and is willing to try something new or unusual. To
give that customer base good stock, good service, good
advice. Second would be to serve the customer who's got
the money but not the time or the inclination to dig in the
dirt. The one who wants to beautify but either doesn't
know where to start or doesn't want the job. We'll go in,
and for a fee we'll work up a design, get the plants, hire the
laborers. We'll guarantee satisfaction."

"All right." Stella studied the long, rolling tables, the
sprinkler heads of the irrigation system, the drains in the
sloping concrete floor.

"When the season starts we have tables of annuals and
perennials along the side of this building. They'll show
from the front as people drive by, or in. We've got a shaded
area for ones that need shade," she continued as she walked
through, boots slapping on concrete. "Over here we keep
our herbs, and through there's a storeroom for extra pots

and plastic flats, tags. Now, out back here's greenhouses for stock plants, seedlings, preparation areas. Those two will open to the public, more annuals sold by the flat."

She crunched along gravel, over more asphalt. Shrubs and ornamental trees. She gestured toward an area on the side where the stock wintering over was screened. "Behind that, closed to the public, are the propagation and grafting areas. We do mostly container planting, but I've culled out an acre or so for field stock. Water's no problem with the pond back there."

They continued to walk, with Stella calculating, dissecting. And the lust in her belly had gone from tangled knot to rock-hard ball.

She could *do* something here. Make her mark over the excellent foundation another woman had built. She could help improve, expand, refine.

Fulfilled? she thought. Challenged? Hell, she'd be so busy, she'd be fulfilled and challenged every minute of every day.

It was perfect.

There were the white scoop-shaped greenhouses, worktables, display tables, awnings, screens, sprinklers. Stella saw it brimming with plants, thronged with customers. Smelling of growth and possibilities.

Then Roz opened the door to the propagation house, and Stella let out a sound, just a quiet one she couldn't hold back. And it was pleasure.

The smell of earth and growing things, the damp heat. The air was close, and she knew her hair would frizz out insanely, but she stepped inside.

Seedlings sprouted in their containers, delicate new growth spearing out of the enriched soil. Baskets already planted were hung on hooks where they'd be urged into early bloom. Where the house teed off there were the stock plants, the parents of these fledglings. Aprons hung on pegs, tools were scattered on tables or nested in buckets.

Silently she walked down the aisles, noting that the containers were marked clearly. She could identify some of the plants without reading the tags. Cosmos and columbine, petunias and penstemon. This far south, in a few short weeks they'd be ready to be laid in beds, arranged in patio pots, tucked into sunny spaces or shady nooks.

Would she? Would she be ready to plant herself here, to root here? To bloom here? Would her sons?

Gardening was a risk, she thought. Life was just a bigger one. The smart calculated those risks, minimized them, and worked toward the goal.

"I'd like to see the grafting area, the stockrooms, the offices."

"All right. Better get you out of here. Your suit's going to wilt."

Stella looked down at herself, spied the green boots. Laughed. "So much for looking professional."

The laugh had Roz angling her head in approval. "You're a pretty woman, and you've got good taste in clothes. That kind of image doesn't hurt. You took the time to put yourself together well for this meeting, which I neglected to do. I appreciate that."

"You hold the cards, Ms. Harper. You can put yourself together any way you like."

"You're right about that." She walked back to the door, gestured, and they stepped outside into a light, chilly drizzle. "Let's go into the office. No point hauling you around in the wet. What are your other reasons for moving back here?"

"I couldn't find any reason to stay in Michigan. We moved there after Kevin and I were married—his work. I think, I suppose, I've stayed there since he died out of a kind of loyalty to him, or just because I was used to it. I'm not sure. I liked my work, but I never felt—it never felt like my place. More like I was just getting from one day to the next."

"Family?"

"No. No, not in Michigan. Just me and the boys.

Kevin's parents are gone, were before we married. My mother lives in New York. I'm not interested in living in the city or raising my children there. Besides that, my mother and I have . . . tangled issues. The way mothers and daughters often do."

"Thank God I had sons."

"Oh, yeah." She laughed again, comfortably now. "My parents divorced when I was very young. I suppose you know that."

"Some of it. As I said, I like your father, and Jolene."

"So do I. So rather than stick a pin in a map, I decided to come here. I was born here. I don't really remember, but I thought, hoped, there might be a connection. That it might be the place."

They walked back through the retail center and into a tiny, cluttered office that made Stella's organized soul wince. "I don't use this much," Roz began. "I've got stuff scattered between here and the house. When I'm over here, I end up spending my time in the greenhouses or the field."

She dumped gardening books off a chair, pointed to it, then sat on the edge of the crowded desk when Stella took the seat.

"I know my strengths, and I know how to do good business. I've built this place from the ground up, in less than five years. When it was smaller, when it was almost entirely just me, I could afford to make mistakes. Now I have up to eighteen employees during the season. People depending on me for a paycheck. So I can't afford to make mistakes. I know how to plant, what to plant, how to price, how to design, how to stock, how to handle employees, and how to deal with customers. I know how to organize."

"I'd say you're absolutely right. Why do you need me— or someone like me?"

"Because of all those things I can—and have done— there are some I don't like. I don't like to organize. And we've gotten too big for it to fall only to me how and what to stock. I want a fresh eye, fresh ideas, and a good head."

"Understood. One of your requests was that your nursery manager live in your house, at least for the first several months. I—"

"It wasn't a request. It was a requirement." In the firm tone, Stella recognized the *difficult* attributed to Rosalind Harper. "We start early, we work late. I want someone on hand, right on hand, at least until I know if we're going to find the rhythm. Memphis is too far away, and unless you're ready to buy a house within ten miles of mine pretty much immediately, there's no other choice."

"I have two active young boys, and a dog."

"I like active young boys, and I won't mind the dog unless he's a digger. He digs in my gardens, we'll have a problem. It's a big house. You'll have considerable room for yourself and your sons. I'd offer you the guest cottage, but I couldn't pry Harper out of it with dynamite. My oldest," she explained. "Do you want the job, Stella?"

She opened her mouth, then took a testing breath. Hadn't she already calculated the risks in coming here? It was time to work toward the goal. The risk of the single condition couldn't possibly outweigh the benefits.

"I do. Yes, Ms. Harper, I very much want the job."

"Then you've got it." Roz held out a hand to shake. "You can bring your things over tomorrow—morning's best—and we'll get y'all settled in. You can take a couple of days, make sure your boys are acclimated."

"I appreciate that. They're excited, but a little scared too." And so am I, she thought. "I have to be frank with you, Ms. Harper. If my boys aren't happy—after a reasonable amount of time to adjust—I'll have to make other arrangements."

"If I thought differently, I wouldn't be hiring you. And call me Roz."

SHE CELEBRATED BY BUYING A BOTTLE OF CHAMPAGNE and a bottle of sparkling cider on the way back to her father's home. The rain, and the detour, put her in a nasty knot of mid-afternoon traffic. It occurred to her that however awkward it might be initially, there were advantages to living essentially where she worked.

She got the job! A dream job, to her point of view. Maybe she didn't know how Rosalind—call me Roz—Harper would be to work for, and she still had a lot of boning up to do about the nursery process in this zone—and she couldn't be sure how the other employees would handle taking orders from a stranger. A Yankee stranger at that.

But she couldn't wait to start.

And her boys would have more room to run around at the Harper . . . estate, she supposed she'd call it. She wasn't ready to buy a house yet—not before she was sure they'd stay, not before she had time to scout out neighborhoods and communities. The fact was, they were crowded in her father's house. Both he and Jolene were more than accommodating, more than welcoming, but they couldn't stay indefinitely jammed into a two-bedroom house.

This was the practical solution, at least for the short term.

She pulled her aging SUV beside her stepmother's snappy little roadster and, grabbing the bag, dashed through the rain to the door.

She knocked. They'd given her a key, but she wasn't comfortable just letting herself in.

Jolene, svelte in black yoga pants and a snug black top, looking entirely too young to be chasing sixty, opened the door.

"I interrupted your workout."

"Just finished. Thank God!" She dabbed at her face with a little white towel, shook back her cloud of honey-blond hair. "Misplace your key, honey?"

"Sorry. I can't get used to using it." She stepped in, listened. "It's much too quiet. Are the boys chained in the basement?"

"Your dad took them into the Peabody to see the afternoon duck walk. I thought it'd be nice for just the three of them, so I stayed here with my yoga tape." She cocked her head to the side. "Dog's snoozing out on the screened porch. You look smug."

"I should. I'm hired."

"I knew it, I knew it! Congratulations!" Jolene threw out her arms for a hug. "There was never any question in my mind. Roz Harper's a smart woman. She knows gold when she sees it."

"My stomach's jumpy, and my nerves are just plain shot. I should wait for Dad and the boys, but . . ." She pulled out the champagne. "How about an early glass of champagne to toast my new job?"

"Oh, twist my arm. I'm so excited for you I could just pop!" Jolene slung an arm around Stella's shoulders as they turned into the great room. "Tell me what you thought of Roz."

"Not as scary in person." Stella set the bottle on the counter to open while Jolene got champagne flutes out of her glass-front display cabinet. "Sort of earthy and direct, confident. And that house!"

"It's a beaut." Jolene laughed when the cork popped. "My, my, what a decadent sound in the middle of the afternoon. Harper House has been in her family for generations. She's actually an Ashby by marriage—the first one. She went back to Harper after her second marriage fizzled."

"Give me the dish, will you, Jolene? Dad won't."

"Plying me with champagne to get me to gossip? Why, thank you, honey." She slid onto a stool, raised her glass. "First, to our Stella and brave new beginnings."

Stella clinked glasses, drank. "Mmmmm. Wonderful. Now, dish."

"She married young. Just eighteen. What you'd call a good match—good families, same social circle. More important, it was a love match. You could see it all over them. It was about the time I fell for your father, and a woman recognizes someone in the same state she's in. She was a late baby—I think her mama was near forty and her daddy heading to fifty when she came along. Her mama was never well after, or she enjoyed playing the frail wife—depending on who you talk to. But in any case, Roz lost them both within two years. She must've been pregnant with her second son. That'd be . . . shoot. Austin, I think. She and John took over Harper House. She had the three boys, and the youngest barely a toddler, when John was killed. You know how hard that must've been for her."

"I do."

"Hardly saw her outside that house for two, three years, I guess. When she did start getting out again, socializing, giving parties and such, there was the expected speculation. Who she'd marry, when. You've seen her. She's a beautiful woman."

"Striking, yes."

"And down here, a lineage like hers is worth its weight and then some. Her looks, her bloodline, she could've had any man she wanted. Younger, older, or in between, single, married, rich, or poor. But she stayed on her own. Raised her boys."

Alone, Stella thought, sipping champagne. She understood the choice very well.

"Kept her private life private," Jolene went on, "much to Memphis society's consternation. Biggest to-do I recall was when she fired the gardener—well, both of them. Went after them with a Weedwacker, according to some reports, and ran them right off the property."

"Really?" Stella's eyes widened in shocked admiration. "Really?"

"That's what I heard, and that's the story that stuck, truth or lie. Down here, we often prefer the entertaining lie to the plain truth. Apparently they'd dug up some of her plants or something. She wouldn't have anybody else after that. Took the whole thing over herself. Next thing you know—though I guess it was about five years later—she's building that garden place over on her west end. She got married about three years ago, and divorced—well, all you had to do was blink. Honey, why don't we make that two early glasses of champagne?"

"Why don't we?" Stella poured. "So, what was the deal with the second husband?"

"Hmmm. Very slick character. Handsome as sin and twice as charming. Bryce Clerk, and he *says* his people are from Savannah, but I don't know as I'd believe a word coming out of his mouth if it was plated with gold. Anyway, they looked stunning together, but it happened he enjoyed looking stunning with a variety of women, and a wedding ring didn't restrict his habits. She booted him out on his ear."

"Good for her."

"She's no pushover."

"That came through loud and clear."

"I'd say she's proud, but not vain, tough-minded but not hard—or not too hard, though there are some who would disagree with that. A good friend, and a formidable enemy. You can handle her, Stella. You can handle anything."

She liked people to think so, but either the champagne or fresh nerves was making her stomach a little queasy. "Well, we're going to find out."

thRee

SHE HAD A CAR FULL OF LUGGAGE, A BRIEFCASE
stuffed with notes and sketches, a very unhappy dog who'd
already expressed his opinion of the move by vomiting on
the passenger seat, and two boys bickering bitterly in the
back.

She'd already pulled over to deal with the dog and the
seat, and despite the January chill had the windows wide
open. Parker, their Boston terrier, sprawled on the floor
looking pathetic.

She didn't know what the boys were arguing about, and
since it hadn't come to blows yet, let them go at it. They
were, she knew, as nervous as Parker about yet another
move.

She'd uprooted them. No matter how carefully you dug,
it was still a shock to the system. Now all of them were
about to be transplanted. She believed they would thrive.
She had to believe it or she'd be as sick as the family dog.

"I hate your slimy, stinky guts," eight-year-old Gavin
declared.

"I hate your big, stupid butt," six-year-old Luke
retorted.

"I hate your ugly elephant ears."

"I hate your whole ugly *face*!"

Stella sighed and turned up the radio.

She waited until she'd reached the brick pillars that flanked the drive to the Harper estate. She nosed in, out of the road, then stopped the car. For a moment, she simply sat there while the insults raged in the backseat. Parker sent her a cautious look, then hopped up to sniff at the air through the window.

She turned the radio off, sat. The voices behind her began to trail off, and after a last, harshly whispered, "And I hate your entire body," there was silence.

"So, here's what I'm thinking," she said in a normal, conversational tone. "We ought to pull a trick on Ms. Harper."

Gavin strained forward against his seat belt. "What kind of trick?"

"A tricky trick. I'm not sure we can pull it off. She's pretty smart; I could tell. So we'd have to be really sneaky."

"I can be sneaky," Luke assured her. And her glance in the rearview mirror told her the battle blood was already fading from his cheeks.

"Okay, then, here's the plan." She swiveled around so she could face both her boys. It struck her, as it often did, what an interesting meld of herself and Kevin they were. Her blue eyes in Luke's face, Kevin's gray-green ones in Gavin's. Her mouth to Gavin, Kevin's to Luke. Her coloring—poor baby—to Luke, and Kevin's sunny blond to Gavin.

She paused, dramatically, noted that both her sons were eagerly focused.

"No, I don't know." She shook her head regretfully. "It's probably not a good idea."

There was a chorus of pleas, protests, and a great deal of seat bouncing that sent Parker into a spate of enthusiastic barking.

"Okay, okay." She held up her hands. "What we do is,

we drive up to the house, and we go up to the door. And when we're inside and you meet Ms. Harper—this is going to have to be really sneaky, really clever."

"We can do it!" Gavin shouted.

"Well, when that happens, you have to pretend to be . . . this is tough, but I think you can do it. You have to pretend to be polite, well-behaved, well-mannered boys."

"We can do it! We . . ." Luke's face scrunched up. "Hey!"

"And I have to pretend not to be a bit surprised by finding myself with two well-behaved, well-mannered boys. Think we can pull it off?"

"Maybe we won't like it there," Gavin muttered.

Guilt roiled up to churn with nerves. "Maybe we won't. Maybe we will. We'll have to see."

"I'd rather live with Granddad and Nana Jo in their house." Luke's little mouth trembled, and wrenched at Stella's heart. "Can't we?"

"We really can't. We can visit, lots. And they can visit us, too. Now that we're going to live down here, we can see them all the time. This is supposed to be an adventure, remember? If we try it, really try it, and we're not happy, we'll try something else."

"People talk funny here," Gavin complained.

"No, just different."

"And there's no snow. How are we supposed to build snowmen and go sledding if it's too stupid to snow?"

"You've got me there, but there'll be other things to do." Had she seen her last white Christmas? Why hadn't she considered that before?

He jutted his chin out. "If she's mean, I'm not staying."

"That's a deal." Stella started the car, took a steadying breath, and continued down the drive.

Moments later she heard Luke's wondering: "It's big!"

No question about that, Stella mused, and wondered how her children saw it. Was it the sheer size of the three-storied structure that overwhelmed them? Or would they notice the details? The pale, pale yellow stone, the majestic columns, the charm of the entrance that was covered by the double stairway leading to the second floor and its pretty wraparound terrace?

Or would they just see the bulk of it—triple the size of their sweet house in Southfield?

"It's really old," she told them. "Over a hundred and fifty years old. And Ms. Harper's family's lived here always."

"Is she a hundred and fifty?" Luke wanted to know and earned a snort and an elbow jab from his brother.

"Dummy. Then she'd be *dead*. And there'd be worms crawling all over her—"

"I have to remind you, polite, well-mannered, well-behaved boys don't call their brothers dummy. See all the lawn? Won't Parker love being taken for walks out here? And there's so much room for you to play. But you have to stay out of the gardens and flower beds, just like at home. Back in Michigan," she corrected herself. "And we'll have to ask Ms. Harper where you're allowed to go."

"There's really big trees," Luke murmured. "Really big."

"That one there? That's a sycamore, and I bet it's even older than the house."

She pulled around the parking circle, admiring the use of Japanese red maple and golden mop cedar along with azaleas in the island.

She clipped on Parker's leash with hands that were a lot more steady than her heart rate. "Gavin, you take Parker. We'll come out for our things after we go in and see Ms. Harper."

"Does she get to boss us?" he demanded.

"Yes. The sad and horrible fate of children is to be bossed by adults. And as she's paying my salary, she gets to boss me, too. We're all in the same boat."

Gavin took Parker's leash when they got out. "I don't like her."

"That's what I love about you, Gavin." Stella ruffled his wavy blond hair. "Always thinking positive. Okay, here we go." She took his hand, and Luke's, gave each a gentle squeeze. The four of them started toward the covered entry.

The doors, a double set painted the same pure and glossy white as the trim, burst open.

"At last!" David flung out his arms. "Men! I'm no longer outnumbered around here."

"Gavin, Luke, this is Mr.—I'm sorry, David, I don't know your last name."

"Wentworth. But let's keep it David." He crouched down, looked the rapidly barking Parker in the eye. "What's your problem, buddy?"

In response, Parker planted his front paws on David's knee and lapped, with great excitement, at his face.

"That's more like it. Come on in. Roz'll be right along. She's upstairs on the phone, skinning some supplier over a delivery."

They stepped into the wide foyer, where the boys simply stood and goggled.

"Pretty ritzy, huh?"

"Is it like a church?"

"Nah." David grinned at Luke. "It's got fancy parts, but it's just a house. We'll get a tour in, but maybe you need some hot chocolate to revive you after your long journey."

"David makes wonderful hot chocolate." Roz started down the graceful stairs that divided the foyer. She was dressed in work clothes, as she'd been the day before. "With lots of whipped cream."

"Ms. Harper, my boys. Gavin and Luke."

"I'm very pleased to meet you. Gavin." She offered a hand to him.

"This is Parker. He's our dog. He's one and a half."

"And very handsome. Parker." She gave the dog a friendly pat.

"I'm Luke. I'm six, and I'm in first grade. I can write my name."

"He cannot either." Gavin sneered in brotherly disgust. "He can only print it."

"Have to start somewhere, don't you? It's very nice to

meet you, Luke. I hope you're all going to be comfortable here."

"You don't look really old," Luke commented, and had David snorting out a laugh.

"Why, thank you. I don't feel really old either, most of the time."

Feeling slightly ill, Stella forced a smile. "I told the boys how old the house was, and that your family's always lived here. He's a little confused."

"I haven't been here as long as the house. Why don't we have that hot chocolate, David? We'll sit in the kitchen, get acquainted."

"Is he your husband?" Gavin asked. "How come you have different last names?"

"She won't marry me," David told him, as he herded them down the hall. "She just breaks my poor, weeping heart."

"He's teasing you. David takes care of the house, and most everything else. He lives here."

"Is she the boss of you, too?" Luke tugged David's hand. "Mom says she's the boss of all of us."

"I let her think so." He led the way into the kitchen with its granite counters and warm cherry wood. A banquette with sapphire leather cushions ranged under a wide window.

Herbs thrived in blue pots along the work counter. Copper pots gleamed.

"This is my domain," David told them. "I'm boss here, just so you know the pecking order. You like to cook, Stella?"

"I don't know if 'like's' the word, but I do know I can't manage anything that would earn a kitchen like this."

Two Sub-Zero refrigerators, what looked to be a restaurant-style stove, double ovens, acres of counter.

And the little details that made a serious work space homey, she noted with relief. The brick hearth with a pretty fire simmering, the old china cupboard filled with antique glassware, forced bulbs of tulips and hyacinths blooming on a butcher block table.

"I live to cook. I can tell you it's pretty frustrating to waste my considerable talents on Roz. She'd just as soon eat cold cereal. And Harper rarely makes an appearance."

"Harper's my oldest son. He lives in the guest house. You'll see him sometimes."

"He's the mad scientist." David got out a pot and chunks of chocolate.

"Does he make monsters? Like Frankenstein?" As he asked, Luke snuck his hand into his mother's again.

"Frankenstein's just pretend," Stella reminded him. "Ms. Harper's son works with plants."

"Maybe one day he'll make a giant one that talks."

Delighted, Gavin sidled over toward David. "Nuh-uh."

" 'There are more things in heaven and earth, Horatio.' Bring that stool over, my fine young friend, and you can watch the master make the world's best hot chocolate."

"I know you probably want to get to work shortly," Stella said to Roz. "I have some notes and sketches I worked on last night I'd like to show you at some point."

"Busy."

"Eager." She glanced over as Luke let go of her hand and went over to join his brother on the stool. "I have an appointment this morning with the principal at the school. The boys should be able to start tomorrow. I thought I could ask at the school office for recommendations for before- and after-school care, then—"

"Hey!" David whipped chocolate and milk in the pot. "These are my men now. I figured they'd hang out with me, providing me with companionship as well as slave labor, when they're not in school."

"I couldn't ask you to—"

"We could stay with David," Gavin piped up. "That'd be okay."

"I don't—"

"Of course, it all depends." David spoke easily as he

added sugar to the pot. "If they don't like PlayStation, the deal's off. I have my standards."

"I like PlayStation," Luke said.

"Actually, they have to *love* PlayStation."

"I do! I do!" They bounced in unison on the stool. "I *love* PlayStation."

"Stella, while they're finishing up here, why don't we get some of your things out of the car?"

"All right. We'll just be a minute. Parker—"

"Dog's fine," David said.

"Well. Be right back, then."

Roz waited until they were at the front door. "David's wonderful with kids."

"Anyone could see." She caught herself twisting the band of her watch, made herself stop. "It just feels like an imposition. I'd pay him, of course, but—"

"You'll work that out between you. I just wanted to say—from one mother to another—that you can trust him to look after them, to entertain them, and to keep them— well, no, you can't trust him to keep them out of trouble. I'll say serious trouble, yes, but not the ordinary sort."

"He'd have to have superpowers for that."

"He practically grew up in this house. He's like my fourth son."

"It would be tremendously easy this way. I wouldn't have to haul them to a sitter." Yet another stranger, she thought.

"And you're not used to things being easy."

"No, I'm not." She heard squeals of laughter rolling out from the kitchen. "But I want my boys to be happy, and I guess that's the deciding vote right there."

"Wonderful sound, isn't it? I've missed it. Let's get your things."

"You have to give me the boundaries," Stella said as they went outside. "Where the boys can go, where they can't. They need chores and rules. They're used to having them at home. Back in Michigan."

"I'll give that some thought. Though David—despite

the fact that I'm the boss of all of you—probably has ideas on all that already. Cute dog, too, by the way." She hauled two suitcases out of the back of the SUV. "My dog died last year, and I haven't had the heart to get another. It's nice having a dog around. Clever name."

"Parker—for Peter Parker. That's—"

"Spider-Man. I did raise three boys of my own."

"Right." Stella grabbed another suitcase and a cardboard carton. She felt her muscles strain even as Roz carried her load with apparent ease.

"I meant to ask who else lives here, or what other staff you have."

"It's just David."

"Oh? He said something about being outnumbered by women before we got here."

"That's right. It would be David, and me, and the Harper Bride."

Roz carried the luggage inside and started up the steps with it. "She's our ghost."

"Your . . ."

"A house this old isn't haunted, it would be a damn shame, I'd think."

"I guess that's one way to look at it."

She decided Roz was amusing herself with a little local color for the new kid on the block. Ghosts would add to the family lore. So she dismissed it.

"You can have your run of the west wing. I think the rooms we've earmarked will suit best. I'm in the east wing, and David's rooms are off the kitchen. Everyone has plenty of privacy, which I've always felt is vital to good relations."

"This is the most beautiful house I've ever seen."

"It is, isn't it?" Roz stopped a moment, looking out the windows that faced one of her gardens. "It can be damp in the winter, and we're forever calling the plumber, the electrician, someone. But I love every inch of it. Some might think it's a waste for a woman on her own."

"It's yours. Your family home."

"Exactly. And it'll stay that way, whatever it takes.
You're just down here. Each room opens to the terrace. I'll
leave it to you to judge if you need to lock the one in the
boys' room. I assumed they'd want to share at this age,
especially in a new place."

"Bull's-eye." Stella walked into the room behind Roz.
"Oh, they'll love this. Lots of room, lots of light." She laid
the carton and the suitcase on one of the twin beds. But
antiques." She ran her fingers over the child-size chest of
drawers. "I'm terrified."

"Furniture's meant to be used. And good pieces
respected."

"Believe me, they'll get the word." Please, God, don't
let them break anything.

"You're next door. The bath connects." Roz gestured,
angled her head. "I thought, at least initially, you'd want to
be close."

"Perfect." She walked into the bath. The generous claw-
foot tub stood on a marble platform in front of the terrace
doors. Roman shades could be pulled down for privacy.
The toilet sat in a tall cabinet built from yellow pine and
had a chain pull—wouldn't the boys get a kick out of that!

Beside the pedestal sink was a brass towel warmer
already draped with fluffy sea-green towels.

Through the connecting door, her room was washed
with winter light. Rhizomes patterned the oak floor.

A cozy sitting area faced the small white-marble fireplace, with a painting of a garden in full summer bloom
above it.

Draped in gauzy white and shell pink, the canopy bed
was accented with a generous mountain of silk pillows in
dreamy pastels. The bureau with its long oval mirror was
gleaming mahogany, as was the charmingly feminine
dressing table and the carved armoire.

"I'm starting to feel like Cinderella at the ball."

"If the shoe fits." Roz set down the suitcases. "I want
you to be comfortable, and your boys to be happy because
I'm going to work you very hard. It's a big house, and

David will show you through at some point. We won't bump into each other, unless we want to."

She shoved up the sleeves of her shirt as she looked around. "I'm not a sociable woman, though I do enjoy the company of people I like. I think I'm going to like you. I already like your children."

She glanced at her watch. "I'm going to grab that hot chocolate—I can't ever resist it—then get to work."

"I'd like to come in, show you some of my ideas, later today."

"Fine. Hunt me up."

SHE DID JUST THAT. THOUGH SHE'D INTENDED TO bring the kids with her after the school meeting, she hadn't had the heart to take them away from David.

So much for her worries about their adjustment to living in a new house with strangers. It appeared that most of the adjustments were going to be on her end.

She dressed more appropriately this time, in sturdy walking shoes that had already seen their share of mud, jeans with considerable wear, and a black sweater. With her briefcase in hand, she headed into the main entrance of the garden center.

The same woman was at the counter, but this time she was waiting on a customer. Stella noted a small dieffenbachia in a cherry-red pot and a quartet of lucky bamboo, tied with decorative hemp, already in a shallow cardboard box.

A bag of stones and a square glass vase were waiting to be rung up.

Good.

"Is Roz around?" Stella asked.

"Oh . . ." Ruby gestured vaguely. "Somewhere or the other."

She nodded to the two-ways behind the counter. "Would she have one of those with her?"

The idea seemed to amuse Ruby. "I don't think so."

"Okay, I'll find her. That's so much fun," she said to the

customer, with a gesture toward the bamboo. "Carefree and interesting. It's going to look great in that bowl."

"I was thinking about putting it on my bathroom counter. Something fun and pretty."

"Perfect. Terrific hostess gifts, too. More imaginative than the usual flowers."

"I hadn't thought of that. You know, maybe I'll get another set."

"You couldn't go wrong." She beamed a smile, then started out toward the greenhouses, congratulating herself as she went. She wasn't in any hurry to find Roz. This gave her a chance to poke around on her own, to check supplies, stock, displays, traffic patterns. And to make more notes.

She lingered in the propagation area, studying the progress of seedlings and cuttings, the type of stock plants, and their health.

It was nearly an hour before she made her way to the grafting area. She could hear music—the Corrs, she thought—seeping out the door.

She peeked in. There were long tables lining both sides of the greenhouse, and two more shoved together to run down the center. It smelled of heat, vermiculite, and peat moss.

There were pots, some holding plants that had been or were being grafted. Clipboards hung from the edges of tables, much like hospital charts. A computer was shoved into a corner, its screen a pulse of colors that seemed to beat to the music.

Scalpels, knives, snippers, grafting tape and wax, and other tools of this part of the trade lay in trays.

She spotted Roz at the far end, standing behind a man on a stool. His shoulders were hunched as he worked. Roz's hands were on her hips.

"It can't take more than an hour, Harper. This place is as much yours as mine, and you need to meet her, hear what she has to say."

"I will, I will, but damn it, I'm in the middle of things here. You're the one who wants her to manage, so let her manage. I don't care."

"There's such a thing as manners." Exasperation rolled into the overheated air. "I'm just asking you to pretend, for an hour, to have a few."

The comment brought Stella's own words to her sons back to her mind. She couldn't stop the laugh, but did her best to conceal it with a cough as she walked down the narrow aisle.

"Sorry to interrupt. I was just . . ." She stopped by a pot, studying the grafted stem and the new leaves. "I can't quite make this one."

"Daphne." Roz's son spared her the briefest glance.

"Evergreen variety. And you've used a splice side-veneer graft."

He stopped, swiveled on his stool. His mother had stamped herself on his face—the same strong bones, rich eyes. His dark hair was considerably longer than hers, long enough that he tied it back with what looked to be a hunk of raffia. Like her, he was slim and seemed to have at least a yard of leg, and like her he dressed carelessly in jeans pocked with rips and a soil-stained Memphis University sweatshirt.

"You know something about grafting?"

"Just the basics. I cleft-grafted a camellia once. It did very well. Generally I stick with cuttings. I'm Stella. It's nice to meet you, Harper."

He rubbed his hand over his jeans before shaking hers. "Mom says you're going to organize us."

"That's the plan, and I hope it's not going to be too painful for any of us. What are you working on here?" She stepped over to a line of pots covered with clean plastic bags held clear of the grafted plant by four split stakes.

"Gypsophilia—baby's breath. I'm shooting for blue, as well as pink and white."

"Blue. My favorite color. I don't want to hold you up. I

was hoping," she said to Roz, "we could find somewhere to go over some of my ideas."

"Back in the annual house. The office is hopeless. Harper?"

"All right, okay. Go ahead. I'll be there in five minutes."

"Harper."

"Okay, ten. But that's my final offer."

With a laugh, Roz gave him a light cuff on the back of the head. "Don't make me come back in here and get you."

"Nag, nag, nag," he muttered, but with a grin.

Outside, Roz let out a sigh. "He plants himself in there, you have to jab a pitchfork in his ass to budge him. He's the only one of my boys who has an interest in the place. Austin's a reporter, works in Atlanta. Mason's a doctor, or will be. He's doing his internship in Nashville."

"You must be proud."

"I am, but I don't see nearly enough of either of them. And here's Harper, practically under my feet, and I have to hunt him like a dog to have a conversation."

Roz boosted herself onto one of the tables. "Well, what've you got?"

"He looks just like you."

"People say. I just see Harper. Your boys with David?"

"Couldn't pry them away with a crowbar." Stella opened her briefcase. "I typed up some notes."

Roz looked at the stack of papers and tried not to wince. "I'll say."

"And I've made some rough sketches of how we might change the layout to improve sales and highlight non-plant purchases. You have a prime location, excellent landscaping and signage, and a very appealing entrance."

"I hear a 'but' coming on."

"But . . ." Stella moistened her lips. "Your first-level retail area is somewhat disorganized. With some changes it would flow better into the secondary area and on through to your main plant facilities. Now, a functional organizational plan—"

"A functional organizational plan. Oh, my God."

"Take it easy, this really won't hurt. What you need is a chain of responsibility for your functional area. That's sales, production, and propagation. Obviously you're a skilled propagator, but at this point you need me to head production and sales. If we increase the volume of sales as I've proposed here—"

"You did charts." There was a touch of wonder in Roz's voice. "And graphs. I'm . . . suddenly afraid."

"You are not," Stella said with a laugh, then looked at Roz's face. "Okay, maybe a little. But if you look at this chart, you see the nursery manager—that's me—and you as you're in charge of everything. Forked out from that is your propagator—you and, I assume, Harper; production manager, me; and sales manager—still me. For now, anyway. You need to delegate and/or hire someone to be in charge of container and/or field production. This section here deals with staff, job descriptions and responsibilities."

"All right." On a little breath, Roz rubbed the back of her neck. "Before I give myself eyestrain reading all that, let me say that while I may consider hiring on more staff, Logan, my landscape designer, has a good handle on the field production at this point. I can continue to head up the container production. I didn't start this place to sit back and have others do all the work."

"Great. Then at some point I'd like to meet with Logan so we can coordinate our visions."

Roz's smile was thin, and just a little wicked. "That ought to be interesting."

"Meanwhile, since we're both here, why don't we take my notes and sketches of the first-level sales section and go through it on the spot? You can see better what I have in mind, and it'll be simpler to explain."

Simpler? Roz thought as she hopped down. She didn't think anything was going to be simpler now.

But it sure as holy hell wasn't going to be boring.

four

Everything was perfect. She worked long hours, but much of it was planning at this stage. There was little Stella loved more than planning. Unless it was *arranging*. She had a vision of things, in her head, of how things could and should be.

Some might see it as a flaw, this tendency to organize and project, to nudge those visions of things into place even when—maybe particularly when—others didn't quite get the picture.

But she didn't see it that way.

Life ran smoother when everything was where it was meant to be.

Her life had—she'd made certain of it—until Kevin's death. Her childhood had been a maze of contradictions, of confusions and irritations. In a very real way she'd lost her father at the age of three when divorce had divided her family.

The only thing she clearly remembered about the move from Memphis was crying for her daddy.

From that point on, it seemed she and her mother had butted heads over everything, from the color of paint on the walls to finances to how to spend holidays and vacations. Everything.

Those same *some people* might say that's what happened with two headstrong women living in the same house. But Stella knew different. While she was practical and organized, her mother was scattered and spontaneous. Which accounted for the four marriages and three broken engagements.

Her mother liked flash and noise and wild romance. Stella preferred quiet and settled and committed.

Not that she wasn't romantic. She was just sensible about it.

It had been both sensible and romantic to fall in love with Kevin. He'd been warm and sweet and steady. They'd wanted the same things. Home, family, future. He'd made her happy, made her feel safe and cherished. And God, she missed him.

She wondered what he'd think about her coming here, starting over this way. He'd have trusted her. He'd always believed in her. They'd believed in each other.

He'd been her rock, in a very real way. The rock that had given her a solid base to build on after a childhood of upheaval and discontent.

Then fate had kicked that rock out from under her. She'd lost her base, her love, her most cherished friend, and the only person in the world who could treasure her children as much as she did.

There had been times, many times, during the first months after Kevin's death when she'd despaired of ever finding her balance again.

Now she was the rock for her sons, and she would do whatever she had to do to give them a good life.

With her boys settled down for the night, and a low fire burning—she was *definitely* having a bedroom fireplace in her next house—she sat on the bed with her laptop.

It wasn't the most businesslike way to work, but she didn't feel right asking Roz to let her convert one of the bedrooms into a home office.

Yet.

She could make do this way for now. In fact, it was cozy and for her, relaxing, to go over the order of business for the next day while tucked into the gorgeous old bed.

She had the list of phone calls she intended to make to suppliers, the reorganization of garden accessories and the houseplants. Her new color-coordinated pricing system to implement. The new invoicing program to install.

She had to speak with Roz about the seasonal employees. Who, how many, individual and group responsibilities.

And she'd yet to corner the landscape designer. You'd think the man could find time in a damn week to return a phone call. She typed in "Logan Kitridge," bolding and underlining the name.

She glanced at the clock, reminded herself that she would put in a better day's work with a good night's sleep.

She powered down the laptop, then carried it over to the dressing table to set it to charge. She really was going to need that home office.

She went through her habitual bedtime routine, meticulously creaming off her makeup, studying her naked face in the mirror to see if the Time Bitch had snuck any new lines on it that day. She dabbed on her eye cream, her lip cream, her nighttime moisturizer—all of which were lined, according to point of use, on the counter. After slathering more cream on her hands, she spent a few minutes searching for gray hairs. The Time Bitch could be sneaky.

She wished she was prettier. Wished her features were more even, her hair straight and a reasonable color. She'd dyed it brown once, and *that* had been a disaster. So, she'd just have to live with . . .

She caught herself humming, and frowned at herself in the mirror. What song was that? How strange to have it stuck in her head when she didn't even know what it was.

Then she realized it wasn't stuck in her head. She *heard* it. Soft, dreamy singing. From the boys' room.

Wondering what in the world Roz would be doing

singing to the boys at eleven at night, Stella reached for the connecting door.

When she opened it, the singing stopped. In the subtle glow of the Harry Potter night-light, she could see her sons in their beds.

"Roz?" she whispered, stepping in.

She shivered once. Why was it so cold in there? She moved, quickly and quietly to the terrace doors, checked and found them securely closed, as were the windows. And the hall door, she thought with another frown.

She could have sworn she'd heard something. *Felt* something. But the chill had already faded, and there was no sound in the room but her sons' steady breathing.

She tucked up their blankets as she did every night, brushed kisses on both their heads.

And left the connecting doors open.

By MORNING SHE'D BRUSHED IT OFF. LUKE COULDN'T find his lucky shirt, and Gavin got into a wrestling match with Parker on their before-school walk and had to change his. As a result, she barely had time for morning coffee and the muffin David pressed on her.

"Will you tell Roz I went in early? I want to have the lobby area done before we open at ten."

"She left an hour ago."

"An hour ago?" Stella looked at her watch. Keeping up with Roz had become Stella's personal mission—and so far she was failing. "Does she *sleep*?"

"With her, the early bird doesn't just catch the worm, but has time to sauté it with a nice plum sauce for breakfast."

"Excuse me, but *eeuw*. Gotta run." She dashed for the doorway, then stopped. "David, everything's going okay with the kids? You'd tell me otherwise, right?"

"Absolutely. We're having nothing but fun. Today, after school, we're going to practice running with scissors, then find how many things we can roughhouse with that can poke our eyes out. After that, we've moving on to flammables."

"Thanks. I feel very reassured." She bent down to give Parker a last pat. "Keep an eye on this guy," she told him.

LOGAN KITRIDGE WAS PRESSED FOR TIME. RAIN HAD delayed his personal project to the point where he was going to have to postpone some of the fine points—again—to meet professional commitments.

He didn't mind so much. He considered landscaping a perpetual work in progress. It was never finished. It *should* never be finished. And when you worked with Nature, Nature was the boss. She was fickle and tricky, and endlessly fascinating.

A man had to be continually on his toes, be ready to flex, be willing to compromise and swing with her moods. Planning in absolutes was an exercise in frustration, and to his mind there were enough other things to be frustrated about.

Since Nature had deigned to give him a good, clear day, he was taking it to deal with his personal project. It meant he had to work alone—he liked that better in any case—and carve out time to swing by the job site and check on his two-man crew.

It meant he had to get over to Roz's place, pick up the trees he'd earmarked for his own use, haul them back to his place, and get them in the ground before noon.

Or one. Two at the latest.

Well, he'd see how it went.

The one thing he couldn't afford to carve out time for was this new manager Roz had taken on. He couldn't figure out why Roz had hired a manager in the first place, and for God's sake a Yankee. It seemed to him that Rosalind Harper knew how to run her business just fine and didn't need some fast-talking stranger screwing with the system.

He liked working with Roz. She was a woman who got things done, and who didn't poke her nose into his end of things any more than was reasonable. She loved the work, just as he did, had an instinct for it. So when she did make a suggestion, you tended to listen and weigh it in.

She paid well and didn't hassle a man over every detail.

He could tell, just *tell*, that this manager was going to be nothing but bumps and ruts in his road.

Wasn't she already leaving messages for him in that cool Yankee voice about time management, invoice systems, and equipment inventory?

He didn't give a shit about that sort of thing, and he wasn't going to start giving one now.

He and Roz had a system, damn it. One that got the job done and made the client happy.

Why mess with success?

He drove his full-size pickup through the parking area, wove through the piles of mulch and sand, the landscape timbers, and around the side loading area.

He'd already eyeballed and tagged what he wanted—but before he loaded them up, he'd take one more look around. Plus there were some young evergreens in the field and a couple of hemlocks in the balled and burlapped area that he thought he could use.

Harper had grafted him a couple of willows and a hedgerow of peonies. They'd be ready to dig in this spring, along with the various pots of cuttings and layered plants Roz had helped him with.

He moved through the rows of trees, then turned around and backtracked.

This wasn't right, he thought. Everything was out of place, changed around. Where were his dogwoods? Where the hell were the rhododendrons, the mountain laurels he'd tagged? Where was his goddamn frigging magnolia?

He scowled at a pussy willow, then began a careful, step-by-step search through the section.

It was all different. Trees and shrubs were no longer in

what he'd considered an interesting, eclectic mix of type and species, but lined up like army recruits, he decided. Alphabetized, for Christ's sweet sake. In frigging Latin.

Shrubs were segregated, and organized in the same anal fashion.

He found his trees and, stewing, carted them to his truck. Muttering to himself, he decided to head into the field, dig up the trees he wanted there. They'd be safer at his place. Obviously.

Bur first he was going to hunt up Roz and get this mess straightened out.

STANDING ON A STEPLADDER, ARMED WITH A BUCKET of soapy water and a rag, Stella attacked the top of the shelf she'd cleared off. A good cleaning, she decided, and it would be ready for her newly planned display. She envisioned it filled with color-coordinated decorative pots, some mixed plantings scattered among them. Add other accessories, like raffia twine, decorative watering spikes, florist stones and marbles, and so on, and you'd have something.

At point of purchase, it would generate impulse sales.

She was moving the soil additives, fertilizers, and animal repellents to the side wall. Those were basics, not impulse. Customers would walk back there for items of that nature, and pass the wind chimes she was going to hang, the bench and concrete planter she intended to haul in. With the other changes, it would all tie together, and with the flow, draw customers into the houseplant section, across to the patio pots, the garden furniture, all before they moved through to the bedding plants.

With an hour and a half until they opened, and if she could shanghai Harper into helping her with the heavy stuff, she'd have it done.

She heard footsteps coming through from the back, blew her hair out of her eyes. "Making progress," she began. "I know it doesn't look like it yet, but . . ."

She broke off when she saw him.

Even standing on the ladder, she felt dwarfed. He had to be six-five. All tough and rangy and fit in faded jeans with bleach stains splattered over one thigh. He wore a flannel shirt jacket-style over a white T-shirt and a pair of boots so dinged and scored she wondered he didn't take pity and give them a decent burial.

His long, wavy, unkempt hair was the color she'd been shooting for the one time she'd dyed her own.

She wouldn't have called him handsome—everything about him seemed rough and rugged. The hard mouth, the hollowed cheeks, the sharp nose, the expression in his eyes. They were green, but not like Kevin's had been. These were moody and deep, and seemed somehow *hot* under the strong line of brows.

No, she wouldn't have said handsome, but arresting, in a big and tough sort of way. The sort of tough that looked like a bunched fist would bounce right off him, doing a lot more damage to the puncher than the punchee.

She smiled, though she wondered where Roz was, or Harper. Or somebody.

"I'm sorry. We're not open yet this morning. Is there something I can do for you?"

Oh, he knew that voice. That crisp, cool voice that had left him annoying messages about functional organizational plans and production goals.

He'd expected her to look like she'd sounded—a usual mistake, he supposed. There wasn't much cool and crisp about that wild red hair she was trying to control with that stupid-looking kerchief, or the wariness in those big blue eyes.

"You moved my damn trees."

"I'm sorry?"

"Well, you ought to be. Don't do it again."

"I don't know what you're talking about." She kept a grip on the bucket—just in case—and stepped down the ladder. "Did you order some trees? If I could have your name, I'll see if I can find your order. We're implementing a new system, so—"

"I don't have to order anything, and I don't like your new system. And what the hell are you doing in here? Where *is* everything?"

His voice sounded local to her, with a definite edge of nasty impatience. "I think it would be best if you came back when we're open. Winter hours start at ten A.M. If you'd leave me your name . . ." She edged toward the counter and the phone.

"It's Kitridge, and you ought to know since you've been nagging me brainless for damn near a week."

"I don't know . . . oh. Kitridge." She relaxed, fractionally. "The landscape designer. And I haven't been nagging," she said with more heat when her brain caught up. "I've been trying to contact you so we could schedule a meeting. You haven't had the courtesy to return my calls. I certainly hope you're not as rude with clients as you are with coworkers."

"Rude? Sister, you haven't seen rude."

"I have two sons," she snapped back. "I've seen plenty of rude. Roz hired me to put some order into her business, to take some of the systemic load off her shoulders, to—"

"Systemic?" His gaze rose to the ceiling like a man sending out a prayer. "Jesus, are you always going to talk like that?"

She took a calming breath. "Mr. Kitridge, I have a job to do. Part of that job is dealing with the landscaping arm of this business. It happens to be a very important and profitable arm."

"Damn right. And it's my frigging arm."

"It also happens to be ridiculously disorganized and apparently run like a circus. I've been finding little scraps of paper and hand-scribbled orders and invoices—if you can call them that—all week."

"So?"

"So, if you'd bothered to return my calls and arrange for

a meeting, I could have explained to you how this arm of the business will now function."

"Oh, is that right?" That west Tennessee tone took on a soft and dangerous hue. "You're going to explain it to me."

"That's exactly right. The system I'm implementing will, in the end, save you considerable time and effort with computerized invoices and inventory, client lists and designs, with—"

He was sizing her up. He figured he had about a foot on her in height, probably a good hundred pounds in bulk. But the woman had a mouth on her. It was what his mother would have called bee stung—pretty—and apparently it never stopped flapping.

"How the hell is having to spend half my time on a computer going to save me anything?"

"Once the data is inputted, it will. At this point, you seem to be carrying most of this information in some pocket, or inside your head."

"So? If it's in a pocket, I can find it. If it's in my head, I can find it there, too. Nothing wrong with my memory."

"Maybe not. But tomorrow you may be run over by a truck and spend the next five years in a coma." That pretty mouth smiled, icily. "Then where will we be?"

"Being as I'd be in a coma, I wouldn't be worried about it. Come out here."

He grabbed her hand, pulled her toward the door. "Hey!" she managed. Then, *"Hey!"*

"This is business." He yanked open the door and kept pulling her along. "I'm not dragging you off to a cave."

"Then let go." His hands were hard as rock, and just as rough. And his legs, she realized, as he strode away from the building, ate up ground in long, hurried bites and forced her into an undignified trot.

"Just a minute. Look at that."

He gestured toward the tree and shrub area while she struggled to get her breath back. "What about it?"

"It's messed up."

"It certainly isn't. I spent nearly an entire day on this area." And had the aching muscles to prove it. "It's cohesively arranged so if a customer is looking for an ornamental tree, he—or a member of the staff—can find the one that suits. If the customer is looking for a spring-blooming shrub or—"

"They're all lined up. What did you use, a carpenter's level? People come in here now, how can they get a picture of how different specimens might work together?"

"That's your job and the staff's. We're here to help and direct the customer to possibilities as well as their more definite wants. If they're wandering around trying to find a damn hydrangea—"

"They might just spot a spirea or camellia they'd like to have, too."

He had a point, and she'd considered it. She wasn't an idiot. "Or they may leave empty-handed because they couldn't easily find what they'd come for in the first place. Attentive and well-trained staff should be able to direct and explore with the customer. Either way has its pros and cons, but I happen to like this way better. And it's my call.

"Now." She stepped back. "If you have the time, we need to—"

"I don't." He stalked off toward his truck.

"Just wait." She jogged after him. "We need to talk about the new purchase orders and invoicing system."

"Send me a frigging memo. Sounds like your speed."

"I don't want to send you a frigging memo, and what are you doing with those trees?"

"Taking them home." He pulled open the truck door, climbed in.

"What do you mean you're taking them home? I don't have any paperwork on these."

"Hey, me neither." After slamming the door, he rolled the window down a stingy inch. "Step back, Red. Wouldn't want to run over your toes."

"Look. You can't just take off with stock whenever you feel like it."

"Take it up with Roz. If she's still the boss. Otherwise, better call the cops." He gunned the engine, and when she stumbled back, zipped into reverse. And left her staring after him.

Cheeks pink with temper, Stella marched back toward the building. Serve him right, she thought, just serve him right if she did call the police. She snapped her head up, eyes hot, as Roz opened the door.

"Was that Logan's truck?"

"Does he work with clients?"

"Sure. Why?"

"You're lucky you haven't been sued. He storms in, nothing but complaints. Bitch, bitch, bitch," Stella muttered as she swung past Roz and inside. "He doesn't like this, doesn't like that, doesn't like any damn thing as far as I can tell. Then he drives off with a truckload of trees and shrubs."

Roz rubbed her earlobe thoughtfully. "He does have his moods."

"Moods? I only saw one, and I didn't like it." She yanked off the kerchief, tossed it on the counter.

"Pissed you off, did he?"

"In spades. I'm trying to do what you hired me to do, Roz."

"I know. And so far I don't believe I've made any comments or complaints that could qualify as bitch, bitch, bitch."

Stella sent her a horrified look. "No! Of course not. I didn't mean—God."

"We're in what I'd call an adjustment period. Some don't adjust as smoothly as others. I like most of your ideas, and others I'm willing to give a chance. Logan's used to doing things his own way, and that's been fine with me. It works for us."

"He took stock. How can I maintain inventory if I don't know what he took, or what it's for? I need paperwork, Roz."

"I imagine he took the specimens he'd tagged for his

personal use. If he took others, he'll let me know. Which is not the way you do things," she continued before Stella could speak. "I'll talk to him, Stella, but you might have to do some adjusting yourself. You're not in Michigan anymore. I'm going to let you get back to work here."

And she was going back to her plants. They generally gave her less trouble than people.

"Roz? I know I can be an awful pain in the ass, but I really do want to help you grow your business."

"I figured out both those things already."

Alone, Stella sulked for a minute. Then she got her bucket and climbed up the ladder again. The unscheduled meeting had thrown her off schedule.

"I DON'T LIKE HER." LOGAN SAT IN ROZ'S PARLOR with a beer in one hand and a boatload of resentment in the other. "She's bossy, rigid, smug, and shrill." At Roz's raised brows, he shrugged. "Okay, not shrill—so far—but I stand by the rest."

"I do like her. I like her energy and her enthusiasm. And I need someone to handle the details, Logan. I've outgrown myself. I'm just asking that the two of you try to meet somewhere in the middle of things."

"I don't think she has any middle. She's extreme. I don't trust extreme women."

"You trust me."

He brooded into his beer. That was true enough. If he hadn't trusted Roz, he wouldn't have come to work for her, no matter what salary and perks she'd dangled under his nose. "She's going to have us filling out forms in triplicate and documenting how many inches we prune off a damn bush."

"I don't think it'll come to that." Roz propped her feet comfortably on the coffee table and sipped her own beer.

"If you had to go and hire some sort of manager, Roz, why the hell didn't you hire local? Get somebody in who understands how things work around here."

"Because I didn't want a local. I wanted her. When she comes down, we're going to have a nice civilized drink followed by a nice civilized meal. I don't care if the two of you don't like each other, but you will learn how to get along."

"You're the boss."

"That's a fact." She gave him a companionable pat on the thigh. "Harper's coming over, too. I browbeat him into it."

Logan brooded a minute longer. "You really like her?"

"I really do. And I've missed the company of women. Women who aren't silly and annoying, anyway. She's neither. She had a tough break, Logan, losing her man at such a young age. I know what that's like. She hasn't broken under it, or gone brittle. So yes, I like her."

"Then I'll tolerate her, but only for you."

"Sweet talker." With a laugh, Roz leaned over to kiss his cheek.

"Only because I'm crazy about you."

Stella came to the door in time to see Logan take Roz's hand in his, and thought, Oh, shit.

She'd gone head-to-head, argued with, insulted, and complained about her boss's lover.

With a sick dread in her stomach, she nudged her boys forward. She stepped inside, plastered on a smile. "Hope we're not late," she said cheerily. "There was a small homework crisis. Hello, Mr. Kitridge. I'd like you to meet my sons. This is Gavin, and this is Luke."

"How's it going?" They looked like normal kids to him rather than the pod-children he'd expected someone like Stella to produce.

"I have a loose tooth," Luke told him.

"Yeah? Let's have a look, then." Logan set down his beer to take a serious study of the tooth Luke wiggled with his tongue. "Cool. You know, I've got me some pliers in my toolbox. One yank and we'd have that out of there."

At the small horrified sound from behind him, Logan turned to smile thinly at Stella.

"Mr. Kitridge is just joking," Stella told a fascinated Luke. "Your tooth will come out when it's ready."

"When it does, the Tooth Fairy comes, and I get a *buck*."

Logan pursed his lips. "A buck, huh? Good deal."

"It makes blood when it comes out, but I'm not scared."

"Miss Roz? Can we go see David in the kitchen?" Gavin shot a look at his mother. "Mom said we had to ask you."

"Sure. You go right on."

"No sweets," Stella called out as they dashed out.

"Logan, why don't you pour Stella a glass of wine?"

"I'll get it. Don't get up," Stella told him.

He didn't look quite as much like an overbearing jerk, she decided. He cleaned up well enough, and she could see why Roz was attracted. If you went for the *über*virile sort.

"Did you say Harper was coming?" Stella asked her.

"He'll be along." Roz gestured with her beer. "Let's see if we can all play nice. Let's get this business out of the way so we can have an enjoyable meal without ruining our digestion. Stella's in charge of sales and production, of managing the day-to-day business. She and I will, for now anyway, share personnel management while Harper and I head up propagation."

She sipped her beer, waited, though she knew her own power and didn't expect an interruption. "Logan leads the landscaping design, both on- and off-site. As such, he has first choice of stock and is authorized to put in for special orders, or arrange trades or purchases or rentals of necessary equipment, material or specimens for outside designs. The changes Stella has already implemented or proposed—and which have been approved by me—will stay or be put in place. Until such time as I decide they don't work. Or if I just don't like them. Clear so far?"

"Perfectly," Stella said coolly.

Logan shrugged.

"Which means you'll cooperate with each other, do what's necessary to work together in such a way for both of you to function in the areas you oversee. I built In the

Garden from the ground up, and I can run it myself if I have to. But I don't choose to. I choose to have the two of you, and Harper, shoulder the responsibilities you've been given. Squabble all you want. I don't mind squabbles. But get the job done."

She finished off her beer. "Questions? Comments?" After a beat of silence, she rose. "Well, then, let's eat."

five

❧

IT WAS, ALL THINGS CONSIDERED, A PLEASANT EVE-
ning. Neither of her kids threw any food or made audible
gagging noises. Always a plus, in Stella's book. Conversation was polite, even lively—particularly when the boys
learned Logan's first name—the same name used by the
X-Men's Wolverine.

It was instant hero status, given polish when it was discovered that Logan shared Gavin's obsession with comic
books.

The fact that Logan seemed more interested in talking
to her sons than her was probably another plus.

"If, you know, the Hulk and Spider-Man ever got into a
fight, I think Spider-Man would win."

Logan nodded as he cut into rare roast beef. "Because
Spider-Man's quicker, and more agile. But if the Hulk ever
caught him, Spidey'd be toast."

Gavin speared a tiny new potato, then held it aloft on
his fork like a severed head on a pike. "If he was under the
influence of some evil guy, like . . ."

"Maybe Mr. Hyde."

"Yeah! Mr. Hyde, then the Hulk could be *forced* to go after Spider-Man. But I still think Spidey would win."

"That's why he's amazing," Logan agreed, "and the Hulk's incredible. It takes more than muscle to battle evil."

"Yeah, you gotta be smart and brave and stuff."

"Peter Parker's the smartest." Luke emulated his brother with the potato head.

"Bruce Banner's pretty smart, too." Since it made the kids laugh, Harper hoisted a potato, wagged it. "He always manages to get new clothes after he reverts from Hulk form."

"If he was really smart," Harper commented, "he'd figure out a way to make his clothes stretch and expand."

"You scientists," Logan said with a grin for Harper. "Never thinking about the mundane."

"Is the Mundane a supervillain?" Luke wanted to know.

"It means the ordinary," Stella told him. "As in, it's more mundane to eat your potatoes than to play with them, but that's the polite thing to do at the table."

"Oh." Luke smiled at her, an expression somewhere between sweet and wicked, and chomped the potato off the fork. "Okay." After the meal, she used the excuse of the boys' bedtime to retreat upstairs. There were baths to deal with, the usual thousand questions to answer, and all that end-of-day energy to burn off, which included one or both of them running around mostly naked.

Then came her favorite time, when she drew a chair between their beds and read to them while Parker began to snore at her feet. The current pick was *Mystic Horse*, and when she closed the book, she got the expected moans and pleas for just a little more.

"Tomorrow, because now I'm afraid it's time for sloppy kisses."

"Not sloppy kisses." Gavin rolled onto his belly to bury his face in the pillow. "Not that!"

"Yes, and you must succumb." She covered the back of his head, the base of his neck with kisses while he giggled.

"And now, for my second victim." She turned to Luke and rubbed her hands together.

"Wait, wait!" He threw out his hand to ward off the attack. "Do you think my tooth will fall out tomorrow?"

"Let's have another look." She sat on the side of his bed, studying soberly as he wiggled the tooth with his tongue. "I think it just might."

"Can I have a horse?"

"It won't fit under your pillow." When he laughed, she kissed his forehead, his cheeks, and his sweet, sweet mouth.

Rising, she switched off the lamp, leaving them in the glow of the night-light. "Only fun dreams allowed."

"I'm gonna dream I get a horse, because dreams come true sometimes."

"Yes, they do. 'Night now."

She walked back to her room, heard the whispers from bed to bed that were also part of the bedtime ritual.

It had become their ritual, over the last two years. Just the three of them at nighttime, where they had once been four. But it was solid now, and good, she thought, as a few giggles punctuated the whispers.

Somewhere along the line she'd stopped aching every night, every morning, for what had been. And she'd come to treasure what was.

She glanced at her laptop, thought about the work she'd earmarked for the evening. Instead, she went to the terrace doors.

It was still too cool to sit out, but she wanted the air, and the quiet, and the night.

Imagine, just imagine, she was standing outside at night in January. And not freezing. Though the forecasters were calling for more rain, the sky was star-studded and graced with a sliver of moon. In that dim light she could see a camellia in bloom. Flowers in winter—now that was something to add to the plus pile about moving south.

She hugged her elbows and thought of spring, when the air would be warm and garden-scented.

She wanted to be here in the spring, to see it, to be part of the awakening. She wanted to keep her job. She hadn't realized how much she wanted to keep it until Roz's firm, no-nonsense sit-down before dinner.

Less than two weeks, and she was already caught up. Maybe too much caught, she admitted. That was always a problem. Whatever she began, she needed to finish. Stella's religion, her mother called it.

But this was more. She was emotional about the place. A mistake, she knew. She was half in love with the nursery, and with her own vision of how it could be. She wanted to see tables alive with color and green, cascading flowers spilling from hanging baskets that would drop down along the aisles to make arbors. She wanted to see customers browsing and buying, filling the wagons and flatbeds with containers.

And, of course, there was that part of her that wanted to go along with each one of them and show them exactly how everything should be planted. But she could control that.

She could admit she also wanted to see the filing system in place, and the spreadsheets, the weekly inventory logs.

And whether he liked it or not, she intended to visit some of Logan's jobs. To get a feel for that end of the business.

That was supposing he didn't talk Roz into firing her.

He'd gotten slapped back, too, Stella admitted. But he had home-field advantage.

In any case, she wasn't going to be able to work, or relax, or think about anything else until she'd straightened things out.

She would go downstairs, on the pretext of making a cup of tea. If his truck was gone, she'd try to have a minute with Roz.

It was quiet, and she had a sudden sinking feeling that they'd gone up to bed. She didn't want that picture in her head. Tiptoeing into the front parlor, she peeked out the window. Though she didn't see his truck, it occurred to her she didn't know where he'd parked, or what he'd driven in the first place.

She'd leave it for morning. That was best. In the morning, she would ask for a short meeting with Roz and get everything back in place. Better to sleep on it, to plan exactly what to say and how to say it.

Since she was already downstairs, she decided to go ahead and make that tea. Then she would take it upstairs and focus on work. Things would be better when she was focused.

She walked quietly back into the kitchen, and let out a yelp when she saw the dim figure in the shaded light. The figure yelped back, then slapped at the switch beside the stove.

"Just draw and shoot next time," Roz said, slapping a hand to her heart.

"I'm sorry. God, you scared me. I knew David was going into the city tonight and I didn't think anyone was back here."

"Just me. Making some coffee."

"In the dark?"

"Stove light was on. I know my way around. You come down to raid the refrigerator?"

"What? No. No!" She was hardly that comfortable here, in another woman's home. "I was just going to make some tea to take up while I do a little work."

"Go ahead. Unless you want some of this coffee."

"If I drink coffee after dinner, I'm awake all night."

It was awkward, standing here in the quiet house, just the two of them. It wasn't her house, Stella thought, her kitchen, even her quiet. She wasn't a guest, but an employee.

However gracious Roz might be, everything around them belonged to her.

"Did Mr. Kitridge leave?"

"You can call him Logan, Stella. You only sound pissy otherwise."

"Sorry. I don't mean to be." Maybe a little. "We got off

on the wrong foot, that's all, and I . . . oh, thanks," she said when Roz handed her the teakettle. "I realize I shouldn't have complained about him."

She filled the kettle, wishing she'd thought through what she wanted to say. Practiced it a few times.

"Because?" Roz prompted.

"Well, it's hardly constructive for your manager and your landscape designer to start in on each other after one run-in, and less so to whine to you about it."

"Sensible. Mature." Roz leaned back on the counter, waiting for her coffee to brew. Young, she thought. She had to remember that despite some shared experiences, the girl was more than a decade younger than she. And a bit tender yet.

"I try to be both," Stella said, and put the kettle on to boil.

"So did I, once upon a time. Then I decided, screw that. I'm going to start my own business."

Stella pushed back her hair. Who was this woman who was elegant to look at even in the hard lights? Who spoke frank words in that debutante-of-the-southern-aristocracy voice and wore ancient wool socks in lieu of slippers? "I can't get a handle on you. I can't figure you out."

"That's what you do, isn't it? Get handles on things." She shifted to reach up and behind into a cupboard for a coffee mug. "That's a good quality to have in a manager. Might be irritating on a personal level."

"You wouldn't be the first." Stella let out a breath. "And on that personal level, I'd like to add a separate apology. I shouldn't have said those things about Logan to you. First off, because it's bad form to fly off about another employee. And second, I didn't realize you were involved."

"Didn't you?" The moment, Roz decided, called for a cookie. She reached into the jar David kept stocked, pulled out a snickerdoodle. "And you realized it when . . ."

"When we came downstairs—before dinner. I didn't mean to eavesdrop, but I happened to notice . . ."

"Have a cookie."

"I don't really eat sweets after—"

"Have a cookie," Roz insisted and handed one over. "Logan and I are involved. He works for me, though he doesn't quite see it that way." An amused smile brushed over her lips. "It's more a *with me* from his point of view, and I don't mind that. Not as long as the work gets done, the money comes in, and the customers are satisfied. We're also friends. I like him very much. But we don't sleep together. We're not, in any way, romantically involved."

"Oh." This time she huffed out a breath. "Oh. Well, I've used up my own, so I'll have to borrow someone else's foot to stuff in my mouth."

"I'm not insulted, I'm flattered. He's an excellent, specimen. I can't say I've ever thought about him in that way."

"Why?"

Roz poured her coffee while Stella took the sputtering kettle off the burner. "I've got ten years on him."

"And your point would be?"

Roz glanced back, a little flicker of surprise running over her face, just ahead of humor. "You're right. That doesn't, or shouldn't, apply. However, I've been married twice. One was good, very good. One was bad, very bad. I'm not looking for a man right now. Too damn much trouble. Even when it's good, they take a lot of time, effort, and energy. I'm enjoying using all that time, effort, and energy on myself."

"Do you get lonely?"

"Yes. Yes, I do. There was a time I didn't think I'd have the luxury of being lonely. Raising my boys, all the running around, the mayhem, the responsibilities."

She glanced around the kitchen, as if surprised to find it quiet, without the noise and debris generated by young boys. "When I'd raised them—not that you're ever really done, but there's a point where you have to step back—I thought I wanted to share my life, my home, myself with someone. That was a mistake." Though her expression stayed easy and pleasant, her tone went hard as granite. "I corrected it."

"I can't imagine being married again. Even a good marriage is a balancing act, isn't it? Especially when you toss in careers, family."

"I never had all of them at once to juggle. When John was alive, it was home, kids, him. I wrapped my life around them. Only wrapped it tighter when it was just me and the boys. I'm not sorry for doing that," she said after a sip of coffee. "It was the way I wanted things. The business, the career, that started late for me. I admire women who can handle all those balls."

"I think I was good at it." There was a pang at remembering, a sweet little slice in the heart. "It's exhausting work, but I hope I was good at it. Now? I don't think I have the skill for it anymore. Being with someone every day, at the end of it." She shook her head. "I can't see it. I could always picture Kevin and me, all the steps and stages. I can't picture anyone else."

"Maybe he just hasn't come into the viewfinder yet."

Stella lifted a shoulder in a little shrug. "Maybe. But I could picture you and Logan together."

"Really?"

There was such humor, with a bawdy edge to it, that Stella forgot any sense of awkwardness and just laughed. "Not that way. Or I started to, then engaged the impenetrable mind block. I meant you looked good together. So attractive and easy. I thought it was nice. It's nice to have someone you can be easy with."

"And you and Kevin were easy together."

"We were. Sort of flowed on the same current."

"I wondered. You don't wear a wedding ring."

"No." Stella looked at her bare finger. "I took it off about a year ago, when I started dating again. It didn't seem right to wear it when I was with another man. I don't feel married anymore. It was gradual, I guess."

At the half question, Roz nodded. "Yes, I know."

"Somewhere along the line I stopped thinking, What would Kevin say about this. Or, What would Kevin do, or think, or want. So I took off my ring. It was hard. Almost as hard as losing him."

"I took mine off on my fortieth birthday," Roz murmured. "I realized I'd stopped wearing it as a tribute. It had become more of a shield against relationships. So I took it off on that black-letter day," she said with a half smile. "Because we move on, or we fade away."

"I'm too busy to worry about all of this most of the time, and I didn't mean to get into it now. I only wanted to apologize."

"Accepted. I'm going to take my coffee up. I'll see you in the morning."

"All right. Good night."

Feeling better, Stella finished making her tea. She would get a good start in the morning, she decided as she carried it upstairs. She'd get a good chunk of the reorganizing done, she'd talk with Harper and Roz about which cuttings should be added to inventory, *and* she'd find a way to get along with Logan.

She heard the singing, quiet and sad, as she started down the hall. Her heart began to trip, and china rattled on the tray as she picked up her pace. She was all but running by the time she got to the door of her sons' room.

There was no one there, just that same little chill to the air. Even when she set her tea down, searched the closet, under the bed, she found nothing.

She sat on the floor between the beds, waiting for her pulse to level. The dog stirred, then climbed up in her lap to lick her hand.

Stroking him, she stayed there, sitting between her boys while they slept.

ON SUNDAY, SHE WENT TO HER FATHER'S FOR brunch. She was more than happy to be handed a mimosa and ordered out of the kitchen by Jolene.

It was her first full day off since she'd started at In the Garden, and she was scheduled to relax.

With the boys running around the little backyard with Parker, she was free to sit down with her father.

"Tell me everything," he ordered.

"Everything will go straight through brunch, into dinner, and right into breakfast tomorrow."

"Give me the highlights. How do you like Rosalind?"

"I like her a lot. She manages to be straightforward and slippery. I'm never quite sure where I stand with her, but I do like her."

"She's lucky to have you. And being a smart woman, she knows it."

"You might be just a tiny bit biased."

"Just a bit."

He'd always loved her, Stella knew. Even when there had been months between visits. There'd always been phone calls or notes, or surprise presents in the mail.

He'd aged comfortably, she thought now. Whereas her mother waged a bitter and protracted war with the years, Will Dooley had made his truce with them. His red hair was overpowered by the gray now, and his bony frame carried a soft pouch in the middle. There were laugh lines around his eyes and mouth, glasses perched on his nose.

His face was ruddy from the sun. The man loved his gardening and his golf.

"The boys seem happy," he commented.

"They love it there. I can't believe how much I worried about it, then they just slide in like they've lived there all their lives."

"Sweetheart, if you weren't worrying about some such thing, you wouldn't be breathing."

"I hate that you're right about that. Anyway, there are still a few bumps regarding school. It's so hard being the new kids, but they like the house, and all that room. And they're crazy about David. You know David Wentworth?"

"Yeah. You could say he's been part of Roz's household since he was a kid, and now he runs it."

"He's great with the kids. It's a weight off knowing they're with someone they like after school. And I like Harper, though I don't see much of him."

"Boy's always been a loner. Happier with his plants. Good looking," he added.

"He is, Dad, but we'll just stick with discussing leaf-bud cuttings and cleft grafting, okay?"

"Can't blame a father for wanting to see his daughter settled."

"I am settled, for the moment." More, she realized, than she would have believed possible. "At some point, though, I'm going to want my own place. I'm not ready to look yet—too much to do, and I don't want to rock the boat with Roz. But it's on my list. Something in the same school district when the time comes. I don't want the boys to have to change again."

"You'll find what you're after. You always do."

"No point in finding what you're not after. But I've got time. Right now I'm up to my ears in reorganizing. That's probably an exaggeration. I'm up to my ears in organizing. Stock, paperwork, display areas."

"And having the time of your life."

She laughed, stretched out her arms and legs. "I really am. Oh, Dad, it's a terrific place, and there's so much untapped potential yet. I'd like to find somebody who has a real head for sales and customer relations, put him or her in charge of that area while I concentrate on rotating stock, keep ahead of the paperwork, and juggle in some of my ideas. I haven't even touched on the landscape area. Except for a head butt with the guy who runs that."

"Kitridge?" Will smiled. "Met him once or twice, I think. Hear he's a prickly sort."

"I'll say."

"Does good work. Roz wouldn't tolerate less, I can promise you. He did a property for a friend of mine about two years ago. Bought this old house, wanted to concentrate on rehabbing it. Grounds were a holy mess. He hired Kitridge for that. Showplace now. Got written up in a magazine."

"What's his story? Logan's?"

"Local boy. Born and bred. Though it seems to me he moved up north for a while. Got married."

"I didn't realize he's married."

"Was," Will corrected. "Didn't take. Don't know the details. Jo might. She's better at ferreting out and remembering that sort of thing. He's been back here six, eight years. Worked for a big firm out of the city until Roz scooped him up. Jo! What do you know about the Kitridge boy who works for Roz?"

"Logan?" Jolene peeked around the corner. She was wearing an apron that said, JO'S KITCHEN. There was a string of pearls around her neck and fuzzy pink slippers on her feet. "He's sexy."

"I don't think that's what Stella wanted to know."

"Well, she could see that for herself. Got eyes in her head and blood in her veins, doesn't she? His folks moved out to Montana, of all places, two, three years ago."

She cocked a hip, tapped a finger on her cheek as she lined up her data. "Got an older sister lives in Charlotte now. He went out with Marge Peters's girl, Terri, a couple times. You remember Terri, don't you, Will?"

"Can't say as I do."

"'Course you do. She was homecoming and prom queen in her day, then Miss Shelby County. First runner-up for Miss Tennessee. Most agree she missed the crown because her talent wasn't as strong as it could've been. Her voice is a little bit, what you'd call slight, I guess."

As Jo talked, Stella just sat back and enjoyed. Imagine knowing all this, or caring. She doubted she could remember who the homecoming or prom queens were from her own high school days. And here was Jo, casually pumping out the information on events that were surely a decade old.

Had to be a southern thing.

"And Terri? She said Logan was too serious-minded for

her," Jo continued, "but then a turnip would be too serious-minded for that girl."

She turned back into the kitchen, lifting her voice. "He married a Yankee and moved up to Philadelphia or Boston or some place with her. Moved back a couple years later without her. No kids."

She came back with a fresh mimosa for Stella and one for herself. "I heard she liked big-city life and he didn't, so they split up. Probably more to it than that. Always is, but Logan's not one to talk, so information is sketchy. He worked for Fosterly Landscaping for a while. You know, Will, they do mostly commercial stuff. Beautifying office buildings and shopping centers and so on. Word is Roz offered him the moon, most of the stars, and a couple of solar systems to bring him into her operation."

Will winked at his daughter. "Told you she'd have the details."

"And then some."

Jo chuckled, waved a hand. "He bought the old Morris place on the river a couple of years ago. Been fixing it up, or having it fixed up. *And* I heard he was doing a job for Tully Scopes. You don't know Tully, Will, but I'm on the garden committee with his wife, Mary. She'll complain the sky's too blue or the rain's too wet. Never satisfied with anything. You want another Bloody Mary, honey?" she asked Will.

"Can't say as I'd mind."

"So I heard Tully wanted Logan to design some shrubbery, and a garden and so on for this property he wanted to turn over."

Jolene kept on talking as she walked back to the kitchen counter to mix the drink. Stella exchanged a mile-wide grin with her father.

"And every blessed day, Tully was down there complaining, or asking for changes, or saying this, that, or the other. Until Logan told him to screw himself sideways, or words to that effect."

"So much for customer relations," Stella declared.

"Walked off the job, too," Jolene continued. "Wouldn't set foot on the property again or have any of his crew plant a daisy until Tully agreed to stay away. That what you wanted to know?"

"That pretty much covers it," Stella said and toasted Jolene with her mimosa.

"Good. Just about ready here. Why don't you go on and call the boys?"

WITH THE INFORMATION FROM JOLENE ENTERED INTO her mental files, Stella formulated a plan. Bright and early Monday morning, armed with her map and a set of MapQuest directions, she set out for the job site Logan had scheduled.

Or, she corrected, the job Roz thought he had earmarked for that morning.

She was going to be insanely pleasant, cooperative, and flexible. Until he saw things her way.

She cruised the neighborhood that skirted the city proper. Charming old houses, closer to each other than to the road. Lovely sloping lawns. Gorgeous old trees. Oak and maple that would leaf and shade, dogwood and Bradford pear that would celebrate spring with blooms. Of course, it wouldn't be the south without plenty of magnolias along with enormous azaleas and rhododendrons.

She tried to picture herself there, with her boys, living in one of those gracious homes, with her lovely yard to tend. Yes, she could see that, could see them happy in such a place, cozy with the neighbors, organizing dinner parties, play dates, cookouts.

Out of her price range, though. Even with the money she'd saved, the capital from the sale of the house in Michigan, she doubted she could afford real estate here. Besides, it would mean changing schools again for the boys, and she would have to spend time commuting to work.

Still, it made a sweet, if brief, fantasy.

She spotted Logan's truck and a second pickup outside a two-story brick house.

She could see immediately it wasn't as well kept as most of its neighbors. The front lawn was patchy. The foundation plantings desperately needed shaping, and what had been flower beds looked either overgrown or stone dead.

She heard the buzz of chain saws and country music playing too loud as she walked around the side of the house. Ivy was growing madly here, crawling its way up the brick. Should be stripped off, she thought. That maple needs to come down, before it falls down, and that fence line's covered with brambles, overrun with honeysuckle.

In the back, she spotted Logan, harnessed halfway up a dead oak. Wielding the chain saw, he speared through branches. It was cool, but the sun and the labor had a dew of sweat on his face, and a line of it darkening the back of his shirt.

Okay, so he was sexy. Any well-built man doing manual labor looked sexy. Add some sort of dangerous tool to the mix, and the image went straight to the lust bars and played a primal tune.

But sexy, she reminded herself, wasn't the point.

His work and their working dynamics were the point. She stood well out of the way while he worked, and scanned the rest of the backyard.

The space might have been lovely once, but now it was neglected, weedy, overgrown with trash trees and dying shrubs. A sagging garden shed tilted in the far corner of a fence smothered in vines.

Nearly a quarter of an acre, she estimated as she watched a huge black man drag lopped branches toward a short, skinny white man working a splitter. Nearby a burly-looking mulcher waited its turn to chew up the rest.

The beauty here wasn't lost, Stella decided. It was just buried.

It needed vision to bring it to life again.

Since the black man caught her eye, Stella wandered over to the ground crew.

"Help you, Miss?"

She extended her hand and a smile. "I'm Stella Rothchild, Ms. Harper's manager."

"'Meetcha. I'm Sam, this here is Dick.'"

The little guy had the fresh, freckled face of a twelve-year-old, with a scraggly goatee that looked as if it might have grown there by mistake. "Heard about you." He sent an eyebrow-wiggling grin toward her coworker.

"Really?" She kept her tone friendly, though her teeth came together tight in the smile. "I thought it would be helpful if I dropped by a couple of the jobs, looked at the work." She scanned the yard again, deliberately keeping her gaze below Logan's perch in the tree. "You've certainly got yours cut out for you with this."

"Got a mess of clearing to do," Sam agreed. Covered with work gloves, his enormous hands settled on his hips. "Seen worse, though."

"Is there a projection on man-hours?"

"Pro*jec*tion." Dick sniggered and elbowed Sam.

From his great height, Sam sent down a pitying look.

"You want to know about the plans and, uh, projections," he said, "you need to talk to the boss. He's got all that worked up."

"All right, then. Thanks. I'll let you get back to work."

Walking away, Stella took the little camera out of her bag and began to take what she thought of as "before" pictures.

HE KNEW SHE WAS THERE. STANDING DOWN THERE all pressed and tidy with her wild hair pulled back and shaded glasses hiding her big blue eyes.

He'd wondered when she would come nag him on a job, as it appeared to him she was a woman born to nag. At least she had the sense not to interrupt.

Then again, she seemed to be nothing *but* sense.

Maybe she'd surprise him. He liked surprises, and he'd gotten one when he met her kids. He'd expected to see a couple of polite little robots. The sort that looked to their domineering mother before saying a word. Instead he'd found them normal, interesting, funny kids. Surely it took some imagination to manage two active boys.

Maybe she was only a pain in the ass when it came to work.

Well, he grinned a little as he cut through a branch. So was he.

He let her wait while he finished. It took him another thirty minutes, during which he largely ignored her. Though he did see her take a camera—Jesus—then a notebook out of her purse.

He also noticed she'd gone over to speak to his men and that Dick sent occasional glances in Stella's direction.

Dick was a social moron, Logan thought, particularly when it came to women. But he was a tireless worker, and he would take on the filthiest job with a blissful and idiotic grin. Sam, who had more common sense in his big toe than Dick had in his entire skinny body, was, thank God, a tolerant and patient man.

They went back to high school, and that was the sort of thing that set well with Logan. The continuity of it, and the fact that because they'd known each other around twenty years, they didn't have to gab all the damn time to make themselves understood.

Explaining things half a dozen times just tried his patience. Which he had no problem admitting he had in short supply to begin with.

Between the three of them, they did good work, often exceptional work. And with Sam's brawn and Dick's energy, he rarely had to take on any more laborers.

Which suited him. He preferred small crews to large. It was more personal that way, at least from his point of view. And in Logan's point of view, every job he took was personal.

It was his vision, his sweat, his blood that went into the land. And his name that stood for what he created with it.

The Yankee could harp about forms and systemic bullshit all she wanted. The land didn't give a rat's ass about that. And neither did he.

He called out a warning to his men, then topped the old, dead oak. When he shimmied down, he unhooked his harness and grabbed a bottle of water. He drank half of it down without taking a breath.

"Mr. . . ." No, friendly, Stella remembered. She boosted up her smile, and started over. "Nice job. I didn't realize you did the tree work yourself."

"Depends. Nothing tricky to this one. Out for a drive?"

"No, though I did enjoy looking at the neighborhood. It's beautiful." She looked around the yard, gestured to encompass it. "This must have been, too, once. What happened?"

"Couple lived here fifty years. He died a while back. She couldn't handle the place on her own, and none of their kids still live close by. She got sick, place got rundown. She got sicker. Kids finally got her out and into a nursing home."

"That's hard. It's sad."

"Yeah, a lot of life is. They sold the place. New owners got a bargain and want the grounds done up. We're doing them up."

"What've you got in mind?"

He took another slug from the water bottle. She noticed the mulcher had stopped grinding, and after Logan sent a long, narrowed look over her shoulder, it got going again.

"I've got a lot of things in mind."

"Dealing with this job, specifically?"

"Why?"

"Because it'll help me do my job if I know more about yours. Obviously you're taking out the oak and I assume the maple out front."

"Yeah. Okay, here's the deal. We clear everything out that can't or shouldn't be saved. New sod, new fencing. We knock down the old shed, replace it. New owners want lots of color. So we shape up the azaleas, put a weeping cherry out front, replacing the maple. Lilac over there, and a magnolia on that side. Plot of peonies on that side, rambling roses along the back fence. See they got that rough little hill toward the back there, on the right? Instead of leveling it, we'll plant it."

He outlined the rest of it quickly, rolling out Latin terms and common names, taking long slugs from his water bottle, gesturing.

He could see it, he always could—the finished land. The small details, the big ones, fit together into one attractive whole.

Just as he could see the work that would go into each and every step, as he could look forward to the process nearly as much as the finished job.

He liked having his hands in the dirt. How else could you respect the landscape or the changes you made in it? And as he spoke he glanced down at her hands. Smirked a little at her tidy fingernails with their coat of glossy pink polish.

Paper pusher, he thought. Probably didn't know crabgrass from sumac.

Because he wanted to give her and her clipboard the full treatment and get her off his ass, he switched to the house and talked about the patio they intended to build and the plantings he'd use to accent it.

When he figured he'd done more talking than he normally did in a week, he finished off the water. Shrugged. He didn't expect her to follow everything he'd said, but she couldn't complain that he hadn't cooperated.

"It's wonderful. What about the bed running on the south side out front?"

He frowned a little. "We'll rip out the ivy, then the clients want to try their hand at that themselves."

"Even better. You've got more of an investment if you dig some yourself."

Because he agreed, he said nothing and only jingled some change in his pocket.

"Except I'd rather see winter creeper than yews around the shed. The variegated leaves would show off well, as would the less uniform shape."

"Maybe."

"Do you work from a landscape blueprint or out of your head?"

"Depends."

Should I pull all his teeth at once, or one at a time, she thought, but maintained the smile. "It's just that I'd like to see one of your designs, on paper, at some point. Which leads me to a thought I'd had."

"Bet you got lots of them."

"My boss told me to play nice," she said, coolly now. "How about you?"

He moved his shoulder again. "Just saying."

"My thought was, with some of the reorganizing and transferring I'm doing, I could cull out some office space for you at the center."

He gave her the same look he'd sent his men over her shoulder. A lesser woman, Stella told herself, would wither under it. "I don't work in a frigging office."

"I'm not suggesting that you spend all your time there, just that you'd have a place to deal with your paperwork, make your phone calls, keep your files."

"That's what my truck's for."

"Are you trying to be difficult?"

"Nope. I can do it without any effort at all. How about you?"

"You don't want the office, fine. Forget the office."

"I already have."

"Dandy. But *I* need an office. *I* need to know exactly what stock and equipment, what materials you'll need for this job." She yanked out her notebook again. "One red maple, one magnolia. Which variety of magnolia?"

"Southern. *Grandiflora gloriosa.*"

"Good choice for the location. One weeping cherry," she continued, and to his surprise and reluctant admiration, she ran down the entire plan he'd tossed out at her.

Okay, Red, he thought. Maybe you know a thing or two about the horticulture end of things after all.

"Yews or winter creeper?"

He glanced back at the shed, tried both out in his head. Damn if he didn't think she was right, but he didn't see why he had to say so right off. "I'll let you know."

"Do, and I'll want the exact number and specimen type of other stock as you take them."

"I'd be able to find you . . . in your office?"

"Just find me." She turned around, started to march off.

"Hey, Stella."

When she glanced back, he grinned. "Always wanted to say that."

Her eyes lit, and she snapped her head around again and kept going.

"Okay, okay. Jesus. Just a little humor." He strode after her. "Don't go away mad."

"Just go away?"

"Yeah, but there's no point in us being pissed at each other. I don't mind being pissed as a rule."

"I never would've guessed."

"But there's no point, right at the moment." As if he'd just remembered he had them on, he tugged off his work gloves, stuck them finger-first in his back pocket. "I'm doing my job, you're doing yours. Roz thinks she needs you, and I set a lot of store by Roz."

"So do I."

"I get that. Let's try to stay out from under each other's skin, otherwise we're just going to give each other a rash."

She inclined her head, lifted her eyebrows. "Is this you being agreeable?"

"Pretty much, yeah. I'm being agreeable so we can both do what Roz pays us to do. And because your kid has a copy of *Spider-Man* Number 121. If you're mad, you won't let him show it to me."

Now she tipped down her sunglasses, peered at him over the tops. "This isn't you being charming, is it?"

"No, this is me being sincere. I really want to see that issue, firsthand. If I was being charming, I guarantee you'd be in a puddle at my feet. It's a terrible power I have over women, and I try to use it sparingly."

"I just bet."

But she was smiling as she got into her car.

SIX

HAYLEY PHILLIPS WAS RIDING ON FUMES AND A DYING transmission. The radio still worked, thank God, and she had it cranked up with the Dixie Chicks blasting out. It kept her energy flowing.

Everything she owned was jammed into the Pontiac Grandville, which was older than she was and a lot more temperamental. Not that she had much at this point. She'd sold everything that could be sold. No point in being sentimental. Money took you a lot more miles than sentiment.

She wasn't destitute. What she'd banked would get her through the rough spots, and if there were more rough spots than she anticipated, she'd earn more. She wasn't aimless. She knew just where she was going. She just didn't know what would happen when she got there.

But that was fine. If you knew everything, you'd never be surprised.

Maybe she was tired, and maybe she'd pushed the rattling old car farther than it wanted to go that day. But if she and it could just hang on a few more miles, they'd get a break.

She didn't expect to get tossed out on her ear. But, well, if she was, she'd just do what needed to be done next.

She liked the look of the area, especially since she'd skirted around the tangle of highways that surrounded Memphis. On this north edge beyond the city, the land rolled a bit, and she'd seen snatches of the river and the steep bluffs that fell toward it. There were pretty houses—the neat spread of the suburbs that fanned out from the city limits, and now the bigger, richer ones. There were plenty of big old trees, and despite some walls of stone or brick, it *felt* friendly.

She sure could use a friend.

When she saw the sign for In the Garden, she slowed. She was afraid to stop, afraid the old Pontiac would just heave up and die if she did. But she slowed enough to get a look at the main buildings, the space in the security lights.

Then she took a lot of slow breaths as she kept driving. Nearly there. She'd planned out what she would say, but she kept changing her mind. Every new approach gave her a dozen different scenes to play out in her head. It had passed the time, but it hadn't gelled for her.

Maybe some could say that changing her mind was part of her problem. But she didn't think so. If you never changed your mind, what was the point of having one? It seemed to Hayley she'd known too many people who were stuck with one way of thinking, and how could that be using the brain God gave you?

As she headed toward the drive, the car began to buck and sputter.

"Come on, come on. Just a little more. If I'd been paying attention I'd've got you gas at the last place."

Then it conked on her, half in, half out of the entrance between the brick pillars.

She gave the wheel a testy little slap, but it was half-hearted. Nobody's fault but her own, after all. And maybe it was a good thing. Tougher to kick her out if her car was out of gas, and blocking the way.

She opened her purse, took out a brush to tidy her hair. After considerable experimentation, she'd settled back on her own oak-bark brown. At least for now. She was glad she'd gotten it cut and styled before she'd headed out. She liked the longish sweep of side bangs and the careless look of the straight bob with its varying lengths.

It made her look easy, breezy. Confident.

She put on lipstick, powdered off the shine.

"Okay. Let's get going."

She climbed out, hooked her purse over her shoulder, then started the walk up the long drive. It took money—old or new—to plant a house so far from the road. The one she'd grown up in had been so close, people driving by could practically reach out and shake her hand.

But she didn't mind that. It had been a nice house. A good house, and part of her had been sorry to sell it. But that little house outside Little Rock was the past. She was heading toward the future.

Halfway up the drive, she stopped. Blinked. This wasn't just a house, she decided as her jaw dropped. It was a mansion. The sheer size of it was one thing—she'd seen big-ass houses before, but nothing like this. This was the most beautiful house she'd ever laid eyes on outside of a magazine. It was Tara and Manderley all in one. Graceful and *female*, and strong.

Lights gleamed against windows, others flooded the lawn. As if it were welcoming her. Wouldn't that be nice?

Even if it wasn't, even if they booted her out again, she'd had the chance to see it. That alone was worth the trip.

She walked on, smelling the evening, the pine and woodsmoke.

She crossed her fingers on the strap of her purse for luck and walked straight up to the ground-level doors.

Lifting one of the brass knockers, she gave three firm raps.

Inside, Stella came down the steps with Parker. It was her turn to walk him. She called out, "I'll get it."

Parker was already barking as she opened the door.

She saw a girl with straight, fashionably ragged brown hair, a sharply angled face dominated by huge eyes the color of a robin's egg. She smiled, showing a bit of an overbite, and bent down to pet Parker when he sniffed at her shoes.

She said, "Hi."

"Hi." Where the hell had she come from? Stella wondered. There was no car parked outside.

The girl looked to be about twelve. And very pregnant.

"I'm looking for Rosalind Ashby. Rosalind Harper Ashby," she corrected. "Is she home?"

"Yes. She's upstairs. Come in."

"Thanks. I'm Hayley." She held out a hand. "Hayley Phillips. Mrs. Ashby and I are cousins, in a complicated southern sort of way."

"Stella Rothchild. Why don't you come in, sit down. I'll go find Roz."

"That'd be great." Swiveling her head back and forth, Hayley tried to see everything as Stella led her into the parlor. "Wow. You've just got to say wow."

"I did the first time I saw it. Do you want anything? Something to drink?"

"I'm okay. I should probably wait until . . ." She stayed on her feet, wandered to the fireplace. It was like something on a television show, or the movies. "Do you work in the house? Are you, like, the housekeeper?"

"No. I work at Roz's nursery. I'm the manager. I'll just go get Roz. You should sit down."

"It's okay." Hayley rubbed her pregnant belly. "We've been sitting."

"Be right back." With Parker in tow, Stella dashed off.

She hurried up the stairs, turned into Roz's wing. She'd only been in there once, when David had taken her on the grand tour, but she followed the sounds of the television and found Roz in her sitting room.

There was an old black-and-white movie on TV. Not that Roz was watching. She sat at an antique secretary, wearing baggy jeans and a sweatshirt as she sketched on a pad. Her feet were bare, and to Stella's surprise, her toenails were painted a bright candy pink.

She knocked on the doorjamb.

"Hmm? Oh, Stella, good. I was just sketching out an idea I had for a cutting garden along the northwest side of the nursery. Thought it might inspire customers. Come take a look."

"I'd love to, but there's someone downstairs to see you. Hayley Phillips. She says she's your cousin."

"Hayley?" Roz frowned. "I don't have a cousin Hayley. Do I?"

"She's young. Looks like a teenager. Pretty. Brown hair, blue eyes, taller than me. She's pregnant."

"Well, for God's sake." Roz rubbed the back of her neck. "Phillips. Phillips. My first husband's grandmother's sister—or maybe it was cousin—married a Phillips. I think."

"Well, she did say you were cousins in a complicated southern sort of way."

"Phillips." She closed her eyes, tapped a finger in the center of her forehead as if to wake up memory. "She must be Wayne Phillips's girl. He died last year. Well, I'd better go see what this is about."

She got up. "Your boys settled down for the night?"

"Yes, just."

"Then come on with me."

"Don't you think you should—"

"You've got a good level head. So come on, bring it with you."

Stella scooped Parker up and, hoping his bladder would hold, went downstairs with Roz.

Hayley turned as they came in. "I think this is the most completely awesome room. It makes you feel cozy and special just to be in it. I'm Hayley. I'm Wayne Phillips's daughter. My daddy was a connection of your first husband's, on his mother's side. You sent me a very nice note of condolence when he passed last year."

"I remember. I met him once. I liked him."

"So did I. I'm sorry to come this way, without calling or asking, and I didn't mean to get here so late. I had some car trouble earlier."

"That's all right. Sit down, Hayley. How far along are you?"

"Heading toward six months. The baby's due end of May. I should apologize, too, because my car ran out of gas right at the front of your driveway."

"We can take care of that. Are you hungry, Hayley? Would you like a little something to eat?"

"No, ma'am, I'm fine. I stopped to eat earlier. Forgot to feed the car. I have money. I don't want you to think I'm broke or here for a handout."

"Good to know. We should have tea, then. It's a cool night. Hot tea would be good."

"If it's not too much trouble. And if you've got decaffeinated." She stroked her belly. "Hardest thing about being pregnant's been giving up caffeine."

"I'll take care of it. Won't be long."

"Thanks, Stella." Roz turned back to Hayley as Stella went out. "So, did you drive all the way from . . . Little Rock, isn't it?"

"I did. I like to drive. Like to better when the car's not acting up, but you have to do what you have to do." She cleared her throat. "I hope you've been well, Cousin Rosalind."

"I have been, very well. And you? Are you and the baby doing well?"

"We're doing great. Healthy as horses, so the doctor said. And I feel just fine. Feel like I'm getting big as a house, but I don't mind that, or not so much. It's kind of interesting. Um, your children, your sons? They're doing fine?"

"Yes, they are. Grown now. Harper, that's my oldest, lives here in the guest house. He works with me at the nursery."

"I saw it—the nursery—when I was driving in." Hayley

caught herself rubbing her hands on the thighs of her jeans and made herself stop. "It looks so big, bigger than I expected. You must be proud."

"I am. What do you do back in Little Rock?"

"I worked in a bookstore, was helping manage it by the time I left. A small independent bookstore and coffee shop."

"Managed? At your age?"

"I'm twenty-four. I know I don't look it," she said with a hint of a smile. "I don't mind that, either. But I can show you my driver's license. I went to college, on partial scholarship. I've got a good brain. I worked summers there through high school and college. I got the job initially because my daddy was friends with the owner. But I earned it after."

"You said managed. You don't work there now."

"No." She was listening, Hayley thought. She was asking the right questions. That was something. "I resigned a couple of weeks ago. But I have a letter of recommendation from the owner. I'd decided to leave Little Rock."

"It seems a difficult time to leave home, and a job you're secure in."

"It seemed like the right time to me." She looked over as Stella wheeled in a tea cart. "Now *that* is just like the movies. I know saying that makes me sound like a hick or something, but I can't help it."

Stella laughed. "I was thinking exactly the same as I loaded it up. I made chamomile."

"Thanks. Stella, Hayley was just telling me she's left her home and her job. I'm hoping she's going to tell us why she thinks this was the right time to make a couple of drastic moves."

"Not drastic," Hayley corrected. "Just big. And I made them because of the baby. Well, because of both of us. You've probably figured out I'm not married."

"Your family isn't supportive?" Stella asked.

"My mother took off when I was about five. You may not remember that," she said to Roz. "Or you were too polite to mention it. My daddy died last year. I've got aunts and uncles, a pair of grandmothers left, and cousins. Some are still in the Little Rock area. Opinion is . . . mixed about my current situation. Thanks," she added after Roz had poured out and offered her a cup.

"Well, the thing is, I was awfully sad when Daddy passed. He got hit by a car, crossing the street. Just one of those accidents that you can never understand and that, well, just don't seem right. I didn't have time to prepare for it. I guess you never do. But he was just gone, in a minute."

She drank tea and felt it soothe her right down to the bones she hadn't realized were so tired. "I was sad, and mad and lonely. And there was this guy. It wasn't a one-night stand or anything like that. We liked each other. He used to come in the bookstore, flirt with me. I used to flirt back. When I was alone, he was comforting. He was sweet. Anyway, one thing led to another. He's a law student. Then he went back to school, and a few weeks later, I found out I was pregnant. I didn't know what I was going to do. How I was going to tell him. Or anybody. I put it off for a few more weeks. I didn't know what I was going to do."

"And when you did?"

"I thought I should tell him face-to-face. He hadn't been coming into the store like he used to. So I went by the college to look him up. Turned out he'd fallen in love with this girl. He was a little embarrassed to tell me, seeing as we'd been sleeping together. But it wasn't like we'd made each other any promises, or been in love or anything. We'd just liked each other, that's all. And when he talked about this other girl, he got all lit up. You could just see how crazy he was about her. So I didn't tell him about the baby."

She hesitated, then took one of the cookies Stella had arranged on a plate. "I can't resist sweets. After I'd thought about it, I didn't see how telling him would do any of us any good."

"That was a very hard decision," Roz told her.

"I don't know that it was. I don't know what I expected

him to do when I went to tell him, except I thought he had a right to know. I didn't want to marry him or anything. I wasn't even sure, back that far, that I was going to keep the baby."

She nibbled on the cookie while she rubbed a hand gently over the mound of her belly. "I guess that's one of the reasons I went out there, to talk to him. Not just to tell him about it, but to see what he thought we should do. But sitting with him, listening to him go on about this girl—"

She stopped, shook her head. "I needed to decide what to do about it. All telling him would've done was made him feel bad, or resentful or scared. Mess up his life when all he'd really tried to do was help me through a bad time."

"And that left you alone," Stella pointed out.

"If I'd told him, I still would've been alone. The thing is, when I decided I'd keep the baby, I thought about telling him again, and asked some people how he was doing. He was still with that girl, and they were talking about getting married, so I think I did the right thing. Still, once I started to show, there was a lot of gossip and questions, a lot of looks and whispers. And I thought, What we need is a fresh start. So I sold the house and just about everything in it. And here I am."

"Looking for that fresh start," Roz concluded.

"I'm looking for a job." She paused, moistened her lips. "I know how to work. I also know a lot of people would step back from hiring a woman nearly six months along. Family, even distant, through-marriage sort of family, might be a little more obliging."

She cleared her throat when Roz said nothing. "I studied literature and business in college. I graduated with honors. I've got a solid employment record. I've got money—not a lot. My partial scholarship didn't cover everything, and my daddy was a teacher, so he didn't make much. But I've got enough to take care of myself, to pay rent, buy food, pay for this baby. I need a job, any kind of a job for now. You've got your business, you've got this house. It takes a lot of people to help run those. I'm asking for a chance to be one of them."

"Know anything about plants, about gardening?"

"We put in flower beds every year. Daddy and I split the yard work. And what I don't know, I can learn. I learn quick."

"Wouldn't you rather work in a bookstore? Hayley managed an independent bookstore back home," Roz told Stella.

"You don't own a bookstore," Hayley pointed out. "I'll work without pay for two weeks."

"Someone works for me, she gets paid. I'll be hiring the seasonal help in a few weeks. In the meantime . . . Stella, can you use her?"

"Ah . . ." Was she supposed to look at that young face and bulging belly and say no? "What were your responsibilities as manager?"

"I wasn't, like, officially the manager. But that's what I did, when you come down to it. It was a small operation, so I did some of everything. Inventory, buying, customer relations, scheduling, sales, advertising. Just the bookstore end of it. There was a separate staff for the coffee shop."

"What would you say were your strengths?"

She had to take a breath, calm her nerves. She knew it was vital to be clear and concise. And just as vital to her pride not to beg. "Customer relations, which keyed into sales. I'm good with people, and I don't mind taking the extra time you need to take to make sure they get what they want. If your customers are happy, they come back, and they buy. You take the extra steps, personalize service, you get customer loyalty."

Stella nodded. "And your weaknesses?"

"The buying," she said without hesitation. "I'd just want to buy everything if it was up to me. I had to keep reminding myself whose money I was spending. But sometimes I didn't hear myself."

"We're in the process of reorganizing, and some

expanding. I could use some help getting the new system in place. There's still a lot of computer inputting—some of it very tedious—to deal with."

"I can handle a keyboard. PC and Mac."

"We'll go for the two weeks," Roz decided. "You'll get paid, but we'll consider the two weeks a trial balloon for all of us. If it doesn't work out, I'll do what I can to help you find another job."

"Can't say fairer than that. Thanks, Cousin Rosalind."

"Just Roz. We've got some gas out in the shed. I'll go get it, and we'll get your car up here so you can get your things in."

"In? In here?" Shaking her head, Hayley set her cup aside. "I said I wasn't after a handout. I appreciate the job, the chance at the job. I don't expect you to put me up."

"Family, even distant-through-marriage family, is welcome here. And it'll give us all a chance to get to know each other, to see if we're going to suit."

"You live here?" Hayley asked Stella.

"Yes. And my boys—eight and six. They're upstairs asleep."

"Are we cousins?"

"No."

"I'll get the gas." Roz got to her feet and started out.

"I'll pay rent." Hayley rose as well, instinctively laying a hand on her belly. "I pay my way."

"We'll adjust your salary to compensate for it."

When she was alone with Stella, Hayley let out a long, slow breath. "I thought she'd be older. And scarier. Though I bet she can be plenty scary when she needs to. You can't have what she has, and keep it, grow it, without knowing how to be scary."

"You're right. I can be scary, too, when it comes to work."

"I'll remember. Ah, you're from up north?"

"Yes. Michigan."

"That's a long way. Is it just you and your boys?"

"My husband died about two and a half years ago."

"That's hard. It's hard to lose somebody you love. I guess all three of us know about that. I think it can make *you* hard if you don't have something, someone else to love. I've got the baby."

"Do you know if it's a boy or a girl?"

"No. Baby had its back turned during the sonogram." She started to chew on her thumbnail, then tucked the thumb in her fist and lowered it. "I guess I should go out, take the gas Roz is getting."

"I'll go with you. We'll take care of it together."

IN AN HOUR THEY HAD HAYLEY SETTLED IN ONE OF the guest rooms in the west wing. She knew she gawked. She knew she babbled. But she'd never seen a more beautiful room, had never expected to be in one. Much less to be able to call it her own, even temporarily.

She put away her things, running her fingers over the gleaming wood of the bureau, the armoire, the etched-glass lampshades, the carving of the headboard.

She would earn this. That was a promise she made to herself, and her child, as she indulged in a long, warm bath. She would earn the chance she'd been given and would pay Roz back in labor and in loyalty.

She was good at both.

She dried off, then rubbed oil over her belly, her breasts. She wasn't afraid of childbirth—she knew how to work hard toward a goal. But she was really hoping she could avoid stretch marks.

She felt a little chill and slipped hurriedly into her nightshirt. Just at the edge of the mirror, just at the corner of her vision, she caught a shadow, a movement.

Rubbing her arms warm, she stepped through to the bedroom. There was nothing, and the door was closed, as she'd left it.

Dog-tired, she told herself and rubbed her eyes. It had been a long trip from the past to the verge of the future.

She took one of the books she'd had in her suitcase—the

rest, ones she hadn't been able to bring herself to sell, were still packed in the trunk of her car—and slipped into bed.

She opened it to where she'd left it bookmarked, prepared to settle herself down, as she did most nights, with an hour of reading.

And was asleep with the light burning before she'd finished the first page.

AT ROZ'S REQUEST, STELLA ONCE AGAIN WENT INTO her sitting room and sat. Roz poured them each a glass of wine.

"Honest impression?" she asked.

"Young, bright, proud. Honest. She could have spun us a sob story about being betrayed by the baby's father, begged for a place to stay, used her pregnancy as an excuse for all manner of things. Instead she took responsibility and asked to work. I'll still check her references."

"Of course. She seemed fearless about the baby."

"It's after you have them you learn to be afraid of everything."

"Isn't that the truth?" Roz scooped her fingers through her hair twice. "I'll make a few calls, find out a little more about that part of the Ashby family. I honestly don't remember very well. We never had much contact, even when he was alive. I do remember the scandal when the wife took off, left him with the baby. From the impression she made on me, and you, apparently he managed very well."

"Her managerial experience could be a real asset."

"Another manager." Roz, in a gesture Stella took as only half mocking, cast her eyes to heaven. "Pray for me."

seven

It didn't take two weeks. After two days, Stella decided Hayley was going to be the answer to her personal prayer. Here was someone with youth, energy, and enthusiasm who understood and appreciated efficiency in the workplace.

She knew how to read and generate spreadsheets, understood instructions after one telling, and respected color codes. If she was half as good relating to customers as she was with filing systems, she would be a jewel.

When it came to plants, she didn't know much more than the basic this is a geranium, and this is a pansy. But she could be taught.

Stella was already prepared to beg Roz to offer Hayley part-time work when May got closer.

"Hayley?" Stella poked her head in the now efficient and tidy office. "Why don't you come out with me? We've got nearly an hour before we open. We'll have a lesson on shade plants in Greenhouse Number Three."

"Cool. We're input through the H's in perennials. I don't know what half of them are, but I'm doing some reading up at night. I didn't know sunflowers were called Helia . . . wait. Helianthus."

"It's more that Helianthus are called sunflowers. The perennial ones can be divided in spring, or propagated by seeds—in the spring—or cuttings in late spring. Seeds from annual Helianthus can be harvested—from that big brown eye—in late summer or early fall. Though the cultivars hybridize freely, they may not come true from the seeds collected. And I'm lecturing."

"That's okay. I grew up with a teacher. I like to learn."

As they passed through the counter area, Hayley glanced out the window. "Truck just pulled in over by the . . . what do y'all call them? Pavers," she said before Stella could answer. "And, mmmm, just *look* at what's getting out of that truck. Mister tall, dark, and totally *built*. Who's the hunk?"

Struggling not to frown, Stella lifted a shoulder in a shrug. "That would be Logan Kitridge, Roz's landscape designer. I suppose he does score fairly high on the hunk-o-meter."

"Rings my bell." At Stella's expression, Hayley pressed a hand to her belly and laughed. "I'm pregnant. Still have all working parts, though. And just because I'm not looking for a man doesn't mean I don't want to look at one. Especially when he's yummy. He really is all tough and broody-looking, isn't he? What is it about tough, broody-looking men that gives you that tickle down in the belly?"

"I couldn't say. What's he doing over there?"

"Looks like he's loading pavers. If it wasn't so cool, he'd pull off that jacket. Bet we'd get a real muscle show. God, I do love my eye candy."

"That sort'll give you cavities," Stella mumbled. "He's not scheduled for pavers. He hasn't put in the order for pavers. Damn it!"

Hayley's eyebrows shot up as Stella stomped to the door and slammed out. Then she pressed her nose to the window, prepared to watch the show.

"Excuse me?"

"Uh-huh?" Hayley's answer was absent as she tried to get a better look outside. Then she popped back from the window, remembering spying was one thing, getting caught at it another. She turned, put on an innocent smile. And decided she'd gotten a double serving of eye candy.

This one wasn't big and broody, but sort of lanky and dreamy. And hot damn. It took an extra beat for her brain to engage, but she was quick.

"Hey! You must be Harper. You look just like your mama. I didn't get a chance to meet you yet, 'cause you never seemed to be around wherever I was around. Or whenever. I'm Hayley. Cousin Hayley from Little Rock? Maybe your mama told you I was working here now."

"Yeah. Yeah." He couldn't think of anything else. Could barely think at all. He felt lightning-struck and stupid.

"Do you just *love* working here? I do already. There's so much of everything, and the customers are so friendly. And Stella, she's just amazing, that's all. Your mama's like, I don't know, a goddess, for giving me a chance this way."

"Yeah." He winced. Could he *be* any more lame? "They're great. It's great." Apparently he could. And damn it, he was good with women. Usually. But one look at this one had given him some sort of concussion. "You, ah, do you need anything?"

"No." She gave him a puzzled smile. "I thought you did."

"I need something? What?"

"I don't know." She laid a hand on the fascinating mound of her belly and laughed, all throaty and free. "You're the one who came in."

"Right. Right. No, nothing. Now. Later. I've got to get back." Outside, in the air, where he should be able to breathe again.

"It was nice meeting you, Harper."

"You, too." He glanced back as he retreated and saw she was already back at the window.

* * *

OUTSIDE, STELLA SPED ACROSS THE PARKING AREA.
She called out twice, and the second time got a quick
glance and an absent wave. Building up steam as she went,
she pumped it out the minute she reached the stacks of
pavers.

"What do you think you're doing?"

"Playing tennis. What does it look like I'm doing?"

"It looks like you're taking material you haven't
ordered, that you haven't been authorized to take."

"Really?" He hauled up another stack. "No wonder my
backhand is rusty." The truck shuddered as he loaded.
"Hey."

Much to her amazement, he leaned toward her, sniffed.
"Different shampoo. Nice."

"Stop smelling me." She waved him away by flapping a
hand at his chin as she stepped back.

"I can't help it. You're standing right there. I have a
nose."

"I need the paperwork on this material."

"Yeah, yeah, yeah. Fine, fine, fine. I'll come in and take
care of it after I'm loaded."

"You're supposed to take care of it *before* you load."

He turned, aimed a hot look with those mossy green
eyes. "Red, you're a pain in the ass."

"I'm supposed to be. I'm the manager."

He had to smile at that, and he tipped down his sunglasses to look over them at her. "You're real good at it,
too. Think of it this way. The pavers are stored on the way
to the building. By loading first, then coming in, I'm actually being more efficient."

The smile morphed into a smirk. "That'd be important,
I'd think, if we were doing, say, a projection of man-
hours."

He took a moment to lean against the truck and study
her. Then he loaded another stack of pavers. "You standing

here watching me means you're wasting time, and likely adding to your own man-hours."

"You don't come in to handle the paperwork, Kitridge, I'll hunt you down."

"Don't tempt me."

He took his time, but he came in.

He was calculating how best to annoy Stella again. Her eyes went the color of Texas bluebonnets when she was pissed off. But when he stepped in, he saw Hayley.

"Hey."

"Hey," she said back and smiled. "I'm Hayley Phillips. A family connection to Roz's first husband? I'm working here now."

"Logan. Nice to meet you. Don't let this Yankee scare you." He nodded toward Stella. "Where are the sacred forms, and the ritual knife so I can slice open a vein and sign them in blood?"

"My office."

"Uh-huh." But he lingered rather than following her. "When's the baby due?" he asked Hayley.

"May."

"Feeling okay?"

"Never better."

"Good. This here's a nice outfit, a good place to work *most* of the time. Welcome aboard." He sauntered into Stella's office, where she was already at her computer, with the form on the screen.

"I'll type this one up to save time. There's a whole stack of them in that folder. Take it. All you have to do is fill them in as needed, date, sign or initial. Drop them off."

"Uh-huh." He looked around the room. The desk was cleared off. There were no cartons, no books sitting on the floor or stacked on chairs.

That was too bad, he thought. He'd liked the workaday chaos of it.

"Where's all the stuff in here?"

"Where it belongs. Those pavers were the eighteen-inch round, number A-23?"

"They were eighteen-inch rounds." He picked up the framed photo on her desk and studied the picture of her boys and their dog. "Cute."

"Yes, they are. Are the pavers for personal use or for a scheduled job?"

"Red, you ever loosen up?"

"No. We Yankees never do."

He ran his tongue over his teeth. "Um-hmm."

"Do you know how *sick* I am of being referred to as 'the Yankee,' as though it were a foreign species, or a disease? Half the customers who come in here look me over like I'm from another planet and may not be coming in peace. Then I have to tell them I was born here, answer all sorts of questions about why I left, why I'm back, who my *people* are, for Christ's sake, before I can get down to any sort of business. I'm from Michigan, not the moon, and the Civil damn War's been over for quite some time."

Yep, just like Texas bluebonnets. "That would be the War Between the damn States this side of the Mason-Dixon, honey. And looks to me like you loosen up just fine when you get riled enough."

"Don't 'honey' me in that southern-fried twang."

"You know, Red, I like you better this way."

"Oh, shut up. Pavers. Personal or professional use?"

"Well, that depends on your point of view." Since there was room now, he edged a hip onto the corner of the desk. "They're for a friend. I'm putting in a walkway for her—my own time, no labor charge. I told her I'd pick up the materials and give her a bill from the center."

"We'll consider that personal use and apply your employee discount." She began tapping keys. "How many pavers?"

"Twenty-two."

She tapped again and gave him the price per paver, before discount, after discount.

Impressed despite himself, he tapped the monitor. "You got a math nerd trapped in there?"

"Just the wonders of the twenty-first century. You'd find it quicker than counting on your fingers."

"I don't know. I've got pretty fast fingers." Drumming them on his thigh, he kept his gaze on her face. "I need three white pine."

"For this same *friend*?"

"No." His grin flashed, fast and crooked. If she wanted to interpret "friend" as "lover," he couldn't see any point in saying the pavers were for Mrs. Kingsley, his tenth-grade English teacher. "Pine's for a client. Roland Guppy. Yes, like the fish. You've probably got him somewhere in your vast and mysterious files. We did a job for him last fall."

Since there was a coffeemaker on the table against the wall, and the pot was half full, he got up, took a mug, and helped himself.

"Make yourself at home," Stella said dryly.

"Thanks. As it happens, I recommended white pine for a windbreak. He hemmed and hawed. Took him this long to decide to go for it. He called me at home yesterday. I said I'd pick them up and work him in."

"We need a different form."

He sampled the coffee. Not bad. "Somehow I knew that."

"Are the pavers all you're taking for personal use?"

"Probably. For today."

She hit Print, then brought up another form. "That's three white pine. What size?"

"We got some nice eight-foot ones."

"Balled and burlapped?"

"Yeah."

Tap, tap, tap, he thought, with wonder, and there you go. Woman had pretty fingers, he noted. Long and tapered, with that glossy polish on them, the delicate pink of the inside of a rose petal.

She wore no rings.

"Anything else?"

He patted his pockets, eventually came up with a scrap of paper. "That's what I told him I could put them in for."

She added the labor, totaled, then printed out three copies while he drank her coffee. "Sign or initial," she told him. "One copy for my files, one for yours, one for the client."

"Gotcha."

When he picked up the pen, Stella waved a hand. "Oh, wait, let me get that knife. Which vein did you plan to open?"

"Cute." He lifted his chin toward the door. "So's she."

"Hayley? Yeah, she is. And entirely too young for you."

"I wouldn't say entirely. Though I do prefer women with a little more . . ." He stopped, smiled again. "We'll just say more, and stay alive."

"Wise."

"Your boys getting a hard time in school?"

"Excuse me?"

"Just considering what you said before. Yankee."

"Oh. A little, maybe, but for the most part the other kids find it interesting that they're from up north, lived near one of the Great Lakes. Both their teachers pulled up a map to show where they came from."

Her face softened as she spoke of it. "Thanks for asking."

"I like your kids."

He signed the forms and found himself amused when she groaned—actually groaned—watching him carelessly fold his and stuff them in his pocket.

"Next time could you wait until you're out of the office to do that? It hurts me."

"No problem." Maybe it was the different tone they were ending on, or maybe it was the way she'd softened up and smiled when she spoke of her children. Later, he might wonder what possessed him, but for now, he went with impulse. "Ever been to Graceland?"

"No. I'm not a big Elvis fan."

"Ssh!" Widening his eyes, he looked toward the door. "Legally, you can't say that around here. You could face fine and imprisonment, or depending on the jury, public flogging."

"I didn't read that in the Memphian handbook."

"Fine print. So, I'll take you. When's your day off?"

"I . . . It depends. You'll take me to Graceland?"

"You can't settle in down here until you've experienced Graceland. Pick a day, I'll work around it."

"I'm trying to understand here. Are you asking me for a date?"

"I wasn't heading into the date arena. I'm thinking of it more as an outing, between associates." He set the empty mug on her desk. "Think about it, let me know."

SHE HAD TOO MUCH TO DO TO THINK ABOUT IT. She couldn't just pop off to Graceland. And if she could, and had some strange desire to do so, she certainly wouldn't pop off to Graceland with Logan.

The fact that she'd admired his work—and all right, his build—didn't mean she liked him. It didn't mean she wanted to spend her very valuable off-time in his company.

But she couldn't help thinking about it, or more, wondering why he'd asked her. Maybe it was some sort of a trick, a strange initiation for the Yankee. You take her to Graceland, then abandon her in a forest of Elvis paraphernalia and see if she can find her way out.

Or maybe, in his weird Logan way, he'd decided that hitting on her was an easier away around her new system than arguing with her.

Except he hadn't seemed to be hitting on her. Exactly. It had seemed more friendly, off the cuff, or impulsive. And he'd asked about her children. There was no quicker way to cut through her annoyance, any shield, any defense than a sincere interest in her boys.

And if he was just being friendly, it seemed only polite, and sensible, to be friendly back.

What did people wear to Graceland, anyway?

Not that she was going. She probably wasn't. But it was smart to prepare. Just in case.

In Greenhouse Three, supervising while Hayley watered propagated annuals, Stella pondered on the situation.

"Ever been to Graceland?"

"Oh, sure. These are impatiens, right?"

Stella looked down at the flat. "Yeah. Those are Busy Lizzies. They're doing really well."

"And these are impatiens too. The New Guinea ones."

"Right. You do learn fast."

"Well, I recognize these easier because I've planted them before. Anyway, I went to Graceland with some pals when I was in college. It's pretty cool. I bought this Elvis bookmark. Wonder what ever happened to that? Elvis is a form of Elvin. It means 'elf-wise friend.' Isn't that strange?"

"Stranger to me that you'd know that."

"Just one of those things you pick up somewhere."

"Okay. So, what's the dress code?"

"Hmm?" She was trying to identify another flat by the leaves on the seedlings. And struggling not to peek at the name on the spike. "I don't guess there is one. People just wear whatever. Jeans and stuff."

"Casual, then."

"Right. I like the way it smells in here. All earthy and damp."

"Then you made the right career choice."

"It could be a career, couldn't it?" Those clear blue eyes shifted to Stella. "Something I could learn to be good at. I always thought I'd run my own place one day. Always figured on a bookstore, but this is sort of the same."

"How's that?"

"Well, like you've got your new stuff, and your classics. You've got genres, when it comes down to it. Annuals, biennials, perennials, shrubs and trees and grasses. Water plants and shade plants. That sort of thing."

"You know, you're right. I hadn't thought of it that way." Encouraged, Hayley walked down the rows. "And you're learning and exploring, the way you do with books. And we—you know, the staff—we're trying to help people find what suits them, makes them happy or at least satisfied. Planting a flower's like opening a book, because either way you're starting something. And your garden's your library. I could get good at this."

"I don't doubt it."

She turned to see Stella smiling at her. "When I am good at it, it won't just be a job anymore. A job's okay. It's cool for now, but I want more than a paycheck at the end of the week. I don't just mean money—though, okay, I want the money too."

"No, I know what you mean. You want what Roz has here. A place, and the satisfaction of being part of that place. Roots," Stella said, touching the leaves of a seedling. "And bloom. I know, because I want it too."

"But you have it. You're so totally smart, and you know where you're going. You've got two great kids, and a . . . a position here. You worked toward this, this place, this position. I feel like I'm just starting."

"And you're impatient to get on with it. So was I at your age."

Hayley's face beamed good humor. "And, yeah, you're so old and creaky now."

Laughing, Stella pushed back her hair. "I've got about ten years on you. A lot can happen, a lot can change—yourself included—in a decade. In some ways I'm just starting, too—a decade after you. Transplanting myself, and my two precious shoots here."

"Do you get scared?"

"Every day." She laid a hand on Hayley's belly. "It comes with the territory."

"It helps, having you to talk to. I mean, you were married when you went through this, but you—well, both you and Roz had to deal with being a single parent. It helps that you know stuff. Helps having other women around who know stuff I need to know."

With the job complete, Hayley walked over to turn off

the water. "So," she asked, "are you going to Graceland?"

"I don't know. I might."

WITH HIS CREW SPLIT BETWEEN THE WHITE PINES AND
the landscape prep on the Guppy job, Logan set to work on
the walkway for his old teacher. It wouldn't take him long,
and he could hit both the other work sites that afternoon.
He liked juggling jobs. He always had.

Going directly start to finish on one too quickly cut out
the room for brainstorms or sudden inspiration. There was
little he liked better than that *pop*, when he just saw something in his head that he knew he could make with his
hands.

He could take what was and make it better, maybe blend
some of what was with the new and create a different
whole.

He'd grown up respecting the land, and the whims of
Nature, but more from a farmer's point of view. When you
grew up on a small farm, worked it, fought with it, he
thought, you understood what the land meant. Or could
mean.

His father had loved the land, too, but in a different way,
Logan supposed. It had provided for his family, cost them,
and in the end had gifted them with a nice bonanza when
his father had opted to sell out.

He couldn't say he missed the farm. He'd wanted more
than row crops and worries about market prices. But he'd
wanted, needed, to work the land.

Maybe he'd lost some of the magic of it when he'd
moved north. Too many buildings, too much concrete, too
many limitations for him. He hadn't been able to acclimate
to the climate or culture any more than Rae had been able
to acclimate here.

It hadn't worked. No matter how much both of them
had tried to nurture things along, the marriage had just
withered on them.

So he'd come home, and ultimately, with Roz's offer,

he'd found his place—personally, professionally, creatively. And was content.

He ran his lines, then picked up his shovel.

And jabbed the blade into the earth again.

What had he been thinking? He'd asked the woman out. He could call it whatever he liked, but when a guy asked a woman out, it was a frigging date.

He had no intention of dating toe-the-line Stella Rothchild. She wasn't his type.

Okay, sure she was. He set to work turning the soil between his lines to prep for leveling and laying the black plastic. He'd never met a woman, really, who wasn't his type.

He just liked the breed, that's all. Young ones and old ones, country girls and city-slicked. Whip smart or bulb dim, women just appealed to him on most every level.

He'd ended up married to one, hadn't he? And though that had been a mistake, you had to make them along the way.

Maybe he'd never been particularly drawn to the structured, my-way-or-the-highway type before. But there was always a first time. And he liked first times. It was the second times and the third times that could wear on a man.

But he wasn't attracted to Stella.

Okay, shit. Yes, he was. Mildly. She was a good-looking woman, nicely shaped, too. And there was the hair. He was really gone on the hair. Wouldn't mind getting his hands on that hair, just to see if it felt as sexy as it looked.

But it didn't mean he wanted to date her. It was hard enough to deal with her professionally. The woman had a rule or a form or a damn system for everything.

Probably had them in bed, too. Probably had a typed list of bullet points, dos and don'ts, all with a mission statement overview.

What the woman needed was some spontaneity, a little shake of the order of things. Not that he was interested in being the one to provide it.

It was just that she'd looked so pretty that morning, and

her hair had smelled good. Plus she'd had that sexy little smile going for her. Before he knew it, he'd been talking about taking her to Graceland.

Nothing to worry about, he assured himself. She wouldn't go. It wasn't the sort of thing a woman like her did, just for the hell of it. As far as he could tell, she didn't do *anything* for the hell of it.

They'd both forget he'd even brought it up.

BECAUSE SHE FELT IT WAS IMPERATIVE, AT LEAST FOR the first six months of her management, Stella insisted on a weekly progress meeting with Roz.

She'd have preferred a specific time for these meetings, and a specific location. But Roz was hard to pin down.

She'd already held them in the propagation house and in the field. This time she cornered Roz in her own sitting room, where she'd be unlikely to escape.

"I wanted to give you your weekly update."

"Oh. Well, all right." Roz set aside a book on hybridizing that was thick as a railroad tie, and took off her frameless reading glasses. "Time's zipping by. Ground's warming up."

"I know. Daffodils are ready to pop. So much earlier than I'm used to. We've been selling a lot of bulbs. Back north, we'd sell most of those late summer or fall."

"Homesick?"

"Now and then, but less and less already. I can't say I'm sorry to be out of Michigan as we slog through February. They got six inches of snow yesterday, and I'm watching daffodils spearing up."

Roz leaned back in the chair, crossed her sock-covered feet at the ankles. "Is there a problem?"

"So much for the illusion that I conceal my emotions under a composed façade. No, no problem. I did the duty call home to my mother a little while ago. I'm still recovering."

"Ah."

It was a noncommittal sound, and Stella decided she could interpret it as complete non-interest or a tacit invitation to unload. Because she was brimming, she chose to unload.

"I spent the almost fifteen minutes she spared me out of her busy schedule listening to her talk about her current boyfriend. She actually calls these men she sees boyfriends. She's fifty-eight years old, and she just had her fourth divorce two months ago. When she wasn't complaining that Rocky—and he's actually named Rocky—isn't attentive enough and won't take her to the Bahamas for a midwinter getaway, she was talking about her next chemical peel and whining about how her last Botox injection hurt. She never asked about the boys, and the only reference she made to the fact that I was living and working down here was to ask if I was tired of being around the jerk and his bimbo—her usual terms for my father and Jolene."

When she'd run out of steam, Stella rubbed her hands over her face. "Goddamn it."

"That's a lot of bitching, whining, and venom to pack into a quarter of an hour. She sounds like a very talented woman."

It took Stella a minute—a minute where she let her hands slide into her lap so she could stare into Roz's face. Then she let her own head fall back with a peal of laughter.

"Oh, yeah. Oh, yeah, she's loaded with talent. Thanks."

"No problem. My mama spent most of her time—at least the time we were on earth together—sighing wistfully over her health. Not that she meant to complain, so she said. I very nearly put that on her tombstone. 'Not That I Mean to Complain.' "

"I could put 'I Don't Ask for Much' on my mother's."

"There you go. Mine made such an impression on me that I went hell-bent in the opposite direction. I could probably cut off a limb, and you wouldn't hear a whimper out of me."

"God, I guess I've done the same with mine. I'll have to think about that later. Okay, on to business. We're sold out of the mixed-bulb planters we forced. I don't know if you want to do others this late in the season."

"Maybe a few. Some people like to pick them up, already done, for Easter presents and so on."

"All right. How about if I show Hayley how it's done? I know you usually do them yourself, but—"

"No, it's a good job for her. I've been watching her." At Stella's expression, she inclined her head. "I don't like to look like I'm watching, but generally I am. I know what's going on in my place, Stella, even if I do occasionally miss crossing a T."

"And I'm there to cross them, so that's all right."

"Exactly. Still, I've left her primarily to you. She working out for you?"

"More than. You don't have to tell her something twice, and when she claimed she learned fast she wasn't kidding. She's thirsty."

"We've got plenty to drink around here."

"She's personable with customers—friendly, never rushed. And she's not afraid to say she doesn't know, but she'll find out. She's outside right now, poking around your beds and shrubs. She wants to know what she's selling."

She moved to the window as she spoke, to look out. It was nearly twilight, but there was Hayley walking the dog and studying the perennials. "At her age, I was planning my wedding. It seems like a million years ago."

"At her age, I was raising two toddlers and was pregnant with Mason. Now *that* was a million years ago. And five minutes ago."

"It's off topic, again, of the update, but I wanted to ask if you'd thought about what you'll do when we get to May."

"That's still high season for us, and people like to freshen up the summer garden. We sell—"

"No, I meant about Hayley. About the baby."

"Oh. Well, she'll have to decide that, but I expect if she

decides to stay on at the nursery, we'll find her sit-down work."

"She'll need to find child care, when she's ready to go back to work. And speaking of nurseries . . ."

"Hmm. That's thinking ahead."

"Time zips by," Stella repeated.

"We'll figure it out."

Because she was curious, Roz rose to go to the window herself. Standing beside Stella she looked out.

It was a lovely thing, she decided, watching a young woman, blooming with child, wandering a winter garden.

She'd once been that young woman, dreaming in the twilight and waiting for spring to bring life.

Time didn't just zip by, she thought. It damn near evaporated on you.

"She seems happy now, and sure of what she's going to do. But could be after she has the baby, she'll change her mind about having the father involved." Roz watched Hayley lay a hand on her belly and look west, to where the sun was sinking behind the trees and into the river beyond them. "Having a live baby in your arms and the prospect of caring for it single-handed's one hell of a reality check. We'll see when the time comes."

"You're right. And I don't suppose either of us knows her well enough to know what's best. Speaking of babies, it's nearly time to get mine in the tub. I'm going to leave the weekly report with you."

"All right. I'll get to it. I should tell you, Stella, I like what you've done. What shows, like in the customer areas, and what doesn't, in the office management. I see spring coming, and for the first time in years, I'm not frazzled and overworked. I can't say I minded being overworked, but I can't say I mind not being, either."

"Even when I bug you with details?"

"Even when. I haven't heard any complaints about Logan in the past few days. Or from him. Am I living in a fool's paradise, or have you two found your rhythm?"

"There are still a few hitches in it, and I suspect there'll be others, but nothing for you to worry about. In fact, he made a very friendly gesture and offered to take me to Graceland."

"He did?" Roz's eyebrows drew together. "Logan?"

"Would that be out of the ordinary for him?"

"I couldn't say, except I don't know that he's dated anyone from work before."

"It's not a date, it's an outing."

Intrigued, Roz sat again. You never knew what you'd learn from a younger woman, she decided. "What's the difference?"

"Well, a date's dinner and a movie with potential, even probable, romantic overtones. Taking your kids to the zoo is an outing."

Roz leaned back, stretched out her legs. "Things do change, don't they? Still, in my book, when a man and a woman go on an outing, it's a date."

"See, that's my quandary." Since conversation seemed welcomed, Stella walked over again, sat on the arm of the chair facing Roz. "Because that's my first thought. But it seemed like just a friendly gesture, and the 'outing' term was his. Like a kind of olive branch. And if I take it, maybe we'd find that common ground, or that rhythm, whatever it is we need to smooth out the rough spots in our working relationship."

"So, if I'm following this, you'd go to Graceland with Logan for the good of In the Garden."

"Sort of."

"And not because he's a very attractive, dynamic, and downright sexy single man."

"No, those would be bonus points." She waited until Roz stopped laughing. "And I'm not thinking of wading in that pool. Dating's a minefield."

"Tell me about it. I've got more years in that war zone than you."

"I like men." She reached back to tug the band ponytailing her hair a little higher. "I like the company of men. But dating's so complicated and stressful."

"Better complicated and stressful than downright boring, which too many of my experiences in the field have been."

"Complicated, stressful, or downright boring, I like the sound of 'outing' much better. Listen, I know Logan's a friend of yours. But I'd just like to ask if you think, if I went with him, I'd be making a mistake, or giving the wrong impression. The wrong signal. Or maybe crossing that line between coworkers. Or—"

"That's an awful lot of complication and stress you're working up over an outing."

"It is. I irritate myself." Shaking her head, she pushed off the chair. "I'd better get bath time started. Oh, and I'll get Hayley going on those bulbs tomorrow."

"That's fine. Stella—are you going on this outing?"

She paused at the doorway. "Maybe. I'll sleep on it."

eight

SHE WAS DREAMING OF FLOWERS. AN ENCHANTING
garden, full of young, vital blooms, flowed around her. It
was perfect, tidied and ordered, its edges ruler-straight to
form a keen verge against the well-trimmed grass.

Color swept into color, whites and pinks, yellows and
silvery greens, all soft and delicate pastels that shimmered
in subtle elegance in the golden beams of the sun.

Their fragrance was calming and drew a pretty bevy of
busy butterflies, the curiosity of a single shimmery hum-
mingbird. No weed intruded on its flawlessness, and every
blossom was full and ripe, with dozens upon dozens of
buds waiting their turn to open.

She'd done this. As she circled the bed it was with a
sense of pride and satisfaction. She'd turned the earth and
fed it, she'd planned and selected and set each plant in
exactly the right place. The garden so precisely matched
her vision, it was like a photograph.

It had taken her years to plan and toil and create. But
now everything she'd wanted to accomplish was here,
blooming at her feet.

Yet even as she watched, a stem grew up, sharp and

green, crowding the others, spoiling the symmetry. Out of place, she thought, more annoyed than surprised to see it breaking out of the ground, growing up, unfurling its leaves.

A dahlia? She'd planted no dahlias there. They belonged in the back. She'd specifically planted a trio of tall pink dahlias at the back of the bed, exactly one foot apart.

Puzzled, she tilted her head, studied it as the stems grew and thickened, as buds formed fat and healthy. Fascinating, so fascinating and unexpected.

Even as she started to smile, she heard—felt?—a whisper over the skin, a murmur through her brain.

It's wrong there. Wrong. It has to be removed. *It will take and take until there's nothing left.*

She shivered. The air around her was suddenly cool, with a hint of raw dampness, with bleak clouds creeping in toward that lovely golden sun.

In the pit of her belly was a kind of dread.

Don't let it grow. It will strangle the life out of everything you've done.

That was right. Of course, that was right. It had no business growing there, muscling the others aside, changing the order.

She'd have to dig it out, find another place for it. Reorganize everything, just when she'd thought she was finished. And look at that, she thought, as the buds formed, as they broke open to spread their deep blue petals. It was entirely the wrong color. Too bold, too dark, too bright.

It was beautiful; she couldn't deny it. In fact, she'd never seen a more beautiful specimen. It looked so strong, so vivid. It was already nearly as tall as she, with flowers as wide as dinner plates.

It lies. It lies.

That whisper, somehow female, somehow raging, slithered into her sleeping brain. She whimpered a little, tossed restlessly in her chilly bed.

Kill it! Kill it. Hurry before it's too late.

No, she couldn't kill something so beautiful, so alive, so vivid. But that didn't mean she could just leave it there, out of its place, upsetting the rest of the bed.

All that work, the preparation, the *planning*, and now this. She'd just have to plan another bed and work it in. With a sigh, she reached out, feathered her fingers over those bold blue petals. It would be a lot of work, she thought, a lot of trouble, but—

"Mom."

"Isn't it pretty?" she murmured. "It's so *blue*."

"Mom, wake up."

"What?" She tumbled out of the dream, shaking off sleep as she saw Luke kneeling in the bed beside her.

God, the room was freezing.

"Luke?" Instinctively she dragged the spread over him. "What's the matter?"

"I don't feel good in my tummy."

"Aw." She sat up, automatically laying a hand on his brow to check for fever. A little warm, she thought. "Does it hurt?"

He shook his head. She could see the gleam of his eyes, the sheen of tears. "It feels sick. Can I sleep in your bed?"

"Okay." She drew the sheets back. "Lie down and bundle up, baby. I don't know why it's so cold in here. I'm going to take your temperature, just to see." She pressed her lips to his forehead as he snuggled onto her pillow. Definitely a little warm.

Switching on the bedside lamp, she rolled out to get the thermometer from the bathroom.

"Let's find out if I can see through your brain." She stroked his hair as she set the gauge to his ear. "Did you feel sick when you went to bed?"

"Nuh-uh, it was . . ." His body tightened, and he made a little groan.

She knew he was going to retch before he did. With a mother's speed, she scooped him up, dashed into the bathroom. They made it, barely, and she murmured and stroked and fretted while he was sick.

Then he turned his pale little face up to hers. "I frew up."

"I know, baby. I'm sorry. We're going to make it all better soon."

She gave him a little water, cooled his face with a cloth, then carried him back to her bed. Strange, she thought, the room felt fine now.

"It doesn't feel as sick in my tummy anymore."

"That's good." Still, she took his temperature—99.1, not too bad—and brought the wastebasket over beside the bed. "Does it hurt anywhere?"

"Nuh-uh, but I don't like to frow up. It makes it taste bad in my throat. And my other tooth is loose, and maybe if I frow up again, it'll come out and I won't have it to put under my pillow."

"Don't you worry about that. You'll absolutely have your tooth for under your pillow, just like the other one. Now, I'll go down and get you some ginger ale. You stay right here, and I'll be back in just a minute. Okay?"

"Okay."

"If you have to be sick again, try to use this." She set the wastebasket beside him on the bed. "I'll be right back, baby."

She hurried out, jogging down the stairs in her nightshirt. One of the disadvantages of a really big house, she realized, was that the kitchen was a mile away from the bedrooms.

She'd see about buying a little fridge, like the one she'd had in her dorm room at college, for the upstairs sitting room.

Low-grade fever, she thought as she rushed into the kitchen. He'd probably be better by tomorrow. If he wasn't, she'd call the doctor.

She hunted up ginger ale, filled a tall glass with ice, grabbed a bottle of water, and dashed back upstairs.

"I get ginger ale," she heard Luke say as she walked back down the hall to her room. "Because I was sick. Even though I feel better, I can still have it. You can have some, too, if you want."

"Thanks, honey, but—" When she swung into the room, she saw Luke was turned away from the door, sitting back against the pillows. And the room was cold again, so cold that she saw the vapor of her own breath.

"She went away," Luke said.

Something that was more than the cold danced up her spine. "Who went away?"

"The lady." His sleepy eyes brightened a bit when he saw the ginger ale. "She stayed with me when you went downstairs."

"What lady, Luke? Miss Roz? Hayley?"

"Nuh-uh. The lady who comes and sings. She's nice. Can I have *all* the ginger ale?"

"You can have some." Her hands shook lightly as she poured. "Where did you see her?"

"Right here." He pointed to the bed, then took the glass in both hands and drank. "This tastes good."

"You've seen her before?"

"Uh-huh. Sometimes I wake up and she's there. She sings the dilly-dilly song."

Lavender's blue, dilly dilly. Lavender's green. That's the song she'd heard, Stella realized with a numb fear. The song she'd caught herself humming.

"Did she—" No, don't frighten him, she warned herself. "What does she look like?"

"She's pretty, I guess. She has yellow hair. I think she's an angel, a lady angel? 'Member the story about the guard angel?"

"Guardian angel."

"But she doesn't have wings. Gavin says she's maybe a witch, but a good one like in *Harry Potter.*"

Her throat went desert dry. "Gavin's seen her too?"

"Yeah, when she comes to sing." He handed the glass back to Stella, rubbed his eyes. "My tummy feels better now, but I'm sleepy. Can I still sleep in your bed?"

"Absolutely." But before she got into bed with him, Stella turned on the bathroom light.

She looked in on Gavin, struggled against the urge to pluck him out of his bed and carry him into hers.

Leaving the connecting doors wide open, she walked back into her room.

She turned off the bedside lamp, then slid into bed with her son.

And gathering him close, she held him as he slept.

HE SEEMED FINE THE NEXT MORNING. BRIGHT AND bouncy, and cheerfully told David over breakfast that he'd thrown up and had ginger ale.

She considered keeping him home from school, but there was no fever and, judging by his appetite, no stomach problems.

"No ill effects there," David commented when the boys ran up to get their books. "You, on the other hand, look like you put in a rough one." He poured her another cup of coffee.

"I did. And not all of it because Luke was sick. After he 'frew up,' he settled down and slept like a baby. But before he settled down, he told me something that kept me awake most of the night."

David rested his elbows on the island counter, leaned forward. "Tell Daddy all."

"He says . . ." She glanced around, cocking an ear so she'd hear the boys when they came back down. "There's a lady with yellow hair who comes into his room at night and sings to him."

"Oh." He picked up his dishcloth and began to mop the counter.

"Don't say 'oh' with that silly little smile."

"Hey, I'll have you know this is my amused smirk. Nothing silly about it."

"David."

"Stella," he said with the same stern scowl. "Roz told you we have a ghost, didn't she?"

"She mentioned it. But there's just one little problem with that. There are no such things as ghosts."

"So, what, some blonde sneaks into the house every night, heads to the boys' room, and breaks out in song? *That's* more plausible?"

"I don't know what's going on. I've heard someone singing, and I've felt . . ." Edgy, she twisted the band of her watch. "Regardless, the idea of a ghost is ridiculous. But something's going on with my boys."

"Is he afraid of her?"

"No. I probably just imagined the singing. And Luke, he's six. He can imagine anything."

"Have you asked Gavin?"

"No. Luke said they'd both seen her, but . . ."

"So have I."

"Oh, please."

David rinsed the dishcloth, squeezed out the excess water, then laid it over the lip of the sink to dry. "Not since I was a kid, but I saw her a few times when I'd sleep over. Freaked me out at first, but she'd just sort of *be* there. You can ask Harper. He saw her plenty."

"Okay. Just who is this fictional ghost supposed to be?" She threw up a hand as she heard the thunder of feet on the stairs. "Later."

SHE TRIED TO PUT IT OUT OF HER MIND, AND SUC-ceeded from time to time when the work took over. But it snuck back into her brain, and played there, like the ghostly lullaby.

By midday, she left Hayley working on bulb planters and Ruby at the counter, and grabbing a clipboard, headed toward the grafting house.

Two birds, she thought, one stone.

The music today was Rachmaninoff. Or was it Mozart? Either way, it was a lot of passionate strings and flutes. She passed the staging areas, the tools, the soils and additives and rooting mediums.

She found Harper down at the far end at a worktable with a pile of five-inch pots, several cacti as stock plants, and a tray of rooting medium. She noted the clothespins, the rubber bands, the raffia, the jar of denatured alcohol.

"What do you use on the Christmas cactus?"

He continued to work, using his knife to cut a shoot from the joint of a scion plant. He had beautiful hands, she noted. Long, artistic fingers. "Apical-wedge, then? Tricky, but probably best with that specimen because of the flat stems. Are you creating a standard, or hybridizing?"

He made his vertical slit into the vascular bundle and still didn't answer.

"I'm just wondering because—" She set her hand on his shoulder, and when he jumped and let out a muffled shout, she stumbled back and rammed into the table behind her.

"Shit!" He dropped the knife and stuck the thumb it had nicked in his mouth. "Shit!" he said again, around his thumb, and tugged headphones off with his free hand.

"I'm sorry. I'm so sorry! How bad are you cut? Let me see."

"It's just a scratch." He took it out of his mouth, rubbed it absently on his grimy jeans. "Not nearly as fatal as the *heart attack* you just brought on."

"Let me see the thumb." She grabbed his hand. "You've got dirt in it now."

He saw her gaze slide over toward the alcohol and ripped his hand out of hers. "Don't even think about it."

"Well, it should at least be cleaned. And I really am sorry. I didn't see the headphones. I thought you heard me."

"It's okay. No big. The classical's for the plants. If I listen to it for too long, my eyes get glassy."

"Oh?" She picked up the headphones, held one side to one ear. "Metallica?"

"Yeah. My kind of classical." Now he looked warily at her clipboard. "What's up?"

"I'm hoping to get an idea of what you'll have ready in here to put out for our big spring opening next month. And what you have at the stage you'd want it moved out to the stock greenhouse."

"Oh, well . . ." He looked around. "A lot of stuff. Probably. I keep the staging records on computer."

"Even better. Maybe you could just make me a copy. Floppy disk would be perfect."

"Yeah, okay. Okay, wait." He shifted his stool toward the computer.

"You don't have to do it this minute, when you're in the middle of something else."

"If I don't, I'll probably forget."

With a skill she admired, he tapped keys with somewhat grungy fingers, found what he was after. He dug out a floppy, slid it into the data slot. "Look, I'd rather you didn't take anything out when I'm not here."

"No problem."

"How's, um, Hayley working out?"

"An answer to a prayer."

"Yeah?" He reached for a can of Coke, took a quick drink. "She's not doing anything heavy or working around toxics. Right?"

"Absolutely not. I've got her doing bulb planters right now."

"Here you go." He handed her the floppy.

"Thanks, Harper. This makes my life easier. I've never done a Christmas cactus graft." She clipped the floppy to her board. "Can I watch?"

"Sure. Want to do one? I'll talk you through."

"I'd really like to."

"I'll finish this one up. See, I cut a two-, maybe two-and-a-half-inch shoot, straight through the joint. I've cut the top couple inches from the stem of the stock plant. And on the way to slicing my finger—"

"Sorry."

"Wouldn't be the first time. I made this fine, vertical cut into the vascular bundle."

"I got that far."

"From here, we pare slivers of skin from both sides of the base of the scion, tapering the end, and exposing the central core." Those long, artistic fingers worked cleverly and patiently. "See?"

"Mmm. You've got good hands for this."

"Came by them naturally. Mom showed me how to graft. We did an ornamental cherry when I was about Luke's age. Now we're going to insert the scion into the slit on the stock stem. We want the exposed tissues of both in contact, and match the cut surfaces as close as you can. I like to use a long cactus spine. . . ." He took one from a tray and pushed it straight into the grafted area.

"Neat and organic."

"Uh-huh. I don't like binding with raffia on these. Weakened clothespins are better. Right across the joint, see, so it's held firm but not too tight. The rooting medium's two parts cactus soil mix to one part fine grit. I've already got the mix. We get our new baby in the pot, cover the mix with a little fine gravel."

"So it stays moist but not wet."

"You got it. Then you want to label it and put it in an airy position, out of full sun. The two plants should unite in a couple of days. Want to give it a shot?"

"Yeah." She took the stool when he vacated it, and began, following his directions carefully. "Ah, David was telling me about the house legend this morning."

"That's good." His gaze stayed focused on her hands, and the plant. "Keep the slice really thin. Legend?"

"You know, woo-woo, ghost."

"Oh, yeah, the sad-eyed blonde. Used to sing to me when I was a kid."

"Come on, Harper."

He shrugged, took another sip of Coke. "You want?" He tipped the can from side to side. "I've got more in the cooler under here."

"No, but thanks. You're saying a ghost used to come in your room and sing to you."

"Up until I was about twelve, thirteen. Same with my brothers. You hit puberty, she stops coming around. You need to taper the scion now."

She paused in her work only long enough to slide a glance up at his face. "Harper, don't you consider yourself a scientist?"

He smiled at her with those somewhat dreamy brown eyes. "Not so much. Some of what I do is science, and some of what I do requires knowing some science. But down at it, I'm a gardener."

He two-pointed the Coke can into his waste bin, then bent down to get another out of his cooler. "But if you're asking if I find ghosts at odds with science, not so much either. Science is an exploration, it's experimentation, it's discovery."

"I can't argue with your definition." She went back to the work. "But—"

He popped the top. "Gonna Scully me?"

She had to laugh. "It's one thing for a young boy to believe in ghosts, and Santa Claus, and—"

"You're trying to say there's no Santa Claus?" He looked horrified. "That's just sick."

"But," she continued, ignoring him, "it's entirely another when it's a grown man."

"Who are you calling a grown man? I think I'm going to have to order you out of my house. Stella." He patted her shoulder, transferred soil, then casually brushed it off her shirt. "I saw what I saw, I know what I know. It's just part of growing up in the house. She was always . . . a benign presence, at least to me and my brothers. She gave Mom grief now and then."

"What do you mean, grief?"

"Ask Mom. But I don't know why you'd bother, since you don't believe in ghosts anyway." He smiled. "That's a good graft. According to family lore, she's supposed to be one of the Harper brides, but she's not in any of the paintings or pictures we have." He lifted a shoulder. "Maybe she was a servant who died there. She sure knows her way around the place."

"Luke told me he saw her."

"Yeah?" His gaze sharpened as Stella labeled the pot. "If you're worried that she might hurt him, or Gavin, don't. She's, I don't know, maternal."

"Perfect, then—an unidentified yet maternal ghost who haunts my sons' room at night."

"It's a Harper family tradition."

AFTER A CONVERSATION LIKE THAT, STELLA NEEDED something sensible to occupy her mind. She grabbed a flat of pansies and some trailing vinca from a greenhouse, found a couple of nice free-form concrete planters in storage, loaded them and potting soil onto a flatbed cart. She gathered tools, gloves, mixed up some starter solution, and hauled everything out front.

Pansies didn't mind a bit of chill, she thought, so if they got a few more frosts, they wouldn't be bothered. And their happy faces, their rich colors would splash spring right at the entryway.

Once she'd positioned the planters, she got her clipboard and noted down everything she'd taken from stock. She'd enter it in her computer when she was finished.

Then she knelt down to do something she loved, something that never failed to comfort her. Something that always made sense.

She planted.

When the first was done, the purple and yellow flowers cheerful against the dull gray of the planter, she stepped back to study it. She wanted its mate to be as close to a mirror image as she could manage.

She was half done when she heard the rumble of tires on gravel. Logan, she thought, as she glanced around and identified his truck. She saw him start to turn toward the material area, then swing back and drive toward the building.

He stepped out, worn boots, worn jeans, bad-boy black-lensed sunglasses.

She felt a little itch right between her shoulder blades.

"Hey," he said.

"Hello, Logan."

He stood there, his thumbs hooked in the front pockets of his work pants and a trio of fresh scratches on his forearms just below the rolled-up sleeves of his shirt.

"Picking up some landscape timbers and some more black plastic for the Dawson job."

"You're moving right along there."

"It's cooking." He stepped closer, studied her work. "Those look good. I could use them."

"These are for display."

"You can make more. I take those over to Miz Dawson, the woman's going to snap them up. Sale's a sale, Red."

"Oh, all right." She'd hardly had a *minute* to think of them as her own. "Let me at least finish them. You tell her she'll need to replace these pansies when it gets hot. They won't handle summer. And if she puts perennials in them, she should cover the planters over for winter."

"It happens I know something about plants myself."

"Just want to make sure the customer's satisfied."

He'd been polite, she thought. Even cooperative. Hadn't he come to give her a materials list? The least she could do was reciprocate. "If Graceland's still on, I can take off some time next Thursday." She kept her eyes on the plants, her tone casual as a fistful of daisies. "If that works for you."

"Thursday?" He'd been all prepared with excuses if she happened to bring it up. Work was jamming him up, they'd do it some other time.

But there she was, kneeling on the ground, with that damn hair curling all over the place and the sun hitting it. Those blue eyes, that cool Yankee voice.

"Sure, Thursday's good. You want me to pick you up here or at the house?"

"Here, if that's okay. What time works best for you?"

"Maybe around one. That way I can put the morning in."

"That'll be perfect." She rose, brushed off her gloves and set them neatly on the cart. "Just let me put together a price for these planters, make you up an order form. If she decides against them, just bring them back."

"She won't. Go ahead and do the paperwork." He dug a many folded note out of his pocket. "On these and the materials I've got down here. I'll load up."

"Good. Fine." She started inside. The itch had moved from her shoulder blades to just under her belly button.

It wasn't a date, it wasn't a date, she reminded herself. It wasn't even an outing, really. It was a gesture. A goodwill gesture on both sides.

And now, she thought as she walked into her office, they were both stuck with it.

NINE

"I don't know how it got to be Thursday."

"It has something to do with Thor, the Norse god." Hayley hunched her shoulders sheepishly. "I know a lot of stupid things. I don't know why."

"I wasn't looking for the origin of the word, more how it got here so fast. Thor?" Stella repeated, turning from the mirror in the employee bathroom.

"Pretty sure."

"I'll just take your word on that one. Okay." She spread out her arms. "How do I look?"

"You look really nice."

"Too nice? You know, too formal or prepared?"

"No, just right nice." The fact was, she envied the way Stella looked in simple gray pants and black sweater. Sort of tailored, and curvy under it. When she wasn't pregnant, she herself tended to be on the bony side and flat-chested.

"The sweater makes you look really built," she added.

"Oh, God!" Horrified, Stella crossed her arms, pressing them against her breasts. "Too built? Like, hey, look at my boobs?"

"No." Laughing, Hayley tugged Stella's arms down. "Cut it out. You've got really excellent boobs."

"I'm nervous. It's ridiculous, but I'm nervous. I *hate* being nervous, which is why I hardly ever am." She tugged at the sleeve of her sweater, brushed at it. "Why do something you hate?"

"It's just a casual afternoon outing." Hayley avoided the D word. They'd been over that. "Just go and have fun."

"Right. Of course. Stupid." She shook herself off before walking out of the room. "You've got my cell number."

"Everybody has your cell number, Stella." She cast a look at Ruby, who answered it with chuckle. "I think the mayor probably has it on speed dial."

"If there are any problems at all, don't hesitate to use it. And if you're not sure about anything, and can't find Roz or Harper, just call me."

"Yes, Mama. And don't worry, the keg's not coming until three." She slapped a hand over her mouth. "Did I say keg? Peg's what I meant. Yeah, I meant Peg."

"Ha ha."

"And the male strippers aren't a definite." She got a hoot of laughter out of Ruby at that and grinned madly. "So you can chill."

"I don't think chilling's on today's schedule."

"Can I ask how long it's been since you've been on a date—I mean, an outing?"

"Not that long. A few months." When Hayley rolled her eyes, Stella rolled hers right back. "I was busy. There was a lot to do with selling the house, packing up, arranging for storage, researching schools and pediatricians down here. I didn't have time."

"And didn't have anyone who made you want to make time. You're making it today."

"It's not like that. Why is he late?" she demanded, glancing at her watch. "I knew he'd be late. He has 'I'm chronically late for mostly everything' written all over him."

When a customer came in, Hayley patted Stella's shoulder. "That's my cue. Have a good time. May I help you?" she asked, strolling over to the customer.

Stella waited another couple of minutes, assuring herself that Hayley had the new customer in hand. Ruby rang up two more. Work was being done where work needed to be done, and she had nothing to do but wait.

Deciding to do her waiting outside, she grabbed her jacket.

Her planters looked good, and she figured her display of them was directly responsible for the flats of pansies they'd moved in the past few days. That being the case, they could add a few more planters, do a couple of half whiskey barrels, add some hanging pots.

Scribbling, she wandered around, picking out the best spots to place displays, to add other touches that would inspire customers to buy.

When Logan pulled up at quarter after one, she was sitting on the steps, listing the proposed displays and arrangements and dividing up the labor of creating them.

She got up even as he climbed out of the truck. "I got hung up."

"No problem. I kept busy."

"You okay riding in the truck?"

"Wouldn't be the first time." She got in, and as she buckled her seat belt, studied the forest of notes and reminders, sketches and math calculations stuck to his dashboard.

"Your filing system?"

"Most of it." He turned on the CD player, and Elvis rocked out with "Heartbreak Hotel." "Seems only right."

"Are you a big fan?"

"You've got to respect the King."

"How many times have you been to Graceland?"

"Couldn't say. People come in from out of town, they want to see it. You visit Memphis, you want Graceland, Beale Street, ribs, the Peabody's duck walk."

Maybe she could chill, Stella decided. They were just talking, after all. Like normal people. "Then this is the first tic on my list."

He looked over at her. Though his eyes were shielded by the black lenses, she knew, from the angle of his head, that they were narrowed with speculation. "You've been here, what, around a month, and you haven't gone for ribs?"

"No. Will I be arrested?"

"You a vegetarian?"

"No, and I like ribs."

"Honey, you haven't had ribs yet if you haven't had Memphis ribs. Don't your parents live down here? I thought I'd met them once."

"My father and his wife, yeah. Will and Jolene Dooley."

"And no ribs?"

"I guess not. Will *they* be arrested?"

"They might, if it gets out. But I'll give you, and them, a break and keep quiet about it for the time being."

"Guess we'll owe you."

"Heartbreak Hotel" moved into "Shake, Rattle, and Roll." This was her father's music, she thought. It was odd, and kind of sweet, to be driving along, tapping her foot, on the way to Memphis listening to the music her father had listened to as a teenager.

"What you do is you take the kids to the Reunion for ribs," Logan told her. "You can walk over to Beale from there, take in the show. But before you eat, you go by the Peabody so they can see the ducks. Kids gotta see the ducks."

"My father's taken them."

"That might keep him out of the slammer."

"Whew." It was easier than she'd thought it would be, and she felt foolish knowing she'd prepared several avenues for small talk. "Except for the time you moved north, you've always lived in the Memphis area?"

"That's right."

"It's strange for me, knowing I was born here, but having no real memory of it. I like it here, and I like to think—overlooking the lack of ribs to date—that there's a connection for me here. Of course, I haven't been through a summer yet—that I can remember—but I like it. I love working for Roz."

"She's a jewel."

Because she heard the affection in his tone, she shifted toward him a bit. "She thinks the same of you. In fact, initially, I thought the two of you were . . ."

His grin spread. "No kidding?"

"She's beautiful and clever, and you've got a lot in common. You've got a history."

"All true. Probably the history makes anything like that weird. But thanks."

"I admire her so much. I like her, too, but I have such admiration for everything she's accomplished. Single-handedly. Raising her family, maintaining her home, building a business from the ground up. And all the while doing it her own way, calling her own shots."

"Is that what you want?"

"I don't want my own business. I thought about it a couple of years ago. But that sort of leap with no parachute and two kids?" She shook her head. "Roz is gutsier than I am. Besides, I realized it wasn't what I really wanted. I like working for someone else, sort of troubleshooting and coming in with a creative and efficient plan for improvement or expansion. Managing is what I do best."

She waited a beat. "No sarcastic comments to that?"

"Only on the inside. That way I can save them up until you tick me off again."

"I can hardly wait. In any case, it's like, I enjoy planting a garden from scratch—that blank slate. But more, I like taking one that's not planned very well, or needs some shaping up, and turning it around."

She paused, frowned. "Funny, I just remembered. I had a dream about a garden a few nights ago. A really strange dream with . . . I don't know, something spooky about it. I can't quite get it back, but there was something . . . this huge, gorgeous blue dahlia. Dahlias are a particular favorite of mine, and blue's my favorite color. Still, it shouldn't have been there, didn't belong there. I hadn't planted it. But there it was. Strange."

"What did you do with it? The dahlia?"

"Can't remember. Luke woke me up, so my garden and the exotic dahlia went poof." And the room, she thought, the room had been so cold. "He wasn't feeling well, a little tummy distress."

"He okay now?"

"Yeah." Another point for his side, Stella thought. "He's fine, thanks."

"How about the tooth?"

Uh-oh, second point. The man remembered her baby'd had a loose tooth. "Sold to the Tooth Fairy for a crisp dollar bill. Second one's about to wiggle out. He's got the cutest little lisp going on right now."

"His big brother teach him how to spit through the hole yet?"

She grimaced. "Not to my knowledge."

"What you don't know . . . I bet it's still there—the magic dahlia—blooming in dreamland."

"That's a nice thought." *Kill it.* God, where did that come from? she wondered, fighting off a shudder. "It was pretty spectacular, as I recall."

She glanced around as he pulled into a parking lot. "Is this it?"

"It's across the road. This is like the visitors' center, the staging area. We get our tickets inside, and they take groups over in shuttles."

He turned off the engine, shifted to look at her. "Five bucks says you're a convert when we come back out."

"An Elvis convert? I don't have anything against him now."

"Five bucks. You'll be buying an Elvis CD, minimum, after the tour."

"That's a bet."

* * *

IT WAS SO MUCH SMALLER THAN SHE'D IMAGINED. She'd pictured something big and sprawling, something mansionlike, close to the level of Harper House. Instead, it was a relatively modest-sized home, and the rooms—at least the ones the tour encompassed—rather small.

She shuffled along with the rest of the tourists, listening to Lisa Marie Presley's recorded memories and observations through the provided headset.

She puzzled over the pleated fabric in shades of curry, blue, and maroon swagged from the ceiling and covering every inch of wall in the cramped, pool-table-dominated game room. Then wondered at the waterfall, the wild-animal prints and tiki-hut accessories all crowned by a ceiling of green shag carpet in the jungle room.

Someone had lived with this, she thought. Not just someone, but an icon—a man of miraculous·talent and fame. And it was sweet to listen to the woman who'd been a child when she'd lost her famous father, talk about the man she remembered, and loved.

The trophy room was astonishing to her, and immediately replaced her style quibbles with awe. It seemed like miles of walls in the meandering hallways were covered, cheek by jowl, with Elvis's gold and platinum records. All that accomplished, all that earned in fewer years, really, than she'd been alive.

And with Elvis singing through her headset, she admired his accomplishments, marveled over his elaborate, splashy, and myriad stage costumes. Then was charmed by his photographs, his movie posters, and the snippets of interviews.

YOU LEARNED A LOT ABOUT SOMEONE WALKING through Graceland with her, Logan discovered. Some snickered over the dated and debatably tacky decor. Some stood glassy-eyed with adoration for the dead King. Others bopped along, rubbernecking or chatting, moving on through so they could get it all in and push on to the souvenir shops. Then they could go home and say, been there, done that.

But Stella looked at everything. And listened. He could tell she was listening carefully to the recording, the way her head would cock just an inch to the right. Listening soberly, he thought, and he'd bet a lot more than five bucks that she followed the instructions on the tape, pressing the correct number for the next segment at exactly the proper time.

It was kind of cute actually.

When they stepped outside to make the short pilgrimage to Elvis's poolside grave, she took off her headphones for the first time.

"I didn't know all that," she began. "Nothing more than the bare basics, really. Over a billion records sold? It's beyond comprehension, really. I certainly can't imagine what it would be like to *do* all that and . . . what are you grinning at?"

"I bet if you had to take an Elvis test right now, you'd ace it."

"Shut up." But she laughed, then sobered again when she walked through the sunlight with him to the Meditation Garden, and the King's grave.

There were flowers, live ones wilting in the sun, plastic ones fading in it. And the little gravesite beside the swimming pool seemed both eccentric and right. Cameras snapped around them now, and she heard someone quietly sobbing.

"People claim to have seen his ghost, you know, back there." Logan gestured. "That is, if he's really dead."

"You don't believe that."

"Oh, yeah, Elvis left the building a long time ago."

"I mean about the ghost."

"Well, if he was going to haunt any place, this would be it."

They wound around toward the shuttle pickup. "People are awfully casual about ghosts around here."

It took him a minute. "Oh, the Harper Bride. Seen her yet?"

"No, I haven't. But that may only be because, you know, she doesn't exist. You're not going to tell me you've seen her."

"Can't say I have. Lot of people claim to, but then some claim to have seen Elvis eating peanut-butter-and-banana sandwiches at some diner ten years after he died."

"Exactly!" She was so pleased with his good sense, she gave him a light punch on the arm. "People see what they want to see, or have been schooled to see, or expect to. Imaginations run wild, especially under the right conditions or atmosphere. They ought to do more with the gardens here, don't you think?"

"Don't get me started."

"You're right. No shop talk. Instead, I'll just thank you for bringing me. I don't know when I'd've gotten around to it on my own."

"What'd you think?"

"Sad and sweet and fascinating." She passed her headphones back to the attendant and stepped on the shuttle. "Some of the rooms were, let's say, unique in decor."

Their arms bumped, brushed, stayed pressed to each other in the narrow confines of the shuttle's seats. Her hair skimmed along his shoulder until she shoved it back. He was sorry when she did.

"I knew this guy, big Elvis fan. He set about duplicating Graceland in his house. Got fabric like you saw in the game room, did his walls and ceilings."

She turned to face him, stared. "You're kidding."

He simply swiped a finger over his heart. "Even put a scar on his pool table to match the one on Elvis's. When he talked about getting those yellow appliances—"

"Harvest gold."

"Whatever. When he starting making noises about putting those in, his wife gave him notice. Her or Elvis."

Her face was alive with humor, and he stopped hearing the chatter of other passengers. There was something about her when she smiled, full out, that blew straight through him.

"And which did he choose?"

"Huh?"

"Which did he choose? His wife or Elvis?"

"Well." He stretched out his legs, but couldn't really shift his body away from hers. The sun was blasting through the window beside her, striking all that curling red hair. "He settled on re-creating it in his basement, and was trying to talk her into letting him put a scale model of the Meditation Garden in their backyard."

She laughed, a delightful roll of sound. When she dropped her head back on the seat, her hair tickled his shoulder again. "If he ever does, I hope we get the job."

"Count on it. He's my uncle."

She laughed again, until she was breathless. "Boy, I can't wait to meet your family." She angled around so she could face him. "I'm going to confess the only reason I came today was because I didn't want to spoil a nice gesture by saying no. I didn't expect to have fun."

"It wasn't a nice gesture so much as a spur of the moment thing. Your hair smelled good, and that clouded my better judgment."

Humor danced over her face as she pushed her hair back. "And? You're supposed to say you had fun, too."

"Actually, I did."

When the shuttle stopped, he got up, stepped back so she could slide out and walk in front of him. "But then, your hair still smells good, so that could be it."

She shot him a grin over her shoulder, and damn it, he felt that clutch in the belly. Usually the clutch meant possibilities of fun and enjoyment. With her, he thought it meant trouble.

But he'd been raised to follow through, and his mama

would be horrified and shocked if he didn't feed a woman he'd spent the afternoon with.

"Hungry?" he asked when he stepped down after her.

"Oh . . . Well, it's too early for dinner, too late for lunch. I really should—"

"Walk on the wild side. Eat between meals." He grabbed her hand, and that was such a surprise she didn't think to protest until he'd pulled her toward one of the on-site eateries.

"I really shouldn't take the time. I told Roz I'd be back around four."

"You know, you stay wrapped that tight for any length of time, you're going to cut your circulation off."

"I'm not wrapped that tight," she objected. "I'm responsible."

"Roz doesn't have a time clock at the nursery, and it doesn't take that long to eat a hot dog."

"No, but . . ." Liking him was so unexpected. As unexpected as the buzz along her skin at the feel of that big, hard hand gripping hers. It had been a long while since she'd enjoyed a man's company. Why cut it short?

"Okay." Though, she realized, her assent was superfluous, as he'd already pulled her inside and up to the counter. "Anyway. Since I'm here, I wouldn't mind looking in the shops for a minute. Or two."

He ordered two dogs, two Cokes and just smiled at her.

"All right, smart guy." She opened her purse, dug out her wallet. And took out a five-dollar bill. "I'm buying the CD. And make mine a Diet Coke."

She ate the hot dog, drank the Coke. She bought the CD. But unlike every other female he knew, she didn't have some religious obligation to look at and paw over everything in the store. She did her business and was done—neat, tidy, and precise.

And as they walked back to his truck, he noticed she glanced at the readout display of her cell phone. Again.

"Problem?"

"No." She slipped the phone back into her bag. "Just

checking to see if I had any messages." But it seemed everyone had managed without her for an afternoon.

Unless something was wrong with the phones. Or they'd lost her number. Or—

"The nursery could've been attacked by psychopaths with a petunia fetish." Logan opened the passenger-side door. "The entire staff could be bound and gagged in the propagation house even as we speak."

Deliberately, Stella zipped her bag closed. "You won't think that's so funny if we get there and that's just what happened."

"Yes, I will."

He walked around the truck, got behind the wheel.

"I have an obsessive, linear, goal-oriented personality with strong organizational tendencies."

He sat for a moment. "I'm glad you told me. I was under the impression you were a scatterbrain."

"Well, enough about me. Why—"

"Why do you keep doing that?"

She paused, her hands up in her hair. "Doing what?"

"Why do you keep jamming those pins in your hair?"

"Because they keep coming out."

To her speechless shock, he reached over, tugged the loosened bobby pins free, then tossed them on the floor of his truck. "So why put them in there in the first place?"

"Well, for God's sake." She scowled down at the pins. "How many times a week does someone tell you you're pushy and overbearing?"

"I don't count." He drove out of the lot and into traffic. "You've got sexy hair. You ought to leave it alone."

"Thanks very much for the style advice."

"Women don't usually sulk when a man tells them they're sexy."

"I'm not sulking, and you didn't say I was sexy. You said my hair was."

He took his eyes off the road long enough to give her an up-and-down glance. "Rest of you works, too."

Okay, something was wrong when that sort of half-assed compliment had heat balling in her belly. Best to return to safe topics. "To return to my question before I was so oddly interrupted, why did you go into landscape design?"

"Summer job that stuck."

She waited a beat, two. Three. "Really, Logan, must you go on and on, boring me with details?"

"Sorry. I never know when to shut up. I grew up on a farm."

"Really? Did you love it or hate it?"

"Was used to it, mostly. I like working outside, and don't mind heavy, sweaty work."

"Blabbermouth," she said when he fell silent again.

"Not that much more to it. I didn't want to farm, and my daddy sold the farm some years back, anyway. But I like working the land. It's what I like, it's what I'm good at. No point in doing something you don't like or you're not good at."

"Let's try this. How did you know you were good at it?"

"Not getting fired was an indication." He didn't see how she could possibly be interested, but since she was pressing, he'd pass the time. "You know how you're in school, say in history, and they're all Battle of Hastings or crossing the Rubicon or Christ knows? In and out," he said, tapping one side of his head, then the other. "I'd jam it in there long enough to skin through the test, then poof. But on the job, the boss would say we're going to put cotoneasters in here, line these barberries over there, and I'd remember. What they were, what they needed. I liked putting them in. It's satisfying, digging the hole, prepping the soil, changing the look of things. Making it more pleasing to the eye."

"It is," she agreed. "Believe it or not, that's the same sort of deal I have with my files."

He slanted her a look that made her lips twitch. "You say. Anyway, sometimes I'd get this idea that, you know, those cotoneasters would look better over there, and instead of barberries, golden mops would set this section off. So I angled off into design."

"I thought about design for a while. Not that good at it," she said. "I realized I had a hard time adjusting my vision to blend with the team's—or the client's. And I'd get too hung up in the math and science of it, and bogged down when it came time to roll over into the art."

"Who did your landscaping up north?"

"I did. If I had something in mind that took machines, or more muscle than Kevin and I could manage, I had a list." She smiled. "A very detailed and specific list, with the design done on graph paper. Then I hovered. I'm a champion hoverer."

"And nobody shoved you into a hole and buried you?"

"No. But then, I'm very personable and pleasant. Maybe, when the time comes and I find my own place, you could consult on the landscaping design."

"I'm not personable and pleasant."

"Already noted."

"And isn't it a leap for an obsessive, linear, detail freak to trust me to consult when you've only seen one of my jobs, and that in its early stages?"

"I object to the term 'freak.' I prefer 'devotee.' And it happens I've seen several of your jobs, complete. I got some of the addresses out of the files and drove around. It's what I do," she said when he braked at a Stop sign and stared at her. "I've spent some time watching Harper work, and Roz, as well as the employees. I made it a point to take a look at some of your completed jobs. I like your work."

"And if you hadn't?"

"If I hadn't, I'd have said nothing. It's Roz's business, and *she* obviously likes your work. But I'd have done some quiet research on other designers, put a file together and presented it to her. That's my job."

"And here I thought your job was to manage the nursery and annoy me with forms."

"It is. Part of that management is to make sure that all

employees and subcontractors, suppliers and equipment are not only suitable for In the Garden but the best Roz can afford. You're pricey," she added, "but your work justifies it."

When he only continued to frown, she poked a finger into his arm. "And men don't usually sulk when a woman compliments their work."

"Huh. Men never sulk, they brood."

But she had a point. Still, it occurred to him that she knew a great deal about him—personal matters. How much he made, for instance. When he asked himself how he felt about that, the answer was, Not entirely comfortable.

"My work, my salary, my prices are between me and Roz."

"Not anymore," she said cheerfully. "She has the last word, no question, but I'm there to manage. I'm saying that, in my opinion, Roz showed foresight and solid business sense in bringing you into her business. She pays you very well because you're worth it. Any reason you can't take that as a compliment and skip the brooding phase?"

"I don't know. What's she paying you?"

"That *is* between her and me, but you're certainly free to ask her." The *Star Wars* theme erupted in her purse. "Gavin's pick," she said as she dug it out. The readout told her the call came from home. "Hello? Hi, baby."

Though he was still a little irked, he watched everything about her light up. "You *did*? You're amazing. Uh-huh. I absolutely will. See you soon."

She closed the phone, put it back in her purse. "Gavin aced his spelling test."

"Yay."

She laughed. "You have *no* idea. I have to pick up pepperoni pizza on the way home. In our family, it's not a carrot at the end of the stick used as motivation—or simple bribery—it's pepperoni pizza."

"You bribe your kids?"

"Often, and without a qualm."

"Smart. So, they're getting along in school?"

"They are. All that worry and guilt wasted. I'll have to set it aside for future use. It was a big move for them—new place, new school, new people. Luke makes friends easily, but Gavin can be a little shy."

"Didn't seem shy to me. Kid's got a spark. Both of them do."

"Comic book connection. Any friend of Spidey's, and so on, so they were easy with you. But they're both sliding right along. So I can scratch traumatizing my sons by ripping them away from their friends off my Things to Worry About list."

"I bet you actually have one."

"Every mother has one." She let out a long, contented sigh as he pulled into the lot at the nursery. "This has been a really good day. Isn't this a great place? Just look at it. Industrious, attractive, efficient, welcoming. I envy Roz her vision, not to mention her guts."

"You don't seem deficient in the guts department."

"Is that a compliment?"

He shrugged. "An observation."

She liked being seen as gutsy, so she didn't tell him she was scared a great deal of the time. Order and routine were solid, defensive walls that kept the fear at bay.

"Well, thanks. For the observation, and the afternoon. I really appreciated both." She opened the door, hopped out. "And I've got a trip into the city for ribs on my list of must-dos."

"You won't be sorry." He got out, walked around to her side. He wasn't sure why. Habit, he supposed. Ingrained manners his mother had carved into him as a boy. But it wasn't the sort of situation where you walked the girl to her door and copped a kiss good night.

She thought about offering her hand to shake, but it seemed stiff *and* ridiculous. So she just smiled. "I'll play the CD for the boys." She shook her bag. "See what they think."

"Okay. See you around."

He started to walk back to his door. Then he cursed under his breath, tossed his sunglasses on the hood, and turned back. "Might as well finish it out."

She wasn't slow, and she wasn't naive. She knew what he intended when he was still a full stride away. But she couldn't seem to move.

She heard herself make some sound—not an actual word—then his hand raked through her hair, his fingers cupping her head with enough pressure to bring her up on her toes. She saw his eyes. There were gold flecks dusted over the green.

Then everything blurred, and his mouth was hard and hot on hers.

Nothing hesitant about it, nothing testing or particularly friendly. It was all demand, with an irritable edge. Like the man, she thought dimly, he was doing what he intended to do, was determined to see it through, but wasn't particularly pleased about it.

And still her heart rammed into her throat, throbbing there to block words, even breath. The fingers of the hand that had lifted to his shoulder in a kind of dazed defense dug in. They slid limply down to his elbow when his head lifted.

With his hand still caught in her hair, he said, "Hell."

He dragged her straight up to her toes again, banded an arm around her so that her body was plastered to his. When his mouth swooped down a second time, any brains that hadn't already been fried drained out of her ears.

He shouldn't have thought of kissing her. But once he had, it didn't seem reasonable to walk away and leave it undone. And now he was in trouble, all wound up in that wild hair, that sexy scent, those soft lips.

And when he deepened the kiss, she let out this sound, this catchy little moan. What the hell was a man supposed to do but want?

Her hair was like a maze of madly coiled silk, and that

pretty, curvy body of hers vibrated against him like a well-tuned machine, revving for action. The longer he held her, the more he tasted her, the dimmer the warning bells sounded to remind him he didn't want to get tangled up with her. On any level.

When he managed to release her, to step back, he saw the flush riding along her cheeks. It made her eyes bluer, bigger. It made him want to toss her over his shoulder and cart her off somewhere, anywhere at all where they could finish what the kiss had started. Because the urge to do so was an ache in the belly, he took another step back.

"Okay." He thought he spoke calmly, but couldn't be sure with the blood roaring in his ears. "See you around."

He walked back to the truck, got in. Managed to turn over the engine and shove into reverse. Then he hit the brakes again when the sun speared into his eyes.

He sat, watching Stella walk forward, retrieve the sunglasses that had bounced off the hood and onto the gravel. He lowered the window as she stepped to it.

His eyes stayed on hers when he reached out to take them from her. "Thanks."

"Sure."

He slipped them on, backed out, turned the wheel and drove out of the lot.

Alone, she let out a long, wheezing breath, sucked in another one; and let that out as she ordered her limp legs to carry her to the porch.

She made it as far as the steps before she simply lowered herself down to sit. "Holy Mother of God," she managed.

She sat, even as a customer came out, as another came in, while everything inside her jumped and jittered. She felt as though she'd fallen off a cliff and was even now, barely—just barely—clinging to a skinny, crumbling ledge by sweaty fingertips.

What was she supposed to do about this? And how could she figure it out when she couldn't think?

So she wouldn't try to figure it out until she could think. Getting to her feet, she rubbed her damp palms on the thighs of her pants. For now, she'd go back to work, she'd order pizza, then go home to her boys. Go home to normal.

She did better with normal.

ten

HARPER SPADED THE DIRT AT THE BASE OF THE clematis that wound its way up the iron trellis. It was quiet on this edge of the garden. The shrubs and ornamental trees, the paths and beds separated what he still thought of as the guest house from the main.

Daffodils were just opening up, with all that bright yellow against the spring green. Tulips would be coming along next. They were one of his favorite things about this leading edge of spring, so he'd planted a bed of bulbs right outside the kitchen door of his place.

It was a small converted carriage house and according to every female he'd ever brought there, it was charming. "Dollhouse" was the usual term. He didn't mind it. Though he thought of it more as a cottage, like a groundskeeper's cottage with its whitewashed cedar shakes and pitched roof. It was comfortable, inside and out, and more than adequate for his needs.

There was a small greenhouse only a few feet out the back door, and that was his personal domain. The cottage was just far enough from the house to be private, so he

didn't have to feel weird having overnight guests of the
female persuasion. And close enough that he could be at
the main house in minutes if his mother needed him.

He didn't like the idea of her being alone, even with
David on hand. And thank God for David. It didn't matter
that she was self-sufficient, the strongest person he knew.
He just didn't like the idea of his mother rattling around in
that big old house alone, day after day, night after night.

Though he certainly preferred that to having her stuck
in it with that asshole she'd married. Words couldn't
describe how he despised Bryce Clerk. He supposed having his mother fall for the guy proved she wasn't infallible,
but it had been a hell of a mistake for someone who rarely
made one.

Though she'd given him the boot, swiftly and without
mercy, Harper had worried how the man would handle
being cut off—from Roz, the house, the money, the whole
ball.

And damned if he hadn't tried to break in once, the
week before the divorce was final. Harper didn't doubt his
mother could've handled it, but it hadn't hurt to be at hand.

And having a part in kicking the greedy, cheating, lying
bastard out on his ass couldn't be overstated.

But maybe enough time had passed now. And she sure
as hell wasn't alone in the house these days. Two women,
two kids made for a lot of company. Between them and the
business, she was busier than ever.

Maybe he should think about getting a place of his own.

Trouble was, he couldn't think of a good reason. He
loved this place, in a way he'd never loved a woman. With
a kind of focused passion, respect, and gratitude.

The gardens were home, maybe even more than the
house, more than his cottage. Most days he could walk out
his front door, take a good, healthy hike, and be at work.

God knew he didn't want to move to the city. All that
noise, all those people. Memphis was great for a night
out—a club, a date, meeting up with friends. But he'd suf-
focate there inside a month.

He sure as hell didn't want suburbia. What he wanted was right where he was. A nice little house, extensive gardens, a greenhouse and a short hop to work.

He sat back on his heels, adjusted the ball cap he wore to keep the hair out of his eyes. Spring was coming. There was nothing like spring at home. The way it smelled, the way it looked, even the way it sounded.

The light was soft now with approaching evening. When the sun went down, the air would chill, but it wouldn't have that bite of winter.

When he was done planting here, he'd go in and get himself a beer. And he'd sit out in the dark and the cool, and enjoy the solitude.

He took a bold yellow pansy out of the cell pack and began to plant.

He didn't hear her walk up. Such was his focus that he didn't notice her shadow fall over him. So her friendly "Hey!" nearly had him jumping out of his skin.

"Sorry." With a laugh, Hayley rubbed a hand over her belly. "Guess you were a million miles away."

"Guess." His fingers felt fat and clumsy all of a sudden, and his brain sluggish. She stood with the setting sun at her back, so when he squinted up at her, her head was haloed, her face shadowed.

"I was just walking around. Heard your music." She nodded toward the open windows where REM spilled out. "I saw them in concert once. Excellent. Pansies? They're a hot item right now."

"Well, they like the cool."

"I know. How come you're putting them here? You've got this vine thing happening."

"Clematis. Likes its roots shaded. So you . . . you know, put annuals over them."

"Oh." She squatted down for a closer look. "What color is the clematis?"

"It's purple." He wasn't sure pregnant women should squat. Didn't it crowd things in there? "Ah, you want a chair or something?"

"No, I'm set. I like your house."

"Yeah, me too."

"It's sort of storybook here, with all the gardens. I mean, the big house is amazing. But it's a little intimidating." She grimaced. "I don't mean to sound ungrateful."

"No, I get you." It helped to keep planting. She didn't *smell* pregnant. She smelled sexy. And that had to be wrong. "It's a great place, and you couldn't get my mother out of it with dynamite and wild mules. But it's a lot of house."

"Took me a week to stop walking about on tiptoe and wanting to whisper. Can I plant one?"

"You don't have any gloves. I can get—"

"Hell, I don't mind a little dirt under my nails. A lady was in today? She said it's like good luck for a pregnant woman to plant gardens. Something about fertility, I guess."

He didn't want to think about fertility. There was something terrifying about it. "Go ahead."

"Thanks. I wanted to say . . ." And it was easier with her hands busy. "Well, just that I know how it might look, me coming out of nowhere, landing on your mama's doorstep. But I'm not going to take advantage of her. I don't want you to think I'd try to do that."

"I've only known one person to manage it, and he didn't manage it for long."

"The second husband." She nodded as she patted the dirt around her plant. "I asked David about him so I wouldn't say something stupid. He said how he'd stuck his hand in the till, and cheated on her with another woman." She chose another pansy. "And when Roz got wind of it, she booted him out so hard and fast he didn't land till he was halfway to Memphis. You gotta admire that, because you know even with a mad on, it had to hurt her feelings. Plus, it's just embarrassing when somebody—oops."

She pressed a hand to her side, and had the blood draining out of Harper's face.

"What? What?"

"Nothing. Baby's moving around. Sometimes it gives me a jolt is all."

"You should stand up. You should sit down."

"Let me just finish this one. Back home, when I started to show? People, some people, just figured I'd got myself in trouble and the boy wouldn't stand up for me. I mean, Jesus, are we in the twenty-first century or what? Anyway, that made me mad, but it was embarrassing, too. I guess that's partly why I left. It's hard being embarrassed all the damn time. There." She patted the dirt. "They look really pretty."

He popped up to help her to her feet. "You want to sit for a minute? Want me to walk you back?"

She patted her belly. "This makes you nervous."

"Looks like."

"Me too. But I'm fine. You'll want to get the rest of those planted before it gets dark." She looked down at the flowers again, at the house, at the gardens surrounding it, and those long, lake-colored eyes seemed to take in everything.

Then they zeroed in on his face and made his throat go dry.

"I really like your place. See you at work."

He stood, rooted, as she walked off, gliding along the path, around the curve of it, into the twilight.

He was exhausted, he realized. Like he'd run some sort of crazed race. He'd just have that beer now, settle himself down. Then he'd finish with the pansies.

WITH THE KIDS OUTSIDE TAKING PARKER FOR HIS after-dinner walk, Stella cleaned up the mess two boys and a dog could make in the kitchen over a pepperoni pizza.

"Next pizza night, I buy," Hayley said as she loaded glasses into the dishwasher.

"That's a deal." Stella glanced over. "When I was carrying Luke, all I wanted was Italian. Pizza, spaghetti, mani-cotti. I was surprised he didn't pop out singing 'That's Amore.' "

"I don't have any specific cravings. I'll just eat any-thing." In the wash of the outside floodlights, she could see boys and dog racing. "The baby's moving around a lot. That's normal, right?"

"Sure. Gavin just sort of snuggled and snoozed. I'd have to poke him or sip some Coke to get him moving. But Luke did gymnastics in there for months. Is it keeping you up nights?"

"Sometimes, but I don't mind. It feels like we're the only two people in the world. Just me and him—or her."

"I know just what you mean. But Hayley, if you're awake, worried or just not feeling well, whatever, you can come get me."

The tightness in her throat loosened instantly. "Really? You mean it?"

"Sure. Sometimes it helps to talk to somebody who's been there and done that."

"I'm not on my own," she said quietly, with her eyes on the boys outside the window. "Not like I thought I'd be. Was ready to be—I think." When those eyes filled, she blinked them, rubbed at them. "Hormones. God."

"Crying can help, too." Stella rubbed Hayley's shoul-ders. "And I want you to tell me if you want someone to go with you to your doctor's appointments."

"He said, when I went in, that everything looks good. Right on schedule. And that I should sign up for the classes, you know? Childbirth classes. But they like you to have a partner."

"Pick me!"

Laughing, Hayley turned. "Really? You're sure? It's a lot to ask."

"I would love it. It's almost as good as having another one of my own."

"Would you? If . . ."

"Yes. Two was the plan, but as soon as Luke was born, I thought, how can I not do this again—and wouldn't it be fun to try for a girl? But another boy would be great." She leaned forward on the counter, looked out the window. "They're terrific, aren't they? My boys."

"They are."

"Kevin was so proud, so in love with them. I think he'd have had half a dozen."

Hayley heard the change in tone, and this time, she rubbed a hand on Stella's shoulder. "Does it hurt to talk about him?"

"Not anymore. It did for a while, for a long while." She picked up the dishrag to wipe the counter. "But now it's good to remember. Warm, I guess. I ought to call those boys in."

But she turned at the sound of heels clicking on wood. When Roz breezed in, Stella's mouth dropped open.

She recalled her first impression of Rosalind Harper had been of beauty, but this was the first time she'd seen Roz exploit her natural attributes.

She wore a sleek, form-fitting dress in a muted copper color that made her skin glow. It, along with ice-pick-heeled sandals, showed off lean, toned legs. A necklace of delicate filigree with a teardrop of citrine lay over her breasts.

"David?" Roz scanned the room, then rolled dark, dramatic eyes. "He's going to make me late."

Stella let out an exaggerated breath. "Just let me say, Wow!"

"Yeah." She grinned, did a little half turn. "I must've been insane when I bought the shoes. They're going to kill me. But when I have to drag myself out to one of these charity deals, I like to make a statement."

"If the statement's 'I'm totally hot,'" Hayley put in, "you hit it dead on."

"That was the target."

"You look absolutely amazing. Sex with class. Every

man there's going to wish he was taking you home to-night."

"Well." With a half laugh, Roz shook her head. "It's great having women in the house. Who knew? I'm going to go nag David. He'll primp for another hour if I don't give his ass a kick."

"Have a wonderful time."

"She sure didn't look like anybody's mother," Stella said under her breath.

WHAT WOULD SHE LOOK LIKE IN TWENTY YEARS? Hayley wondered.

She studied herself in the mirror while she rubbed Vitamin E oil over her belly and breasts. Would she still be able to fix herself up and know she looked good?

Of course, she didn't have as much to work with as Roz. She remembered her grandmother saying once that beauty was in the bones. Looking at Roz helped her understand just what that meant.

She'd never be as stunning as Roz, or as eye-catching as Stella, but she looked okay. She took care of her skin, tried out the makeup tricks she read about in magazines.

Guys were attracted.

Obviously, she thought with a self-deprecating smile as she looked down at her belly.

Or had been. Most guys didn't get the hots for pregnant women. And that was fine, because she wasn't interested in men right now. The only thing that mattered was her baby.

"It's all about you now, kid," she said as she pulled on an oversized T-shirt.

After climbing into bed, plumping up her pillows, she reached for one of the books stacked on her nightstand. She had books on childbirth, on pregnancy, on early-childhood development. She read from one of them every night.

When her eyes began to droop, she closed the book.

Switching off the light, she snuggled down. "'Night, baby," she whispered.

And felt it just as she was drifting off. The little chill, the absolute certainty that she wasn't alone. Her heartbeat quickened until she could hear it in her ears. Gathering courage, she let her eyes open to slits.

She saw the figure standing over the bed. The light-colored hair, the lovely sad face. She thought about screaming, just as she did every time she saw the woman. But she bit it back, braced herself, and reached out.

When her hand passed through the woman's arm, Hayley did let out a muffled scream. Then she was alone, shivering in bed and fumbling for the light.

"I'm not imagining it. I'm not!"

STELLA CLIMBED UP THE STEPSTOOL TO HOOK ANOTHER hanging basket for display. After looking over last year's sales, crunching numbers, she'd decided to increase the number offered by 15 percent.

"I could do that," Hayley insisted. "I'm not going to fall off a stupid stepstool."

"No chance. Hand me up that one. The begonias."

"They're really pretty. So lush."

"Roz and Harper started most of these over the winter. Begonias and impatiens are big-volume sellers. With growers like Roz and Harper, we can do them in bulk, and our cost is low. These are bread-and-butter plants for us."

"People could make up their own cheaper."

"Sure." Stella climbed down, moved the ladder, climbed up again. "Ivy geranium," she decided. "But it's tough to resist all this color and bloom. Even avid gardeners, the ones who do some propagating on their own, have a hard time passing up big, beautiful blooms. Blooms, my young apprentice, sell."

"So we're putting these baskets everywhere."

"Seduction. Wait until we move some of the annuals

outside, in front. All that color will draw the customers. Early-blooming perennials too."

She selected another basket. "I've got this. Page Roz, will you? I want her to see these, and get her clearance to hang a couple dozen in Greenhouse Three with the extra stock. And pick out a pot. One of the big ones that didn't move last year. I want to do one up, put it by the counter. I'll move that sucker. In fact, pick out two. Clean off the discount price. When I'm done, they'll not only move, they'll move at a fat profit."

"Gotcha."

"Make sure one of them's that cobalt glaze," she called out. "You know the one? And don't pick it up yourself."

In her mind, Stella began to plan it. White flowers— heliotrope, impatiens, spills of sweet alyssum, silvery accents from dusty miller and sage. Another trail of white petunias. Damn, she should've told Hayley to get one of the stone-gray pots. Good contrast with the cobalt. And she'd do it up hot. Bold red geraniums, lobelia, verbena, red New Guineas.

She added, subtracted plants in her mind, calculated the cost of pots, stock, soil. And smiled to herself as she hung another basket.

"Shouldn't you be doing paperwork?"

She nearly tipped off the stool, might have if a hand hadn't slapped onto her butt to keep her upright.

"It's not all I do." She started to get down, but realized being on the stool kept her at eye level with him. "You can move your hand now, Logan."

"It doesn't mind being there." But he let it fall, slipped it into his pocket. "Nice baskets."

"In the market?"

"Might be. You had a look on your face when I came in."

"I usually do. That's why it's called a face."

"No, the kind of look a woman gets when she's thinking about how to make some guy drool."

"Did I? Mind?" she added, gesturing to a basket. "You're off the mark. I was thinking how I was going to turn two over-stock pots on the discount rack into stupendous displays and considerable profit."

Even as she hung the basket, he was lifting another, and by merely raising his arm, set it in place. "Showoff."

"Shorty."

Hayley came through the doorway, turned briskly on her heel and headed out.

"Hayley."

"Forgot something," she called out and kept going.

Stella blew out a breath and would've asked for another basket, but he'd already picked one up, hung it. "You've been busy," she said.

"Cool, dry weather the last week."

"If you're here to pick up the shrubs for the Pitt job, I can get the paperwork."

"My crew's out loading them. I want to see you again."

"Well. You are."

He kept his eyes on hers. "You're not dim."

"No, I'm not. I'm not sure—"

"Neither am I," he interrupted. "Doesn't seem to stop me from wanting to see you again. It's irritating, thinking about you."

"Thanks. That really makes me want to sigh and fall into your arms."

"I don't want you to fall into them. If I did, I'd just kick your feet out from under you."

She laid a hand on her heart, fluttered her lashes, and did her best woman of the south accent. "My goodness, all this soppy romance is too much for me."

Now he grinned. "I like you, Red. Some of the time. I'll pick you up at seven."

"What? Tonight?" Reluctant amusement turned to outright panic in a fingersnap. "I can't possibly just go out, spur of the moment. I have two kids."

"And three adults in the house. Any reason you can think of why any or all of them can't handle your boys for a few hours tonight?"

"No. But I haven't *asked*, a concept you appear to be

unfamiliar with. And—" She shoved irritably at her hair. "I might have plans."

"Do you?"

She angled her head, looked down her nose. "I always have plans."

"I bet. So flex them. You take the boys for ribs yet?"

"Yes, last week after—"

"Good."

"Do you know how often you interrupt me in the middle of a sentence?"

"No, but I'll start counting. Hey, Roz."

"Logan. Stella, these look great." She stopped in the center of the aisle, scanning, nodding as she absently slapped her dirty gloves against her already dirt-smeared jeans. "I wasn't sure displaying so many would work, but it does. Something about the abundance of bloom."

She took off her ball cap, stuffed it in the back pocket of her work pants, stuffed the gloves in the other. "Am I interrupting?"

"No."

"Yes," Logan corrected. "But it's okay. You up to watching Stella's boys tonight?"

"I haven't said—"

"Absolutely. It'll be fun. You two going out?"

"A little dinner. I'll leave the invoice on your desk," he said to Stella. "See you at seven."

Tired of standing, Stella sat on the stool and scowled at Roz when Logan sauntered out. "You didn't help."

"I think I did." Reaching up, she turned one of the baskets to check the symmetry of the plants. "You'll go out, have a good time. Your boys'll be fine, and I'll enjoy spending some time with them. If you didn't want to go out with Logan, you wouldn't go. You know how to say no loud enough."

"That may be true, but I might've liked a little more notice. A little more . . . something."

"He is what he is." She patted Stella's knee. "And the good thing about that is you don't have to wonder what he's hiding, or what kind of show he's putting on. He's . . . I can't say he's a nice man, because he can be incredibly difficult. But he's an honest one. Take it from me, there's a lot to be said for that."

eLeveN

THIS, STELLA THOUGHT, WAS WHY DATING WAS VERY rarely worth it. In her underwear, she stood in front of her closet, debating, considering, despairing over what to wear.

She didn't even know where she was going. She *hated* not knowing where she was going. How was she supposed to know what to prepare for?

"Dinner" was not enough information. Was it little-black-dress dinner, or dressy-casual on-sale-designer-suit dinner? Was it jeans and a shirt and jacket dinner, or jeans and a silk blouse dinner?

Added to that, by picking her up at seven, he'd barely left her enough time to change, much less decide what to change into.

Dating. How could something that had been so desired, so exciting and so damn much fun in her teens, so easy and natural in her early twenties, have become such a complicated, often irritating chore in her thirties?

It wasn't just that marriage had spoiled her, or rusted her dating tools. Adult dating was complex and exhausting because the people involved in the stupid date had almost certainly been through at least one serious relationship, and breakup, and carried that extra baggage on their backs. They were already set in their ways, had defined their expectations, and had performed this societal dating ritual so often that they really just wanted to cut to the chase—or go home and watch Letterman.

Add to that a man who dropped the date on your head out of the clear blue, then didn't have the sense to give you some guidelines so you knew how to present yourself, and it was just a complete mess before it started.

Fine, then. *Fine*. He'd just get what he got.

She was stepping into the little black dress when the connecting bathroom door burst open and Gavin rushed in. "Mom! I finished my homework. Luke didn't, but I did. Can I go down now? Can I?"

She was glad she'd decided on the open-toed slides and no hose, as Parker was currently trying to climb up her leg. "Did you forget something?" she asked Gavin.

"Nuh-uh. I did all the vocabulary words."

"The knocking something?"

"Oh." He smiled, big and innocent. "You look pretty."

"Smooth talker." She bent down to kiss the top of his head. "But when a door's closed, you knock."

"Okay. Can I go down now?"

"In a minute." She walked over to her dresser to put on the silver hoops she'd laid out. "I want you to promise you'll be good for Miss Roz."

"We're going to have cheeseburgers and play video games. She says she can take us in Smackdown, but I don't think so."

"No fighting with your brother." Hope springs, she thought. "Consider this your night off from your mission in life."

"Can I go *down*?"

"Get." She gave him a light slap on the rump. "Remember, I'll have my phone if you need me."

When he rushed out, she slipped on her shoes and a thin black sweater. After a check in the mirror, she decided the accessories took the dress into the could-be-casual, could-be-more area she'd been shooting for.

She picked up her bag and, checking the contents as she went, walked into the next bedroom. Luke was sprawled belly-down on the floor—his favored position—frowning miserably over his arithmetic book.

"Trouble, handsome?"

He lifted his head, and his face was aggrieved in the way only a young boy could manage. "I hate homework."

"Me too."

"Gavin did the touchdown dance, with his fingers in the air, 'cause he finished first."

Understanding the demoralization, she sat on the floor beside him. "Let's see what you've got."

"How come I have to know two plus three, anyway?"

"How else would you know how many fingers you have on each hand?"

His brow beetled, then cleared with a delighted smile. "Five!"

With the crisis averted, she helped him with the rest of the problems. "There, all done. That wasn't so bad."

"I still hate homework."

"Maybe, but what about the touchdown dance?"

On a giggle, he leaped up and did his strut around the room.

And all, she thought, was right in her little world once more.

"How come you're not going to eat here? We're having cheeseburgers."

"I'm not entirely sure. You'll behave for Miss Roz?"

"Uh-huh. She's nice. Once she came out in the yard and threw the ball for Parker. And she didn't even mind when it got slobbered. Some girls do. I'm going down now, okay? 'Cause I'm hungry."

"You bet."

Alone, she got to her feet, automatically picking up the scatter of toys and clothes that hadn't made it back onto the shelf or into the closet.

She ran her fingers over some of their treasures. Gavin's beloved comic books, his ball glove. Luke's favorite truck, and the battered bear he wasn't yet ashamed to sleep with.

The prickle between her shoulder blades had her stiffening. Even under the light sweater her arms broke out in gooseflesh. Out of the corner of her eye, she saw a shape— a reflection, a shadow—in the mirror over the bureau.

When she spun, Hayley swung around the door and into the room.

"Logan's just pulling up in front of the house," she began, then stopped. "You okay? You look all pale."

"Fine. I'm fine." But she pushed a not-quite-steady hand at her hair. "I just thought . . . nothing. Nothing. Besides pale, how do I look?" And she made herself turn to the mirror again. Saw only herself, with Hayley moving toward her.

"Two thumbs up. I just love your hair."

"Easy to say when you don't wake up with it every morning. I thought about putting it up, but it seemed too formal."

"It's just right." Hayley edged closer, tipping her head toward Stella's. "I did the redhead thing once. Major disaster. Made my skin look yellow."

"That deep, dense brown's what's striking on you." And look at that face, Stella thought with a tiny twist of envy. Not a line on it.

"Yeah, but the red's so now. Anyway, I'm going to go on down. I'll keep Logan busy until. You wait just a few more minutes before you head down, then we'll all be back in the kitchen. Big burger feast."

She didn't intend to make an entrance, for heaven's sake. But Hayley had already gone off, and she did want to check her lipstick. And settle herself down.

At least her nerves over this date—it *was* a date this

time—had taken a backseat to others. It hadn't been Hayley's reflection in the mirror. Even that quick glimpse had shown her the woman who'd stood there had blond hair.

Steadier, she walked out, started down the hall. From the top of the steps, she heard Hayley laugh.

"She'll be right down. I guess you know how to make yourself at home. I'm going on back to the kitchen with the rest of the gang. Let Stella know I'll say bye from her to everyone. Y'all have fun."

Was the girl psychic? Stella wondered. Hayley had timed her exit so adroitly that as she walked down the hall, Stella hit the halfway point on the steps.

And Logan's attention shifted upward.

Good black trousers, she noted. Nice blue shirt, no tie, but with a casual sport coat over it. And still he didn't look quite tame.

"Nice," he said.

"Thanks. You, too."

"Hayley said she'd tell everyone you were leaving. You ready?"

"Sure."

She stepped out with him, then studied the black Mustang. "You own a car."

"This is not merely a car, and to call it such is very female."

"And to say that is very sexist. Okay, if it's not a car, what is it?"

"It's a machine."

"I stand corrected. You never said where we were going."

He opened her door. "Let's find out."

HE DROVE INTO THE CITY, WITH MUSIC SHE DIDN'T recognize on low. She knew it was blues—or supposed it was, but she didn't know anything about that area of music. Mentioning that, casually, not only seemed to shock him but kept conversation going through the trip.

She got a nutshell education on artists like John Lee Hooker and Muddy Waters, B. B. King and Taj Mahal.

And it occurred to her after they'd crossed into the city, that conversation between them never seemed to be a problem. After he parked, he shifted to take a long look at her. "You sure you were born down here?"

"It says so on my birth certificate."

He shook his head and climbed out. "Since you're that ignorant of the blues, you better check it again."

He took her inside a restaurant where the tables were already crowded with patrons and the noise level high with chatter. Once they were seated, he waved the waiter away. "Why don't we just wait on drinks until you know what you want to eat. We'll get a bottle of wine to go with it."

"All right." Since it seemed he'd nixed the pre-dinner conversation, she opened her menu.

"They're known for their catfish here. Ever had it?" he asked.

She lifted her gaze over the top of her menu, met his. "No. And whether or not that makes me a Yankee, I'm thinking I'll go for the chicken."

"Okay. You can have some of mine to give you a sample of what you've been missing. There's a good California Chardonnay on their wine list that'll go with both the fish and the bird. It's got a nice finish."

She set her menu down, leaned forward. "Do you really know that, or are you just making it up?"

"I like wine. I make it a point to know what I like."

She sat back when he motioned the waiter over. Once they'd ordered, she angled her head. "What are we doing here, Logan?"

"Speaking for myself, I'm going to have a really fine catfish dinner and a glass of good wine."

"We've had some conversations, mostly business-oriented."

"We've had some conversations, and some arguments," he corrected.

"True. We had an outing, an enjoyable one, which ended on a surprisingly personal note."

"I do like listening to you talk sometimes, Red. It's almost like listening to a foreign language. Are you laying all those things down like pavers, trying to make some sort of path from one point to the next?"

"Maybe. The fact is, I'm sitting here with you, on a date. That wasn't my intention twenty-four hours ago. We've got a working relationship."

"Uh-huh. And speaking of that, I still find your system mostly annoying."

"Big surprise. And speaking of that, you neglected to put that invoice on my desk this afternoon."

"Did I?" He moved a shoulder. "I've got it somewhere."

"My point is—"

She broke off when the waiter brought the wine to the table, turned the label toward Logan.

"That's the one. Let the lady taste it."

She bided her time, then picked up the glass holding the testing sip. She sampled, lifted her eyebrows. "It's very good . . . has a nice finish."

Logan grinned. "Then let's get started on it."

"The point I was trying to make," she began again, "is that while it's smart and beneficial all around for you and me to develop a friendly relationship, it's probably not either for us to take it to any other level."

"Uh-huh." He sampled the wine himself, kept watching her with those big-cat eyes. "You think I'm not going to kiss you again because it might not be smart or beneficial?"

"I'm in a new place, with a new job. I've taken my kids to a new place. They're first with me."

"I expect they would be. But I don't expect this is your first dinner with a man since you lost your husband."

"I'm careful."

"I never would've guessed. How'd he die?"

"Plane crash. Commuter plane. He was on his way back from a business trip. I had the TV on, and there was a bulletin. They didn't give any names, but I knew it was Kevin's plane. I knew he was gone before they came to tell me."

"You know what you were wearing when you heard the bulletin, what you were doing, where you were standing." His voice was quiet, his eyes were direct. "You know every detail about that day."

"Why do you say that?"

"Because it was the worst day of your life. You'll be hazy on the day before, the day after, but you'll never forget a single detail of that day."

"You're right." And his intuition surprised her, touched her. "Have you lost someone?"

"No, not like what you mean, or how you mean. But a woman like you? She doesn't get married, stay married, unless the man's at the center of her life. Something yanks that center out of you, you never forget."

"No, I won't." It was carved into her heart. "That's the most insightful and accurate, and comforting expression of sympathy anyone's given me. I hope I don't insult you by saying it comes as a surprise."

"I don't insult that easy. You lost their father, but you've built a life—looks like a good one—for your kids. That takes work. You're not the first woman I've been interested in who's had children. I respect motherhood, and its priorities. Doesn't stop me from looking across this table and wondering when I'm going to get you naked."

She opened her mouth, closed it again. Cleared her throat, sipped wine. "Well. Blunt."

"Different sort of woman, I'd just go for the mattress." At her strangled half laugh, he lifted his wine. And waited while their first course was served. "But as it is, you're a . . . since we're having this nice meal together I'll say you're a cautious sort of woman."

"You wanted to say tight-ass."

He grinned, appreciating her. "You'll never know. Added to that, we both work for Roz, and I wouldn't do anything to mess her up. Not intentionally. You've got two kids to worry about. And I don't know how tender you might be yet over losing your husband. So instead of my hauling you off to bed, we're having dinner conversation."

She took a minute to think it through. At the root, she couldn't find anything wrong with his logic. In fact, she agreed with it. "All right. First Roz. I won't do anything to mess her up either. So whatever happens here, we agree to maintain a courteous working relationship."

"Might not always be courteous, but it'll be about the work."

"Fair enough. My boys are my priority, first and last. Not only because they have to be," she added, "but because I want them to be. Nothing will change that."

"Anything did, I wouldn't have much respect for you."

"Well." She waited just a moment because his response had not only been blunt again, but was one she appreciated a great deal. "As for Kevin, I loved him very much. Losing him cut me in two, the part that just wanted to lie down and die, and the part that had to go through the grief and the anger and the motions—and live."

"Takes courage to live."

Her eyes stung, and she took one very careful breath. "Thank you. I had to put myself back together. For the kids, for myself. I'll never feel for another man exactly what I felt for him. I don't think I should. But that doesn't mean I can't be interested in and attracted to someone else. It doesn't mean I'm fated to live my life alone."

He sat for a moment. "How can such a sensible woman have an emotional attachment to forms and invoices?"

"How can such a talented man be so disorganized?" More relaxed than she'd imagined, she enjoyed her salad. "I drove by the Dawson job again."

"Oh, yeah?"

"I realize you still have a few finishing touches that have to wait until all danger of frost is over, but I wanted to tell you it's good work. No, that's wrong. It's not. It's exceptional work."

"Thanks. You take more pictures?"

"I did. We'll be using some of them—before and

after—in the landscaping section of the Web site I'm designing."

"No shit."

"None whatsoever. I'm going to make Roz more money, Logan. She makes more, you make more. The site's going to generate more business for the landscaping arm. I guarantee it."

"It's hard to find a downside on that one."

"You know what I envy you most?"

"My sparkling personality."

"No, you don't sparkle in the least. Your muscle."

"You envy my muscle? I don't think it'd look so good on you, Red."

"Whenever I'd start a project at home—back home—I couldn't do it all myself. I have vision—not as creative as yours, maybe, but I can see what I want, and I've got considerable skill. But when it comes to the heavy, manual labor of it, I'm out. It's frustrating because with some of it, I'd really like to do it all myself. And I can't. So I envy you the muscle that means you can."

"I imagine whether you're doing it or directing it, it's done the way you want."

She smiled into her wine. "Goes without saying. I've heard you've got a place not far from Roz's."

"About two miles out." When their main courses were served, Logan cut a chunk off his catfish, laid it on her plate.

Stella stared at it. "Well. Hmmm."

"I bet you tell your kids they don't know if they like something or not until they've tried it."

"One of the advantages of being a grown-up is being able to say things like that without applying them to yourself. But okay." She forked off a tiny bite, geared herself up for the worst, and ate it. "Interestingly," she said after a moment, "it tastes nothing like cat. Or like what one assumes cat might taste like. It's actually good."

"You might just get back some of your southern. We'll have you eating grits next."

"I don't think so. Those I have tried. Anyway, are you doing the work yourself? On your house."

"Most of it. Land's got some nice gentle rises, good drainage. Some fine old trees on the north side. A couple of pretty sycamores and some hickory, with some wild azalea and mountain laurel scattered around. Some open southern exposure. Plenty of frontage, and a small creek running on the back edge."

"What about the house?"

"What?"

"The house. What kind of house is it?"

"Oh. Two-story frame. It's probably too much space for me, but it came with the land."

"It sounds like the sort of thing I'll be looking for in a few months. Maybe if you hear of anything on the market you could let me know."

"Sure, I can do that. Kids doing all right at Roz's?"

"They're doing great. But at some point we'll need to have our own place. It's important they have their own. I don't want anything elaborate—couldn't afford it, anyway. And I don't mind fixing something up. I'm fairly handy. And I'd really prefer it wasn't haunted."

She stopped herself when he sent her a questioning look. Then shook her head. "Must be the wine because I didn't know *that* was in my head."

"Why is it?"

"I saw—thought I saw," she corrected, "this ghost reputed to haunt the Harper house. In the mirror, in my bedroom, just before you picked me up. It wasn't Hayley. She came in an instant later, and I tried to convince myself it had been her. But it wasn't. And at the same time, it could hardly have been anyone else because . . . it's just not possible."

"Sounds like you're still trying to convince yourself."

"Sensible woman, remember." She tapped a finger on the side of her head. "Sensible women don't see ghosts, or hear them singing lullabies. Or feel them."

"Feel them how?"

"A chill, a . . . *feeling*." She gave a quick shudder and tried to offset it with a quick laugh. "I can't explain it because it's not rational. And tonight, that feeling was very intense. Brief, but intense. And hostile. No, that's not right. 'Hostile' is too strong a word. Disapproving."

"Why don't you talk to Roz about it? She could give you the history, as far as she knows it."

"Maybe. You said you've never seen it?"

"Nope."

"Or felt it?"

"Can't say I have. But sometimes when I've been working a job, walking some land, digging into it, I've felt something. You plant something, even if it dies off, it leaves something in the soil. Why shouldn't a person leave something behind?"

It was something to think about, later, when her mind wasn't so distracted. Right now she had to think about the fact that she was enjoying his company. And there was the basic animal attraction to consider. If she continued to enjoy his company, and the attraction didn't fade off, they were going to end up in bed.

Then there were all the ramifications and complications that would entail. In addition, their universe was finite. They worked for the same person in the same business. It wasn't the sort of atmosphere where two people could have an adult affair without everyone around them knowing they were having it.

So she'd have to think about *that*, and just how uncomfortable it might be to have her private life as public knowledge.

After dinner, they walked over to Beale Street to join the nightly carnival. Tourists, Memphians out on the town, couples, and clutches of young people wandered the street lit by neon signs. Music trickled out of doorways, and people flooded in and out of shops.

"Used to be a club along here called the Monarch. Those shoes going to give you any trouble with this?"

"No."

"Good. Great legs, by the way."

"Thanks. I've had them for years."

"So, the Monarch," he continued. "Happened it shared a back alley with an undertaker. Made it easy for the owners to dispose of gunshot victims."

"That's a pretty piece of Beale Street trivia."

"Oh, there's plenty more. Blues, rock—it's the home of both—voodoo, gambling, sex, scandal, bootleg whiskey, pickpockets, and murder."

Music pumped out of a club as he talked, and struck Stella as southern-fried in the best possible way.

"It's all been right here," he continued. "But you oughta just enjoy the carnival the way it is now."

They joined a crowd lining the sidewalk to watch three boys do running flips and gymnastics up and down the center of the street.

"I can do that." She nodded toward one of the boys as he walked on his hands back to their tip box.

"Uh-huh."

"I can. I'm not going to demonstrate here and now, but I certainly can. Six years of gymnastic lessons. I can bend my body like a pretzel. Well, half a pretzel now, but at one time . . ."

"You trying to get me hot?"

She laughed. "No."

"Just a side effect, then. What does half a pretzel look like?"

"Maybe I'll show you sometime when I'm more appropriately dressed."

"You *are* trying to make me hot."

She laughed again and watched the performers. After Logan dropped money in the tip box, they strolled along the sidewalk. "Who's Betty Paige and why is her face on these shirts?"

He stopped dead. "You've got to be kidding."

"I'm not."

"I guess you didn't just live up north, you lived up north in a cave. Betty Paige, legendary fifties pinup and general sex goddess."

"How do you know? You weren't even born in the fifties."

"I make it a point to learn my cultural history, especially when it involves gorgeous women who strip. Look at that face. The girl next door with the body of Venus."

"She probably couldn't walk on her hands," Stella said, and casually strolled away when he laughed.

They walked off the wine, and the meal, meandering down one side of the street and back up the other. He tempted her with a blues club, but after a brief, internal debate she shook her head.

"I really can't. It's already later than I'd planned. I've got a full day tomorrow, and I've imposed on Roz long enough tonight."

"We'll rain-check it."

"And a blues club will go on my list. Got more checks tonight. Beale Street and catfish. I'm practically a native now."

"Next thing you know you'll be frying up the cat and putting peanuts in your Coke."

"Why in the world would I put peanuts in my Coke? Never mind." She waved him away as he drove out of town. "It's a southern thing. How about if I just say I had a good time tonight?"

"That'll work."

It hadn't been complicated, she realized, or boring, or stressful. At least not after the first few minutes. She'd forgotten, or nearly, what it could be like to be both stimulated and relaxed around a man.

Or to wonder, and there was no point pretending she wasn't wondering, what it would be like to have those hands—those big, work-hardened hands—on her.

Roz had left lights on for her. Front porch, foyer, her own bedroom. She saw the gleam of them as they drove up, and found it a motherly thing to do. Or big sisterly, Stella supposed, as Roz wasn't nearly old enough to be her mother.

Her mother had been too busy with her own life and interests to think about little details like front porch lights. Maybe, Stella thought, that was one of the reasons she herself was so compulsive about them.

"Such a beautiful house," Stella said. "The way it sort of glimmers at night. It's no wonder she loves it."

"No place else quite like it. Spring comes in, the gardens just blow you away."

"She ought to hold a house and garden tour."

"She used to, once a year. Hasn't done it since she peeled off that asshole Clerk. I wouldn't bring it up," he said before Stella spoke. "If she wants to do that kind of thing again, she will."

Knowing his style now, Stella waited for him to come around and open her door. "I'm looking forward to seeing the gardens in their full glory. And I'm grateful for the chance to live here a while and have the kids exposed to this kind of tradition."

"There's another tradition. Kiss the girl good night."

He moved a little slower this time, gave her a chance to anticipate. Those sexy nerves were just beginning to dance over her skin when his mouth met hers.

Then they raced in a shivering path to belly, to throat as his tongue skimmed over her lips to part them. His hands moved through her hair, over her shoulders, and down her body to her hips to take a good, strong hold.

Muscles, she thought dimly. Oh, God. He certainly had them. It was like being pressed against warm, smooth steel. Then he moved in so she swayed back and was trapped between the wall of him and the door. Imprisoned there, her blood sizzling as he devastated her mouth, she felt fragile and giddy, and alive with need.

"Wait a minute," she managed. "Wait."

"Just want to finish this out first."

He wanted a great deal more than that, but already knew he'd have to hold himself at a kiss. So he didn't intend to rush through it. Her mouth was sumptuous, and that slight tremor in her body brutally erotic. He imagined himself gulping her down whole, with violence, with greed. Or savoring her nibble by torturous nibble until he was half mad from the flavor.

When he eased back, the drugged, dreamy look in her eyes told him he could do either. Some other time, some other place.

"Any point in pretending we're going to stop things here?"

"I can't—"

"I don't mean tonight," he said when she glanced back at the door.

"Then, no, there'd be no point in that."

"Good."

"But I can't just jump into something like this. I need to—"

"Plan," he finished. "Organize."

"I'm not good at spontaneity, and spontaneity—this sort—is nearly impossible when you have two children."

"Then plan. Organize. And let me know. I'm good at spontaneity." He kissed her again until she felt her knees dissolve from the knee down.

"You've got my numbers. Give me a call." He stepped back. "Go on inside, Stella. Traditionally, you don't just kiss the girl good night, you wait until she's inside before you walk off wondering when you'll have the chance to do it again."

"Good night then." She went inside, drifted up the stairs, and forgot to turn off the lights.

She was still floating as she started down the hall so the singing didn't register until she was two paces away from her sons' bedroom.

She closed the distance in one leap. And she *saw*, she saw the silhouette, the glint of blond hair in the nightlight, the gleam of eyes that stared into hers.

The cold hit her like a slap, angry and sharp. Then, it, and she, were gone.

On unsteady legs, she rushed between the beds, stroked Gavin's hair, Luke's. Laid her hands on their cheeks, then their backs as she'd done when they were infants. A nervous mother's way to assure herself that her child breathed.

Parker rolled lazily over, gave a little greeting growl, a single thump of his tail, then went back to sleep.

He senses me, smells me, knows me. Is it the same with her? Why doesn't he bark at her?

Or am I just losing my mind?

She readied for bed, then took a blanket and pillow into their room. She laid down between her sons and passed the rest of the night between them, guarding them against the impossible.

twelve

IN THE GREENHOUSE, ROZ WATERED FLATS OF ANNU-als she'd grown over the winter. It was nearly time to put them out for sale. Part of her was always a little sad to know she wouldn't be the one planting them. And she knew that not all of them would be tended properly.

Some would die of neglect, others would be given too much sun, or not enough. Now they were lush and sweet and full of potential.

And hers.

She had to let them go, the way she'd let her sons go. She had to hope, as with her boys, that they found their potential and bloomed, lavishly.

She missed her little guys. More than she'd realized now that her house had boys in it again with all their chatter and scents and debris. Having Harper close helped, so much at times that it was hard for her not to lean too heavily on him, not to surround him with need.

But he'd passed the stage when he was just hers. Though he lived within shouting distance, and they often worked together side by side, he would never be just hers again.

She had to content herself with occasional visits, with

phone calls and e-mails from her other sons. And with the knowledge that they were happy building their own lives.

She'd rooted them, and tended them, nurtured and trained. And let them go.

She wouldn't be one of those overbearing, smothering mothers. Sons, like plants, needed space and air. But oh, sometimes she wanted to go back ten years, twenty, and just hold on to those precious boys a little bit longer.

And sentiment was only going to make her blue, she reminded herself. She switched off the water just as Stella came into the greenhouse.

Roz drew a deep breath. "Nothing like the smell of damp soil, is there?"

"Not when you're us. Look at these marigolds. They're going to fly out the door. I missed you this morning."

"I wanted to get here early. I've got that Garden Club meeting this afternoon. I want to put together a couple dozen six-inch pots as centerpieces."

"Good advertising. I just wanted to thank you again for watching the boys for me last night."

"I enjoyed it. A lot. Did you have a good time?"

"I really did. Is it going to be a problem for you if Logan and I see each other socially?"

"Why would it be?"

"In a work situation . . ."

"Adults should be able to live their own lives, just like in any situation. You're both unattached adults. I expect you'll figure out for yourself if there's any problem with you socializing."

"And we're both using 'socializing' as a euphemism."

Roz began pinching back some petunias. "Stella, if you didn't want to have sex with a man who looks like Logan, I'd worry about you."

"I guess you've got nothing to worry about, then. Still, I want to say . . . I'm working for you, I'm living in your house, so I want to say I'm not promiscuous."

"I'm sure you aren't." She glanced up briefly from her

work. "You're too careful, too deliberate, and a bit too bound up to be promiscuous."

"Another way of calling me a tight-ass," Stella muttered.

"Not precisely. But if you were promiscuous, it would still be your business and not mine. You don't need my approval."

"I want it—because I'm working for you and living in your house. And because I respect you."

"All right, then." Roz moved on to impatiens. "You have it. One of the reasons I wanted you to live in the house was because I wanted to get to know you, on a personal level. When I hired you, I was giving you a piece of something very important to me, personally important. So if I'd decided, after the first few weeks, that you weren't the sort of person I could like and respect, I'd have fired you." She glanced back. "No matter how competent you were. Competent just isn't that hard to find."

"Thanks. I think."

"I think I'll take in some of these geraniums that are already potted. Saves me time and trouble, and we've got a good supply of them."

"Let me know how many, and I'll adjust the inventory. Roz, there was something else I wanted to talk to you about."

"Talk away," Roz invited as she started to select her plants.

"It's about the ghost."

Roz lifted a salmon-pink geranium, studied it from all sides. "What about her?"

"I feel stupid even talking about this, but . . . have you ever felt threatened by her?"

"Threatened? No. I wouldn't use a word that strong." Roz set the geranium in a plastic tray, chose another. "Why?"

"Because, apparently, I've seen her."

"That's not unexpected. The Harper Bride tends to

show herself to mothers, and young boys. Young girls, occasionally. I saw her myself a few times when I was a girl, then fairly regularly once the boys started coming along."

"Tell me what she looks like."

"About your height." As she spoke, Roz continued to select her geraniums for the Garden Club. "Thin. Very thin. Mid- to late twenties at my guess, though it's hard to tell. She doesn't look well. That is," she added with an absent smile, "even for a ghost. She strikes me as a woman who had a great deal of beauty, but was ill for some time. She's blond, and her eyes are somewhere between green and gray. And very sad. She wears a gray dress—or it looks gray, and it hangs on her as if she'd lost weight."

Stella let out a breath. "That's who I saw. What I saw. It's too fantastic, but I *saw*."

"You should be flattered. She rarely shows herself to anyone outside the family—or so the legend goes. You shouldn't feel threatened, Stella."

"But I did. Last night, when I got home, and went in to check on the boys. I heard her first. She sings some sort of lullaby."

" 'Lavender's Blue.' It's what you could call her trademark." Taking out small clippers, Roz trimmed off a weak side stem. "She's never spoken that I've heard, or heard of, but she sings to the children of the house at night."

" 'Lavender's Blue.' Yes, that's it. I heard her, and rushed in. There she was, standing between their beds. She looked at me. It was only for a second, but she looked at me. Her eyes weren't sad, Roz, they were angry. There was a blast of cold, like she'd thrown something at me in temper. Not like the other times, when I'd just felt a chill."

Interested now, Roz studied Stella's face. "I felt as if I'd annoyed her a few times, on and off. Just a change of tone. Very like you described, I suppose."

"It happened."

"I believe you, but primarily, from most of my experiences, she's always been a benign sort of presence. I always took those temper snaps to be a kind of moodiness. I expect ghosts get moody."

"You expect ghosts get moody," Stella repeated slowly. "I just don't understand a statement like that."

"People do, don't they? Why should that change when they're dead?"

"Okay," Stella said after a moment. "I'm going to try to roll with all this, like it's not insanity. So, maybe she doesn't like me being here."

"Over the last hundred years or so, Harper House has had a lot of people live in it, a lot of houseguests. She ought to be used to it. If you'd feel better moving to the other wing—"

"No. I don't see how that would make a difference. And though I was unnerved enough last night to sleep in the boys' room with them, she wasn't angry with them. It was just me. Who was she?"

"Nobody knows for sure. In polite company, she's referred to as the Harper Bride, but it's assumed she was a servant. A nurse or governess. My theory is one of the men in the house seduced her, maybe cast her off, especially if she got pregnant. There's the attachment to children, so it seemed most logical she had a connection to kids. It's a sure bet she died in or around the house."

"There'd be records, right? A family Bible, birth and death records, photographs, tintypes, whatever."

"Oh, tons."

"I'd like to go through them, if it's all right with you. I'd like to try to find out who she was. I want to know who, or what, I'm dealing with."

"All right." Clippers still in hand, Roz set a fist on her hip. "I guess it's odd no one's ever done it before, including myself. I'll help you with it. It'll be interesting."

"THIS IS SO AWESOME." HAYLEY LOOKED AROUND the library table, where Stella had arranged the photograph albums, the thick Bible, the boxes of old papers, her laptop, and several notebooks. "We're like the Scooby gang."

"I can't believe you saw her, too, and didn't say any-thing."

Hayley hunched up her shoulders and continued to wander the room. "I figured you'd think I'd wigged. Besides, except for the once, I only caught a glimpse, like over here." She held up a hand at the side of her head. "I've never been around an actual ghost. This is completely cool."

"I'm glad someone's enjoying herself."

She really was. As she and her father had both loved books, they'd used their living room as a kind of library, stuffing the shelves with books, putting in a couple of big, squishy chairs.

It had been nice, cozy and nice.

But this was a *library*. Beautiful bookcases of deep, dark wood flanked long windows, then rose up and around the walls in a kind of platform where the long table stood. There had to be hundreds of books, but it didn't seem over-whelming, not with the dark, restful green of the walls and the warm cream granite of the fireplace. She liked the big black candlesticks and the groupings of family pictures on the mantel.

There were more pictures scattered around here and there, and *things*. Fascinating things like bowls and statues and a dome-shaped crystal clock. Flowers, of course. There were flowers in nearly every room of the house. These were tulips with deep, deep purple cups that sort of spilled out of a wide, clear glass vase.

There were lots of chairs, wide, butter-soft leather chairs, and even a leather sofa. Though a chandelier dripped from the center of the tray ceiling, and even the bookcases lit up, there were lamps with those cool shades that looked like stained glass. The rugs were probably really old, and so interesting with their pattern of exotic birds around the borders.

She couldn't imagine what it must have been like to

have a room like this, much less to know just how to decorate it so it would be—well, gorgeous was the only word
she could think of—and yet still be as cozy as the little
library she'd had at home.

But Roz knew. Roz, in Hayley's opinion, was the
absolute bomb.

"I think this is my favorite room of the house," she
decided. "Of course, I think that about every room after
I'm in it for five minutes. But I really think this wins the
prize. It's like a picture out of *Southern Living* or something, but the accent's on *living*. You wouldn't be afraid to
take a nap on the couch."

"I know what you mean." Stella set aside the photo
album she'd looked through. "Hayley, you have to remember not to say anything about this to the kids."

"Of course, I won't." She came back to the table, and
finally sat. "Hey, maybe we could do a séance. That would
be so spooky and great."

"I'm not that far gone yet," Stella replied. She glanced
over as David came in.

"Ghost hunter snacks," he announced and set the tray on
the table. "Coffee, tea, cookies. I considered angel food
cake, but it seemed too obvious."

"Having fun with this?"

"Damn right. But I'm also willing to roll up my sleeves
and dive into all this stuff. It'll be nice to put a name to her
after all this time." He tapped a finger on Stella's laptop.
"And this is for?"

"Notes. Data, facts, speculation. I don't know. It's my
first day on the job."

Roz came in, carting a packing box. There was a
smudge of dust on her cheek and silky threads of cobwebs
in her hair. "Household accounts, from the attic. There's
more up there, but this ought to give us a start."

She dumped the box on the table, grinned. "This should
be fun. Don't know why I haven't thought of it before.
Where do y'all want to start?"

"I was thinking we could have a séance," Hayley began. "Maybe she'll just tell us who she is and why her spirit's, you know, trapped on this plane of existence. That's the thing with ghosts. They get trapped, and sometimes they don't even know they're dead. How creepy is that?"

"A séance." David rubbed his hands together. "Now where did I leave my turban?"

When Hayley burst into throaty laughter, Stella rapped her knuckles on the table. "If we could control the hilarity? I thought we'd start with something a little more mundane. Like trying to date her."

"I've never dated a ghost," David mused, "but I'm up for it."

"Get her time period," Stella said with a slanted look for David. "By what she's wearing. We might be able to pinpoint when she lived, or at least get an estimate."

"Discovery through fashion." Roz nodded as she picked up a cookie. "That's good."

"Smart," Hayley agreed. "But I didn't really notice what she had on. I only got a glimpse."

"A gray dress," Roz put in. "High-necked. Long sleeves."

"Can any of us sketch?" Stella asked. "I'm all right with straight lines and curves, but I'd be hopeless with figures."

"Roz is your girl." David patted Roz on the shoulder.

"Can you draw her, Roz? Your impression of her?"

"I can sure give it a shot."

"I bought notebooks." Stella offered one and made Roz smile.

"Of course you did. And I bet your pencils are all nicely sharpened, too. Just like the first day of school."

"Hard to write with them otherwise. David, while she's doing that, why don't you tell us your experiences with . . . I guess we'll call her the Harper Bride for now."

"Only had a few, and all back when I was a kid, hanging out here with Harper."

"What about the first time?"

"You never forget your first." He winked at her, and

after sitting, poured himself coffee. "I was bunking in with Harper, and we were pretending to be asleep so Roz didn't come in and lower the boom. We were whispering—"

"They always thought they were," Roz said as she sketched.

"I think it was spring. I remember we had the windows open, and there was a breeze. I'd have been around nine. I met Harper in school, and even though he was a year behind me, we hit it off. We hadn't known each other but a few weeks when I came over to spend the night. So we were there, in the dark, thinking we were whispering, and he told me about the ghost. I thought he was making it up to scare me, but he swore all the way up to the needle in his eye that it was true, and he'd seen her lots of times.

"We must've fallen asleep. I remember waking up, thinking somebody had stroked my head. I thought it was Roz, and I was a little embarrassed, so I squinted one eye open to see."

He sipped coffee, narrowing his eyes as he searched for the memory. "And I saw her. She walked over to Harper's bed and bent over him, the way you do when you kiss a child on the top of the head. Then she walked across the room. There was a rocking chair over in the corner. She sat down and started to rock, and sing."

He set the coffee down. "I don't know if I made some sound, or moved, or what, but she looked right at me. She smiled. I thought she was crying, but she smiled. And she put her finger to her lips as if to tell me to hush. Then she disappeared."

"What did you do?" Hayley whispered the question, reverently.

"I pulled the covers over my head, and stayed under till morning."

"You were afraid of her?" Stella prompted.

"Nine-year-old, ghost—and I have a sensitive nature, so sure. But I didn't stay afraid. In the morning it seemed like a dream, but a nice one. She'd stroked my hair and sung to me. And she was pretty. No rattling chains or bloodless howls. She seemed a little like an angel, so I wasn't afraid of her. I told Harper about it in the morning, and he said we must be brothers, because none of his other friends got to see her."

He smiled at the memory. "I felt pretty proud of that, and looked forward to seeing her again. I saw her a few more times when I was over. Then, when I was about thirteen the—we'll say visitations—stopped."

"Did she ever speak to you?"

"No, she'd just sing. That same song."

"Did you only see her in the bedroom, at night?"

"No. There was this time we all camped out back. It was summer, hot and buggy, but we nagged Roz until she let all of us sleep out there in a tent. We didn't make it through the night 'cause Mason cut his foot on a rock. Remember that, Roz?"

"I do. Two o'clock in the morning, and I'm packing four kids in the car so I can take one of them to the ER for stitches."

"We were out there before sunset, out near the west edge of the property. By ten we were all of us half sick on hot dogs and marshmallows, and had spooked ourselves stupid with ghost stories. Lightning bugs were out," he murmured, closing his eyes. "Past midsummer then, and steamy. We'd all stripped down to our underwear. The younger ones fell asleep, but Harper and I stayed up for a while. A long while. I must've conked out, because the next thing I knew, Harper was shaking my shoulder. 'There she is,' he said, and I saw her, walking in the garden."

"Oh, my God," Hayley managed, and edged closer to David as Stella continued to type. "What happened then?"

"Well, Harper's hissing in my ear about how we should go follow her, and I'm trying to talk him out of it without sacrificing my manhood. The other two woke up, and Harper said he was going, and we could stay behind if we were yellow coward dogs."

"I bet that got you moving," Stella commented.

"Being a yellow coward dog isn't an option for a boy in

the company of other boys. We all got moving. Mason couldn't've been but six, but he was trotting along at the rear, trying to keep up. There was moonlight, so we could see her, but Harper said we had to hang back some, so she didn't see us.

"I swear there wasn't a breath of air that night, not a whisper of it to stir a leaf. She didn't make a sound as she walked along the paths, through the shrubs. There was something different about her that night. I didn't realize what it was until long after."

"What?" Breathless, Hayley leaned forward, gripped his arm. "What was different about her that night?"

"Her hair was down. Always before, she'd had it up. Sort of sweet and old-fashioned ringlets spiraling down from the top of her head. But that night it was down, and kind of wild, spilling down her back, over her shoulders. And she was wearing something white and floaty. She looked more like a ghost that night than she ever did otherwise. And I was afraid of her, more than I was the first time, or ever was again. She moved off the path, walked over the flowers without touching them. I could hear my own breath pant in and out, and I must've slowed down because Harper was well ahead. She was going toward the old stables, or maybe the carriage house."

"The carriage house?" Hayley almost squealed it. "Where Harper lives?"

"Yeah. He wasn't living there then," he added with a laugh. "He wasn't more than ten. It seemed like she was heading for the stables, but she'd have to go right by the carriage house. So, she stopped, and she turned around, looking back. I know I stopped dead then, and the blood just drained out of me."

"I guess!" Hayley said, with feeling.

"She looked crazy, and that was worse than dead somehow. Before I could decide whether to run after Harper, or hightail it like a yellow coward dog, Mason screamed. I thought somehow she'd gotten him, and damn near screamed myself. But Harper came flying back. Turned out

Mason had gashed his foot open on a rock. When I looked back toward the old stables, she was gone."

He stopped, shuddered, then let out a weak laugh. "Scared myself."

"Me, too," Hayley managed.

"He needed six stitches." Roz scooted the notebook toward Stella. "That's how she looks to me."

"That's her." Stella studied the sketch of the thin, sad-eyed woman. "Is this how she looked to you, David?"

"Except that one night, yeah."

"Hayley?"

"Best I can tell."

"Same for me. This shows her in fairly simple dress, nipped-in waist, high neck, front buttons. Okay, the sleeves are a little poufed down to the elbow, then snug to the wrist. Skirt's smooth over the hips, then widens out some. Her hair's curly, lots of curls that are scooped up in a kind of topknot. I'm going to do an Internet search on fashion, but it's obviously after the 1860s, right? Scarlett O'Hara hoop skirts were the thing around then. And it'd be before, say, the 1920s and the shorter skirts."

"I think it's near the turn of the century," Hayley put in, then shrugged when gazes shifted to her. "I know a lot of useless stuff. That looks like what they called hourglass style. I mean, even though she's way thin, it looks like that's the style. Gay Nineties stuff."

"That's good. Okay, let's look it up and see." Stella tapped keys, hit Execute.

"I gotta pee. Don't find anything important until I get back." Hayley dashed out, as fast as her condition would allow.

Stella scanned the sites offered, and selected one on women's fashion in the 1890s.

"Late Victorian," she stated as she read and skimmed pictures. "Hourglass. These are all what I'd think of as more stylish, but it seems like the same idea."

She moved to the end of the decade, and over into the early twentieth century. "No, see, these sleeves are a lot bigger at the shoulder. They're calling them leg-o'-mutton, and the bodices on the daywear seem a little sleeker."

She backtracked in the other direction. "No, we're getting into bustles here. I think Hayley may have it. Somewhere in the 1890s."

"Eighteen-nineties?" Hayley hurried back in. "Score one for me."

"Not so fast. If she was a servant," Roz reminded them, "she might not have been dressed fashionably."

"Damn." Hayley mimed erasing a scoreboard.

"But even so, we could say between 1890 and, what, 1910?" Stella suggested. "And if we go with that, and an approximate age of twenty-five, we could estimate that she was born between 1865 and 1885."

She huffed out a breath. "That's too much scope, and too much margin for error."

"Hair," David said. "She may have been a servant, may have had secondhand clothes, but there'd be nothing to stop her from wearing her hair in the latest style."

"Excellent." She typed again, picked through sites. "Okay, the Gibson Girl deal—the smooth pompadour— was popularized after 1895. If we take a leap of faith, and figure our heroine dressed her hair stylishly, we'd narrow this down to between 1890 and 1895, or up to, say '98 if she was a little behind the times. Then we'd figure she died in that decade, anyway, between the ages of . . . oh, let's say between twenty-two and twenty-six."

"Family Bible first," Roz decided. "That should tell us if any of the Harper women, by blood or marriage, and of that age group, died in that decade."

She dragged it in front of her. The binding was black leather, ornately carved. Someone—Stella imagined it was Roz herself—kept it dusted and oiled.

Roz paged through to the family genealogy. "This goes back to 1793 and the marriage of John Andrew Harper to Fiona MacRoy. It lists the births of their eight children."

"Eight?" Hayley widened her eyes and laid a hand on her belly. "Holy God."

"You said it. Six of them lived to adulthood," Roz continued. "Married and begat, begat, begat." She turned the thin pages carefully. "Here we've got several girl children born through Harper marriages between 1865 and 1870. And here, we've got an Alice Harper Doyle, died in childbirth October of 1893, at the age of twenty-two."

"That's awful," Hayley said. "She was younger than me."

"And already gave birth twice," Roz stated. "Tough on women back then, before Margaret Sanger."

"Would she have lived here, in this house?" Stella asked. "Died here?"

"Might have. She married Daniel Francis Doyle, of Natchez, in 1890. We can check the death records on her. I've got three more who died during the period we're using, but the ages are wrong. Let's see here, Alice was Reginald Harper's youngest sister. He had two more, no brothers. He'd have inherited the house, and the estate. A lot of space between Reggie and each of his sisters. Probably miscarriages."

At Hayley's small sound, Roz looked up sharply. "I don't want this to upset you."

"I'm okay. I'm okay," she said again and took a long breath. "So Reginald was the only son on that branch of the family tree?"

"He was. Lots of cousins, and the estate would've passed to one of them after his death, but he had a son—several daughters first, then the boy, in 1892."

"What about his wife?" Stella put in. "Maybe she's the one."

"No, she lived until 1925. Ripe age."

"Then we look at Alice first," Stella decided.

"And see what we can find on servants during that period. Wouldn't be a stretch for Reginald to have diddled around with a nurse or a maid while his wife was breeding. Seeing as he was a man."

"Hey!" David objected.

"Sorry, honey. Let me say he was a Harper man, and

lived during a period where men of a certain station had mistresses and didn't think anything of taking a servant to bed."

"That's some better. But not a lot."

"Are we sure he and his family lived here during that period?"

"A Harper always lived in Harper House," Roz told Stella. "And if I remember my family history, Reginald's the one who converted from gaslight to electricity. He'd have lived here until his death in . . ." She checked the book. "Nineteen-nineteen, and the house passed to his son, Reginald Junior, who'd married Elizabeth Harper McKinnon—fourth cousin—in 1916."

"All right, so we find out if Alice died here, and we go through records to find out if there were any servants of the right age who died during that period." Using her notebook now, Stella wrote down the points of the search. "Roz, do you know when the—let's call them sightings for lack of better. Do you know when they began?"

"I don't, and I'm just realizing that's odd. I should know, and I should know more about her than I do. Harper family history gets passed down, orally and written. But here we have a ghost who as far as I know's been wandering around here for more than a century, and I know next to nothing about her. My daddy just called her the Harper Bride."

"What do you know about her?" Stella readied herself to take notes.

"What she looks like, the song she sings. I saw her when I was a girl, when she came in my room to sing that lullaby, just as she's reputed to have done for generations before. It was . . . comforting. There was a gentleness about her. I tried to talk to her sometimes, but she never talked back. She'd just smile. Sometimes she'd cry. Thanks, sweetie," she said when David poured her more coffee. "I didn't see her through my teenage years, and being a teenage girl I didn't think about her much. I had my mind on other things. But I remember the next time I saw her."

"Don't keep us in suspense," Hayley demanded.

"It was early in the summer, end of June. John and I hadn't been married very long, and we were staying here. It was already hot, one of those hot, still nights where the air's like a wet blanket. But I couldn't sleep, so I left the cool house for the hot garden. I was restless and nervy. I thought I might be pregnant. I wanted it—we wanted it so much, that I couldn't think about anything else. I went out to the garden and sat on this old teak glider, and dreamed up at the moon, praying it was true and we'd started a baby."

She let out a little sigh. "I was barely eighteen. Anyway, while I sat there, she came. I didn't see or hear her come, she was just there, standing on the path. Smiling. Something in the way she smiled at me, something about it, made me know—absolutely know—I had child in me. I sat there, in the midnight heat and cried for the joy of it. When I went to the doctor a couple weeks later, I already knew I was carrying Harper."

"That's so nice." Hayley blinked back tears. "So sweet."

"I saw her off and on for years after, and always saw her at the onset of a pregnancy, before I was sure. I'd see her, and I'd know there was a baby coming. When my youngest hit adolescence, I stopped seeing her regularly."

"It has to be about children," Stella decided, underlining "pregnancy" twice in her notes. "That's the common link. Children see her, women with children, or pregnant women. The died-in-childbirth theory is looking good." Immediately she winced. "Sorry, Hayley, that didn't sound right."

"I know what you mean. Maybe she's Alice. Maybe what she needs to pass over is to be acknowledged by name."

"Well." Stella looked at the cartons and books. "Let's dig in."

* * *

SHE DREAMED AGAIN THAT NIGHT, WITH HER MIND full of ghosts and questions, of her perfect garden with the blue dahlia that grew stubbornly in its midst.

A weed is a flower growing in the wrong place.

She heard the voice inside her head, a voice that wasn't her own.

"It's true. That's true," she murmured. "But it's so beautiful. So strong and vivid."

It seems so now, but it's deceptive. If it stays, it changes everything. It will take over, and spoil everything you've done. Everything you have. Would you risk that, risk all, for one dazzling flower? One that will only die away at the first frost?

"I don't know." Studying the garden, she rubbed her arms as her skin pricked with unease. "Maybe I could change the plan. I might be able to use it as a focal point."

Thunder boomed and the sky went black, as she stood by the garden, just as she'd once stood through a stormy evening in her own kitchen.

And the grief she'd felt then stabbed into her as if someone had plunged a knife into her heart.

Feel it? Would you feel it again? Would you risk that kind of pain, for this?

"I can't breathe." She sank to her knees as the pain radiated. "I can't breathe. What's happening to me?"

Remember it. Think of it. Remember the innocence of your children and hack it down. Dig it out. Before it's too late! Can't you see how it tries to overshadow the rest? Can't you see how it steals the light? Beauty can be poison.

She woke, shivering with cold, with her heart beating against the pain that had ripped awake with her.

And knew she hadn't been alone, not even in dreams.

thirteen

ON HER DAY OFF, STELLA TOOK THE BOYS TO MEET her father and his wife at the zoo. Within an hour, the boys were carting around rubber snakes, balloons, and chowing down on ice cream cones.

Stella had long since accepted that a grandparent's primary job was to spoil, and since fate had given her sons only this one set, she let them have free rein.

When the reptile house became the next objective, she opted out, freely handing the controls of the next stage to Granddad.

"Your mom's always been squeamish about snakes," Will told the boys.

"And I'm not ashamed to admit it. You all just go ahead. I'll wait."

"I'll keep you company." Jolene adjusted her baby-blue ball cap. "I'd rather be with Stella than a boa constrictor any day."

"Girls." Will exchanged a pitying look with each of his grandsons. "Come on, men, into the snake pit!"

On a battle cry, the three of them charged the building.

"He's so good with them," Stella said. "So natural and

easy. I'm so glad we're living close now, and they can see each other regularly."

"You couldn't be happier about it than we are. I swear that man's been like a kid himself the last couple of days, just waiting for today to get here. He couldn't be more proud of the three of you."

"I guess we both missed out on a lot when I was growing up."

"It's good you're making up for it now."

Stella glanced at Jolene as they walked over to a bench. "You never say anything about her. You never criticize."

"Sugar pie, I bit my tongue to ribbons more times than I can count in the last twenty-seven years."

"Why?"

"Well, honey, when you're the second wife, and the stepmama on top of that, it's the smartest thing you can do. Besides, you grew up to be a strong, smart, generous woman raising the two most handsome, brightest, most charming boys on God's green earth. What's the point of criticizing?"

She does you, Stella thought. "Have I ever told you I think you're the best thing that ever happened to my father?"

"Maybe once or twice." Jolene pinked prettily. "But I never mind hearing it repeated."

"Let me add, you're one of the best things that ever happened to me. And the kids."

"Oh, now." This time Jolene's eyes filled. "Now you've got me going." She dug in her purse, dug out a lace hankie. "That's the sweetest thing. The sweetest thing." She sniffled, tried to dab at her eyes and hug Stella at the same time. "I just love you to pieces. I always did."

"I always felt it." Tearing up herself, Stella pushed through her own purse for a more mundane tissue. "God, look at the mess we've made of each other."

"It was worth it. Sometimes a good little cry's as good as some sex. Do I have mascara all down my face?"

"No. Just a little . . ." Stella used the corner of her tissue to wipe away a smear under Jolene's eye. "There. You're fine."

"I feel like a million tax-free dollars. Now, tell me how you're getting on before I start leaking again."

"Work-wise it couldn't be better. It really couldn't. We're about to hit the spring rush dead-on, and I'm so revved for it. The boys are happy, making friends at school. Actually, between you and me, I think Gavin's got a crush on this little curly-headed blond in his class. Her name's Melissa, and the tips of his ears get red when he mentions her."

"That's so sweet. Nothing like your first crush, is there? I remember mine. I was crazy for this boy. He had a face full of freckles and a cowlick. I just about died with joy the day he gave me a little hop-toad in a shoe box."

"A toad."

"Well, honey, I was eight and a country girl, so it was a thoughtful gift all in all. He ended up marrying a friend of mine. I was in the wedding and had to wear the most god-awful pink dress with a hoop skirt wide enough I could've hidden a horse under it and rode to the church. It was covered with ruffles, so I looked like a human wedding cake."

She waved a hand while Stella rolled with laughter. "I don't know why I'm going on about that, except it's the sort of traumatic experience you never forget, even after more than thirty years. Now they live on the other side of the city. We get together every now and then for dinner. He's still got the freckles, but the cowlick went, along with most of his hair."

"I guess you know a lot of the people and the history of the area, since you've lived here all your life."

"I guess I do. Can't go to the Wal-Mart, day or night, without seeing half a dozen people I know."

"What do you know about the Harper ghost?"

"Hmm." Jolene took out a compact and her lipstick and freshened her face. "Just that she's always roamed around there, or at least as far back as anybody can remember. Why?"

"This is going to sound insane, especially coming from me, but . . . I've seen her."

"Oh my goodness." She snapped the compact closed. "Tell me everything."

"There isn't a lot to tell."

But she told her what there was, and what she'd begun to do about it.

"This is so exciting! You're like a detective. Maybe your father and I could help. You know how he loves playing on that computer of his. Stella!" She clamped a hand on Stella's arm. "I bet she was *murdered*, just hacked to death with an ax or something and buried in a shallow grave. Or dumped in the river—pieces of her. I've always thought so."

"Let me just say—ick—and her ghost, at least is whole. Added to that, our biggest lead is the ancestor who died in childbirth," Stella reminded her.

"Oh, that's right." Jolene sulked a moment, obviously disappointed. "Well, if it turns out it's her, that'd be sad, but not nearly as thrilling as murder. You tell your daddy all about this, and we'll see what we can do. We've both got plenty of time on our hands. It'll be fun."

"It's a departure for me," Stella replied. "I seem to be doing a lot of departing from the norm recently."

"Any of that departing have to do with a man? A tall, broad-shouldered sort of man with a wicked grin?"

Stella's eyes narrowed. "And why would you ask?"

"My third cousin, Lucille? You met her once. She happened to be having dinner in the city a couple nights ago and told me she saw you in the same restaurant with a very good-looking young man. She didn't come by your table because she was with her latest beau. And he's not altogether divorced from his second wife. Fact is, he hasn't been altogether divorced for a year and a half now, but that's Lucille for you."

Jolene waved it away. "So, who's the good-looking young man?"

"Logan Kitridge."

"Oh." It came out in three long syllables. "That *is* a good-looking young man. I thought you didn't like him."

"I didn't not like him, I just found him annoying and difficult to work with. We're getting along a little better at work, and somehow we seem to be dating. I've been trying to figure out if I want to see him again."

"What's to work out? You do or you don't."

"I do, but . . . I shouldn't ask you to gossip."

Jolene wiggled closer on the bench. "Honey, if you can't ask me, who can you ask?"

Stella snickered, then glanced toward the reptile house to be sure her boys weren't heading out. "I wondered, before I get too involved, if he sees a lot of women."

"You want to know if he cats around."

"I guess that's the word for it."

"I'd say a man like that gets lucky when he has a mind to, but you don't hear people saying, 'That Logan Kitridge is one randy son of a gun.' Like they do about my sister's boy, Curtis. Most of what you hear about Logan is people—women mostly—wondering how that wife of his let him get loose, or why some other smart woman hasn't scooped him up. You thinking about scooping?"

"No. No, definitely not."

"Maybe he's thinking about scooping you up."

"I'd say we're both just testing the ground." She caught sight of her men. "Here come the Reptile Hunters. Don't say anything about any of this in front of the boys, okay?"

"Lips are sealed."

IN THE GARDEN OPENED AT EIGHT, PREPARED FOR ITS advertised spring opening as for a war. Stella had mustered the troops, supervised with Roz the laying out of supplies. They had backups, seasoned recruits, and the field of combat was—if she said so herself—superbly organized and displayed.

By ten they were swamped, with customers swarming

the showrooms, the outside areas, the public greenhouses. Cash registers rang like church bells.

She marched from area to area, diving in where she felt she was most needed at any given time. She answered questions from staff and from customers, restacked wagons and carts when the staff was too overwhelmed to get to them, and personally helped countless people load purchases in their cars, trucks, or SUVs.

She used the two-way on her belt like a general.

"Miss? Do you work here?"

Stella paused and turned to the woman wearing baggy jeans and a ragged sweatshirt. "Yes, ma'am, I do. I'm Stella. How can I help you?"

"I can't find the columbine, or the foxglove or . . . I can't find half of what's on my list. Everything's changed around."

"We did do some reorganizing. Why don't I help you find what you're looking for?"

"I've got that flat cart there loaded already." She nodded toward it. "I don't want to have to be hauling it all over creation."

"You're going to be busy, aren't you?" Stella said cheerfully. "And what wonderful choices. Steve? Would you take this cart up front and tag it for Mrs . . . I'm sorry?"

"Haggerty." She pursed her lips. "That'd be fine. Don't you let anybody snatch stuff off it, though. I spent a good while picking all that out."

"No, ma'am. How are you doing, Mrs. Haggerty?"

"I'm doing fine. How's your mama and your daddy?"

"Doing fine, too," Steve lifted the handle of her cart. "Mrs. Haggerty's got one of the finest gardens in the county," he told Stella.

"I'm putting in some new beds. You mind my cart, Steve, or I'll come after you. Now where the hell's the columbine?"

"It's out this way. Let me get you another cart, Mrs. Haggerty."

Stella grabbed one on the way.

"You that new girl Rosalind hired?"

"Yes, ma'am."

"From up north."

"Guilty."

She pursed her lips, peered around with obvious irritation. "You sure have shuffled things around."

"I know. I hope the new scheme will save the customer time and trouble."

"Hasn't saved me any today. Hold on a minute." She stopped, adjusting the bill of her frayed straw hat against the sun as she studied pots of yarrow.

"That achillea's good and healthy, isn't it? Does so well in the heat and has a nice long blooming season."

"Wouldn't hurt to pick up a few things for my daughter while I'm here." She chose three of the pots, then moved on. As they did, Stella chatted about the plants, managed to draw Mrs. Haggerty into conversation. They'd filled the second cart and half of a third by the time they'd wound through the perennial area.

"I'll say this, you know your plants."

"I can certainly return the compliment. And I envy you the planting you've got ahead of you."

Mrs. Haggerty stopped, peering around again. But this time with speculation. "You know, the way you got things set up here, I probably bought half again as much as I planned on."

This time Stella offered a wide, wide smile. "Really?"

"Sneaky. I like that. All your people up north?"

"No, actually my father and his wife live in Memphis. They're natives."

"Is that so. Well. Well. You come on by and see my gardens sometime. Roz can tell you where to find me."

"I'd absolutely love to. Thanks."

BY NOON STELLA ESTIMATED SHE'D WALKED TEN miles.

By three, she gave up wondering how many miles she'd walked, how many pounds she'd lifted, how many questions she'd answered.

She began to dream about a long, cool shower and a bottomless glass of wine.

"This is wild," Hayley managed as she dragged wagons away from the parking area.

"When did you take your last break?"

"Don't worry, I've been getting plenty of sit-down time. Working the counter, chatting up the customers. I wanted to stretch my legs, to tell you the truth."

"We're closing in just over an hour, and things are slowing down a bit. Why don't you find Harper or one of the seasonals and see about restocking?"

"Sounds good. Hey, isn't that Mr. Hunky's truck pulling in?"

Stella looked over, spotted Logan's truck. "Mr. Hunky?"

"When it fits, it fits. Back to work for me."

It should have been for her, too. But she watched as Logan drove over the gravel, around the mountains formed by huge bags of mulch and soil. He climbed out one side of the truck, and his two men piled out the other. After a brief conversation, he wandered across the gravel lot toward her.

So she wandered across to him.

"Got a client who's decided on that red cedar mulch. You can put me down for a quarter ton."

"Which client?"

"Jameson. We're going to swing back by and get it down before we knock off. I'll get the paperwork to you tomorrow."

"You could give it to me now."

"Have to work it up. I take time to work it up, we're not going to get the frigging mulch down today. Client won't be happy."

She used her forearm to swipe at her forehead. "Fortunately for you I don't have the energy to nag."

"Been busy."

"There's no word for what we've been. It's great. I'm betting we broke records. My feet feel like a couple of smoked sausages. By the way, I was thinking I'd like to come by, see your house."

His eyes stared into hers until she felt fresh pricks of heat at the base of her spine. "You could do that. I've got time tonight."

"I can't tonight. Maybe Wednesday, after we close? If Roz is willing to watch the boys."

"Wednesday's no problem for me. Can you find the place all right?"

"Yeah, I'll find it. About six-thirty?"

"Fine. See you."

As he walked back to his truck, Stella decided it was the strangest conversation she'd ever had about sex.

THAT EVENING, AFTER HER KIDS WERE FED, AND engaged in their play hour before bed, Stella indulged in that long shower. As the aches and fatigue of the day washed away, her excitement over it grew.

They'd kicked *ass*! she thought.

She was still a little concerned about overstock in some areas, and what she saw as understock in others. But flushed with the day's success, she told herself not to question Roz's instincts as a grower.

If today was any indication, they were in for a rock-solid season.

She pulled on her terry-cloth robe, wrapped her hair in a towel, then did a kind of three-step boogie out of the bathroom.

And let out a short, piping scream at the woman in her bedroom doorway.

"Sorry. Sorry." Roz snorted back a laugh. "Flesh and blood here."

"God!" Since her legs had gone numb, Stella sank onto the side of the bed. "*God!* My heart just about stopped."

"I got something that should start it up again." From behind her back, Roz whipped out a bottle of champagne.

"Dom Perignon? Woo, and two hoos! Yes, I think I detect a beat."

"We're going to celebrate. Hayley's across in the sitting room. And I'm giving her half a glass of this. No lectures."

"In Europe pregnant women are allowed, if not encouraged, to have a glass of wine a week. I'm willing to pretend we're in France if I get a full glass of that."

"Come on over. I sent the boys down to David. They're having a video game contest."

"Oh. Well, I guess that's all right. They've got a half hour before bath and bed. Is that caviar?" she asked when she stepped into the sitting room.

"Roz says I can't have any." Hayley leaned over and sniffed the silver tray with its silver bowl of glossy black caviar. "Because it's not good for the baby. I don't know as I'd like it, anyway."

"Good. More for me. Champagne and caviar. You're a classy boss, Ms. Harper."

"It was a great day. I always start off the first of the season a little blue." She popped the cork. "All my babies going off like that. Then I get too busy to think about it." She poured the glasses. "And by the end I'm reminded that I got into this to sell and to make a profit—while doing something I enjoy doing. Then I come on home and start feeling a little blue again. But not tonight."

She passed the glasses around. "I may not have the figures and the facts and the data right at my fingertips, but I know what I know. We've just had the best single day ever."

"Ten percent over last year." Stella lifted her glass in a toast. "I happen to have facts and data at my fingertips."

"Of course you do." With a laugh, Roz stunned Stella by throwing an arm around her shoulders, squeezing once, then pressing a kiss to her cheek. "Damn right you do. You did a hell of a job. Both of you. Everyone. And it's fair to say, Stella, that I did myself and In the Garden a favor the day I hired you."

"Wow!" She took a sip to open her throat. "I won't argue with that." Then another to let the wine fizz on her tongue before she went for the caviar. "However, as much as I'd love to take full credit for that ten percent increase, I can't. The stock is just amazing. You and Harper are exceptional growers. I'll take credit for five of the ten percent."

"It was fun," Hayley put in. "It was crazy a lot of the time, but fun. All those people, and the noise, and carts sailing out the door. Everybody seemed so happy. I guess being around plants, thinking about having them for yourself, does that."

"Good customer service has a lot to do with those happy faces. And you"—Stella tipped her glass to Hayley—"have that knocked."

"We've got a good team." Roz sat, wiggled her bare toes. They were painted pale peach today. "We'll take a good overview in the morning, see what areas Harper and I should add to." She leaned forward to spread caviar on a toast point. "But tonight we'll just bask."

"This is the best job I've ever had. I just want to say that." Hayley looked at Roz. "And not just because I get to drink fancy champagne and watch y'all eat caviar."

Roz patted her arm. "I should bring up another subject. I've already told David. The calls I've made about Alice Harper Doyle's death certificate? Natchez," she said. "According to official records, she died in Natchez, in the home she shared with her husband and two children."

"Damn." Stella frowned into her wine. "I guess it was too easy."

"We'll just have to keep going through the household records, noting down the names of the female servants during that time period."

"Big job," Stella replied.

"Hey, we're good." Hayley brushed off the amount of work. "We can handle it. And, you know, I was thinking. David said they saw her going toward the old stables, right? So maybe she had a thing going with one of the sta-blehands. They got into a fight over something, and he killed her. Maybe an accident, maybe not. Violent deaths are supposed to be one of the things that trap spirits."

"Murder," Roz speculated. "It might be."

"You sound like my stepmother. I talked to her about it," Stella told Roz. "She and my father are willing and able to help with any research if we need them. I hope that's all right."

"It's all right with me. I wondered if she'd show herself to one of us, since we started looking into it. Try to point us in the right direction."

"I had a dream." Since it made her feel silly to talk about it, Stella topped off her glass of champagne. "A kind of continuation of one I had a few weeks ago. Neither of them was very clear—or the details of them go foggy on me. But I know it—they—have to do with a garden I've planted, and a blue dahlia."

"Do dahlias come in blue?" Hayley wondered.

"They do. They're not common," Roz explained, "but you can hybridize them in shades of blue."

"This was like nothing I've ever seen. It was . . . elec-tric, intense. This wildly vivid blue, and huge. And she was in the dream. I didn't see her, but I felt her."

"Hey!" Hayley pushed herself forward. "Maybe her name was Dahlia."

"That's a good thought," Roz commented. "If we're researching ghosts, it's not a stretch to consider that a dream's connected in some way."

"Maybe." Frowning, Stella sipped again. "I could hear her, but I couldn't see her. Even more, I could feel her, and there was something dark about it, something frightening. She wanted me to get rid of it. She was insistent, angry, and, I don't know how to explain it, but she was *there*. How could she be in a dream?"

"I don't know," Roz replied. "But I don't care for it."

"Neither do I. It's too . . . intimate. Hearing her inside my head that way, whispering." Even now, she shivered.

"When I woke up, I knew she'd been there, in the room, just as she'd been there, in the dream."

"It's scary," Hayley agreed. "Dreams are supposed to be personal, just for ourselves, unless we want to share them. Do you think the flower had something to do with her? I don't get why she wants you to get rid of it."

"I wish I knew. It could've been symbolic. Of the gardens here, or the nursery. I don't know. But dahlias are a particular favorite of mine, and she wanted it gone."

"Something else to put in the mix." Roz took a long sip of champagne. "Let's give it a rest tonight, before we spook ourselves completely. We can try to carve out some time this week to look for names."

"Ah, I've made some tentative plans for Wednesday after work. If you wouldn't mind watching the boys for a couple of hours."

"I think between us we can manage them," Roz agreed.

"Another date with Mr. Hunky?"

With a laugh, Roz ate more caviar. "I assume that would be Logan."

"According to Hayley," Stella stated. "I was going to go by and see his place. I'd like a firsthand look at how he's landscaping it." She downed more champagne. "And while that's perfectly true, the main reason I'm going is to have sex with him. Probably. Unless I change my mind. Or he changes his. So." She set down her empty glass. "There it is."

"I'm not sure what you'd like us to say," Roz said after a moment.

"Have fun?" Hayley suggested. Then looked down at her belly. "And play safe."

"I'm only telling you because you'd know anyway, or suspect, or wonder. It seems better not to dance around it. And it doesn't seem right for me to ask you to watch my kids while I'm off . . . while I'm off without being honest about it."

"It is your life, Stella," Roz pointed out.

"Yeah." Hayley took the last delicious sip of her champagne. "Not that I wouldn't be willing to hear the details. I think hearing about sex is as close as I'm getting to it for a long time. So if you want to share . . ."

"I'll keep that in mind. Now I'd better go down and round up my boys. Thanks for the celebration, Roz."

"We earned it."

As Stella walked away, she heard Roz's questioning "Mr. Hunky?" And the dual peals of female laughter.

fourteen

GUILT TUGGED AT STELLA AS SHE BUZZED HOME TO clean up before her date with Logan. No, not date, she corrected as she jumped into the shower. It wasn't a date unless there were plans. This was a drop-by.

So now they'd had an outing, a date, and a drop-by. It was the strangest relationship she'd ever had.

But whatever she called it, she felt guilty. She wasn't the one giving her kids their evening meal and listening to their day's adventures while they ate.

It wasn't that she had to be with them every free moment, she thought as she jumped back out of the shower again. That sort of thing wasn't good for them—or for her. It wasn't as if they'd starve if she wasn't the one to put food in front of them.

But still, it seemed awfully selfish of her to give them over to someone else's care just so she could be with a man.

Be intimate with a man, if things went as she expected.

Sorry, kids, Mom can't have dinner with you tonight. She's going to go have some hot, sweaty sex.

God.

She slathered on cream as she struggled between antici-
pation and guilt.

Maybe she should put it off. Unquestionably she was
rushing this step, and that wasn't like her. When she did
things that weren't like her, it was usually a mistake.

She was thirty-three years old, and entitled to a physical
relationship with a man she liked, a man who stirred her
up, a man, who it turned out, she had considerable in common with.

Thirty-three. Thirty-four in August, she reminded herself and winced. Thirty-four wasn't early thirties anymore.
It was mid-thirties. Shit.

Okay, she wasn't going to think about that. Forget the
numbers. She'd just say she was a grown woman. That was
better.

Grown woman, she thought, and tugged on her robe so
she could work on her face. Grown, single woman. Grown,
single man. Mutual interests between them, reasonable
sense of companionship. Intense sexual tension.

How could a woman think straight when she kept imagining what it would be like to have a man's hands—

"Mom!"

She stared at her partially made-up face in the mirror.
"Yes?"

The knocking was like machine-gun fire on the bathroom door.

"Mom! Can I come in? Can I? Mom!"

She pulled open the door herself to see Luke, rosy with
rage, his fists bunched at his side. "What's the matter?"

"He's *looking* at me."

"Oh, Luke."

"With the face, Mom. With . . . the . . . *face.*"

She knew the face well. It was the squinty-eyed, smirky
sneer that Gavin had designed to torment his brother. She
knew damn well he practiced it in the mirror.

"Just don't look back at him."

"Then he makes the noise."

The noise was a hissing puff, which Gavin could keep up for hours if called for. Stella was certain that even the most hardened CIA agent would crack under its brutal power.

"All right." How the hell was she supposed to gear herself up for sex when she had to referee? She swung out of the bath, through the boys' room and into the sitting room across the hall, where she'd hoped her sons could spend the twenty minutes it took her to get dressed companionably watching cartoons.

Foolish woman, she thought. Foolish, foolish woman.

Gavin looked up from his sprawl on the floor when she came in. His face was the picture of innocence under his mop of sunny hair.

Haircuts next week, she decided, and noted it in her mental files.

He held a Matchbox car and was absently spinning its wheels while cartoons rampaged on the screen. There were several other cars piled up, lying on their sides or backs as if there'd been a horrendous traffic accident. Unfortunately the miniature ambulance and police car appeared to have had a nasty head-on collision.

Help was not on the way.

"Mom, your face looks crooked."

"Yes, I know. Gavin, I want you to stop it."

"I'm not doing anything."

She felt, actually felt, the sharp edges of the shrill scream razor up her throat. Choke it back, she ordered herself. Choke it back. She would *not* scream at her kids the way her mother had screamed at her.

"Maybe you'd like to not do anything in your room, alone, for the rest of the evening."

"I wasn't—"

"Gavin!" She cut off the denial before it dragged that scream out of her throat. Instead her voice was full of weight and aggravation. "Don't look at your brother. Don't hiss at your brother. You know it annoys him, which is exactly why you do it, and I want you to stop."

Innocence turned into a scowl as Gavin rammed the last car into the tangle of disabled vehicles. "How come I always get in trouble?"

"Yes, how come?" Stella shot back, with equal exasperation.

"He's just being a baby."

"I'm not a baby. You're a dickhead."

"Luke!" Torn between laughter and shock, Stella rounded on Luke. "Where did you hear that word?"

"Somewhere. Is it a swear?"

"Yes, and I don't want you to say it again." Even when it's apt, she thought as she caught Gavin making the face.

"Gavin, I can cancel my plans for this evening. Would you like me to do that, and stay home?" She spoke in calm, almost sweet tones. "We can spend your play hour cleaning your room."

"No." Outgunned, he poked at the pileup. "I won't look at him anymore."

"Then if it's all right with you, I'll go finish getting ready."

She heard Luke whisper, "What's a dickhead?" to Gavin as she walked out. Rolling her eyes to the ceiling, she kept going.

"THEY'RE AT EACH OTHER TONIGHT," STELLA WARNED Roz.

"Wouldn't be brothers if they weren't at each other now and then." She looked over to where the boys, the dog, and Hayley romped in the yard. "They seem all right now."

"It's brewing, under the surface, like a volcano. One of them's just waiting for the right moment to spew over the other."

"We'll see if we can distract them. If not, and they get out of hand, I'll just chain them in separate corners until you get back. I kept the shackles I used on my boys. Sentimental."

Stella laughed, and felt completely reassured. "Okay.

But you'll call me if they decide to be horrible brats. I'll be home in time to put them to bed."

"Go, enjoy yourself. And if you're not back, we can manage it."

"You make it too easy," Stella told her.

"No need for it to be hard. You know how to get there now?"

"Yes. That's the easy part."

She got in her car, gave a little toot of the horn and a wave. They'd be fine, she thought, watching in the rearview as her boys tumbled onto the ground with Parker. She couldn't have driven away if she wasn't sure of that.

It was tougher to be sure she'd be fine.

She could enjoy the drive. The early-spring breeze sang through the windows to play across her face. Tender green leaves hazed the trees, and the redbuds and wild dogwoods teased out blooms to add flashes of color.

She drove past the nursery and felt the quick zip of pride and satisfaction because she was a part of it now.

Spring had come to Tennessee, and she was here to experience it. With her windows down and the wind streaming over her, she thought she could smell the river. Just a hint of something great and powerful, contrasting with the sweet perfume of magnolia.

Contrasts, she supposed, were the order of the day now. The dreamy elegance and underlying strength of the place that was now her home, the warm air that beat the calendar to spring while the world she'd left behind still shoveled snow.

Herself, a careful, practical-natured woman driving to the bed of a man she didn't fully understand.

Nothing seemed completely aligned any longer. Blue dahlias, she decided. Her life, like her dreams, had big blue dahlias cropping up to change the design.

For tonight at least, she was going to let it bloom.

She followed the curve of the road, occupying her mind with how they would handle the weekend rush at the nursery.

Though "rush," she admitted, wasn't precisely the word. No one, staff or customer, seemed to rush—unless she counted herself.

They came, they meandered, browsed, conversed, ambled some more. They were served, with unhurried graciousness and a lot more conversation.

The slower pace sometimes made her want to grab something and just get the job done. But the fact that it often took twice as long to ring up an order than it should—in her opinion—didn't bother anyone.

She had to remind herself that part of her duties as manager was to blend efficiency with the culture of the business she managed.

One more contrast.

In any case, the work schedule she'd set would ensure that there were enough hands and feet to serve the customers. She and Roz had already poured another dozen concrete planters, and would dress them tomorrow. She could have Hayley do a few. The girl had a good eye.

Her father and Jolene were going to take the boys on Saturday, and *that* she couldn't feel guilty about, as all involved were thrilled with the arrangement.

She needed to check on the supply of plastic trays and carrying boxes, oh, and take a look at the field plants, and . . .

Her thoughts trailed off when she saw the house. She couldn't say what she'd been expecting, but it hadn't been this.

It was gorgeous.

A little run-down, perhaps, a little tired around the edges, but beautiful. Bursting with potential.

Two stories of silvered cedar stood on a terraced rise, the weathered wood broken by generous windows. On the wide, covered porch—she supposed it might be called a veranda—were an old rocker, a porch swing, a high-backed bench. Pots and baskets of flowers were arranged among them.

On the side, a deck jutted out, and she could see a short span of steps leading from it to a pretty patio.

More chairs there, more pots—oh, she was falling in love—then the land took over again and spread out to a lovely grove of trees.

He was doing shrubberies in the terraces—Japanese andromeda with its urn-shaped flowers already in bud, glossy-leaved bay laurels, the fountaining old-fashioned weigela, and a sumptuous range of azalea just waiting to explode into bloom.

And clever, she thought, creeping the car forward, clever and creative to put phlox and candytuft and ground junipers on the lowest terrace to base the shrubs and spill over the wall.

He'd planted more above in the yard—a magnolia, still tender with youth, and a dogwood blooming Easter pink. On the far side was a young weeping cherry.

Some of these were the very trees he'd hammered her over moving the first time they'd met. Just what did it say about her feelings for him that it made her smile to remember that?

She pulled into the drive beside his truck and studied the land.

There were stakes, with thin rope riding them in a kind of meandering pattern from drive to porch. Yes, she saw what he had in mind. A lazy walkway to the porch, which he would probably anchor with other shrubs or dwarf trees. Lovely. She spotted a pile of rocks and thought he must be planning to build a rock garden. There, just at the edge of the trees, would be perfect.

The house needed its trim painted, and the fieldstone that rose from its foundation repointed. A cutting garden over there, she thought as she stepped out, naturalized daffodils just inside the trees. And along the road, she'd do ground cover and shrubs, and plant daylilies, maybe some iris.

The porch swing should be painted, too, and there should be a table there—and there. A garden bench near

the weeping cherry, maybe another path leading from there
to around the back. Flagstone, perhaps. Or pretty stepping-
stones with moss or creeping thyme growing between
them.

She stopped herself as she stepped onto the porch. He'd
have his own plans, she reminded herself. His house, his
plans. No matter how much the place called to her, it
wasn't hers.

She still had to find hers.

She took a breath, fluffed a hand through her hair, and
knocked.

It was a long wait, or it seemed so to her while she
twisted her watchband around her finger. Nerves began to
tap-dance in her belly as she stood there in the early-
evening breeze.

When he opened the door, she had to paint an easy
smile on her face. He looked so *male*. The long, muscled
length of him clad in faded jeans and a white T-shirt. His
hair was mussed; she'd never seen it any other way. There
was too much of it, she thought, to be tidy. And tidy would
never suit him.

She held out the pot of dahlias she'd put together. "I've
had dahlias on the mind," she told him. "I hope you can use
them."

"I'm sure I can. Thanks. Come on in."

"I love the house," she began, "and what you're doing
with it. I caught myself mentally planting—"

She stopped. The door led directly into what she supposed was a living room, or family room. Whatever it was,
it was completely empty. The space consisted of bare dry-
wall, scarred floors, and a smoke-stained brick fireplace
with no mantel.

"You were saying?"

"Great views." It was all she could think of, and true
enough. Those generous windows brought the outdoors in.
It was too bad *in* was so sad.

"I'm not using this space right now."

"Obviously."

"I've got plans for it down the road, when I get the time, and the inclination. Why don't you come on back before you start crying or something."

"Was it like this, when you bought it?"

"Inside?" He shrugged a shoulder as he walked back through a doorway into what might have been a dining room. It, too, was empty, its walls covered with faded, peeling wallpaper. She could see brighter squares on it where pictures must have hung.

"Wall-to-wall carpet over these oak floors," he told her. "Leak upstairs had water stains all over the ceiling. And there was some termite damage. Tore out the walls last winter."

"What's this space?"

"Haven't decided yet."

He went through another door, and Stella let out a whistle of breath.

"Figured you'd be more comfortable in here." He set the flowers on a sand-colored granite counter and just leaned back to let her look.

It was his mark on the kitchen, she had no doubt. It was essentially male and strongly done. The sand tones of the counters were echoed in the tiles on the floor and offset by a deeper taupe on the walls. Cabinets were a dark, rich wood with pebbled-glass doors. There were herbs growing in small terra-cotta pots on the wide sill over the double sinks, and a small stone hearth in the corner.

Plenty of workspace on the long L of the counter, she calculated, plenty of eating space in the diagonal run of the counter that separated the kitchen area from a big, airy sitting space where he'd plopped down a black leather couch and a couple of oversized chairs.

And best of all, he'd opened the back wall with glass. You would sit there, Stella thought, and be a part of the gardens he was creating outside. Step through to the flagstone terrace and wander into flowers and trees.

"This is wonderful. Wonderful. Did you do it yourself?"

Right at the moment, seeing that dreamy look on her

face, he wanted to tell her he'd gathered the sand to make the glass. "Some. Work slows down in the winter, so I can deal with the inside of the place when I get the urge. I know people who do good work. I hire, or I barter. Want a drink?"

"Hmm. Yes. Thanks. The other room has to be your formal dining room, for when you entertain, or have people over for dinner. Of course, everyone's going to end up in here. It's irresistible."

She wandered back into the kitchen and took the glass of wine he offered. "It's going to be fabulous when you're done. Unique, beautiful, and welcoming. I love the colors you've picked in here."

"Last woman I had in here said they seemed dull."

"What did she know?" Stella sipped and shook her head. "No, they're earthy, natural—which suits you and the space."

She glanced toward the counter, where there were vegetables on a cutting board. "And obviously you cook, so the space needs to suit you. Maybe I can get a quick tour along with this wine, then I'll let you get to your dinner."

"Not hungry? I got some yellowfin tuna's going to go to waste, then."

"Oh." Her stomach gave a little bounce. "I didn't intend to invite myself to dinner. I just thought . . ."

"You like grilled tuna?"

"Yes. Yes, I do."

"Fine. You want to eat before or after?"

She felt the blood rush to her cheeks, then drain out again. "Ah . . ."

"Before or after I show you around?"

There was enough humor in his voice to tell her he knew just where her mind had gone. "After." She took a bracing sip of wine. "After. Maybe we could start outside, before we lose the light."

He took her out on the terrace, and her nerves eased back again as they talked about the lay of his land, his plans for it.

She studied the ground he'd tilled and nodded as he spoke of kitchen gardens, rock gardens, water gardens. And her heart yearned.

"I'm getting these old clinker bricks," he told her. "There's a mason I know. I'm having him build a three-sided wall here, about twenty square feet inside it."

"You're doing a walled garden? God, I am going to cry. I always wanted one. The house in Michigan just didn't work for one. I promised myself when I found a new place I'd put one in. With a little pool, and stone benches and secret corners."

She took a slow turn. A lot of hard, sweaty work had already gone into this place, she knew. And a lot of hard, sweaty work was still to come. A man who could do this, would do it, wanted to do this, was worth knowing.

"I envy you—and admire you—every inch of this. If you need some extra hands, give me a call. I miss gardening for the pleasure of it."

"You want to come by sometime, bring those hands and the kids, I'll put them to work." When she just lifted her eyebrows, he added. "Kids don't bother me, if that's what you're thinking. And there's no point planning a yard space where kids aren't welcome."

"Why don't you have any? Kids?"

"Figured I would by now." He reached out to touch her hair, pleased that she hadn't bothered with pins. "Things don't always work out like you figure."

She walked with him back toward the house. "People often say divorce is like death."

"I don't think so." He shook his head, taking his time on the walk back. "It's like an end. You make a mistake, you fix it, end it, start over from there. It was her mistake as well as mine. We just didn't figure that out until we were already married."

"Most men, given the opportunity, will cheerfully trash an ex."

"Waste of energy. We stopped loving each other, then we stopped liking each other. That's the part I'm sorry about," he added, then opened the wide glass door to the kitchen. "Then we stopped being married, which was the best thing for both of us. She stayed where she wanted to be, I came back to where I wanted to be. It was a couple years out of our lives, and it wasn't all bad."

"Sensible." But marriage was a serious business, she thought. Maybe the most serious. The ending of it should leave some scars, shouldn't it?

He poured more wine into their glasses, then took her hand. "I'll show you the rest of the house."

Their footsteps echoed as they moved through empty spaces. "I'm thinking of making a kind of library here, with work space. I could do my designs here."

"Where do you do them now?"

"Out of the bedroom mostly, or in the kitchen. Whatever's handiest. Powder room over there, needs a complete overhaul, eventually. Stairs are sturdy, but need to be sanded and buffed up."

He led her up, and she imagined paint on the walls, some sort of technique, she decided, that blended earthy colors and brought out the tones of wood.

"I'd have files and lists and clippings and dozens of pictures cut out of magazines." She slanted him a look. "I don't imagine you do."

"I've got thoughts, and I don't mind giving them time to stew a while. I grew up on a farm, remember? Farm's got a farmhouse, and my mama loved to buy old furniture and fix it up. Place was packed with tables—she had a weakness for tables. For now, I'm enjoying having nothing much but space around."

"What did she do with all of it when they moved? Ah, someone mentioned your parents moved to Montana," she added when he stopped to give her a speculative look.

"Yeah, got a nice little place in Helena. My daddy goes fly-fishing nearly every damn day, according to my mama, anyway. And she took her favorite pieces with her, filled a frigging moving van with stuff. She sold some, gave some to my sister, dumped some on me. I got it stored. Gotta get around to going through it one of these days, see what I can use."

"If you went through it, you'd be able to decide how you want to paint, decorate, arrange your rooms. You'd have some focal points."

"Focal points." He leaned against the wall, just grinned at her.

"Landscaping and home decorating have the same basic core of using space, focal points, design—and you know that very well or you couldn't have done what you did with your kitchen. So I'll shut up now."

"Don't mind hearing you talk."

"Well, I'm done now, so what's the next stop on the tour?"

"Guess this would be. I'm sort of using this as an office." He gestured to a door. "And I don't think you want to look in there."

"I can take it."

"I'm not sure I can." He tugged her away, moved on to another door. "You'll get all steamed up about filing systems and in and out boxes or whatever, and it'll screw up the rhythm. No point in using the grounds as foreplay if I'm going to break the mood by showing you something that'll insult your sensibilities."

"The grounds are foreplay?"

He just smiled and drew her through a door.

It was his bedroom and, like the kitchen, had been finished in a style that mirrored him. Simple, spacious, and male, with the outdoors blending with the in. The deck she'd seen was outside atrium doors, and beyond it the spring green of trees dominated the view. The walls were a dull, muted yellow, set off by warm wood tones in trim, in floor, in the pitched angles of the ceiling, where a trio of skylights let in the evening glow.

His bed was wide. A man of his size would want room there, she concluded. For sleeping, and for sex. Black iron head- and footboards and a chocolate-brown spread.

There were framed pencil drawings on the walls, gardens in black and white. And when she moved closer, she saw the scrawled signature at the lower corner. "You did these? They're wonderful."

"I like to get a visual of projects, and sometimes I sketch them up. Sometimes the sketches aren't half bad."

"These are a lot better than half bad, and you know it." She couldn't imagine those big, hard hands drawing anything so elegant, so lovely and fresh. "You're a constant surprise to me, Logan. A study of contrasts. I was thinking about contrasts on the way over here tonight, about how things aren't lined up the way I thought they would be. Should be."

She turned back to him, gestured toward his sketches. "These are another blue dahlia."

"Sorry—not following you. Like the one in your dream?"

"Dreams. I've had two now, and neither was entirely comfortable. In fact, they're getting downright scary. But the thing is the dahlia, it's so bold and beautiful, so unexpected. But it's not what I planned. Not what I imagined. Neither is this."

"Planned, imagined, or not, I wanted you here."

She took another sip of wine. "And here I am." She breathed slow in and out. "Maybe we should talk about . . . what we expect and how we'll—"

He moved in, pulled her against him. "Why don't we plant another blue dahlia and just see what happens."

Or we could try that, she thought when his mouth was on hers. The low tickle in her belly spread, and the needy part of her whispered, Thank God, inside her head.

She rose on her toes, all the way up, like a dancer on point, to meet him. And angling her body more truly to his, let him take the glass out of her hand.

Then his hands were in her hair, fingers streaming through it, clutching at it, and her arms were locked around him.

"I feel dizzy," she whispered. "Something about you makes me dizzy."

His blood fired, blasting a bubbling charge of lust straight to his belly. "Then you should get off your feet." In one quick move he scooped her up in his arms. She was, he thought, the sort of woman a man wanted to scoop up. Feminine and slight and curvy and soft. Holding her made him feel impossibly strong, uncommonly tender.

"I want to touch you everywhere. Then start right back at the beginning and touch you everywhere again." When he carried her to the bed, he felt sexy little tremors run through her. "Even when you annoy me, I want my hands on you."

"You must want them on me all the time, then."

"Truer words. Your hair drives me half crazy." He buried his face in it as he lowered the two of them to the bed.

"Me too." Her skin sprang to life with a thousand nerves as his lips wandered down to her throat. "But probably for different reasons."

He bit that sensitive skin, lightly, like a man helping himself to a sample. And the sensation rippled through her in one long, sweet stream. "We're grown-ups," she began.

"Thank God."

A shaky laugh escaped. "What I mean is we . . ." His teeth explored the flesh just above her collarbone in that same testing nibble, and had a lovely fog settling over her brain. "Never mind."

He touched, just as he'd told her he wanted to. A long, smooth stroke from her shoulders down to her fingertips. A lazy pass over her hips, her thigh, as if he were sampling her shape as he'd sampled her flavor.

Then his mouth was on hers again, hot and greedy. Those nerve endings exploded, electric jolts as his hands, his lips ran over her as if he were starved now for each separate taste. Hard hands, rough at the palms, rushed over her with both skill and desperation.

Just as she'd imagined. Just as she'd wanted.

Desires she'd ruthlessly buried broke the surface and screamed into life. Riding on the thrill, she dragged at his shirt until her hands found the hot, bare skin and dug in.

Man and muscle.

He found her breast, had her arching in delicious pleasure as his teeth nipped over shirt and bra to tantalize the
flesh beneath, to stir the blood beneath into feverish, pulsing life. Everything inside her went full, and ripe, and
ready.

As senses awakened, slashing one against the other in
an edgy tangle of needs, she gave herself over to them, to
him. And she yearned for him, for that promise of release,
in a way she hadn't yearned for in so long. She wanted,
craved, the heat that washed through her as the possessive
stroke of those labor-scarred hands, the demanding crush
of those insatiable lips, electrified her body.

She wanted, craved, all these quivering aches, these
madly churning needs and the freedom to meet them.

She rose with him, body to body, moved with him, flesh
to flesh. And drove him toward delirium with that creamy
skin, those lovely curves. In the softening light, she looked
beyond exquisite lying against the dark spread—that bright
hair tumbled, those summer-blue eyes clouded with pleasure.

Passion radiated from her, meeting and matching his
own. And so he wanted to give her more, and take more,
and simply drown himself in what they brought to each
other. The scent of her filled him like breath.

He murmured her name, savoring and exploiting as they
explored each other. And there was more, he discovered,
more than he'd expected.

Her heart lurched as those rugged hands guided her up,
over, through the steep rise of desire. The crest rolled
through her, a long, endless swell of sultry heat. She
arched up again, crying out as she clamped her arms
around him, pulses galloping.

Her mouth took his in a kind of ravenous madness, even
as her mind screamed—Again!

He held on, held strong while she rode the peak, and the
thrill her response brought him made him tremble. He
ached, heart, mind, loins, ached to the point of pain.

And when he could bear it no longer, he drove into her.

She cried out once more, a sound of both shock and triumph. And she was already moving with him, a quick piston of hips, as her hands came up to frame his face.

She watched him, those blue eyes swimming, those lush lips trembling with each breath as they rose and fell together.

In the whole of his life, he'd never seen such beauty bloom.

When those eyes went blind, when they closed on a sobbing moan, he let himself go.

HE WAS HEAVY. VERY HEAVY. STELLA LAY STILL beneath Logan and pondered the wonder of being pinned, helplessly, under a man. She felt loose and sleepy and utterly relaxed. She imagined there was probably a nice pink light beaming quietly out of her fingers and toes.

His heart was thundering still. What woman wouldn't feel smug and satisfied knowing she'd caused a big, strong man to lose his breath?

Cat-content, she stroked her hands over his back.

He grunted, and rolled off of her.

She felt immediately exposed and self-conscious. Reaching out, she started to give the spread a little tug, to cover herself at least partially. Then he did something that froze her in place, and had her heart teetering.

He took her hand and kissed her fingers.

He said nothing, nothing at all, and he stayed very still while she tried to swallow her heart back into place.

"Guess I'd better feed you now," he said at length.

"Ah, I should call and make sure the boys are all right."

"Go ahead." He sat up, patting her naked thigh before he rolled out of bed and reached for his jeans. "I'll go get things started in the kitchen."

He didn't bother with his shirt, but started out. Then he stopped, turned and looked at her.

"What?" She lifted an arm, casually, she hoped, over her breasts.

"I just like the way you look there. All mussed and flushed. Makes me want to muss and flush you some more, first chance I get."

"Oh." She tried to formulate a response, but he was already sauntering off. And whistling.

fifteeN

THE MAN COULD COOK. WITH LITTLE HELP FROM
Stella, Logan put together a meal of delicately grilled tuna,
herbed-up brown rice, and chunks of sautéed peppers and
mushrooms. He was the sort of cook who dashed and
dumped ingredients in by eye, or impulse, and seemed to
enjoy it.

The results were marvelous.

She was an adequate cook, a competent one. She measured everything and considered cooking just one of her
daily chores.

It was probably a good analogy for who they were, she
decided. And another reason why it made little sense for her
to be eating in his kitchen or being naked in his bed.

The sex had been . . . incredible. No point in being less
than honest about it. And after good, healthy sex she
should've been feeling relaxed and loose and comfortable.
Instead she felt tense and tight and awkward.

It had been so intense, then he'd just rolled out of bed
and started dinner. They might just as easily have finished
a rousing match of tennis.

Except he'd kissed her fingers, and that sweet, affectionate gesture had arrowed straight to her heart.

Her problem, her problem, she reminded herself. Over-analyzing, over-compensating, over-something. But if she didn't analyze something how did she know what it was?

"Dinner okay?"

She broke out of her internal debate to see him watching her steadily, with those strong jungle-cat eyes. "It's terrific."

"You're not eating much."

Deliberately she forked off more tuna. "I've never understood people who cook like you, like they do on some of the cooking shows. Tossing things together, shaking a little of this in, pinches of that. How do you know it's right?"

If that was really what she'd been thinking about with her mouth in that sexy sulk, he'd go outside and eat a shovelful of mulch. "I don't know. It usually is, or different enough to be right some other way."

Maybe he couldn't get inside her head, but he had to figure whatever was in there had to do with sex, or the ramifications of having it. But they'd play it her way for the moment. "If I'm going to cook, and since I don't want to spend every night in a restaurant, I'm going to cook, I want to enjoy it. If I regimented it, it'd start to piss me off."

"If I don't regiment it to some extent, I get nervous. Is it going to be too bland, or overly spiced? Overcooked, underdone? I'd be a wreck by the time I had a meal on the table." Worry flickered over her face. "I don't belong here, do I?"

"Define here."

"Here, here." She gestured wide with both arms. "With you, eating this really lovely and inventive meal, in your beautifully designed kitchen in your strangely charming and neglected house after relieving some sort of sexual insanity upstairs in your I'm-a-man-and-I-know-it bedroom."

He sat back and decided to clear the buzz from his head with a long drink of wine. He'd figured her right, he decided, but he just never seemed to figure her enough. "I've never heard that definition of here before. Must come from up north."

"You know what I mean," she fired back. "This isn't . . . It isn't—"

"Efficient? Tidy? Organized?"

"Don't take that placating tone with me."

"That wasn't my placating tone, it was my exasperated tone. What's your problem, Red?"

"You *confuse* me."

"Oh." He shrugged a shoulder. "If that's all." And went back to his meal.

"Do you think that's funny?"

"No, but I think I'm hungry, and that I can't do a hell of a lot about the fact that you're confused. Could be I don't mind all that much confusing you, anyway, since otherwise you'd start lining things up in alphabetical order."

Those bluebell eyes went to slits. "A, you're arrogant and annoying. B, you're bossy and bullheaded. C—"

"C, you're contrary and constricting, but that doesn't bother me the way it once did. I think we've got something interesting between us. Neither one of us was looking for it, but I can roll with that. You pick it apart. Hell if I know why I'm starting to like that about you."

"I've got more to risk than you do."

He sobered. "I'm not going to hurt your kids."

"If I believed you were the sort of man who would, or could, I wouldn't be with you on this level."

"What's 'this level'?"

"Evening sex and kitchen dinners."

"You seemed to handle the sex better than the meal."

"You're exactly right. Because I don't know what you expect from me now, and I'm not entirely sure what I expect from you."

"And this is your equivalent of tossing ingredients in a pot."

She huffed out a breath. "Apparently you understand me better than I do you."

"I'm not that complicated."

"Oh, please. You're a maze, Logan." She leaned forward until she could see the gold flecks on the green of his eyes. "A goddamn maze without any geometric pattern. Professionally, you're one of the most creative, versatile, and knowledgeable landscape designers I've ever worked with, but you do half of your designing and scheduling on the fly, with little scraps of papers stuffed into your truck or your pockets."

He scooped up more rice. "It works for me."

"Apparently, but it shouldn't work for anyone. You thrive in chaos, which this house clearly illustrates. Nobody should thrive in chaos."

"Now wait a minute." This time he gestured with his fork. "Where's the chaos? There's barely a frigging thing in the place."

"Exactly!" She jabbed a finger at him. "You've got a wonderful kitchen, a comfortable and stylish bedroom—"

"Stylish?" Mortification, clear as glass, covered his face. "Jesus."

"And empty rooms. You should be tearing your hair out wondering what you're going to do with them, but you're not. You just—just—" She waved her hand in circles. "Mosey along."

"I've never moseyed in my life. Amble sometimes," he decided. "But I never mosey."

"Whatever. You know wine and you read comic books. What kind of sense does that make?"

"Makes plenty if you consider I *like* wine and comic books."

"You were married, and apparently committed enough to move away from your home."

"What's the damn point in getting married if you're not ready and willing to do what makes the other person happy? Or at least try."

"You loved her," Stella said with a nod. "Yet you walked

away from a divorce unscarred. It was broken, too bad, so you ended it. You're rude and abrupt one minute, and accommodating the next. You knew why I'd come here tonight, yet you went to the trouble to fix a meal—which was considerate and, and civilized—there, put *that* in the C column."

"Christ, Red, you kill me. I'd move on to D, and say you're delicious, but right now it's more like demented."

Despite the fact he was laughing, she was wound up and couldn't stop. "And we have incredible, blow-the-damn-roof-off sex, then you bounce out of bed as if we'd been doing this every night for years. I can't keep up."

Once he decided she'd finished, he picked up his wine, drank thoughtfully. "Let's see if I can work my way back through that. Though I've got to tell you, I didn't detect any geometric pattern."

"Oh, shut up."

His hand clamped over hers before she could shove back from the table. "No, you just sit still. It's my turn. If I didn't work the way I do? I wouldn't be able to do what I do, and I sure as hell wouldn't love it. I found that out up north. My marriage was a failure. Nobody likes to fail, but nobody gets through life without screwing up. We screwed it up, didn't hurt anybody but ourselves. We took our lumps and moved on."

"But—"

"Hush. If I'm rude and abrupt it's because I feel rude and abrupt. If I'm accommodating, it's because I want to be, or figure I have to be at some point."

He thought, What the hell, and topped off his wine. She'd barely touched hers. "What was next? Oh, yeah, you being here tonight. Yeah, I knew why. We're not teenagers, and you're a pretty straightforward woman, in your way. I wanted you, and made that clear. You wouldn't come knocking on my door unless you were ready. As for the meal, there are a couple of reasons for that. One, I like to eat. And two, I wanted you here. I wanted to be with you here, like this. Before, after, in between. However it worked out."

Somewhere, somehow, during his discourse, her temper had ebbed. "How do you make it all sound sane?"

"I'm not done. While I'm going to agree with your take on the sex, I object to the word 'bounce.' I don't bounce anymore than I mosey. I got out of bed because if I'd breathed you in much longer, I'd have asked you to stay. You can't, you won't. And the fact is, I don't know that I'm ready for you to stay anyway. If you're the sort who needs a lot of postcoital chat, like 'Baby, that was amazing'—"

"I'm not." There was something in his aggravated tone that made her lips twitch. "I can judge for myself, and I destroyed you up there."

His hand slid up to her wrist, back down to her fingers. "Any destruction was mutual."

"All right. Mutual destruction. The first time with a man, and I think this holds true for most women, is as nerve-racking as it is exciting. It's more so afterward if what happened between them touched something in her. You touched something in me, and it scares me."

"Straightforward," he commented.

"Straightforward, to your maze. It's a difficult combination. Gives us a lot to think about. I'm sorry I made an issue out of all of this."

"Red, you were born to make issues out of every damn thing. It's kind of interesting now that I'm getting used to it."

"That may be true, and I could say that the fact your drummer certainly bangs a different tune's fairly interesting, too. But right now, I'm going to help you clean up your kitchen. Then I have to get home."

He rose when she did, then simply took her shoulders and backed her into the refrigerator. He kissed her blind and deaf—pent-up temper, needs, frustration, longings all boiled together.

"Something else to think about," he said.

"I'll say."

* * *

ROZ DIDN'T PRY INTO OTHER PEOPLE'S BUSINESS. SHE didn't mind hearing about it when gossip came her way, but she didn't pry. She didn't like—more she didn't permit—others to meddle in her life, and afforded them the same courtesy.

So she didn't ask Stella any questions. She thought of plenty, but she didn't ask them.

She observed.

Her manager conducted business with her usual calm efficiency. Roz imagined Stella could be standing in the whirling funnel of a tornado and would still be able to conduct business efficiently.

An admirable and somewhat terrifying trait.

She'd grown very fond of Stella, and she'd come—unquestionably—to depend on her to handle the details of the business so she herself could focus on the duties, and pleasures, of being the grower. She adored the children. It was impossible for her not to. They were charming and bright, sly and noisy, entertaining and exhausting.

Already, she was so used to them, and Stella and Hayley, being in her house she could hardly imagine them not being there.

But she didn't pry, even when Stella came home from her evening at Logan's with the unmistakable look of a woman who'd been well pleasured.

But she didn't hush Hayley, or brush her aside when the girl chattered about it.

"She won't get specific," Hayley complained while she and Roz weeded a bed at Harper House. "I really like it when people get specific. But she said he cooked for her. I always figure when a man cooks, he's either trying to get you between the sheets, or he's stuck on you."

"Maybe he's just hungry."

"A man's hungry, he sends out for pizza. At least the guys I've known. I think he's stuck on her." She waited, the pause obviously designed for Roz to comment. When there was none, Hayley blew out a breath. "Well? You've known him a long time."

"A few years. I can't tell you what's in his mind. But I can tell you he's never cooked for me."

"Was his wife a real bitch?"

"I couldn't say. I didn't know her."

"I'd like it if she was. A real stone bitch who tore him apart and left him all wounded and resentful of women. Then Stella comes along and gets him all messed up in the head even as she heals him."

Roz sat back on her heels and smiled. "You're awfully young, honey."

"You don't have to be young to like romance. Um . . . your second husband, he was terrible, wasn't he?"

"He was—is—a liar, a cheat, and a thief. Other than that he's charming."

"Did he break your heart?"

"No. He bruised my pride and pissed me off. Which was worse, in my opinion. That's yesterday's news, Hayley. I'm going to plug some *silene armeria* in these pockets," she continued. "They've got a long blooming season, and they'll fill in nice here."

"I'm sorry."

"No need to be sorry."

"It's just that this woman was in this morning, Mrs. Peebles?"

"Oh, yes, Roseanne." After studying the space, Roz picked up her trowel and began to turn the earth in the front of the mixed bed. "Did she actually buy anything?"

"She dithered around for an hour, said she'd come back."

"Typical. What did she want? It wouldn't have been plants."

"I clued in there. She's the nosy sort, and not the kind with what you'd call a benign curiosity. Just comes in for gossip—to spread it or to harvest it. You see her kind most everywhere."

"I suppose you do."

"So, well. She'd gotten word I was living here, and was a family connection, so she was pumping me. I don't pump so easy, but I let her keep at it."

Roz grinned under the brim of her cap as she reached for a plant. "Good for you."

"I figured what she really wanted was for me to pass on to you the news that Bryce Clerk is back in Memphis."

A jerk of her fingers broke off part of the stem. "Is he?" Roz said, very quietly.

"He's living at the Peabody for now and has some sort of venture in the works. She was vague about that. She says he plans to move back permanent, and he's taking office space. Said he looked very prosperous."

"Likely he hosed some other brainless woman."

"You aren't brainless, Roz."

"I was, briefly. Well, it's no matter to me where he is or what he's doing. I don't get burned twice by the same crooked match."

She set the plant, then reached for another. "Common name for these is none-so-pretty. Feel these sticky patches on the stems? They catch flies. Shows that something that looks attractive can be dangerous, or at least a big pain in the ass."

SHE BURIED IT AS SHE CLEANED UP. SHE WASN'T CON-cerned with a scoundrel she'd once been foolish enough to marry. A woman was entitled to a few mistakes along the way, even if she made them out of loneliness or foolishness, or—screw it—vanity.

Entitled, Roz thought, as long as she corrected the mistakes and didn't repeat them.

She put on a fresh shirt, skimmed her fingers through her damp hair as she studied herself in the mirror. She could still look good, damn good, if she worked at it. If she wanted a man, she could have one—and not because he assumed she was dim-witted and had a depthless well of money to draw from. Maybe what had happened with Bryce had shaken her confidence and self-esteem for a little while, but she was all right now. Better than all right.

She hadn't needed a man to fill in the pockets of her life before he'd come along. She didn't need one now. Things were back the way she liked them. Her kids were happy and productive, her business was thriving, her home was secure. She had friends she enjoyed and acquaintances she tolerated.

And right now, she had the added interest of researching her family ghost.

Giving her hair another quick rub, she went downstairs to join the rest of the crew in the library. She heard the knock as she came to the base of the stairs, and detoured to the door.

"Logan, what a nice surprise."

"Hayley didn't tell you I was coming?"

"No, but that doesn't matter. Come on in."

"I ran into her at the nursery today, and she asked if I'd come by tonight, give y'all a hand with your research and brainstorming. I had a hard time resisting the idea of being a ghostbuster."

"I see." And she did. "I'd best warn you that our Hayley's got a romantic bent and she currently sees you as Rochester to Stella's Jane Eyre."

"Oh. Uh-oh."

She only smiled. "Jane's still with the boys, getting them settled down for the night. Why don't you go on up to the West wing? Just follow the noise. You can let her know we'll entertain ourselves until she comes down."

She walked away before he could agree or protest.

She didn't pry into other people's business. But that didn't mean she didn't sow the occasional seeds.

Logan stood where he was for a moment, tapping his fingers on the side of his leg. He was still tapping them as he started up the stairs.

Roz was right about the noise. He heard the laughter

and squeals, the stomping feet before he'd hit the top. Following it, he strolled down the hall, then paused in the open doorway.

It was obviously a room occupied by boys. And though it was certainly tidier than his had been at those tender ages, it wasn't static or regimented. A few toys were scattered on the floor, books and other debris littered the desk and shelves. It smelled of soap, shampoo, wild youth, and crayons.

In the midst of it, Stella sat on the floor, mercilessly tickling a pajama-clad Gavin while a blissfully naked Luke scrambled around the room making crazed hooting sounds through his cupped hands.

"What's my name?" Stella demanded as she sent her oldest son into helpless giggles.

"Mom!"

She made a harsh buzzing sound and dug fingers into his ribs. "Try again, small, helpless boy child. What is my name?"

"Mom, Mom, Mom, Mom, Mom!" He tried to wiggle away and was flipped over.

"I can't hear you."

"Empress," he managed on hitching giggles.

"And? The rest, give it all or the torment continues."

"Empress Magnificent of the Entire Universe!"

"And don't you forget it." She gave him a loud, smacking kiss on his cotton-clad butt, and sat back. "And now you, short, frog-faced creature." She got to her feet, rubbing her hands together as Luke screamed in delight.

And stumbled back with a scream of her own when she saw Logan in the doorway. "Oh, my God! You scared me to death!"

"Sorry, just watching the show. Your Highness. Hey, kid." He nodded at Gavin, who lay on the floor. "How's it going?"

"She defeated me. Now I have to go to bed, 'cause that's the law of the land."

"I've heard that." He picked up the bottom half of a pair

of X-Men pj's, lifted an eyebrow at Luke. "These your mom's?"

Luke let out a rolling gut laugh, and danced, happy with his naked state. "Uh-*uh*. They're mine. I don't have to wear them unless she catches me."

Luke started to make a break for the adjoining bath and was scooped up, one-armed, by his mother.

Stronger than she looks, Logan mused as she hoisted her son over her head.

"Foolish boy, you'll never escape me." She lowered him. "Into the pj's, and into bed." She glanced over at Logan. "Is there something . . ."

"I got invited to the . . . get-together downstairs."

"Is it a party?" Luke wanted to know when Logan handed him the pajama bottoms. "Are there cookies?"

"It's a meeting, a grown-up meeting, and if there are cookies," Stella said as she turned down Luke's bed, "you can have some tomorrow."

"David makes really good cookies," Gavin commented. "Better than Mom's."

"If that wasn't true, I'd have to punish you severely." She turned to his bed, where he sat grinning at her, and using the heel of her hand shoved him gently onto his back.

"But you're prettier than he is."

"Clever boy. Logan, could you tell everyone I'll be down shortly? We're just going to read for a bit first."

"Can he read?" Gavin asked.

"I can. What's the book?"

"Tonight we get *Captain Underpants*." Luke grabbed the book and hurried over to shove it into Logan's hands.

"So is he a superhero?"

Luke's eyes widened like saucers. "You don't know about Captain Underpants?"

"Can't say I do." He turned the book over in his hands, but he was looking at the boy. He'd never read to kids before. It might be entertaining. "Maybe I should read it, then I can find out. If that suits the Empress."

"Oh, well, I—"

"Please, Mom! Please!"

At the chorus on either side of her, Stella eased back with the oddest feeling in her gut. "Sure. I'll just go straighten up the bath."

She left them to it, mopping up the wet, gathering bath toys, while Logan's voice, deep and touched with ironic amusement, carried to her.

She hung damp towels, dumped bath toys into a plastic net to dry, fussed. And she felt the chill roll in around her. A hard, needling cold that speared straight to her bones.

Her creams and lotions tumbled over the counter as if an angry hand swept them. The thuds and rattles sent her springing forward to grab at them before they fell to the floor.

And each one was like a cube of ice in her hand.

She'd seen them move. Good God, she'd seen them *move*.

Shoving them back, she swung instinctively to the connecting doorway to shield her sons from the chill, from the fury she felt slapping the air.

There was Logan, with the chair pulled between the beds, as she did herself, reading about the silly adventures of Captain Underpants in that slow, easy voice, while her boys lay tucked in and drifting off.

She stood there, blocking that cold, letting it beat against her back until he finished, until he looked up at her.

"Thanks." She was amazed at how calm her voice sounded. "Boys, say good night to Mr. Kitridge."

She moved into the room as they mumbled it. When the cold didn't follow her, she took the book, managed a smile. "I'll be down in just a minute."

"Okay. See you later, men."

The interlude left him feeling mellow and relaxed. Reading bedtime stories was a kick. Who knew? Captain Underpants. Didn't that beat all.

He wouldn't mind doing it again sometime, especially

if he could talk Mama into letting them read a graphic novel.

He'd liked seeing her wrestling on the floor with her boy. Empress Magnificent, he thought with a half laugh.

Then the breath was knocked out of him. The force of the cold came like a tidal wave at his back, swamping him even as it shoved him forward.

He pitched at the top of the stairs, felt his head go light at the thought of the fall. Flailing out, he managed to grab the rail and, spinning his body, hook his other hand over it while tiny black dots swam in front of his eyes. For another instant he feared he would simply tumble over the railing, pushed by the momentum.

Out of the corner of his eye, he saw a shape, vague but female. And from it he felt a raw and bitter rage.

Then it was gone.

He could hear his own breath heaving in and out, and feel the clamminess of panic sweat down his back. Though his legs wanted to fold on him, he stayed where he was, working to steady himself until Stella came out.

Her half smile faded the minute she saw him. "What is it?" She moved to him quickly. "What happened?"

"She—this ghost of yours—has she ever scared the boys?"

"No. Exactly the opposite. She's . . . comforting, even protective of them."

"All right. Let's go downstairs." He took her hand firmly in his, prepared to drag her to safety if necessary.

"Your hand's cold."

"Yeah, tell me about it."

"You tell me."

"I intend to."

HE TOLD THEM ALL WHEN THEY SAT AROUND THE library table with their folders and books and notes. And he dumped a good shot of brandy in his coffee as he did.

"There's been nothing," Roz began, "in all the years she's been part of this house, that indicates she's a threat. People have been frightened or uneasy, but no one's ever been physically attacked."

"Can ghosts physically attack?" David wondered.

"You wouldn't ask if you'd been standing at the top of the stairs with me."

"Poltergeists can cause stuff to fly around," Hayley commented. "But they usually manifest around adolescent kids. Something about puberty can set them off. Anyway, this isn't that. It might be that an ancestor of Logan's did something to her. So she's paying him back."

"I've been in this house dozens of times. She's never bothered with me before."

"The children." Stella spoke softly as she looked over her own notes. "It centers on them. She's drawn to children, especially little boys. She's protective of them. And she almost, you could say, envies me for having them, but not in an angry way. More sad. But she was angry the night I was going out to dinner with Logan."

"Putting a man ahead of your kids." Roz held up a hand. "I'm not saying that's what I think. We have to think like she does. We talked about this before, Stella, and I've been thinking back on it. The only times I remember feeling anything angry from her was when I went out with men now and again, when my boys were coming up. But I didn't experience anything as direct or upsetting as this. But then, there was nothing to it. I never had any strong feelings for any of them."

"I don't see how she could know what I feel or think."

But the dreams, Stella thought. She's been in my dreams.

"Let's not get irrational now," David interrupted. "Let's follow this line through. Let's say she believes things are serious, or heading that way, between you and Logan. She doesn't like it, that's clear enough. The only people who've felt threatened, or been threatened are the two of you. Why? Does it make her angry? Or is she jealous?"

"A jealous ghost." Hayley drummed her hands on the table. "Oh, that's good. It's like she sympathizes, relates to you being a woman, a single woman, with kids. She'll help you look after them, even sort of look after you. But then you put a man in the picture, and she's all bitchy about it. She's like, you're not supposed to have a nice, standard family—mom, dad, kids—because I didn't."

"Logan and I hardly . . . All he did was read them a story."

"The sort of thing a father might do," Roz pointed out.

"I . . . well, when he was reading to them, I was putting the bathroom back in shape. And she was there. I felt her. Then, well, my things. The things I keep on the counter started to jump. *I* jumped."

"Holy shit," Hayley responded.

"I went to the door, and in the boy's room, everything was calm, normal. I could feel the warmth on the front of me, and this, this raging cold against my back. She didn't want to frighten them. Only me."

But buying a baby monitor went on her list. From now on, she wanted to hear everything that went on in that room when her boys were up there without her.

"This is a good angle, Stella, and you're smart enough to know we should follow it." Roz laid her hands on the library table. "Nothing we've turned up indicates this spirit is one of the Harper women, as has been assumed all these years. Yet someone knew her, knew her when she was alive, knew that she died. So was it hushed up, ignored? Either way, it might explain her being here. If it was hushed up or ignored, it seems most logical she was a servant, a mistress, or a lover."

"I bet she had a child." Hayley laid a hand over her own. "Maybe she died giving birth to it, or had to give it up, and died from a broken heart. It would have been one of the Harper men who got her into trouble, don't you think? Why would she stay here if it wasn't because she lived here or—"

"Died here," Stella finished. "Reginald Harper was head of the house during the period when we think she died. Roz, how the hell do we go about finding out if he had a mistress, a lover, or an illegitimate child?"

sixteen

LOGAN HAD BEEN IN LOVE TWICE IN HIS LIFE. HE'D been in lust a number of times. He'd experienced extreme interest or heavy like, but love had only knocked him down and out twice. The first had been in his late teens, when both he and the girl of his dreams had been too young to handle it.

They'd burned each other and their love out with passion, jealousies, and a kind of crazed energy. He could look back at that time now and think of Lisa Anne Lauer with a sweet nostalgia and affection.

Then there was Rae. He'd been a little older, a little smarter. They'd taken their time, two years of time before heading into marriage. They'd both wanted it, though some who knew him were surprised, not only by the engagement but by his agreement to move north with her.

It hadn't surprised Logan. He'd loved her, and north was where she'd wanted to be. Needed to be, he corrected, and he'd figured, naively as it turned out, that he could plant himself anywhere.

He'd left the wedding plans up to her and her mother,

with some input from his own. He wasn't crazy. But he'd enjoyed the big, splashy, crowded wedding with all its pomp.

He'd had a good job up north. At least in theory. But he'd been restless and dissatisfied in the beehive of it, and out of place in the urban buzz.

The small-town boy, he thought as he and his crew finished setting the treated boards on the roof of a twelve-foot pergola. He was just too small-town, too small-time, to fit into the urban landscape.

He hadn't thrived there, and neither had his marriage. Little things at first, picky things—things he knew in retrospect they should have dealt with, compromised on, overcome. Instead, they'd both let those little things fester and grow until they'd pushed the two of them, not just apart, he thought, but in opposite directions.

She'd been in her element, and he hadn't. At the core he'd been unhappy, and she'd been unhappy he wasn't acclimating. Like any disease, unhappiness spread straight down to the roots when it wasn't treated.

Not all her fault. Not all his. In the end they'd been smart enough, or unhappy enough, to cut their losses.

The failure of it had hurt, and the loss of that once-promising love had hurt. Stella was wrong about the lack of scars. There were just some scars you had to live with.

The client wanted wisteria for the pergola. He instructed his crew where to plant, then took himself off to the small pool the client wanted outfitted with water plants.

He was feeling broody, and when he was feeling broody, he liked to work alone as much as possible. He had the cattails in containers and, dragging on boots, he waded in to sink them. Left to themselves, the cats would spread and choke out everything, but held in containers they'd be a nice pastoral addition to the water feature. He dealt with a trio of water lilies the same way, then dug in the yellow flags. They liked their feet wet, and would dance with color on the edge of the pool.

The work satisfied him, centered him as it always did. It let another part of his mind work out separate problems. Or at least chew on them for a while.

Maybe he'd put a small pool in the walled garden he planned to build at home. No cattails, though. He might try some dwarf lotus, and some water canna as a background plant. It seemed to him it was more the sort of thing Stella would like.

He'd been in love twice before, Logan thought again. And now he could sense those delicate taproots searching inside him for a place to grow. He could probably cut them off. Probably. He probably should.

What was he going to do with a woman like Stella and those two ridiculously appealing kids? They were bound to drive each other crazy in the long term with their different approaches to damn near everything. He doubted they'd burn each other out, though, God, when he'd had her in bed, he'd felt singed. But they might wilt, as he and Rae had wilted. That was more painful, more miserable, he knew, than the quick flash.

And this time there were a couple of young boys to consider.

Wasn't that why the ghost had given him a good kick in the ass? It was hard to believe he was sweating in the steamy air under overcast skies and thinking about an encounter with a ghost. He'd thought he was open-minded about that sort of thing—until he'd come face-to-face, so to speak, with it.

The fact was, Logan realized now, as he hauled mulch over for the skirt of the pool, he hadn't believed in the ghost business. It had all been window dressing or legendary stuff to him. Old houses were supposed to have ghosts because it made a good story, and the south loved a good story. He'd accepted it as part of the culture, and maybe, in some strange way, as something that might happen to someone else. Especially if that someone else was a little drunk, or very susceptible to atmosphere.

He'd been neither. But he'd felt her breath, the ice of it, and her rage, the power of it. She'd wanted to cause him harm, she'd wanted him away. From those children, and their mother.

So he was invested now in helping to find the identity of what walked those halls.

But a part of him wondered if whoever she was was right. Would they all be better off if he stayed away?

The phone on his belt beeped. Since he was nearly done, he answered instead of ignoring, dragging off his filthy work gloves and plucking the phone off his belt.

"Kitridge."

"Logan, it's Stella."

The quick and helpless flutter around his heart irritated him. "Yeah. I've got the frigging forms in my truck."

"What forms?"

"Whatever damn forms you're calling to nag me about."

"It happens I'm not calling to nag you about anything." Her voice had gone crisp and businesslike, which only caused the flutter and the irritation to increase.

"Well, I don't have time to chat, either. I'm on the clock."

"Seeing as you are, I'd like you to schedule in a consult. I have a customer who'd like an on-site consultation. She's here now, so if you could give me a sense of your plans for the day, I could let her know if and when you could meet with her."

"Where?"

She rattled off an address that was twenty minutes away. He glanced around his current job site, calculated. "Two o'clock."

"Fine. I'll tell her. The client's name is Marsha Fields. Do you need any more information?"

"No."

"Fine."

He heard the firm click in his ear and found himself even more annoyed he hadn't thought to hang up first.

* * *

BY THE TIME LOGAN GOT HOME THAT EVENING, HE was tired, sweaty, and in a better mood. Hard physical work usually did the job for him, and he'd had plenty of it that day. He'd worked in the steam, then through the start of a brief spring storm. He and his crew broke for lunch during the worst of it and sat in his overheated truck, rain lashing at the windows, while they ate cold po'boy sandwiches and drank sweet tea.

The Fields job had strong possibilities. The woman ran that roost and had very specific ideas. Since he liked and agreed with most of them, he was eager to put some of them on paper, expand or refine them.

And since it turned out that Marsha's cousin on her mother's side was Logan's second cousin on his father's, the consult had taken longer than it might have, and had progressed cheerfully.

It didn't hurt that she was bound to send more work his way.

He took the last curve of the road to his house in a pleasant frame of mind, which darkened considerably when he saw Stella's car parked behind his.

He didn't want to see her now. He hadn't worked things out in his head, and she'd just muck up whatever progress he'd made. He wanted a shower and a beer, a little quiet. Then he wanted to eat his dinner with ESPN in the background and his work spread out on the kitchen table.

There just wasn't room in that scenario for a woman.

He parked, fully intending to shake her off. She wasn't in the car, or on the porch. He was trying to determine if going to bed with him gave a woman like her the notion that she could waltz into his house when he wasn't there. Even as he'd decided it wouldn't, not for Stella, he heard the watery hiss of his own garden hose.

Shoving his hands in his pockets, he wandered around the side of the house.

She was on the patio, wearing snug gray pants—the sort that stopped several inches above the ankle—and a loose blue shirt. Her hair was drawn back in a bright, curling tail, which for reasons he couldn't explain he found desperately sexy. As the sun had burned its way through the clouds, she'd shaded her eyes with gray-tinted glasses.

She looked neat and tidy, careful to keep her gray canvas shoes out of the wet.

"It rained today," he called out.

She kept on soaking his pots. "Not enough."

She finished the job, released the sprayer on the hose, but continued to hold it as she turned to face him. "I realize you have your own style, and your own moods, and that's your business. But I won't be spoken to the way you spoke to me today. I won't be treated like some silly female who calls her boyfriend in the middle of the workday to coo at him, or like some anal business associate who interrupts you to harangue you about details. I'm neither."

"Not my girlfriend or not my business associate?"

He could see, quite clearly, the way her jaw tightened when she clenched her teeth. "If and when I contact you during the workday, it will be for a reason. As it most certainly was this morning."

She was right, but he didn't have to say so. "We got the Fields job."

"Hooray."

He bit the inside of his cheek to hold back the grin at her sour cheer. "I'll be working up a design for her, with a bid. You'll get a copy of both. That suit you?"

"It does. What doesn't—"

"Where are the kids?"

It threw her off stride. "My father and his wife picked them up from school today. They're having dinner there, and spending the night, as I have a birthing class with Hayley later."

"What time?"

"What time what?"

"Is the class?"

"At eight-thirty. I'm not here for small talk, Logan, or to be placated. I feel very strongly that—" Her eyes widened, then narrowed as she stepped back. He'd stepped forward, and there was no mistaking the tone of that slow smile.

"Don't even think about it. I couldn't be less interested in kissing you at the moment."

"Then I'll kiss you, and maybe you'll get interested."

"I mean it." She aimed the hose like a weapon. "Just keep your distance. I want to make myself perfectly clear."

"I'm getting the message. Go ahead and shoot," he invited. "I sweated out a gallon today, I won't mind a shower."

"Just stop it." She danced back several steps as he advanced. "This isn't a game, this isn't funny."

"I just get stirred right up when your voice takes on that tone."

"I don't have a tone."

"Yankee schoolteacher. I'm going to be sorry if you ever lose it." He made a grab, and instinctively she tightened her fist on the nozzle. And nailed him.

The spray hit him mid-chest and had a giggle bubbling out of her before she could stop it. "I'm not going to play with you now. I'm serious, Logan."

Dripping, he made another grab, feinted left. This time she squealed, dropped the hose, and ran.

He snagged her around the waist, hauled her off her feet at the back end of the patio. Caught somewhere between shock and disbelief, she kicked, wiggled, then lost her breath as she landed on the grass on top of him.

"Let me go, you moron."

"Don't see why I should." God, it felt good to be horizontal. Better yet to have her horizontal with him. "Here you are, trespassing, watering my pots, spouting off lectures." He rolled, pinning her. "I ought to be able to do what I want on my own land."

"Stop it. I haven't finished fighting with you."

"I bet you can pick it up where you left off." He gave her a playful nip on the chin, then another.

"You're wet, you're sweaty, I'm getting grass stains on my—"

The rest of the words were muffled against his mouth, and she would have sworn the water on both of them went to steam.

"I can't—we can't—" But the reasons why were going dim. "In the backyard."

"Wanna bet?"

He couldn't help wanting her, so why was he fighting it? He wanted the solid, sensible core of her, and the sweet edges. He wanted the woman obsessed with forms who would wrestle on the floor with her children. He wanted the woman who watered his pots even while she skinned him with words.

And the one who vibrated beneath him on the grass when he touched her.

He touched her, his hands possessive as they molded her breasts, as they roamed down her to cup her hips. He tasted her, his lips hungry on her throat, her shoulder, her breast.

She melted under him, and even as she went fluid seemed to come alive with heat, with movement.

It was insane. It was rash and it was foolish, but she couldn't stop herself. They rolled over the grass, like two frenzied puppies. He smelled of sweat, of labor and damp. And, God, of man. Pungent and gorgeous and sexy.

She clamped her hands in that mass of waving hair, already showing streaks from the sun, and dragged his mouth back to hers.

She nipped his lip, his tongue.

"Your belt." She had to fight to draw air. "It's digging—"

"Sorry."

He levered up to unbuckle it, then just stopped to look at her.

Her hair had come out of its band; her eyes were sultry, her skin flushed. And he felt those roots take hold.

"Stella."

He didn't know what he might have said, the words were jumbled in his brain and tangled with so much feeling he couldn't translate them.

But she smiled, slow and sultry as her eyes. "Why don't I help you with that?"

She flipped open the button of his jeans, yanked down the zipper. Her hand closed over him, a velvet vise. His body was hard as steel, and his mind and heart powerless.

She arched up to him, her lips skimmed over his bare chest, teeth scoring a hot little line that was a whisper away from pain.

Then she was over him, destroying him. Surrounding him.

She heard birdsong and breeze, smelled grass and damp flesh. And heliotrope that wafted on the air from the pot she'd watered. She felt his muscles, taut ropes, the broad plane of his shoulders, the surprisingly soft waves of his hair.

And she saw, as she looked down, that he was lost in her.

Throwing her head back, she rode, until she was lost as well.

SHE LAY SPRAWLED OVER HIM, DAMP AND NAKED AND muzzy-headed. Part of her brain registered that his arms were clamped around her as if they were two survivors of a shipwreck.

She turned her head to rest it on his chest. Maybe they'd wrecked each other. She'd just made wild love with a man in broad daylight, outside in the yard.

"This is insane," she murmured, but couldn't quite convince herself to move. "What if someone had come by?"

"People come by without an invitation have to take potluck."

There was a lazy drawl to his voice in direct opposition to his grip on her. She lifted her head to study. His eyes were closed. "So this is potluck?"

The corners of his mouth turned up a little. "Seems to me this pot was plenty lucky."

"I feel sixteen. Hell, I never did anything like this when I was sixteen. I need my sanity. I need my clothes."

"Hold on." He nudged her aside, then rose.

Obviously, she thought, it doesn't bother him to walk around outside naked as a deer. "I came here to talk to you, Logan. Seriously."

"You came here to kick my ass," he corrected. "Seriously. You were doing a pretty good job of it."

"I hadn't finished." She turned slightly, reached out for her hairband. "But I will, as soon as I'm dressed and—"

She screamed, the way a woman screams when she's being murdered with a kitchen knife.

Then she gurgled, as the water he'd drenched her with from the hose ran into her astonished mouth.

"Figured we could both use some cooling off."

It simply wasn't in her, even under the circumstances, to run bare-assed over the grass. Instead, she curled herself up, knees to breast, arms around knees, and cursed him with vehemence and creativity.

He laughed until he thought his ribs would crack. "Where'd a nice girl like you learn words like that? How am I supposed to kiss that kind of mouth?"

She seared him with a look even when he held the hose over his own head and took an impromptu shower. "Feels pretty good. Want a beer?"

"No, I don't want a beer. I certainly don't want a damn beer. I want a damn towel. You insane idiot, now my clothes are wet."

"We'll toss 'em into the dryer." He dropped the hose, scooped them up. "Come on inside, I'll get you a towel."

Since he sauntered across the patio to the door, still unconcerned and naked, she had no choice but to follow.

"Do you have a robe?" she asked in cold and vicious tones.

"What would I do with a robe? Hang on, Red."

He left her, dripping and beginning to shiver in his kitchen.

He came back a few minutes later, wearing ratty gym pants and carrying two huge bath sheets. "These ought to do the trick. Dry off, I'll toss these in for you."

He carried her clothes through a door. Laundry room, she assumed as she wrapped one of the towels around her. She used the other to rub at her hair—which would be hopeless, absolutely hopeless now—while she heard the dryer click on.

"Want some wine instead?" he asked as he stepped back in. "Coffee or something."

"Now you listen to me—"

"Red, I swear I've had to listen to you more than any woman I can remember in the whole of my life. It beats the living hell out of me why I seem to be falling in love with you."

"I don't like being . . . Excuse me?"

"It was the hair that started it." He opened the refrigerator, took out a beer. "But that's just attraction. Then the voice." He popped the top and took a long drink from the bottle. "But that's just orneriness on my part. It's a whole bunch of little things, a lot of big ones tossed in. I don't know just what it is, but every time I'm around you I get closer to the edge."

"I—you—you think you're falling in love with me, and your way of showing it is to toss me on the ground and carry on like some sex addict, and when you're done to drench me with a hose?"

He took another sip, slower, more contemplative, rubbed a hand over his bare chest. "Seemed like the thing to do at the time."

"Well, that's very charming."

"Wasn't thinking about charm. I didn't say I wanted to

be in love with you. In fact, thinking about it put me in a lousy mood most of the day."

Her eyes narrowed until the blue of them was a hot, intense light. "Oh, really?"

"Feel better now, though."

"Oh, that's fine. That's lovely. Get me my clothes."

"They're not dry yet."

"I don't care."

"People from up north are always in a hurry." He leaned back comfortably on the counter. "There's this other thing I thought today."

"I don't care about that either."

"The other thing was how I've only been in love—the genuine deal—twice before. And both times it . . . let's not mince words. Both times it went to shit. Could be this'll head the same way."

"Could be we're already there."

"No." His lips curved. "You're pissed and you're scared. I'm not what you were after."

"I wasn't after anything."

"Me either." He set the beer down, then killed her temper by stepping to her, framing her face with his hands. "Maybe I can stop what's going on in me. Maybe I should try. But I look at you, I touch you, and the edge doesn't just get closer, it gets more appealing."

He touched his lips to her forehead, then released her and stepped back.

"Every time I figure some part of you out, you sprout something off in another direction," she said. "I've only been in love once—the genuine deal—and it was everything I wanted. I haven't figured out what I want now, beyond what I have. I don't know, Logan, if I've got the courage to step up to that edge again."

"Things keep going the way they are for me, if you don't step up, you might get pushed."

"I don't push easily, Logan." It was she who stepped to him now, and she took his hand. "I'm so touched that you'd tell me, so churned up inside that you might feel that way about me. I need time to figure out what's going on inside me, too."

"It'd help," he decided after a moment, "if you could work on keeping the pace."

HER CLOTHES WERE DRY BUT IMPOSSIBLY WRINKLED, her hair had frizzed and was now, in Stella's opinion, approximately twice its normal volume.

She dashed out of the car, mortified to see both Hayley and Roz sitting on the glider drinking something out of tall glasses.

"Just have to change," she called out. "I won't be long."

"There's plenty of time," Hayley called back, and pursed her lips as Stella raced into the house. "You know," she began, "what it means when a woman shows up with her clothes all wrinkled to hell and grass stains on the ass of her pants?"

"I assume she went by Logan's."

"Outdoor nookie."

Roz choked on a sip of tea, wheezed in a laugh. "Hayley. Jesus."

"You ever do it outdoors?"

Roz only sighed now. "In the dim, dark past."

STELLA WAS SHARP ENOUGH TO KNOW THEY WERE talking about her. As a result, the flush covered not only her face but most of her body as she ran into the bedroom. She stripped off her clothes, threw them into a hamper.

"No reason to be embarrassed," she muttered to herself as she threw open her armoire. "Absolutely none." She dug out fresh underwear and felt more normal after she put it on.

And reaching for her blouse, felt the chill.

She braced, half expecting a vase or lamp to fly across the room at her this time.

But she gathered her courage and turned, and she saw the Harper Bride. Clearly, for the first time, clearly, though the dusky light slipped through her as if she were smoke. Still, Stella saw her face, her form, the bright ringlets, the shattered eyes.

The Bride stood at the doorway that connected to the bath, then the boys' room.

But it wasn't anger Stella saw on her face. It wasn't disapproval she felt quivering on the air. It was utter and terrible grief.

Her own fear turned to pity. "I wish I could help you. I want to help." With her blouse pressed against her breasts, Stella took a tentative step forward. "I wish I knew who you were, what happened to you. Why you're so sad."

The woman turned her head, looked back with swimming eyes to the room beyond.

"They're not gone," Stella heard herself say. "I'd never let them go. They're my life. They're with my father and his wife—their grandparents. A treat for them, that's all. A night where they can be pampered and spoiled and eat too much ice cream. They'll be back tomorrow."

She took a cautious second step, even as her throat burned dry. "They love being with my father and Jolene. But it's so quiet when they're not around, isn't it?"

Good God, she was talking to a ghost. Trying to draw a ghost into conversation. How had her life become so utterly strange?

"Can't you tell me something, anything that would help? We're all trying to find out, and maybe when we do . . . Can't you tell me your name?"

Though Stella's hand trembled, she lifted it, reached out. Those shattered eyes met hers, and Stella's hand passed through. There was cold, and a kind of snapping shock. Then there was nothing at all.

"You can speak," Stella said to the empty room. "If you can sing, you can speak. Why won't you?"

Shaken, she dressed, fought her hair into a clip. Her

heart was still thudding as she did her makeup, half expecting to see that other heartbroken face in the mirror.

Then she slipped on her shoes and went downstairs. She would leave death behind, she thought, and go prepare for new life.

seventeen

THE PACE MIGHT HAVE BEEN SLOW, BUT THE HOURS were the killer. As spring turned lushly green and temperatures rose toward what Stella thought of as high summer, garden-happy customers flocked to the nursery, as much, she thought, to browse for an hour or so and chat with the staff and other customers as for the stock.

Still, every day flats of bedding plants, pots of perennials, forests of shrubs and ornamental trees strolled out the door.

She watched the field stock bagged and burlapped, and scurried to plug holes on tables by adding greenhouse stock. As mixed planters, hanging baskets, and the concrete troughs were snapped up, she created more.

She made countless calls to suppliers for more: more fertilizers, more grass seed, more root starter, more everything.

With her clipboard and careful eye she checked inventory, adjusted, and begged Roz to release some of the younger stock.

"It's not ready. Next year."

"At this rate, we're going to run out of columbine, astilbes, hostas—" She waved the board. "Roz, we've sold out a good thirty percent of our perennial stock already. We'll be lucky to get through May with our current inventory."

"And things will slow down." Roz babied cuttings from a stock dianthus. "If I start putting plants out before they're ready, the customer's not going to be happy."

"But—"

"These dianthus won't bloom till next year. Customers want bloom, Stella, you know that. They want to plug it in while it's flowering or about to. They don't want to wait until next year for the gratification."

"I do know. Still . . ."

"You're caught up." With her gloved hand, Roz scratched an itch under her nose. "So's everyone else. Lord, Ruby's beaming like she's been made a grandmother again, and Steve wants to high-five me every time I see him."

"They love this place."

"So do I. The fact is, this is the best year we've ever had. Weather's part of it. We've had a pretty spring. But we've also got ourselves an efficient and enthusiastic manager to help things along. But end of the day, quality's still the byword here. Quantity's second."

"You're right. Of course you're right. I just can't stand the thought of running out of something and having to send a customer somewhere else."

"Probably won't come to that, especially if we're smart enough to lead them toward a nice substitution."

Stella sighed. "Right again."

"And if we do need to recommend another nursery . . ."

"The customers will be pleased and impressed with our efforts to satisfy them. And this is why you're the owner of a place like this, and I'm the manager."

"It also comes down to being born and bred right here. In a few more weeks, the spring buying and planting season will be over. Anyone who comes in after mid-May's going to be looking mostly for supplies, or sidelines, maybe a basket or planter already made up, or a few plants to replace something that's died or bloomed off. And once that June heat hits, you're going to want to be putting what we've got left of spring and summer bloomers on sale before you start pushing the fall stock."

"And in Michigan, you'd be taking a big risk to put anything in before mid-May."

Roz moved to the next tray of cuttings. "You miss it?"

"I want to say yes, because it seems disloyal otherwise. But no, not really. I didn't leave anything back there except memories."

It was the memories that worried her. She'd had a good life, with a man she'd loved. When she'd lost him that life had shattered—under the surface. It had left her shaky and unstable inside. She'd kept that life together, for her children, but in her heart had been more than grief. There'd been fear.

She'd fought the fear, and embraced the memories.

But she hadn't just lost her husband. Her sons had lost their father. Gavin's memory of him was dimmer—dimmer every year—but sweet. Luke was too young to remember his father clearly. It seemed so unfair. If she moved forward in her relationship with Logan while her boys were still so young . . .

It was a little like no longer missing home, she supposed. It seemed disloyal.

As she walked into the showroom, she spotted a number of customers with wagons, browsing the tables, and Hayley hunkering down to lift a large strawberry pot already planted.

"Don't!"

Her sharp command had heads turning, but she marched right through the curious and, slapping her hands on her hips, glared at Hayley. "Just what do you think you're doing?"

"We sold the point-of-purchase planters. I thought this one here would be good out by the counter."

"I'm sure it would. Do you know how pregnant you are?"

Hayley glanced down at her basketball belly. "Kind of hard to miss."

"You want to move a planter, then you ask somebody to move it for you."

"I'm strong as an ox."

"And eight months pregnant."

"You listen to her, honey." One of the customers patted Hayley on the arm. "You don't want to take chances. Once that baby pops out, you'll never stop hauling things around. Now's the time to take advantage of your condition and let people spoil you a little bit."

"I've got to watch her like a hawk," Stella said. "That lobelia's wonderful, isn't it?"

The woman looked down at her flatbed. "I just love that deep blue color. I was thinking I'd get some of that red salvia to go beside it, maybe back it up with cosmos?"

"Sounds perfect. Charming and colorful, with a whole season of bloom."

"I've got some more room in the back of the bed, but I'm not sure what to put in." She bit her lip as she scanned the tables loaded with options. "I wouldn't mind some suggestions, if you've got the time."

"That's what we're here for. We've got some terrific mixed hollyhocks, tall enough to go behind the cosmos. And if you want to back up the salvia, I think those marigolds there would be fabulous. And have you seen the perilla?"

"I don't even know what it is," the woman said with a laugh.

Stella showed her the deep-purple foliage plant, had Hayley gather up several good marigolds. Between them, they filled another flatbed.

"I'm glad you went with the alyssum, too. See the way

the white pops the rest of your colors? Actually, the arrangement there gives you a pretty good idea what you'll have in your garden." Stella nodded toward the flatbeds. "You can just see the way those plants will complement each other."

"I can't wait to get them in. My neighbors are going to be *green* with envy."

"Just send them to us."

"Wouldn't be the first time. I've been coming here since you opened. Used to live about a mile from here, moved down toward Memphis two years ago. It's fifteen miles or more now, but I always find something special here, so I keep coming back."

"That's so nice to hear. Is there anything else Hayley or I can help you with? Do you need any starter, mulch, fertilizer?"

"Those I can handle on my own. But actually"—she smiled at Hayley—"since this cart's full, if you'd have one of those strong young boys cart that pot out to the counter—and on out to my car after—I'll take it."

"Let me arrange that for you." Stella gave Hayley a last telling look. "And you, behave yourself."

"Y'all sisters?" the woman asked Hayley.

"No. She's my boss. Why?"

"Reminded me of my sister and me, I guess. I still scold my baby sister the way she did you, especially when I'm worried about her."

"Really?" Hayley looked off toward where Stella had gone. "I guess we sort of are, then."

WHILE SHE AGREED THAT EXERCISE WAS GOOD FOR expectant mothers, Stella wasn't willing to have Hayley work all day and then walk close to half a mile home at this stage of her pregnancy. Hayley groused, but every evening Stella herded her to the car and drove her home.

"I *like* walking."

"And after we get home and you have something to eat, you can take a nice walk around the gardens. But you're not walking all that way, and through the woods alone, on my watch, kid."

"Are you going to be pestering me like this for the next four weeks?"

"I absolutely am."

"You know Mrs. Tyler? The lady who bought all those annuals we helped her with?"

"Mmm-hmm."

"She said how she thought we were sisters because you give me grief like she does her baby sister. At the time, I thought that was nice. Now, it's irritating."

"That's a shame."

"I'm taking care of myself."

"Yes, and so am I."

Hayley sighed. "If it's not you giving me the hairy eye, it's Roz. Next thing, people'll start thinking she's my mama."

Stella glanced down to see Hayley slip her feet out of her shoes. "Feet hurt?"

"They're all right."

"I've got this wonderful foot gel. Why don't you use it when we get home, and put your feet up for a few minutes?"

"I can't hardly reach them anymore. I feel . . ."

"Fat and clumsy and sluggish," Stella finished.

"And stupid and bitchy." She pushed back her damp bangs, thought about whacking them off. Thought about whacking all her hair off. "And hot and nasty."

When Stella reached over, bumped up the air-conditioning, Hayley's eyes began to sting with remorse and misery. "You're being so sweet to me—everyone is— and I don't even appreciate it. And I just feel like I've been pregnant my whole life and I'm going to stay pregnant forever."

"I can promise you won't."

"And I . . . Stella, when they showed that video at birthing class and we watched that woman go through it? I don't see how I can do that. I just don't think I can."

"I'll be there with you. You'll be just fine, Hayley. I'm not going to tell you it won't be hard, but it's going to be exciting, too. Thrilling."

She turned into the drive. And there were her boys, racing around the yard with the dog and Harper in what seemed to be a very informal game of Wiffle ball.

"And so worth it," she told her. "The minute you hold your baby in your arms, you'll know."

"I just can't imagine being a mama. Before, I could, but now that it's getting closer, I just can't."

"Of course you can't. Nobody can really imagine a miracle. You're allowed to be nervous. You're supposed to be."

"Then I'm doing a good job."

When she parked, the boys ran over. "Mom, Mom! We're playing Wiffle Olympics, and I hit the ball a *million* times."

"A million?" She widened her eyes at Luke as she climbed out. "That must be a record."

"Come on and play, Mom." Gavin grabbed her hand as Parker leaped up to paw at her legs. "Please!"

"All right, but I don't think I can hit the ball a million times."

Harper skirted the car to get to Hayley's side. His hair curled damply from under his ball cap, and his shirt showed stains from grass and dirt. "Need some help?"

She couldn't get her feet back in her shoes. They felt hot and swollen and no longer hers. Cranky tears flooded her throat. "I'm pregnant," she snapped, "not handicapped."

She left her shoes on the mat as she struggled out. Before she could stop herself, she slapped at Harper's offered hand. "Just leave me be, will you?"

"Sorry." He stuffed his hands in his pockets.

"I can't breathe with everybody hovering around me night and day." She marched toward the house, trying hard not to waddle.

"She's just tired, Harper." Whether it was hovering or not, Stella watched Hayley until she'd gotten inside. "Tired and out of sorts. It's just being pregnant."

"Maybe she shouldn't be working right now."

"If I suggested that, she'd explode. Working keeps her mind busy. We're all keeping an eye on her to make sure she doesn't overdo, which is part of the problem. She feels a little surrounded, I imagine."

"Mom!"

She held up a hand to her impatient boys. "She'd have snapped at anybody who offered her a hand just then. It wasn't personal."

"Sure. Well, I've got to go clean up." He turned back to the boys, who were already squabbling over the plastic bat. "Later. And next time I'm taking you both down."

THE AFTERNOON WAS SULTRY, A SLY HINT OF THE summer that waited just around the corner. Even with the air-conditioning, Stella sweltered in her little office. As a surrender to the weather, she wore a tank top and thin cotton pants. She'd given up on her hair and had bundled it as best she could on top of her head.

She'd just finished outlining the next week's work schedule and was about to update one of her spreadsheets when someone knocked on her door.

"Come in." Automatically, she reached for the thermos of iced coffee she'd begun to make every morning. And her heart gave a little jolt when Logan stepped in. "Hi. I thought you were on the Fields job today."

"Got rained out."

"Oh?" She swiveled around to her tiny window, saw the sheets of rain. "I didn't realize."

"All those numbers and columns can be pretty absorbing."

"To some of us."

"It's a good day to play hookey. Why don't you come out and play in the rain, Red?"

"Can't." She spread her arms to encompass her desk. "Work."

He sat on the corner of it. "Been a busy spring so far. I don't figure Roz would blink if you took a couple hours off on a rainy afternoon."

"Probably not. But I would."

"Figured that, too." He picked up an oddly shaped and obviously child-made pencil holder, examined it. "Gavin or Luke?"

"Gavin, age seven."

"You avoiding me, Stella?"

"No. A little," she admitted. "But not entirely. We've been swamped, here and at home. Hayley's only got three weeks to go, and I like to stick close."

"Do you think you could manage a couple of hours away, say, Friday night? Take in a movie?"

"Well, Friday nights I usually try to take the kids out."

"Good. The new Disney flick's playing. I can pick y'all up at six. We'll go for pizza first."

"Oh, I . . ." She sat back, frowned at him. "That was sneaky."

"Whatever works."

"Logan, have you ever been to the movies with a couple of kids on a Friday night?"

"Nope." He pushed off the desk and grinned. "Should be an experience."

He came around the desk and, cupping his hands under her elbows, lifted her straight out of the chair with a careless strength that had her mouth watering. "I've started to miss you."

He touched his mouth to hers, heating up the contact as he let her slide down his body until her feet hit the floor. Her arms lifted to link around his neck, banding there for a moment until her brain engaged again.

"It looks like I've started to miss you, too," she said as she stepped back. "I've been thinking."

"I just bet you have. You keep on doing that." He tugged at a loose lock of her hair. "See you Friday."

She sat down again when he walked out. "But I have trouble remembering what I'm thinking."

HE WAS RIGHT. IT WAS AN EXPERIENCE. ONE HE HAN-dled, in Stella's opinion, better than she'd expected. He didn't appear to have a problem with boy-speak. In fact, during the pizza interlude she got the feeling she was odd man out. Normally she could hold her own in intense discussions of comic books and baseball, but this one headed to another level.

At one point she wasn't entirely sure the X-Men's Wolverine hadn't signed on to play third base for the Atlanta Braves.

"I can eat fifty pieces of pizza," Luke announced as the pie was divvied up. "And after, five *gallons* of popcorn."

"Then you'll puke!"

She started to remind Gavin that puke wasn't proper meal conversation, but Logan just plopped a slice on his own plate. "Be smarter to puke after the pizza to make room for the popcorn."

The wisdom and hilarity of this sent the boys off into delighted gagging noises.

"Hey!" Luke's face went mutinous. "Gavin has more pepperoni on his piece. I have two and he has three!"

As Gavin snorted and set his face into the look, Logan nodded. "You know, you're right. Doesn't seem fair. Let's just fix that." He plucked a round of pepperoni off Gavin's piece and popped it into his own mouth. "Now you're even."

More hilarity ensued. The boys ate like stevedores, made an unholy mess, and were so overstimulated by the time they got to the theater, she expected them to start a riot.

"You've got to remember to be quiet during the movie," she warned. "Other people are here to see it."

"I'll try," Logan said solemnly. "But sometimes I just can't help talking."

The boys giggled all the way to the concession counter.

She knew some men who put on a show for a woman's children—to get to the woman. And, she thought as they settled into seats with tubs of popcorn, she knew some who sincerely tried to charm the kids because they were an interesting novelty.

Still, he seemed to be easy with them, and you had to give a man in his thirties points for at least appearing to enjoy a movie with talking monkeys.

Halfway through, as she'd expected, Luke began to squirm in his seat. Two cups of pop, she calculated, one small bladder. He wouldn't want to go, wouldn't want to miss anything. So there'd be a short, whispered argument.

She leaned toward him, prepared for it. And Logan beat her to it. She didn't hear what he said in Luke's ear, but Luke giggled, and the two of them rose.

"Be right back," he murmured to Stella and walked out with his hand over Luke's.

Okay, that was it, she decided as her eyes misted. The man was taking her little boy to pee.

She was a goner.

TWO VERY HAPPY BOYS PILED INTO THE BACK OF Logan's car. As soon as they were strapped in, they were bouncing and chattering about their favorite parts of the movie.

"Hey, guys." Logan slipped behind the wheel, then draped his arm over the seat to look in the back. "You might want to brace yourselves, 'cause I'm gonna kiss your mama."

"How come?" Luke wanted to know.

"Because, as you might have observed yourselves, she's pretty, and she tastes good."

He leaned over, amusement in his eyes. When Stella would have offered him a cheek, he turned her face with one hand and gave her a soft, quick kiss on the mouth.

"You're not pretty." Luke snorted through his nose. "How come she kissed you?"

"Son, that's because I'm one fine-looking hunk of man." He winked into the rearview mirror, noted that Gavin was watching him with quiet speculation, then started the engine.

LUKE WAS NODDING OFF WHEN THEY GOT TO THE house, his head bobbing as he struggled to stay awake.

"Let me cart him up."

"I can get him." Stella leaned in to unbuckle his seat belt. "I'm used to it. And I don't know if you should go upstairs again."

"She'll have to get used to me." He nudged Stella aside and hoisted Luke into his arms. "Come on, pizza king, let's go for a ride."

"I'm not tired."

"'Course not."

Yawning, he laid his head on Logan's shoulder. "You smell different from Mom. And you got harder skin."

"How about that?"

Roz wandered into the foyer as they came in. "Well, it looks like everyone had a good time. Logan, why don't you come down for a drink once you settle those boys down. I'd like to talk to the both of you."

"Sure. We'll be right down."

"I can take them," Stella began, but he was already carrying Luke up the stairs.

"I'll just get us some wine. 'Night, cutie," Roz said to Gavin, and smiled at Stella's back as she followed Logan.

He was already untying Luke's Nikes. "Logan, I'll do that. You go on down with Roz."

He continued to remove the shoes, wondering if the nerves he heard in her voice had to do with the ghost or with him. But it was the boy standing beside her, unusually silent, who had his attention.

"Go ahead and settle him in, then. Gavin and I want to have a little conversation. Don't we, kid?"

Gavin jerked a shoulder. "Maybe. I guess."

"He needs to get ready for bed."

"Won't take long. Why don't you step into my office?" he said to Gavin, and when he gestured toward the bathroom, he saw the boy's lip twitch.

"Logan," Stella began.

"Man talk. Excuse us." And he closed the door in her face.

Figuring it would be easier on them both if they were more eye-to-eye, Logan sat on the edge of the tub. He wasn't sure, but he had to figure the boy was about as nervous as he was himself.

"Did me kissing your mama bother you?"

"I don't know. Maybe. I saw this other guy kiss her once, when I was little. She went out to dinner with him or something, and we had a babysitter, and I woke up and saw him do it. But I didn't like him so much because he smiled *all* the time." He demonstrated, spreading his lips and showing his teeth.

"I don't like him either."

"Do you kiss all the girls because they're pretty?" Gavin blurted out.

"Well, now, I've kissed my share of girls. But your mama's special."

"How come?"

The boy wanted straight answers, Logan decided. So he'd do his best to give them. "Because she makes my heart feel funny, in a good kind of way, I guess. Girls make us feel funny in lots of ways, but when they make your heart feel funny, they're special."

Gavin looked toward the closed door and back again. "My dad kissed her. I remember."

"It's good you do." He had an urge, one that surprised him, to stroke a hand over Gavin's hair. But he didn't think it was the right time, for either of them.

There was more than one ghost in this house, he knew.

"I expect he loved her a lot, and she loved him. She told me how she did."

"He can't come back. I thought maybe he would, even though she said he couldn't. I thought when the lady started coming, he could come, too. But he hasn't."

Could there be anything harder for a child to face, he wondered, than losing a parent? Here he was, a grown man, and he couldn't imagine the grief of losing one of his.

"Doesn't mean he isn't watching over you. I believe stuff like that. When people who love us have to go away, they still look out for us. Your dad's always going to look out for you."

"Then he'd see you kiss Mom, because he'd watch over her, too."

"I expect so." Logan nodded. "I like to think he doesn't mind, because he'd know I want her to be happy. Maybe when we get to know each other some better, you won't mind too much either."

"Do you make Mom's heart feel funny?"

"I sure hope so, because I'd hate to feel like this all by myself. I don't know if I'm saying this right. I never had to say it before, or think about it. But if we decide to be happy together, all of us, your dad's still your dad, Gavin. Always. I want you to understand I know that, and respect that. Man-to-man."

"Okay." He smiled slowly when Logan offered a hand. When he shook it, the smile became a grin. "Anyway, I like you better than the other guy."

"Good to know."

Luke was tucked in and sleeping when they came back in. Logan merely lifted his eyebrows at Stella's questioning look, then stepped back as she readied Gavin for bed.

Deliberately he took her hand as they stepped into the hall. "Ask him if you want to know," he said before she could speak. "It's his business."

"I just don't want him upset."

"He seem upset to you when you tucked him in?"

"No." She sighed. "No."

At the top of the stairs, the cold blew through them. Protectively, Logan's arm came around her waist, pulling her firmly to his side. It passed by, with a little lash, like a flicked whip.

Seconds later, they heard the soft singing.

"She's angry with us," Stella whispered when he turned, prepared to stride back. "But not with them. She won't hurt them. Let's leave her be. I've got a baby monitor downstairs, so I can hear them if they need me."

"How do you sleep up here?"

"Well, strangely enough. First it was because I didn't believe it. Now it's knowing that in some strange way, she loves them. The night they stayed at my parents', she came into my room and cried. It broke my heart."

"Ghost talk?" Roz asked. "That's just what I had in mind." She offered them wine she'd already poured. Then pursed her lips when Stella switched on the monitor. "Strange to hear that again. It's been years since I have."

"I gotta admit," Logan said with his eyes on the monitor, "creeps me out some. More than some, to tell the truth."

"You get used to it. More or less. Where's Hayley?" she asked Roz.

"She was feeling tired—and a little blue, a little cross, I think. She's settled in upstairs with a book and a big tall glass of decaffeinated Coke. I've already talked to her about this, so . . ." She gestured to seats. On the coffee table was a tray of green grapes, thin crackers, and a half round of Brie.

She sat herself, plucked a grape. "I've decided to do something a little more active about our permanent houseguest."

"An exorcism?" Logan asked, sending a sideways glance toward the monitor and the soft voice singing out of it.

"Not quite that active. We want to find out about her history and her connection to this house. Seems to me we're not making any real progress, mostly because we can't really figure out a direction."

"We haven't been able to spend a lot of time on it," Stella pointed out.

"Another reason for outside help. We're busy, and we're amateurs. So why not go to somebody who knows what to do and has the time to do it right?"

"Concert's over for the night." Logan gestured when the monitor went silent.

"Sometimes she comes back two or three times." Stella offered him a cracker. "Do you know somebody, Roz? Someone you want to take this on?"

"I don't know yet. But I've made some inquiries, using the idea that I want to do a formal sort of genealogy search on my ancestry. There's a man in Memphis whose name's come up. Mitchell Carnegie. Dr. Mitchell Carnegie," she added. "He taught at the university in Charlotte, moved here a couple of years ago. I believe he taught at the University of Memphis for a semester or two and may still give the occasional lecture. Primarily, he writes books. Biographies and so on. He's touted as an expert family historian."

"Sounds like he might be our man." Stella spread a little Brie on a cracker for herself. "Having someone who knows what he's doing should be better than us fumbling around."

"That would depend," Logan put in, "on how he feels about ghosts."

"I'm going to make an appointment to see him." Stella lifted her wineglass. "Then I guess we'll find out."

eighteen

THOUGH HE FELT LIKE HE WAS TAKING HIS LIFE IN his hands, Harper followed instructions and tracked Hayley down at the checkout counter. She was perched on a stool, a garden of container pots and flats around her, ringing out the last customers. Her shirt—smock? tunic? he didn't know what the hell you called maternity-type clothes—was a bright, bold red.

Funny, it was the color that brought her to mind for him. Vivid, sexy red. Those spiky bangs made her eyes seem enormous, and there were big silver hoops in her ears that peeked and swung through her hair when she moved.

With the high counter blocking the target area, you could hardly tell she was pregnant. Except her eyes looked tired, he thought. And her face was a little puffy—maybe weight gain, maybe lack of sleep. Either way, he didn't figure it was the sort of thing he should mention. The fact was, everything and anything that came out of his mouth these days, at least when he was around her, was the wrong thing.

He didn't expect their next encounter to go well either.

But he'd promised to throw himself on the sword for the cause.

He waited until she'd finished with the customers and, girding his loins, he approached the counter.

"Hey."

She looked at him, and he couldn't say her expression was particularly welcoming. "Hey. What're you doing out of your cave?"

"Finished up for the day. Actually my mother just called. She asked if I'd drive you on home when I finished."

"Well, *I'm* not finished," she said testily. "There are at least two more customers wandering around, and Saturday's my night to close out."

It wasn't the tone she'd used to chat up the customers, he noted. He was beginning to think it was the tone she reserved just for him. "Yeah, but she said she needed you at home for something as soon as you could, and to have Bill and Larry finish up and close out."

"What does she want? Why didn't she call me?"

"I don't know. I'm just the messenger." And he knew what often happened to the messenger. "I told Larry, and he's helping the last couple of stragglers. So he's on it."

She started to lever herself off the stool, and though his hands itched to help her, he imagined she'd chomp them off at the wrists. "I can walk."

"Come on. Jesus." He jammed his hands in his pockets and gave her scowl for scowl. "Why do you want to put me on the spot like that? If I let you walk, my mama's going to come down on me like five tons of bricks. And after she's done flattening me, she'll ream you. Let's just go."

"Fine." The truth was, she didn't know why she was feeling so mean and spiteful, and tired and achy. She was terrified something was wrong with her or with the baby, despite all the doctor's assurances to the contrary.

The baby would be born sick or deformed, because she'd . . .

She didn't know what, but it would be her fault.

She snatched her purse and did her best to sail by Harper and out the door.

"I've got another half hour on the clock," she complained and wrenched open the door of his car. "I don't know what she could want that couldn't wait a half hour."

"I don't know either."

"She hasn't seen that genealogy guy yet."

He got in, started the car. "Nope. She'll get to it when she gets to it."

"You don't seem all that interested, anyway. How come you don't come around when we have our meetings about the Harper Bride?"

"I guess I will, when I can think of something to say about it."

She smelled vivid, too, especially closed up in the car with him like this. Vivid and sexy, and it made him edgy. The best that could be said about the situation was the drive was short.

Amazed he wasn't sweating bullets, he swung in and zipped in front of the house.

"You drive a snooty little car like this that fast, you're just begging for a ticket."

"It's not a snooty little car. It's a well-built and reliable sports car. And I wasn't driving that fast. What the hell is it about me that makes you crawl up my ass?"

"I wasn't crawling up your ass; I was making an observation. At least you didn't go for red." She opened the door, managed to get her legs out. "Most guys go for the red, the flashy. The black's probably why you don't have speeding tickets spilling out of your glove compartment."

"I haven't had a speeding ticket in two years."

She snorted.

"Okay, eighteen months, but—"

"Would you stop arguing for five damn seconds and come over here and help me out of this damn car? I can't get up."

Like a runner off the starting line, he sprinted around

the car. He wasn't sure how to manage it, especially when she was sitting there, red in the face and flashing in the eyes. He started to take her hands and tug, but he thought he might . . . jar something.

So he leaned down, hooked his hands under her armpits, and lifted.

Her belly bumped him, and now sweat did slide down his back.

He felt what was in there move—a couple of hard bumps.

It was . . . extraordinary.

Then she was brushing him aside. "Thanks."

Mortifying, she thought. She just hadn't been able to shift her center of gravity, or dig down enough to get out of a stupid car. Of course, if he hadn't insisted she get in that boy toy in the first place, she wouldn't have been mortified.

She wanted to eat a pint of vanilla fudge ice cream and sit in a cool bath. For the rest of her natural life.

She shoved open the front door, stomped inside.

The shouts of *Surprise!* had her heart jumping into her throat, and she nearly lost control of her increasingly tricky bladder.

In the parlor pink and blue crepe paper curled in artful swags from the ceiling, and fat white balloons danced in the corners. Boxes wrapped in pretty paper and streaming with bows formed a colorful mountain on a high table. The room was full of women. Stella and Roz, all the girls who worked at the nursery, even some of the regular customers.

"Don't look stricken, girl." Roz strolled over to wrap an arm around Hayley's shoulders. "You don't think we'd let you have that baby without throwing you a shower, do you?"

"A baby shower." She could feel the smile blooming on her face, even as tears welled up in her eyes.

"You come on and sit down. You're allowed one glass of David's magical champagne punch before you go to the straight stuff."

"This is . . ." She saw the chair set in the center of the

room, festooned with voile and balloons, like a party throne. "I don't know what to say."

"Then I'm sitting beside you. I'm Jolene, darling, Stella's stepmama." She patted Hayley's hand, then her belly. "And I never run out of things to say."

"Here you go." Stella stepped over with a glass of punch.

"Thanks. Thank you so much. This is the nicest thing anyone's ever done for me. In my whole life."

"You have a good little cry." Jolene handed her a lace-edged hankie. "Then we're going to have us a hell of a time."

They did. Ooohing and awwing over impossibly tiny clothes, soft-as-cloud blankets, hand-knit booties, cooing over rattles and toys and stuffed animals. There were fool-ish games that only women at a baby shower could enjoy, and plenty of punch and cake to sweeten the evening.

The knot that had been at the center of Hayley's heart for days loosened.

"This was the best time I ever had." Hayley sat, giddy and exhausted, and stared at the piles of gifts Stella had neatly arranged on the table again. "I know it was all about me. I liked that part, but everyone had fun, don't you think?"

"Are you kidding?" From her seat on the floor, Stella continued to meticulously fold discarded wrapping paper into neat, flat squares. "This party rocked."

"Are you going to save all that paper?" Roz asked her.

"She'll want it one day, and I'm just saving what she didn't rip to shreds."

"I couldn't help it. I was so juiced up. I've got to get thank-you cards, and try to remember who gave what."

"I made a list while you were tearing in."

"Of course she did." Roz helped herself to one more glass of punch, then sat and stretched out her legs. "God. I'm whipped."

"Y'all worked so hard. It was all so awesome." Feeling

herself tearing up again, Hayley waved both hands. "Everyone was—I guess I forgot people could be so good, so generous. Man, look at all those wonderful things. Oh, that little yellow gown with the teddy bears on it! The matching hat. And the baby swing. Stella, I just can't thank you enough for the swing."

"I'd have been lost without mine."

"It was so sweet of you, both of you, to do this for me. I just had no idea. I couldn't've been more surprised, or more grateful."

"You can guess who planned it out," Roz said with a nod at Stella. "David started calling her General Rothchild."

"I have to thank him for all the wonderful food. I can't believe I ate two pieces of cake. I feel like I'm ready to explode."

"Don't explode yet, because we're not quite done. We need to go up, so you can have my gift."

"But the party was—"

"A joint effort," Roz finished. "But there's a gift I hope you'll like upstairs."

"I snapped at Harper," Hayley began as they helped her up and started upstairs.

"He's been snapped at before."

"But I wish I hadn't. He was helping you surprise me, and I gave him a terrible time. He said I was always crawling up his ass, and that's just what I was doing."

"You'll tell him you're sorry." Roz turned them toward the west wing, moved passed Stella's room, and Hayley's. "Here you are, honey."

She opened the door and led Hayley inside.

"Oh, God. Oh, my God." Hayley pressed both hands to her mouth as she stared at the room.

It was painted a soft, quiet yellow, with lace curtains at the windows.

She knew the crib was antique. Nothing was that beautiful, that rich unless it was old and treasured. The wood gleamed, deep with red highlights. She recognized the layette as one she'd dreamed over in a magazine and had known she could never afford.

"The furniture's a loan while you're here. I used it for my children, as my mama did for hers, and hers before her, back more than eighty-five years now. But the linens are yours, and the changing table. Stella added the rug and the lamp. And David and Harper, bless their hearts, painted the room, and hauled the furniture down from the attic."

As emotions swamped her, Hayley could only shake her head.

"Once we bring your gifts up here, you'll have yourself a lovely nursery." Stella rubbed Hayley's back.

"It's so beautiful. More than I ever dreamed of. I—I've been missing my father so much. The closer the baby gets, the more I've been missing him. It's this ache inside. And I've been feeling sad and scared, and mostly just sorry for myself."

She used her hands to rub the tears from her cheeks. "Now today, all this, it just makes me feel . . . It's not the things. I love them, I love everything. But it's that you'd do this, both of you would do this for us."

"You're not alone, Hayley." Roz laid a hand on Hayley's belly. "Neither one of you."

"I know that. I think, well, I think, we'd have been okay on our own. I'd've worked hard to make sure of it. But I never expected to have real family again. I never expected to have people care about me and the baby like this. I've been stupid."

"No," Stella told her. "Just pregnant."

With a half laugh, Hayley blinked back the rest of the tears. "I guess that accounts for a lot of it. I won't be able to use that excuse too much longer. And I'll never, I'll just never be able to thank you, or tell you, or repay you. Never."

"Oh, I think naming the baby after us will clear the decks," Roz said casually. "Especially if it's a boy. Rosalind Stella might be a little hard for him to handle in school, but it's only right."

"Hey, I was thinking Stella Rosalind."

Roz arched a brow at Stella. "This is one of those rare cases when it pays to be the oldest."

THAT NIGHT, HAYLEY TIPTOED INTO THE NURSERY. Just to touch, to smell, to sit in the rocking chair with her hands stroking her belly.

"I'm sorry I've been so nasty lately. I'm better now. We're going to be all right now. You've got two fairy godmothers, baby. The best women I've ever known. I may not be able to pay them back for all they've done for us, not in some ways. But I swear, there's nothing either of them could ask that I wouldn't do. I feel safe here. It was stupid of me to forget that. We're a team, you and me. I shouldn't've been afraid of you. Or for you."

She closed her eyes and rocked. "I want to hold you in my arms so much they hurt. I want to dress you in one of those cute little outfits and hold you, and smell you, and rock you in this chair. Oh, God, I hope I know what I'm doing."

The air turned cold, raising gooseflesh on her arms. But it wasn't fear that had her opening her eyes; it was pity. She stared at the woman who stood beside the crib.

Her hair was down tonight, golden blond and wildly tangled. She wore a white nightgown, muddy at the hem. And there was a look of—Hayley would have said madness—in her eyes.

"You didn't have anyone to help you, did you?" Her hands trembled a bit, but she kept stroking her belly, kept her eyes on the figure, kept talking.

"Maybe you didn't have anyone to be there with you when you were afraid like I've been. I guess I might've gone crazy, too, all on my own. And I don't know what I'd do if anything happened to my baby. Or how I'd stand it, if something happened to take me away from him—her. Even if I were dead I couldn't stand it. So I guess I understand, a little."

At her words, Hayley heard a keening sound, a sound that made her think of a soul, or a mind, shattering.

Then she was alone.

ON MONDAY, HAYLEY SAT PERCHED ON HER STOOL once more. When her back ached, she ignored it. When she had to call for a relief clerk so she could waddle to the bathroom, again, she made a joke out of it.

Her bladder felt squeezed down to the size of a pea.

On the way back, she detoured outside, not only to stretch her legs and back but to see Stella.

"Is it okay if I take my break now? I want to hunt down Harper and apologize." She'd spent all morning dreading the moment, but she couldn't put it off any longer. "He wasn't anywhere to be found on Sunday, but he's probably back in his cave now."

"Go ahead. Oh, I just ran into Roz. She called that professor. Dr. Carnegie? She has an appointment to see him later this week. Maybe we'll make some progress in that area."

Then she narrowed her eyes on Hayley's face. "I tell you what, one of us is going with you to your doctor's appointment tomorrow. I don't want you driving anymore."

"I still fit behind the wheel." Barely.

"That may be, but either Roz or I will take you. And I'm thinking it's time you go part-time."

"You might as well put me in the loony bin as take work away from me now. Come on, Stella, a lot of women work right up to the end. Besides, I'm sitting on my butt most all day. Best thing about finding Harper is walking."

"Walk," Stella agreed. "Don't lift. Anything."

"Nag, nag, nag." But she said it with a laugh as she started toward the grafting house.

Outside the greenhouse she paused. She'd practiced

what she wanted to say. She thought it best to think it all through. He'd accept her apology. His mama had raised him right, and from what she'd seen he had a good heart. But she wanted, very much, for him to understand she'd just been in some sort of mood.

She opened the door. She loved the smell in here. Experimentation, possibilities. One day, she hoped either Harper or Roz would teach her something about this end of the growing.

She could see him down at the end, huddled over his work. He had his headphones on and was tapping one foot to whatever beat played in his ears.

God, he was so cute. If she'd met him in the bookstore, before her life had changed, she'd have hit on him, or worked it around so he'd hit on her. All that dark, messed-up hair, the clean line of jaw, the dreamy eyes. And those artistic hands.

She'd bet he had half a dozen girls dangling on a string, and another half dozen waiting in line for a chance.

She started down toward him and was surprised enough to pull up short when his head snapped up, and he swung around to her.

"Christ on a crutch, Harper! I thought I was going to startle you."

"What? What?" His eyes were dazzled as he dragged off his headset. "What?"

"I didn't think you could hear me."

"I—" He hadn't. He'd smelled her. "Do you need something?"

"I guess I do. I need to say I'm sorry for jumping down your throat every time you opened your mouth the last couple of weeks. I've been an awful bitch."

"No. Well, yeah. It's okay."

She laughed and edged closer to try to see what he was doing. It just looked like he had a bunch of stems tied together. "I guess I had the jumps. What am I going to do, how am I going to do it? Why do I have to feel so fat and ugly all the time?"

"You're not fat. You could never be ugly."

"That's awful nice of you. But being pregnant doesn't affect my eyesight, and I know what I see in the mirror every damn day."

"Then you know you're beautiful."

Her eyes sparkled when she smiled. "I must've been a pitiful case if you're obliged to flirt with a pregnant woman who's got a bad disposition."

"I'm not—I wouldn't." He wanted to, at the very least. "Anyway, I guess you're feeling better."

"So much better. Mostly I was feeling sorry for myself, and I just hate that poor-me crap. Imagine your mama and Stella throwing me a baby shower. I cried all over myself. Got Stella going, too. But then we had the best time. Who knew a baby shower could rock?" She pressed both hands to her belly and laughed. "You ever met Stella's stepmama?"

"No."

"She's just a hoot and a half. I laughed till I thought I'd shoot the baby right out then and there. And Mrs. Haggerty—"

"Mrs. Haggerty? Our Mrs. Haggerty was there?"

"Not only, but she won the song title game. You have to write down the most song titles with 'baby' in it. You'll never guess one she wrote down."

"Okay. I give."

" 'Baby Got Back.' "

Now he grinned. "Get out. Mrs. Haggerty wrote down a rap song?"

"Then rapped it."

"Now you're lying."

"She *did*. Or at least a couple lines. I nearly peed my pants. But I'm forgetting why I'm here. There you were, just trying to help with the best surprise I ever had, and I was bitching and whining. Crawling up your ass, just like you said. I'm really sorry."

"It's no big. I have a friend whose wife had a baby a few

months ago. I swear you could see fangs growing out of her mouth toward the end. And I think her eyes turned red a couple times."

She laughed again, pressed a hand to her side. "I hope I don't get that bad before . . ."

She broke off, a puzzled expression covering her face as she felt a little snap inside. Heard it, she realized. Like a soft, echoing ping.

Then water pooled down between her legs.

Harper made a sound of his own, like that of a man whose words were strangled off somewhere in his throat. He sprang to his feet, babbling as Hayley stared down at the floor.

"Uh-oh," she said.

"Um, that's okay, that's all right. Maybe I should . . . maybe you should . . ."

"Oh, for heaven's sake, Harper, I didn't just pee on the floor. My water broke."

"What water?" He blinked, then went pale as a corpse. "*That* water. Oh, God. Oh, Jesus. Oh, shit. Sit. Sit, or . . . I'll get—"

An ambulance, the marines.

"My mother."

"I think I'd better go with you. We're a little early." She forced a smile so she wouldn't scream. "Just a couple of weeks. I guess the baby's impatient to get out and see what all the fuss is about. Give me a hand, okay? Oh, Jesus, Harper, I'm scared to death."

"It's fine." His arm came around her. "Just lean on me. You hurting anywhere?"

"No. Not yet."

Inside he was still pale, and half sick. But his arm stayed steady around her, and when he turned his head, his smile was easy. "Hey." Very gently, he touched her belly. "Happy birthday, baby."

"Oh, my God." Her face simply illuminated as they stepped outside. "This is *awesome*."

* * *

SHE COULDN'T ACTUALLY HAVE THE BABY, BUT STELLA
figured she could do nearly everything else—or delegate it
done. Hayley hadn't put a hospital bag together, but Stella
had a list. A call to David got that ball rolling even as she
drove Hayley to the hospital. She called the doctor to let
him know the status of Hayley's labor, left a voice mail on
her father's cell phone, and a message on his home answer-
ing machine to arrange for her own children, and coached
Hayley through her breathing as the first contractions
began.

"If I ever get married, or buy a house, or start a war, I
hope you'll be in charge of the details."

Stella glanced over as Hayley rubbed her belly. "I'm
your girl. Doing okay?"

"Yeah. I'm nervous and excited and . . . Oh, wow, I'm
having a baby!"

"You're going to have a fabulous baby."

"The books say things can get pretty tricky during tran-
sition, so if I yell at you or call you names—"

"Been there. I won't take it personally."

By the time Roz arrived, Hayley was ensconced in a
birthing room. The television was on—an old *Friends*
episode. Beneath it on the counter was an arrangement of
white roses. Stella's doing, she had no doubt.

"How's Mama doing?"

"They said I'm moving fast." Flushed and bright-eyed,
Hayley reached out a hand for Roz's. "And everything's
just fine. The contractions are coming closer together, but
they don't hurt all that much."

"She doesn't want the epidural," Stella told her.

"Ah." Roz gave Hayley's hand a pat. "That'll be up to
you. You can change your mind if it gets to be too much."

"Maybe it's silly, and maybe I'll be sorry, but I want to
feel it. Wow! I feel that."

Stella moved in, helped her breathe through it. Hayley

sighed out the last breath, closed her eyes just as David strode in.

"This here the party room?" He set down an overnight case, a tote bag, and a vase of yellow daisies before he leaned over the bed to kiss Hayley's cheek. "You're not going to kick me out 'cause I'm a man, are you?"

"You want to stay?" Delighted color bloomed on Hayley's cheeks. "Really?"

"Are you kidding?" From his pocket he pulled a little digital camera. "I nominate myself official photographer."

"Oh." Biting her lip, Hayley rubbed a hand over her belly. "I don't know as pictures are such a good idea."

"Don't you worry, sugar, I won't take anything that's not G-rated. Give me a big smile."

He took a couple of shots, directed Roz and Stella to stand beside the bed and took a couple more. "By the way, Stella, Logan's taking the boys back to his place after school."

"What?"

"Your parents are at some golf tournament. They were going to come back, but I told them not to worry, I'd take care of the kids. Then apparently Logan came by the nursery, ran into Harper—he's coming by shortly."

"Logan?" Hayley asked. "He's coming here?"

"No, Harper. Logan's taking kid duty. He said he'd take them over to his place, put them to work, and not to worry. We're supposed to keep him updated on baby progress."

"I don't know if—" But Stella broke off as another contraction started.

Her job as labor coach kept her busy, but part of her mind niggled on the idea of Logan riding herd on her boys. What did he mean, 'put them to work'? How would he know what to do if they got into a fight—which, of course, they would at some point. How could he watch them properly if he took them to a job site? They could fall into a ditch, or out of a tree, or cut off an appendage, for God's sake, with some sharp tool.

When the doctor came in to check Hayley's progress, she dashed out to call Logan's cell phone.

"Kitridge."

"It's Stella. My boys—"

"Yeah, they're fine. Got them right here. Hey, Gavin, don't chase your brother with that chain saw." At Stella's horrified squeak, Logan's laughter rolled over the phone. "Just kidding. I've got them digging a hole, and they're happy as pigs in mud and twice as dirty. We got a baby yet?"

"No, they're checking her now. Last check she was at eight centimeters dilated and seventy percent effaced."

"I have no idea what that means, but I'll assume it's a good thing."

"It's very good. She's breezing through it. You'd think she had a baby once a week. Are you sure the kids are all right?"

"Listen."

She assumed he'd held out the phone as she heard giggles and her boys' voices raised in excited argument over just what they could bury in the hole. An elephant. A brontosaurus. Fat Mr. Kelso from the grocery store.

"They shouldn't call Mr. Kelso fat."

"We have no time for women here. Call me when we've got a baby."

He hung up, leaving her scowling at the phone. Then she turned and nearly rammed into Harper. Or into the forest of red lilies he balanced in both hands.

"Harper? Are you in there?"

"She okay? What's going on? Am I too late?"

"She's fine. The doctor's just checking on her. And you're in plenty of time."

"Okay. I thought lilies because they're exotic, and she likes red. I think she likes red."

"They're extremely gorgeous. Let me guide you in."

"Maybe I shouldn't. Maybe you should just take them."

"Don't be silly. We've got a regular party going on. She's a sociable girl, and having people with her is taking her mind off the pain. When I left, David had the Red Hot Chili Peppers on a CD player and a bottle of champagne icing down in the bathroom sink.

She steered him in. It was still the Red Hot Chili Peppers, and David turned his camera to the door to snap a picture of Harper peering nervously through a wonder of red lilies.

"Oh! Oh! Those are the most beautiful things I've ever seen!" A little pale, but beaming, Hayley struggled to sit up in bed.

"They'll make a great focal point, too." Stella helped Harper set them on a table. "You can focus on them during contractions."

"The doctor says I'm nearly there. I can start pushing soon."

He stepped up to the bedside. "You okay?"

"A little tired. It's a lot of work, but not as bad as I thought." Abruptly, her hand clamped down on his. "Oh-oh. Stella."

Roz stood at the foot of the bed. She looked at her son's hand holding Hayley's, looked at his face. She felt something inside her tighten, release painfully. Then she sighed and began to rub Hayley's feet as Stella murmured instructions and encouragement.

The pain increased. Stella watched the arc of contractions on the monitor and felt her own belly tighten in sympathy. The girl was made of iron, she thought. She was pale now, and her skin sheathed in sweat. There were times when Hayley gripped Stella's hand so hard she was surprised her fingers didn't snap. But Hayley stayed focused and rode the contractions out.

An hour passed into another, with the contractions coming fast, coming hard, with Hayley chugging through the breathing like a train. Stella offered ice chips and cool cloths while Roz gave the laboring mother a shoulder massage.

"Harper!" General Rothchild snapped out orders. "Rub her belly."

He goggled at her as if she'd asked him to personally deliver the baby. "Do what?"

"Gently, in circles. It helps. David, the music—"

"No, I like the music." Hayley reached for Stella's hand as she felt the next coming on. "Turn it up, David, in case I start screaming. Oh, oh, *fuck!* I want to push. I want to push it the hell out, *now!*"

"Not yet. Not yet. Focus, Hayley, you're doing great. Roz, maybe we need the doctor."

"Already on it," she said on her way out the door.

When it was time to push, and the doctor sat between Hayley's legs, Stella noted that both men went a little green. She gave Hayley one end of a towel, and took the other, to help her bear down while she counted to ten.

"Harper! You get behind her, support her back."

"I . . ." He was already edging for the door, but his mother blocked him.

"You don't want to be somewhere else when a miracle happens." She gave him a nudge forward.

"You're doing great," Stella told her. "You're amazing." She nodded when the doctor called for Hayley to push again. "Ready now. Deep breath. Hold it, and push!"

"God almighty." Even with the babble of voices, David's swallow was audible. "I've never seen the like. I've gotta call my mama. Hell, I gotta send her a truckload of flowers."

"Jesus!" Harper sucked in a breath along with Hayley. "There's a head."

Hayley began to laugh, with tears streaming down her face. "Look at all that hair! Oh, God, oh, Lord, can't we get him the rest of the way out?"

"Shoulders next, honey, then that's it. Another good push, okay? Listen! He's already crying. Hayley, that's your baby crying." And Stella was crying herself as with a last desperate push, life rushed into the room.

"It's a girl," Roz said softly as she wiped the dampness from her own cheeks. "You've got a daughter, Hayley. And she's beautiful."

"A girl. A little girl." Hayley's arms were already reaching. When they laid her on her belly so Roz could cut the cord, she kept laughing even as she stroked the baby from head to foot. "Oh, just *look* at you. Look at you. No, don't take her."

"They're just going to clean her up. Two seconds." Stella bent down to kiss the top of Hayley's head. "Congratulations, Mom."

"Listen to her." Hayley reached back, gripped Stella's hand, then Harper's. "She even sounds beautiful."

"Six pounds, eight ounces," the nurse announced and carried the wrapped bundle to the bed. "Eighteen inches. And a full ten on the Apgar."

"Hear that?" Hayley cradled the baby in her arms, kissed her forehead, her cheeks, her tiny mouth. "You aced your first test. She's looking at me! Hi. Hi, I'm your mama. I'm so glad to see you."

"Smile!" David snapped another picture. "What name did you decide on?"

"I picked a new one when I was pushing. She's Lily, because I could see the lilies, and I could smell them when she was being born. So she's Lily Rose Star. Rose for Rosalind, Star for Stella."

NINETEEN

EXHAUSTED AND EXHILARATED, STELLA STEPPED INTO the house. Though it was past their bedtime, she expected her boys to come running, but had to make do with an ecstatic Parker. She picked him up, kissed his nose as he tried to bathe her face.

"Guess what, my furry little pal? We had a baby today. Our first girl."

She shoved at her hair, and immediately got the guilts. Roz had left the hospital before she had, and was probably upstairs dealing with the kids.

She started toward the steps when Logan strolled into the foyer. "Big day."

"The biggest," she agreed. She hadn't considered he'd be there, and was suddenly and acutely aware that her duties as labor coach had sweated off all of her makeup. In addition, she couldn't imagine she was smelling her freshest.

"I can't thank you enough for taking on the boys."

"No problem. I got a couple of good holes out of them. You may need to burn their clothes."

"They've got more. Is Roz up with them?"

"No. She's in the kitchen. David's back there whipping something together, and I heard a rumor about champagne."

"More champagne? We practically swam in it at the hospital. I'd better go up and settle down the troops."

"They're out for the count. Have been since just before nine. Digging holes wears a man out."

"Oh. I know you said you'd bring them back when I called to tell you about the baby, but I didn't expect you to put them to bed."

"They were tuckered. We had ourselves a manly shower, then they crawled into bed and were out in under five seconds."

"Well. I owe you big."

"Pay up."

He crossed to her, slid his arms around her and kissed her until her already spinning head lifted off her shoulders.

"Tired?" he asked.

"Yeah. But in the best possible way."

He danced his fingers over her hair, and kept his other arm around her. "How's the new kid on the block and her mama?"

"They're great. Hayley's a wonder. Steady as a rock through seven hours of labor. And the baby might be a couple weeks early, but she came through like a champ. Only a few ounces shy of Gavin's birth weight, though it took me twice as long to convince him to come out."

"Make you want to have another?"

She went a few shades more pale. "Oh. Well."

"Now I've scared you." Amused, he slung an arm around her shoulder. "Let's go see what's on the menu with that champagne."

HE HADN'T SCARED HER, EXACTLY. BUT HE HAD MADE her vaguely uneasy. She was just getting used to having a relationship, and the man was making subtle hints about babies.

Of course, it could have been just a natural, offhand remark under the circumstances. Or a kind of joke.

Whatever the intent, it got her thinking. Did she want more children? She'd crossed that possibility off her list when Kevin died and had ruthlessly shut down her biological clock. Certainly she was capable, physically, of having another child. But it took more than physical capability, or should, to bring a child into the world.

She had two healthy, active children. And was solely and wholly responsible for them—emotionally, financially, morally. To consider having another meant considering a permanent relationship with a man. Marriage, a future, sharing not only what she had but building more, and in a different direction.

She'd come to Tennessee to visit her own roots, and to plant her family in the soil of her own origins. To be near her father, and to allow her children the pleasure of being close to grandparents who wanted to know them.

Her mother had never been particularly interested, hadn't enjoyed seeing herself as a grandmother. It spoiled the youthful image, Stella thought.

If a man like Logan had blipped onto her mother's radar, he'd have been snapped right up.

And if that's why Stella was hesitating, it was a sad state of affairs. Undoubtedly part of it, though, she decided. Otherwise she wouldn't be thinking it.

She hadn't disliked any of her stepfathers. But she hadn't bonded with them either, or they with her. How old had she been the first time her mother had remarried? Gavin's age, she remembered. Yes, right around eight.

She'd been plucked out of her school and plunked down in a new one, a new house, new neighborhood, and dazed by it all while her mother had been in the adrenaline rush of having a new husband.

That one had lasted, what? Three years, four? Somewhere between, she decided, with another year or so of upheaval while her mother dealt with the battle and debris of divorce, another new place, a new job, a new start.

And another new school for Stella.

After that, her mother had stuck with *boyfriends* for a long stretch. But that itself had been another kind of upheaval, having to survive her mother's mad dashes into love, her eventual bitter exit from it.

And they were always bitter, Stella remembered.

At least she'd been in college, living on her own, when her mother had married yet again. And maybe that was part of the reason that marriage had lasted nearly a decade. There hadn't been a child to crowd things. Yet eventually there'd been another acrimonious divorce, with the split nearly coinciding with her own widowhood.

It had been a horrible year, in every possible way, which her mother had ended with yet one more brief, tumultuous marriage.

Strange that even as an adult, Stella found she couldn't quite forgive being so consistently put into second or even third place behind her mother's needs.

She wasn't doing that with her own children, she assured herself. She wasn't being selfish and careless in her relationship with Logan, or shuffling her kids to the back of her heart because she was falling in love with him.

Still, the fact was it was all moving awfully fast. It would make more sense to slow things down a bit until she had a better picture.

Besides, she was going to be too busy to think about marriage. And she shouldn't forget he hadn't asked her to marry him and have his children, for God's sake. She was blowing an offhand comment way out of proportion.

Time to get back on track. She rose from her desk and started for the door. It opened before she reached it.

"I was just going to find you," she said to Roz. "I'm on my way to pick up the new family and take them home."

"I wish I could go with you. I nearly postponed this

meeting so I could." She glanced at her watch as if considering it again.

"By the time you get back from your meeting with Dr. Carnegie, they'll be all settled in and ready for some quality time with Aunt Roz."

"I have to admit I want my hands on that baby. So, now, what've you been fretting about?"

"Fretting?" Stella opened a desk drawer to retrieve her purse. "Why do you think I've been fretting about anything?"

"Your watch is turned around, which means you've been twisting at it. Which means you've been fretting. Something going on around here I don't know about?"

"No." Annoyed with herself, Stella turned her watch around. "No, it's nothing to do with work. I was thinking about Logan, and I was thinking about my mother."

"What does Logan have to do with your mother?" As she asked, Roz picked up Stella's thermos. After opening it and taking a sniff, she poured a few swallows of iced coffee in the lid.

"Nothing. I don't know. Do you want a mug for that?"

"No, this is fine. Just want a taste."

"I think—I sense—I'm wondering . . . and I already sound like an ass." Stella took a lipstick from the cosmetic bag in her purse, and walking to the mirror she'd hung on the wall, she began to freshen her makeup. "Roz, things are getting serious between me and Logan."

"As I've got eyes, I've seen that for myself. Do you want me to say *and*, or do you want me to mind my own business?"

"And. I don't know if I'm ready for serious. I don't know that he is, either. It's surprising enough it turned out we like each other, much less . . ." She turned back. "I've never felt like this about anyone. Not this churned up and edgy, and, well, fretful."

She replaced the lipstick and zipped the bag shut. "With Kevin, everything was so clear. We were young and in love, and there wasn't a single barrier to get over, not really. It wasn't that we never fought or had problems, but it was all relatively simple for us."

"And the longer you live, the more complicated life gets."

"Yes. I'm afraid of being in love again, and of crossing that line from this is mine to this is ours. That sounds incredibly selfish when I say it out loud."

"Maybe, but I'd say it's pretty normal."

"Maybe. Roz, my mother was—is—a mess. I know, in my head, that a lot of the decisions I've made have been because I knew they were the exact opposite of what she'd have done. That's pathetic."

"I don't know that it is, not if those decisions were right for you."

"They were. They have been. But I don't want to step away from something that might be wonderful just because I know my mother would leap forward without a second thought."

"Honey, I can look at you and remember what it was like, and the both of us can look at Hayley and wonder how she has the courage and fortitude to raise that baby on her own."

Stella let out a little laugh. "God, isn't that the truth?"

"And since it's turned out the three of us have connected as friends, we can give each other all kinds of support and advice and shoulders to cry on. But the fact is, each one of us has to get through what we get through. Me, I expect you'll figure this out soon enough. Figuring out how to make things come out right's what you do."

She set the thermos lid on the desk, gave Stella two light pats on the cheek. "Well, I'm going to scoot home and clean up a bit."

"Thanks, Roz. Really. If Hayley's doing all right once I get them home, I'll leave David in charge. I know we're shorthanded around here today."

"No, you stay home with her and Lily. Harper can handle things here. It's not every day you bring a new baby home."

* * *

AND THAT WAS SOMETHING ROZ CONSIDERED AS SHE hunted for parking near Mitchell Carnegie's downtown apartment. It had been a good many years since there had been an infant in Harper House. Just how would the Harper Bride deal with that?

How would they all deal with it?

How would she herself handle the idea of her firstborn falling for that sweet single mother and her tiny girl? She doubted that Harper knew he was sliding in that direction, and surely Hayley was clueless. But a mother knew such things; a mother could read them on her son's face.

Something else to think about some other time, she decided, and cursed ripely at the lack of parking.

She had to hoof it nearly three blocks and cursed again because she'd felt obliged to wear heels. Now her feet were going to hurt, *and* she'd have to waste more time changing into comfortable clothes once this meeting was done.

She was going to be late, which she deplored, and she was going to arrive hot and sweaty.

She would have loved to have passed the meeting on to Stella. But it wasn't the sort of thing she could ask a manager to do. It dealt with her home, her family. She'd taken this particular aspect of it for granted for far too long.

She paused at the corner to wait for the light.

"Roz!"

The voice on the single syllable had her hackles rising. Her face was cold as hell frozen over as she turned and stared at—stared through—the slim, handsome man striding quickly toward her in glossy Ferragamos.

"I thought that was you. Nobody else could look so lovely and cool on a hot afternoon."

He reached out, this man she'd once been foolish enough to marry, and gripped her hand in both of his. "Don't you look gorgeous!"

"You're going to want to let go of my hand, Bryce, or you're going to find yourself facedown and eating sidewalk. The only one who'll be embarrassed by that eventuality is yourself."

His face, with its smooth tan and clear features, hardened. "I'd hoped, after all this time, we could be friends."

"We're not friends, and never will be." Quite deliberately, she took a tissue out of her purse and wiped the hand he'd touched. "I don't count lying, cheating sons of bitches among my friends."

"A man just can't make a mistake or find forgiveness with a woman like you."

"That's exactly right. I believe that's the first time you've been exactly right in your whole miserable life."

She started across the street, more resigned than surprised when he fell into step beside her. He wore a pale gray suit, Italian in cut. Canali, if she wasn't mistaken. At least that had been his designer of the moment when she'd been footing the bills.

"I don't see why you're still upset, Roz, honey. Unless there are still feelings inside you for me."

"Oh, there are, Bryce, there are. Disgust being paramount. Go away before I call a cop and have you arrested for being a personal annoyance."

"I'd just like another chance to—"

She stopped then. "That will never happen in this lifetime, or a thousand others. Be grateful you're able to walk the streets in your expensive shoes, Bryce, and that you're wearing a tailored suit instead of a prison jumpsuit."

"There's no cause to talk to me that way. You got what you wanted, Roz. You cut me off without a dime."

"Would that include the fifteen thousand, six hundred and fifty-eight dollars and twenty-two cents you transferred out of my account the week before I kicked your sorry ass out of my house? Oh, I knew about that one, too," she said when his face went carefully blank. "But I let that one go, because I decided I deserved to pay something for my own stupidity. Now you go on, and you stay out of my way, you stay out of my sight, and you stay out of my hearing, or I promise you, you'll regret it."

She clipped down the sidewalk, and even the "Frigid bitch" he hurled at her back didn't break her stride.

But she was shaking. By the time she'd reached the right address her knees and hands were trembling. She hated that she'd allowed him to upset her. Hated that the sight of him brought any reaction at all, even if it was rage.

Because there was shame along with it.

She'd taken him into her heart and her home. She'd let herself be charmed and seduced—and lied to and deceived. He'd stolen more than her money, she knew. He'd stolen her pride. And it was a shock to the system to realize, after all this time, that she didn't quite have it back. Not all of it.

She blessed the cool inside the building and rode the elevator to the third floor.

She was too frazzled and annoyed to fuss with her hair or check her makeup before she knocked. Instead she stood impatiently tapping her foot until the door opened.

He was as good-looking as the picture on the back of his books—several of which she'd read or skimmed through before arranging this meeting. He was, perhaps, a bit more rumpled in rolled-up shirtsleeves and jeans. But what she saw was a very long, very lanky individual with a pair of horn-rims sliding down a straight and narrow nose. Behind the lenses, bottle-green eyes seemed distracted. His hair was plentiful, in a tangle of peat-moss brown around a strong, sharp-boned face that showed a black bruise along the jaw.

The fact that he wasn't wearing any shoes made her feel hot and overdressed.

"Dr. Carnegie?"

"That's right. Ms. . . . . Harper. I'm sorry. I lost track of time. Come in, please. And don't look at anything." There was a quick, disarming smile. "Part of losing track means I didn't remember to pick up out here. So we'll go straight back to my office, where I can excuse any disorder in the name of the creative process. Can I get you anything?"

His voice was coastal southern, she noted. That easy

drawl that turned vowels into warm liquid. "I'll take something cold, whatever you've got."

Of course, she looked as he scooted her through the living room. There were newspapers and books littering an enormous brown sofa, another pile of them along with a stubby white candle on a coffee table that looked as if it might have been Georgian. There was a basketball and a pair of high-tops so disreputable she doubted even her sons would lay claim to them in the middle of a gorgeous Turkish rug, and the biggest television screen she'd ever seen eating up an entire wall.

Though he was moving her quickly along, she caught sight of the kitchen. From the number of dishes on the counter, she assumed he'd recently had a party.

"I'm in the middle of a book," he explained. "And when I come up for air, domestic chores aren't a priority. My last cleaning team quit. Just like their predecessors."

"I can't imagine why," she said with schooled civility as she stared at his office space.

There wasn't a clean surface to be seen, and the air reeked of cigar smoke. A dieffenbachia sat in a chipped pot on the windowsill, withering. Rising above the chaos of his desk was a flat-screen monitor and an ergonomic keyboard.

He cleaned off the chair, dumping everything unceremoniously on the floor. "Hang on one minute."

As he dashed out, she lifted her brows at the half-eaten sandwich and glass of—maybe it was tea—among the debris on his desk. She was somewhat disappointed when with a crane of her neck she peered around to his monitor. His screen saver was up. But that, she supposed, was interesting enough, as it showed several cartoon figures playing basketball.

"I hope tea's all right," he said as he came back.

"That's fine, thank you." She took the glass and hoped it had been washed sometime in the last decade. "Dr. Carnegie, you're killing that plant."

"What plant?"

"The dieffenbachia in the window."

"Oh? Oh. I didn't know I had a plant." He gave it a baffled look. "Wonder where that came from? It doesn't look very healthy, does it?"

He picked it up, and she saw, with horror, that he intended to dump it in the overflowing wastebasket beside his desk.

"For God's sake, don't just throw it out. Would you bury your cat alive?"

"I don't have a cat."

"Just give it to me." She rose, grabbed the pot out of his hand. "It's dying of thirst and heat, and it's rootbound. This soil's hard as a brick."

She set it beside her chair and sat again. "I'll take care of it," she said, and her legs were an angry slash as she crossed them. "Dr. Carnegie—"

"Mitch. If you're going to take my plant, you ought to call me Mitch."

"As I explained when I contacted you, I'm interested in contracting for a thorough genealogy of my family, with an interest in gathering information on a specific person."

"Yes." All business, he decided, and sat at his desk. "And I told you I only do personal genealogies if something about the family history interests me. I'm—obviously—caught up in a book right now and wouldn't have much time to devote to a genealogical search and report."

"You didn't name your fee."

"Fifty dollars an hour, plus expenses."

She felt a quick clutch in the belly. "That's lawyer steep."

"An average genealogy doesn't take that long, if you know what you're doing and where to look. In most cases, it can be done in about forty hours, depending on how far back you want to go. If it's more complicated, we could arrange a flat fee—reevaluating after that time is used. But as I said—"

"I don't believe you'll have to go back more than a century."

"Chump change in this field. And if you're only dealing with a hundred years, you could probably do this yourself. I'd be happy to direct you down the avenues. No charge."

"I need an expert, which I'm assured you are. And I'm willing to negotiate terms. Since you took the time out of your busy schedule to speak to me, I'd think you'd hear me out before you nudge me out the door."

All business, he thought again, and prickly with it. "That wasn't my intention—the nudging. Of course I'll hear you out. If you're not in any great rush for the search and report, I may be able to help you out in a few weeks."

When she inclined her head, he began to rummage on, through, under the desk. "Just let me . . . how the hell did that get there?"

He unearthed a yellow legal pad, then mined out a pen. "That's Rosalind, right? *As You Like It*?"

A smile whisked over her mouth. "As in Russell. My daddy was a fan."

He wrote her name on the top of the pad. "You said a hundred years back. I'd think a family like yours would have records, journals, documents—and considerable oral family history to cover a century."

"You would, wouldn't you? Actually, I have quite a bit, but certain things have led me to believe some of the oral history is either incorrect or is missing details. I will, however, be glad to have you go through what I do have. We've already been through a lot of it."

"We?"

"Myself, and other members of my household."

"So, you're looking for information on a specific ancestor."

"I don't know as she was an ancestor, but I am certain she was a member of the household. I'm certain she died there."

"You have her death record?"

"No."

He shoved at his glasses as he scribbled. "Her grave?"

"No. Her ghost."

She smiled serenely when he blinked up at her. "Doesn't a man who digs into family histories believe in ghosts?"

"I've never come across one."

"If you take on this job, you will. What might your fee be, Dr. Carnegie, to dig up the history and identity of a family ghost?"

He leaned back in his chair, tapping the pen on his chin. "You're not kidding around."

"I certainly wouldn't kid around to the tune of fifty dollars an hour, plus expenses. I bet you could write a very interesting book on the Harper family ghost, if I were to sign a release and cooperate."

"I just bet I could," he replied.

"And it seems to me that you might consider finding out what I'm after as a kind of research. Maybe I should charge you."

His grin flashed again. "I have to finish this book before I actively take on another project. Despite evidence to the contrary, I finish what I start."

"Then you ought to start washing your dishes."

"Told you not to look. First, let me say that in my opinion the odds of you having an actual ghost in residence are about, oh, one in twenty million."

"I'd be happy to put a dollar down at those odds, if you're willing to risk the twenty million."

"Second, if I take this on, I'd require access to all family papers—personal family papers, and your written consent for me to dig into public records regarding your family."

"Of course."

"I'd be willing to waive my fee for, let's say, the first twenty hours. Until we see what we've got."

"Forty hours."

"Thirty."

"Done."

"And I'd want to see your house."

"Perhaps you'd like to come to dinner. Is there any day next week that would suit you?"

"I don't know. Hold on." He swiveled to his computer, danced his fingers over keys. "Tuesday?"

"Seven o'clock, then. We're not formal, but you will need shoes." She picked up the plant, then rose. "Thank you for your time," she said, extended a hand.

"Are you really going to take that thing?"

"I certainly am. And I have no intention of giving it back and letting you take it to death's door again. Do you need directions to Harper House?"

"I'll find it. Seems to me I drove by it once." He walked her to the door. "You know, sensible women don't usually believe in ghosts. Practical women don't generally agree to pay someone to trace the history of said ghost. And you strike me as a sensible, practical woman."

"Sensible men don't usually live in pigsties and conduct business meetings barefoot. We'll both have to take our chances. You ought to put some ice on that bruise. It looks painful."

"It is. Vicious little . . ." He broke off. "Got clipped going up for a rebound. Basketball."

"So I see. I'll expect you Tuesday, then, at seven."

"I'll be there. Good-bye, Ms. Harper."

"Dr. Carnegie."

He kept the door open long enough to satisfy his curiosity. He was right, he noted. The rear view was just as elegant and sexy as the front side, and both went with that steel-spined southern belle voice.

A class act, top to toe, he decided as he shut the door.

Ghosts. He shook his head and chuckled as he wound his way through the mess back to his office. Wasn't that a kick in the ass.

twenty

LOGAN STUDIED THE TINY FORM BLINKING IN A patch of dappled sunlight. He'd seen babies before, even had his share of personal contact with them. To him, newborns bore a strange resemblance to fish. Something about the eyes, he thought. And this one had all that black hair going for her, so she looked like a human sea creature. Sort of exotic and otherworldly.

If Gavin had been around, and Hayley out of hearing distance, he'd have suggested that this particular baby looked something like the offspring of Aquaman and Wonder Woman.

The kid would've gotten it.

Babies always intimidated him. Something about the way they looked right back at you, as if they knew a hell of a lot more than you did and were going to tolerate you until they got big enough to handle things on their own.

But he figured he had to come up with something better than an encounter between superheros, as the mother was standing beside him, anticipating.

"She looks as if she might've dropped down from Venus, where the grass is sapphire blue and the sky a bowl of gold dust." True enough, Logan decided, and a bit more poetic than the Aquaman theory.

"Aw, listen to you. Go ahead." Hayley gave him a little elbow nudge. "You can pick her up."

"Maybe I'll wait on that until she's more substantial."

With a chuckle, Hayley slipped Lily out of her carrier. "Big guy like you shouldn't be afraid of a tiny baby. Here. Now, make sure you support her head."

"Got long legs for such a little thing." And they kicked a bit in transfer. "She's picture pretty. Got a lot of you in her."

"I can hardly believe she's mine." Hayley fussed with Lily's cotton hat, then made herself stop touching. "Can I open the present now?"

"Sure. She all right in the sun like this?"

"We're baking the baby," Hayley told him as she tugged at the shiny pink ribbon on the box Logan had set on the patio table.

"Sorry?"

"She's got a touch of jaundice. The sun's good for her. Stella said Luke had it too, and they took him out in the sunshine for a little while a few times a day." She went to work on the wrapping paper. "Seems like she and Roz know everything there is to know about babies. I can ask the silliest question and one of them knows the answer. We're blessed, Lily and I."

Three women, one baby. Logan imagined Lily barely got out a burp before one of them was rushing to pick her up.

"Logan, do you think things happen because they're meant to, or because you make them happen?"

"I guess I think you make them happen because they're meant to."

"I've been thinking. There's a lot of thinking time when you're up two or three times in the middle of the night. I just wanted—needed—to get gone when I left Little Rock, and I headed here because I hoped Roz might give me a job. I could just as well have headed to Alabama. I've got closer kin there—blood kin—than Roz. But I came here, and I think I was meant to. I think Lily was supposed to be born here, and have Roz and Stella in her life."

"We'd all be missing out on something if you'd pointed your car in another direction."

"This feels like family. I've missed that since my daddy died. I want Lily to have family. I think—I know—we'd have been all right on our own. But I don't want things to just be all right for her. All right doesn't cut it anymore."

"Kids change everything."

Her smile bloomed. "They do. I'm not the same person I was a year ago, or even a week ago. I'm a mother." She pulled off the rest of the wrapping and let out a sound Logan thought of as distinctly female.

"Oh, what a sweet baby-doll! And it's so soft." She took it out of the box to cradle it much as Logan was cradling Lily.

"Bigger than she is."

"Not for long. Oh, she's so pink and pretty, and look at her little hat!"

"You pull the hat, and it makes music."

"Really?" Delighted, Hayley pulled the peaked pink hat, and "The Cradle Song" tinkled out. "It's perfect." She popped up to give Logan a kiss. "Lily's going to love her. Thank you, Logan."

"I figured a girl can't have too many dolls."

He glanced over as the patio door slammed open. Parker scrambled out a foot ahead of two shouting, racing boys.

They'd been this small once, he realized with a jolt. Small enough to curl in the crook of an arm, as helpless as, well, a fish out of water.

They ran to Logan as Parker sped in circles of delirious freedom.

"We saw your truck," Gavin announced. "Are we going to go work with you?"

"I knocked off for the day." Both faces fell, comically, and the buzz of pleasure it gave him had him adjusting his weekend plans. "But I've got to build me an arbor tomorrow, out in my yard. I could use a couple of Saturday slaves."

"We can be slaves." Luke tugged on Logan's pant leg. "I know what an arbor is, too. It's a thing stuff grows on."

"There you go, then, I've got a couple of expert slaves. We'll see what your mama says."

"She won't mind. She has to work 'cause Hayley's on turnkey."

"Maternity," Hayley explained.

"Got that."

"Can I see her?" Luke gave another tug.

"Sure." Logan crouched down with the baby in his arms. "She sure is tiny, isn't she?"

"She doesn't do anything yet." Gavin frowned thoughtfully as he tapped a gentle finger on Lily's cheek. "She cries and sleeps."

Luke leaned close to Logan's ear. "Hayley feeds her," he said in a conspirator's whisper, "with milk out of her *booby*."

With an admirably straight face, Logan nodded. "I think I heard about that somewhere. It's a little hard to believe."

"It's *true*. That's why they have them. Girls. Guys don't get boobies because they can't make milk, no matter how much they drink."

"Huh. That explains that."

"Fat Mr. Kelso's got boobies," Gavin said and sent his brother into a spasm of hilarity.

Stella stepped to the door and saw Logan holding the baby with her boys flanking him. All three of them had grins from ear-to-ear. The sun was shimmering down through the scarlet leaves of a red maple, falling in a shifting pattern of light and shadow on the stone. Lilies had burst into bloom in a carnival of color and exotic shapes. She could smell them, and the early roses, freshly cut grass, and verbena.

She heard birdsong and the giggling whispers of her boys, the delicate music of the wind chime hung from one of the maple's branches.

Her first clear thought as she froze there, as if she'd walked into an invisible frame of a picture was, Uh-oh.

Maybe she'd said it out loud, as Logan's head turned toward her. When their eyes met, his foolish grin transformed into a smile, easy and warm.

He looked too big crouched there, she thought. Too big, too rough with that tiny child in his arms, too *male* centered between her precious boys.

And so . . . dazzling somehow. Tanned and fit and strong.

He belonged in a forest, beating a path over rocky ground. Not here, in this elegant scene with flowers scenting the air and a baby dozing in the crook of his arm.

He straightened and walked toward her. "Your turn."

"Oh." She reached for Lily. "There you are, beautiful baby girl. There you are." She laid her lips on Lily's brow, and breathed in. "How's she doing today?" she asked Hayley.

"Good as gold. Look here, Stella. Look what Logan bought her."

Yeah, a female thing, Logan mused as Stella made nearly the identical sound Hayley had over the doll. "Isn't that the most precious thing?"

"And watch this." Hayley pulled the hat so the tune played out.

"Mom. Mom." Luke deserted Logan to tug on his mother.

"Just a minute, baby."

They fussed over the doll and Lily while Luke rolled his eyes and danced in place.

"I think Lily and I should go take a nap." Hayley tucked the baby in her carrier, then lifted it and the doll. "Thanks again, Logan. It was awfully sweet of you."

"Glad you like it. You take care now."

"Dolls are lame," Gavin stated, but he was polite enough to wait until Hayley was inside.

"Really?" Stella reached over to flick the bill of his baseball cap over his eyes. "And what are those little people you've got all over your shelves and your desk?"

"Those aren't dolls." Gavin looked as horrified as an eight-year-old boy could manage. "Those are action figures. Come *on*, Mom."

"My mistake."

"We want to be Saturday slaves and build an arbor." Luke pulled on her hand and to get her attention. "Okay?"

"Saturday slaves?"

"I'm building an arbor tomorrow," Logan explained. "Could use some help, and I got these two volunteers. I hear they work for cheese sandwiches and Popsicles."

"Oh. Actually, I was planning to take them to work with me tomorrow."

"An *arbor*, Mom." Luke gazed up pleadingly, as if he'd been given the chance to build the space shuttle and then ride it to Pluto. "I never, ever built one before."

"Well . . ."

"Why don't we split it up?" Logan suggested. "You take them on in with you in the morning, and I'll swing by and get them around noon."

She felt her stomach knot. It sounded normal. Like parenting. Like family. Dimly, she heard her boys begging and pleading over the buzzing in her ears.

"That'll be fine," she managed. "If you're sure they won't be in your way."

He cocked his head at the strained and formal tone. "They get in it, I just kick them out again. Like now. Why don't you boys go find that dog and see what he's up to, so I can talk to your mama a minute?"

Gavin made a disgusted face. "Let's go, Luke. He's probably going to kiss her."

"Why, I'm transparent as glass to that boy," Logan said. He tipped her chin up with his fingers, laid his lips on hers, and watched her watch him. "Hello, Stella."

"Hello, Logan."

"Are you going to tell me what's going on in that head of yours, or do I have to guess?"

"A lot of things. And nothing much."

"You looked poleaxed when you came outside."

"'Poleaxed.' Now there's a word you don't hear every day."

"Why don't you and I take a little walk?"

"All right."

"You want to know why I came by this afternoon?"

"To bring Lily a doll." She walked along one of the paths with him. She could hear her boys and the dog, then the quick thwack of Luke's Wiffle bat. They'd be fine for a while.

"That, and to see if I could sponge a meal off Roz, which was a roundabout way of having a meal with you. I don't figure I'm going to be able to pry you too far away from the baby for a while yet."

She had to smile. "Apparently I'm transparent, too. It's so much fun having a baby in the house. If I manage to steal her away from Hayley for an hour—and win out over Roz—I can play with her like, well, a doll. All those adorable little clothes. Never having had a girl, I didn't realize how addicting all those little dresses can be."

"When I asked you if Lily made you want another, you panicked."

"I didn't panic."

"Clutched, let's say. Why is that?"

"It's not unusual for a woman of my age with two half-grown children to clutch, let's say, at the idea of another baby."

"Uh-huh. You clutched again when I said I wanted to take the kids to my place tomorrow."

"No, it's just that I'd already planned—"

"Don't bullshit me, Red."

"Things are moving so fast and in a direction I hadn't planned to go."

"If you're going to plan every damn thing, maybe I should draw you a frigging map."

"I can draw my own map, and there's no point in being annoyed. You asked." She stopped by a tower of madly climbing passionflower. "I thought things were supposed to move slow in the south."

"You irritated me the first time I set eyes on you."

"Thanks so much."

"That should've given me a clue," he continued. "You were an itch between my shoulder blades. The one in that spot you can't reach and scratch away no matter how you contort yourself. I'd've been happy to move slow. Generally, I don't see the point in rushing through something. But you know, Stella, you can't schedule how you're going to fall in love. And I fell in love with you."

"Logan."

"I can see that put the fear of God in you. I figure there's one of two reasons for that. One, you don't have feelings for me, and you're afraid you'll hurt me. Or you've got plenty of feelings for me, and they scare you."

He snapped off a passionflower with its white petals and long blue filaments, stuck it in the spiraling curls of her hair. A carelessly romantic gesture at odds with the frustration in his voice. "I'm going with number two, not only because it suits me better, but because I know what happens to both of us when I kiss you."

"That's attraction. It's chemistry."

"I know the frigging difference." He took her shoulders, held her still. "So do you. Because we've both been here before. We've both been in love before, so we know the difference."

"That may be right, that may be true. And it's part of why this is too much, too fast." She curled her hands on his forearms, felt solid strength, solid will. "I knew Kevin a full year before things got serious, and another year before we started talking about the future."

"I had about the same amount of time with Rae. And here we are, Stella. You through tragedy, me through circumstance. We both know there aren't any guarantees, no matter how long or how well you plan it out beforehand."

"No, there aren't. But it's not just me now. I have more than myself to consider."

"You come as a package deal." He rubbed his hands up and down her arms, then stepped away. "I'm not dim, Stella. And I'm not above making friends with your boys to get you. But the fact is, I like them. I enjoy having them around."

"I know that." She gave his arms a squeeze, then eased back. "I know that," she repeated. "I can tell when someone's faking. It's not you. It's me."

"That's the goddamnedest thing to say."

"You're right, but it's also true. I know what it's like to be a child and have my mother swing from man to man. That's not what we're doing here," she said, lifting her hands palms out as fresh fury erupted on his face. "I know that, too. But the fact is, my life centers on those boys now. It has to."

"And you don't think mine can? If you don't think I can be a father to them because they didn't come out of me, then it is you."

"I think it takes time to—"

"You know how you get a strong, healthy plant like this to increase, to fill out strong?" He jerked a thumb toward the passionflower vine. "You can layer it, and you end up with new fruit and flower. By hybridizing it, it gets stronger, maybe you get yourself a new variety out of it."

"Yes. But it takes time."

"You have to start. I don't love those boys the way you do. But I can see how I could, if you gave me the chance. So I want the chance. I want to marry you."

"Oh, God. I can't—we don't—" She had to press the heel of her hand on her heart and gulp in air. But she couldn't seem to suck it all the way into her lungs. "Marriage. Logan. I can't get my breath."

"Good. That means you'll shut up for five minutes. I love you, and I want you and those boys in my life. If anybody had suggested to me, a few months ago, that I'd want to take on some fussy redhead and a couple of noisy kids,

I'd've laughed my ass off. But there you go. I'd say we could live together for a while until you get used to it, but I know you wouldn't. So I don't see why we don't just do it and start living our lives."

"Just do it," she managed. "Like you just go out and buy a new truck?"

"A new truck's got a better warranty than marriage."

"All this romance is making me giddy."

"I could go buy a ring, get down on one knee. I figured that's how I'd deal with this, but I'm into it now. You love me, Stella."

"I'm beginning to wonder why."

"You've always wondered why. It wouldn't bother me if you keep right on wondering. We could make a good life together, you and me. For ourselves." He jerked his head in the direction of the smack of plastic bat on plastic ball. "For the boys. I can't be their daddy, but I could be a good father. I'd never hurt them, or you. Irritate, annoy, but I'd never hurt any of you."

"I know that. I couldn't love you if you weren't a good man. And you are, a very good man. But marriage. I don't know if it's the answer for any of us."

"I'm going to talk you into it sooner or later." He stepped back to her now, twined her hair around his finger in a lightning change of mood. "If it's sooner, you'd be able to decide how you want all those bare rooms done up in that big house. I'm thinking of picking one and getting started on it next rainy day."

She narrowed her eyes. "Low blow."

"Whatever works. Belong to me, Stella." He rubbed his lips over hers. "Let's be a family."

"Logan." Her heart was yearning toward him even as her body eased away. "Let's take a step back a minute. A family's part of it. I saw you with Lily."

"And?"

"I'm heading toward my middle thirties, Logan. I have an eight- and a six-year-old. I have a demanding job. A career, and I'm going to keep it. I don't know if I want to have more children. You've never had a baby of your own, and you deserve to."

"I've thought about this. Making a baby with you, well, that would be a fine thing if we both decide we want it. But it seems to me that right now I'm getting the bonus round. You, and two entertaining boys that are already house-broken. I don't have to know everything that's going to happen, Stella. I don't want to know every damn detail. I just have to know I love you, and I want them."

"Logan." Time for rational thinking, she decided. "We're going to have to sit down and talk this out. We haven't even met each other's family yet."

"We can take care of that easy enough, at least with yours. We can have them over for dinner. Pick a day."

"You don't have any *furniture*." She heard her voice pitch, and deliberately leveled herself again. "That's not important."

"Not to me."

"The point is we're skipping over a lot of the most basic steps." And at the moment, all of them were jumbled and muzzy in her mind.

Marriage, changing things for her boys once more, the possibility of another child. How could she keep up?

"Here you are talking about taking on two children. You don't know what it's like to live in the same house as a couple of young boys."

"Red, I *was* a young boy. I tell you what, you go ahead and make me a list of all those basic steps. We'll take them, in order, if that's what you need to do. But I want you to tell me, here and now, do you love me?"

"You've already told me I do."

He set his hands on her waist, drew her in, drew her up in the way that made her heart stutter. "Tell me."

Did he know, could he know, how huge it was for her to say the words? Words she'd said to no man but the one she'd lost. Here he was, those eyes on hers, waiting for the simple acknowledgment of what he already knew.

"I love you. I do, but—"

"That'll do for now." He closed his mouth over hers and rode out the storm of emotion raging inside him. Then he stepped back. "You make that list, Red. And start thinking what color you want on those living room walls. Tell the boys I'll see them tomorrow."

"But . . . weren't you going to stay for dinner?"

"I've got some things to do," he said as he strode away. "And so do you." He glanced over his shoulder. "You need to worry about me."

ONE OF THE THINGS HE HAD TO DO WAS WORK OFF the frustration. When he'd asked Rae to marry him, it was no surprise for either of them and her acceptance had been instant and enthusiastic.

Of course, look where that had gotten them.

But it was hard on a man's ego when the woman he loved and wanted to spend his life with countered every one of his moves with a block of stubborn, hardheaded *sense*.

He put in an hour on his cross-trainer, sweating, guzzling water, and cursing the day he'd had the misfortune to fall in love with a stiff-necked redhead.

Of course, if she wasn't stiff-necked, stubborn, and sensible, he probably wouldn't have fallen in love with her. That still made the whole mess her fault.

He'd been happy before she'd come along. The house hadn't seemed empty before she'd been in it. Her and those noisy kids. Since when had he voluntarily arranged to spend a precious Saturday off, a solitary Saturday at his own house with a couple of kids running around getting into trouble?

Hell. He was going to have to go out and pick up some Popsicles.

He was a doomed man, he decided as he stepped into the shower. Hadn't he already picked the spot in the backyard for a swing set? Hadn't he already started a rough sketch for a tree house?

He'd started thinking like a father.

Maybe he'd liked the sensation of holding that baby in his arms, but having one wasn't a deal breaker. How was either one of them supposed to know how they'd feel about that a year from now?

Things happen, he thought, remembering Hayley's words, because they're meant to happen.

Because, he corrected as he yanked on fresh jeans, you damn well made them happen.

He was going to start making things happen.

In fifteen minutes, after a quick check of the phone book, he was in his car and heading into Memphis. His hair was still wet.

WILL HAD BARELY STARTED ON HIS AFTER-DINNER decaf and the stingy sliver of lemon meringue pie Jolene allowed him when he heard the knock on the door.

"Now who the devil could that be?"

"I don't know, honey. Maybe you should go find out."

"If they want a damn piece of pie, then I want a bigger one."

"If it's the Bowers boy about cutting the grass, tell him I've got a couple of cans of Coke cold in here."

But when Will opened the door, it wasn't the gangly Bowers boy, but a broad-shouldered man wearing an irritated scowl. Instinctively, Will edged into the opening of the door to block it. "Something I can do for you?"

"Yeah. I'm Logan Kitridge, and I've just asked your daughter to marry me."

"Who is it, honey?" Fussing with her hair, Jolene walked up to the door. "Why it's Logan Kitridge, isn't it? We met you a time or two over at Roz's. Been some time back, though. I know your mama a little. Come on in."

"He says he asked Stella to marry him."

"Is that so!" Her face brightened like the sun, with her

eyes wide and avid with curiosity. "Why, that's just marvelous. You come on back and have some pie."

"He didn't say if she'd said yes," Will pointed out.

"Since when does Stella say anything as simple as yes?" Logan demanded, and had Will grinning.

"That's my girl."

They sat down, ate pie, drank coffee, and circled around the subject at hand with small talk about his mother, Stella, the new baby.

Finally, Will leaned back. "So, am I supposed to ask you how you intend to support my daughter and grandsons?"

"You tell me. Last time I did this, the girl's father'd had a couple of years to grill me. Didn't figure I'd have to go through this part of it again at my age."

"Of course you don't." Jolene gave her husband a little slap on the arm. "He's just teasing. Stella can support herself and those boys just fine. And you wouldn't be here looking so irritated if you didn't love her. I guess one question, if you don't mind me asking, is how you feel about being stepfather to her boys."

"About the same way, I expect, you feel being their stepgrandmother. And if I'm lucky, they'll feel about me the way they do about you. I know they love spending time with you, and I hear their Nana Jo bakes cookies as good as David's. That's some compliment."

"They're precious to us," Will said. "They're precious to Stella. They were precious to Kevin. He was a good man."

"Maybe it'd be easier for me if he hadn't been. If he'd been a son of a bitch and she'd divorced him instead of him being a good man who died too young. I don't know, because that's not the case. I'm glad for her that she had a good man and a good marriage, glad for the boys that they had a good father who loved them. I can live with his ghost, if that's what you're wondering. Fact is, I can be grateful to him."

"Well, I think that's just smart." Jolene patted Logan's hand with approval. "And I think it shows good character, too. Don't you, Will?"

On a noncommittal sound, Will pulled on his bottom lip. "You marry my girl, am I going to get landscaping and such at the family rate?"

Logan's grin spread slowly. "We can make that part of the package."

"I've been toying with redoing the patio."

"First I've heard of it," Jolene muttered.

"I saw them putting on one of those herringbone patterns out of bricks on one of the home shows. I liked the look of it. You know how to handle that sort of thing?"

"Done a few like it. I can take a look at what you've got now if you want."

"That'd be just fine." Will pushed back from the table.

twenty-one

STELLA CHEWED AT IT, STEWED OVER IT, AND WORRIED about it. She was prepared to launch into another discussion regarding the pros and cons of marriage when Logan came to pick up the boys at noon.

She knew he was angry with her. Hurt, too, she imagined. But oddly enough, she knew he'd be by—somewhere in the vicinity of noon—to get the kids. He'd told them he would come, so he would come.

A definite plus on his side of the board, she decided. She could, and did, trust him with her children.

They would argue, she knew. They were both too worked up to have a calm, reasonable discussion over such an emotional issue. But she didn't mind an argument. A good argument usually brought all the facts and feelings out. She needed both if she was going to figure out the best thing to do for all involved.

But when he hunted them down where she had the kids storing discarded wagons—at a quarter a wagon—he was perfectly pleasant. In fact, he was almost sunny.

"Ready for some man work?" he asked.

With shouts of assent, they deserted wagon detail for more interesting activities. Luke proudly showed him the plastic hammer he'd hooked in a loop of his shorts.

"That'll come in handy. I like a man who carries his own tools. I'll drop them off at the house later."

"About what time do you think—"

"Depends on how long they can stand up to the work." He pinched Gavin's biceps. "Ought to be able to get a good day's sweat out of this one."

"Feel mine! Feel mine!" Luke flexed his arm.

After he'd obliged, given an impressed whistle, he nodded to Stella. "See you."

And that was that.

So she chewed at it, stewed over it, and worried about it for the rest of the day. Which, not being a fool, she deduced was exactly what he'd wanted.

THE HOUSE WAS ABNORMALLY QUIET WHEN SHE GOT home from work. She wasn't sure she liked it. She showered off the day, played with the baby, drank a glass of wine, and paced until the phone rang.

"Hello?"

"Hi there, is this Stella?"

"Yes, who—"

"This is Trudy Kitridge. Logan's mama? Logan said I should give you a call, that you'd be home from work about this time of day."

"I . . . oh." Oh, God, oh, God. Logan's *mother*?

"Logan told me and his daddy he asked you to marry him. Could've knocked me over with a feather."

"Yes, me, too. Mrs. Kitridge, we haven't decided . . . or I haven't decided . . . anything."

"Woman's entitled to some time to make up her mind, isn't she? I'd better warn you, honey, when that boy sets his mind on something, he's like a damn bulldog. He said you wanted to meet his family before you said yes or no. I think that's a sweet thing. Of course, with us living out here now, it's not so easy, is it? But we'll be coming back sometime during the holidays. Probably see Logan for Thanksgiving, then our girl for Christmas. Got grandchildren in Charlotte, you know, so we want to be there for Christmas."

"Of course." She had no idea, no idea whatsoever what to say. How could she with no time to prepare?

"Then again, Logan tells me you've got two little boys. Said they're both just pistols. So maybe we'll have ourselves a couple of grandchildren back in Tennessee, too."

"Oh." Nothing could have touched her heart more truly. "That's a lovely thing to say. You haven't even met them yet, or me, and—"

"Logan has, and I raised my son to know his own mind. He loves you and those boys, then we will, too. You're working for Rosalind Harper, I hear."

"Yes. Mrs. Kitridge—"

"Now, you just call me Trudy. How you getting along down there?"

Stella found herself having a twenty-minute conversation with Logan's mother that left her baffled, amused, touched, and exhausted.

When it was done, she sat limply on the sofa, like, she thought, the dazed victim of an ambush.

Then she heard Logan's truck rumble up.

She had to force herself not to dash to the door. He'd be expecting that. Instead she settled herself in the front parlor with a gardening magazine and the dog snoozing at her feet as if she didn't have a care in the world.

Maybe she'd mention, oh so casually, that she'd had a conversation with his mother. Maybe she wouldn't, and let him stew over it.

And all right, it had been sensitive and sweet for him to arrange the phone call, but for God's *sake*, couldn't he have given her some warning so she wouldn't have spent the first five minutes babbling like an idiot?

The kids came in with all the elegance of an army battalion on a forced march.

"We built a *whole* arbor." Grimy with sweat and dirt,

Gavin rushed to scoop up Parker. "And we planted the stuff to grow on it."

"Carol Jessmint."

Carolina Jessamine, Stella interpreted from Luke's garbled pronunciation. Nice choice.

"And I got a splinter." Luke held out a dirty hand to show off the Band-Aid on his index finger. "A *big* one. We thought we might have to hack it out with a *knife*. But we didn't."

"Whew, that was close. We'll go put some antiseptic on it."

"Logan did already. And I didn't cry. And we had submarines, except he says they're poor boys down here, but I don't see why they're poor because they have *lots* of stuff in them. And we had Popsicles."

"And we got to ride in the wheelbarrow," Gavin took over the play-by-play. "And I used a real hammer."

"Wow. You had a busy day. Isn't Logan coming in?"

"No, he said he had other stuff. And look." Gavin dug in his pocket and pulled out a wrinkled five-dollar bill. "We each got one, because he said we worked so good we get to be cheap labor instead of slaves."

She couldn't help it, she had to laugh. "That's quite a promotion. Congratulations. I guess we'd better go clean up."

"Then we can eat like a bunch of barnyard pigs." Luke put his hand in hers. "That's what Logan said when it was time for lunch."

"Maybe we'll save the pig-eating for when you're on the job."

They were full of Logan and their day through bathtime, through dinner. And then were too tuckered out from it all to take advantage of the extra hour she generally allowed them on Saturday nights.

They were sound asleep by nine, and for the first time in her memory, Stella felt she had nothing to do. She tried to read, she tried to work, but couldn't settle into either.

She was thrilled when she heard Lily fussing.

When she stepped into the hall, she saw Hayley heading down, trying to comfort a squalling Lily. "She's hungry. I thought I'd curl up in the sitting room, maybe watch some TV while I feed her."

"Mind company?"

"Twist my arm. It was lonely around here today with David off at the lake for the weekend, and you and Roz at work, the boys away." She sat, opened her shirt and settled Lily on her breast. "There. That's better, isn't it? I put her in that baby sling I got at the shower, and we took a nice walk."

"It's good for both of you. What did you want to watch?"

"Nothing, really. I just wanted the voices."

"How about one more?" Roz slipped in, walked over to Lily to smile. "I wanted to take a peek at her. Look at her go!"

"Nothing wrong with her appetite," Hayley confirmed. "She smiled at me today. I know they say it's just gas, but—"

"What do they know?" Roz sprawled in a chair. "They inside that baby's head?"

"Logan asked me to marry him."

She didn't know why she blurted it out—hadn't known it was pushing from her brain to her tongue.

"Holy cow!" Hayley exploded, then immediately soothed Lily and lowered her voice. "When? How? Where? This is just awesome. This is the biggest of the big news. Tell us everything."

"There's not a lot of every anything. He asked me yesterday."

"After I went inside to put the baby down? I just knew something was up."

"I don't think he meant to. I think it just sort of happened, then he was irritated when I tried to point out the very rational reasons we shouldn't rush into anything."

"What are they?" Hayley wondered.

"You've only known each other since January," Roz began, watching Stella. "You have two children. You've each been married before and bring a certain amount of baggage from those marriages."

"Yes." Stella let out a long sigh. "Exactly."

"When you know you know, don't you?" Hayley argued. "Whether it's five months or five years. And he's great with your kids. They're nuts about him. Being married before ought to make both of you understand the pitfalls or whatever. I don't get it. You love him, don't you?"

"Yes. And yes to the rest, to a point, but . . . it's different when you're young and unencumbered. You can take more chances. Well, if you're not me you can take more chances. And what if he wants children and I don't? I have to think about that. I have to know if I'm going to be able to consider having another child at this stage, or if the children I do have would be happy and secure with him in the long term. Kevin and I had a game plan."

"And your game was called," Roz said. "It isn't an easy thing to walk into another marriage. I waited a long time to do it, then it was the wrong decision. But I think, if I could have fallen, just tumbled into love with a man at your age, one who made me happy, who cheerfully spent his Saturday with my children, and who excited me in bed, I'd have walked into it, and gladly."

"But you just said, before, you gave the exact reasons why it's too soon."

"No, I gave the reasons you'd give—and ones I understand, Stella. But there's something else you and I understand, or should. And that is that love is precious, and too often stolen away. You've got a chance to grab hold of it again. And I say lucky you."

SHE DREAMED AGAIN OF THE GARDEN, AND THE BLUE dahlia. It was ladened with buds, fat and ripe and ready to burst into bloom. At the top, a single stunning flower swayed electric in the quiet breeze. Her garden, though no longer tidy and ordered, spread out from its feet in waves and flows and charming bumps of color and shape.

Then Logan was beside her, and his hands were warm and rough as he drew her close. His mouth was strong and exciting as it feasted on hers. In the distance she could hear her children's laughter, and the cheerful bark of the dog.

She lay on the green grass at the garden's edge, her senses full of the color and scent, full of the man.

There was such heat, such pleasure as they loved in the sunlight. She felt the shape of his face with her hands. Not fairy-tale handsome, not perfect, but beloved. Her skin shivered as their bodies moved, flesh against flesh, hard against soft, curve against angle.

How could they fit, how could they make such a glorious whole, when there were so many differences?

But her body merged with his, joined, and thrived.

She lay in the sunlight with him, on the green grass at the edge of her garden, and hearing the thunder of her own heartbeat, knew bliss.

The buds on the dahlia burst open. There were so many of them. Too many. Other plants were being shaded, crowded. The garden was a jumble now, anyone could see it. The blue dahlia was too aggressive and prolific.

It's fine where it is. It's just a different plan.

But before she could answer Logan, there was another voice, cold and hard in her mind.

His plan. Not yours. His wants. Not yours. Cut it down, before it spreads.

No, it wasn't her plan. Of course it wasn't. This garden was meant to be a charming spot, a quiet spot.

There was a spade in her hand, and she began to dig.

That's right. Dig it out, dig it up.

The air was cold now, cold as winter, so that Stella shuddered as she plunged the spade into the ground.

Logan was gone, and she was alone in the garden with the Harper Bride, who stood in her white gown and tangled hair, nodding. And her eyes were mad.

"I don't want to be alone. I don't want to give it up."

*Dig! Hurry. Do you want the pain, the poison? Do you
want it to infect your children? Hurry! It will spoil everything, kill everything, if you let it stay.*

She'd get it out. It was best to get it out. She'd just plant
it somewhere else, she thought, somewhere better.

But as she lifted it out, taking care with the roots, the
flowers went black, and the blue dahlia withered and went
to dust in her hands.

KEEPING BUSY WAS THE BEST WAY NOT TO BROOD.
And keeping busy was no problem for Stella with the
school year winding down, the perennial sale at the nursery
about to begin, and her best saleswoman on maternity
leave.

She didn't have time to pick apart strange, disturbing
dreams or worry about a man who proposed one minute,
then vanished the next. She had a business to run, a family
to tend, a ghost to identify.

She sold the last three bay laurels, then put her mind
and her back into reordering the shrub area.

"Shouldn't you be pushing papers instead of camel-
lias?"

She straightened, knowing very well she'd worked up a
sweat, that there was soil on her pants, and that her hair
was frizzing out of the ball cap she'd stuck on. And faced
Logan.

"I manage, and part of managing is making sure our
stock is properly displayed. What do you want?"

"Got a new job worked up." He waved the paperwork,
and the breeze from it made her want to moan out loud.
"I'm in for supplies."

"Fine. You can put the paperwork on my desk."

"This is as far as I'm going." He shoved it into her hand.
"Crew's loading up some of it now. I'm going to take that
Japanese red maple, and five of the hardy pink oleanders."

He dragged the flatbed over and started to load.

"Fine," she repeated, under her breath. Annoyed, she glanced at the bid, blinked, then reread the client information.

"This is my father."

"Uh-huh."

"What are you doing planting oleander for my father?"

"My job. Putting in a new patio, too. Your stepmama's already talking about getting new furniture for out there. And a fountain. Seems to me a woman can't see a flat surface without wanting to buy something to put on it. They were still talking about it when I left the other night."

"You—what were *you* doing there?"

"Having pie. Gotta get on. We need to get started on this if I'm going to make it home and clean up before this dinner with the professor guy tonight. See you later, Red."

"Hold it. You just hold it. You had your mother call me, right out of the blue."

"How's it out of the blue when you said you wanted us to meet each other's families? Mine's a couple thousand miles away right now, so the phone call seemed the best way."

"I'd just like you to explain . . ." Now she waved the papers. "All this."

"I know. You're a demon for explanations." He stopped long enough to grab her hair, crush his mouth to hers. "If that doesn't make it clear enough, I'm doing something wrong. Later."

"THEN HE JUST WALKED AWAY, LEAVING ME STAND-ing there like an idiot." Still stewing hours later, Stella changed Lily's diaper while Hayley finished dressing for dinner.

"You said you thought you should meet each other's families and stuff," Hayley pointed out. "So now you talked to his mama, and he talked to your daddy."

"I know what I said, but he just went tromping over

there. And he had her call me without letting me know first. He just goes off, at the drop of a hat." She picked up Lily, cuddled her. "He gets me stirred up."

"I kinda miss getting stirred up that way." She turned sideways in the mirror, sighed a little over the post-birth pudge she was carrying. "I guess I thought, even though the books said different, that everything would just spring back where it was after Lily came out."

"Nothing much springs after having a baby. But you're young and active. You'll get your body back."

"I hope." She reached for her favorite silver hoops while Stella nuzzled Lily. "Stella, I'm going to tell you something, because you're my best friend and I love you."

"Oh, sweetie."

"Well, it's true. Last week, when Logan came by to bring Lily her doll, and you and the boys came outside? Before I went in and he popped the big Q? You know what the four of you looked like?"

"No."

"A family. And I think whatever your head's running around with, in your heart you know that. And that that's the way it's going to be."

"You're awfully young to be such a know-it-all."

"It's not the years, it's the miles." Hayley tossed a cloth over her shoulder. "Come here, baby girl. Mama's going to show you off to the dinner guests before you go to sleep. You ready?" she asked Stella.

"I guess we'll find out."

They started toward the stairs, with Stella gathering her boys on the way, and met Roz on the landing.

"Well, don't we all look fine."

"We had to wear new shirts," Luke complained.

"And you look so handsome in them. I wonder if I can be greedy and steal both these well-dressed young men as my escorts." She held out both her hands for theirs. "It's going to storm," she said with a glance out the window. "And look here, I believe that must be our Dr. Carnegie, and right on time. What in the world is that man driving? It looks like a rusty red box on wheels."

"I think it's a Volvo." Hayley moved in to spy over Roz's shoulder. "A really old Volvo. They're like one of the safest cars, and so dopey-looking, they're cool. Oh, my, look at that!" Her eyebrows lifted when Mitch got out of the car. "Serious hottie alert."

"Good God, Hayley, he's old enough to be your daddy." Hayley just smiled at Roz. "Hot's hot. And he's hot."

"Maybe he needs a drink of water," Luke suggested.

"And we'll get one for Hayley, too." Amused, Roz walked down to greet her first guest.

He brought a good white wine as a hostess gift, which she approved of, but he opted for mineral water when she offered him a drink. She supposed a man who drove a car manufactured about the same time he'd been born needed to keep his wits about him. He made appropriate noises over the baby, shook hands soberly with the boys.

She gave him points for tact when he settled into small talk rather than asking more about the reason she wanted to hire him.

By the time Logan arrived, they were comfortable enough.

"I don't think we'll wait for Harper." Roz got to her feet. "My son is chronically late, and often missing in action."

"I've got one of my own," Mitch said. "I know how it goes."

"Oh, I didn't realize you had children."

"Just the one. Josh is twenty. He goes to college here. You really do have a beautiful home, Ms. Harper."

"Roz, and thank you. It's one of my great loves. And here," she added as Harper dashed in from the kitchen, "is another."

"Late. Sorry. Almost forgot. Hey, Logan, Stella. Hi, guys." He kissed his mother, then looked at Hayley. "Hi. Where's Lily?"

"Sleeping."

"Dr. Carnegie, my tardy son, Harper."

"Sorry. I hope I didn't hold you up."

"Not at all," Mitch said as they shook hands. "Happy to meet you."

"Why don't we sit down? It looks like David's outdone himself."

An arrangement of summer flowers in a long, low bowl centered the table. Candles burned, slim white tapers in gleaming silver, on the sideboard. David had used her white-on-white china with pale yellow and green linens for casual elegance. A cool and artful lobster salad was already arranged on each plate. David sailed in with wine.

"Who can I interest in this very nice Pinot Grigio?"

The doctor, Roz noted, stuck with mineral water.

"You know," Harper began as they enjoyed the main course of stuffed pork, "you look awfully familiar." He narrowed his eyes on Mitch's face. "I've been trying to figure it out. You didn't teach at the U of M while I was there, did you?"

"I might have, but I don't recall you being in any of my classes."

"No. I don't think that's it anyway. Maybe I went to one of your lectures or something. Wait. Wait. I've got it. Josh Carnegie. Power forward for the Memphis Tigers."

"My son."

"Strong resemblance. Man, he's a killer. I was at the game last spring, against South Carolina, when he scored thirty-eight points. He's got moves."

Mitch smiled, rubbed a thumb over the fading bruise on his jaw. "Tell me."

Conversation turned to basketball, boisterously, and gave Logan the opportunity to lean toward Stella. "Your daddy says he's looking forward to seeing you and the boys on Sunday. I'll drive you in, as I've got an invitation to Sunday dinner, too."

"Is that so?"

"He likes me." He picked up her free hand, brushed his lips over his fingers. "We're bonding over oleanders."

She didn't try to stop the smile. "You hit him where it counts."

"You, the kids, his garden. Yeah, I'd say I got it covered. You write that list for me yet, Red?"

"Apparently you're doing fine crossing things off without consulting me."

His grin flashed. "Jolene thinks we should go traditional and have a June wedding."

When Stella's mouth dropped open, he turned away to talk to her kids about the latest issues of Marvel Comics.

Over dessert, a rustling, then a long, shrill cry sounded from the baby monitor standing on the buffet. Hayley popped up as if she were on springs. "That's my cue. I'll be back down after she's fed and settled again."

"Speaking of cues." Stella rose as well. "Time for bed, guys. School night," she added even before the protests could be voiced.

"Going to bed before it's dark is a gyp," Gavin complained.

"I know. Life is full of them. What comes next?"

Gavin heaved a sigh. "Thanks for dinner, it was really good, and now we have to go to bed because of stupid school."

"Close enough," Stella decided.

"'Night. I liked the finger potatoes 'specially," Luke said to David.

"Want a hand?" Logan called out.

"No." But she stopped at the doorway, turned back and just looked at him a moment. "But thanks."

She herded them up, beginning the nightly ritual as thunder rumbled in. And Parker scooted under Luke's bed to hide from it. Rain splatted, fat juicy drops, against the windows as she tucked them in.

"Parker's a scaredy-cat." Luke snuggled his head in the pillow. "Can he sleep up here tonight?"

"All right, just for tonight, so he isn't afraid." She lured him out from under the bed, and stroking him as he trembled, laid him in with Luke. "Is that better now?"

"Uh-huh. Mom?" He broke off, petting the dog, and exchanging a long look with his brother.

"What? What are you two cooking up?"

"You ask her," Luke hissed.

"Nuh-uh. You."

"You."

"Ask me what? If you've spent all your allowances and work money on comics, I—"

"Are you going to marry Logan?" Gavin blurted out.

"Am I—where did you get an idea like that?"

"We heard Roz and Hayley talking about how he asked you to." Luke yawned, blinked sleepily at her. "So are you?"

She sat on the side of Gavin's bed. "I've been thinking about it. But I wouldn't decide something that important without talking to both of you. It's a lot to think about, for all of us, a lot to discuss."

"He's nice, and he plays with us, so it's okay if you do."

Stella let out a laugh at Luke's rundown. All right, she thought, maybe not such a lot to discuss from certain points of view.

"Marriage is a very big deal. It's a really big promise."

"Would we go live in his house?" Luke wondered.

"Yes, I suppose we would if . . ."

"We like it there. And I like when he holds me upside down. And he got the splinter out of my finger, and it hardly hurt at all. He even kissed it after, just like he's supposed to."

"Did he?" she murmured.

"He'd be our stepdad." Gavin drew lazy circles with his finger on top of his sheet. "Like we have Nana Jo for a stepgrandmother. She loves us."

"She certainly does."

"So we decided it'd be okay to have a stepdad, if it's Logan."

"I can see you've given this a lot of thought," Stella managed. "And I'm going to think about it, too. Maybe we'll talk about it more tomorrow." She kissed Gavin's cheek.

"Logan said Dad's always watching out for us."

Tears burned the back of her eyes. "Yes. Oh, yes, he is, baby."

She hugged him, hard, then turned to hug Luke. "Good night. I'll be right downstairs."

But she walked through to her room first to catch her breath, compose herself. Treasures, she thought. She had the most precious treasures. She pressed her fingers to her eyes and thought of Kevin. A treasure she'd lost.

Logan said Dad's always watching out for us.

A man who would know that, would accept that and say those words to a young boy was another kind of treasure.

He'd changed the pattern on her. He'd planted a bold blue dahlia in the middle of her quiet garden. And she wasn't digging it out.

"I'm going to marry him," she heard herself say, and laughed at the thrill of it.

Through the next boom of thunder, she heard the singing. Instinctively, she stepped into the bath, to look into her sons' room. She was there, ghostly in billowing white, her hair a tangle of dull gold. She stood between the beds, her voice calm and sweet, her eyes insane as she stared through the flash of lightning at Stella.

Fear trickled down Stella's back. She stepped forward, and was shoved back by a blast of cold.

"No." She raced forward again, and hit a solid wall. "No!" She battered at it. "You won't keep me from my babies." She flung herself against the frigid shield, screaming for her children who slept on, undisturbed.

"You bitch! Don't you touch them."

She ran out of the room, ignoring Hayley, who raced down toward her, ignoring the clatter of feet on the stairs. She knew only one thing. She had to get to her children, she had to get through the barrier and get to her boys.

At a full run she hit the open doorway, and was knocked back against the far wall.

"What the hell's going on?" Logan grabbed her, pushing her aside as he rushed the room himself.

"She won't let me in." Desperate, Stella beat her fists against the cold until her hands were raw and numb. "She's got my babies. Help me."

Logan rammed his shoulder against the opening. "It's like fucking steel." Rammed it again as Harper and David hit it with him.

Behind them, Mitch stared into the room, at the figure in white, who glowed now with a wild light. "Name of God."

"There has to be another way. The other door." Roz grabbed Mitch's arm and pulled him down the hall.

"This ever happen before?"

"No. Dear God. Hayley, keep the baby away."

Frantic, her hands throbbing from pounding, Stella ran. Another way, she thought. Force wouldn't work. She could beat against that invisible ice, rage and threaten, but it wouldn't crack.

Oh, please, God, her babies.

Reason. She would try reason and begging and promises. She dashed out into the rain, yanked open the terrace doors. And though she knew better, hurled herself at the opening.

"You can't have them!" she shouted over the storm. "They're mine. Those are my children. My life." She went down on her knees, ill with fear. She could see her boys sleeping still, and the hard, white light pulsing from the woman between them.

She thought of the dream. She thought of what she and her boys had talked about shortly before the singing. "It's not your business what I do." She struggled to keep her voice firm. "Those are my children, and I'll do what's best for them. You're not their mother."

The light seemed to waver, and when the figure turned, there was as much sorrow as madness in her eyes. "They're not yours. They need me. They need their mother. Flesh and blood."

She held up her hands, scraped and bruised from the beating. "You want me to bleed for them? I will. I am." On her knees, she pressed her palms to the cold while the rain sluiced over her.

"They belong to me, and there's nothing I won't do to keep them safe, to keep them happy. I'm sorry for what happened to you. Whatever it was, whoever you lost, I'm sorry. But you can't have what's mine. You can't take my children from me. You can't take me from my children."

Stella pushed her hand out, and it slid through as if slipping through ice water. Without hesitation, she shoved into the room.

She could see beyond her, Logan still fighting to get through, Stella pressed against the other doorway. She couldn't hear them, but she could see the anguish on Logan's face, and that his hands were bleeding.

"He loves them. He might not have known until tonight, but he loves them. He'll protect them. He'll be a father to them, one they deserve. This is my choice, our choice. Don't ever try to keep me from my children again."

There were tears now as the figure flowed across the room toward the terrace doors. Stella laid a trembling hand on Gavin's head, on Luke's. Safe, she thought as her knees began to shake. Safe and warm.

"I'll help you," she stated firmly, meeting the grieving eyes again. "We all will. If you want our help, give us something. Your name, at least. Tell me your name."

The Bride began to fade, but she lifted a hand to the glass of the door. There, written in rain that dripped like tears, was a single word.

Amelia

When Logan burst through the door behind her, Stella spun toward him, laid a hand quickly on his lips. "Ssh. You'll wake them."

Then she buried her face against his chest and wept.

epilogue

"Amelia." Stella shivered, despite the dry clothes and the brandy Roz had insisted on. "Her name. I saw it written on the glass of the door just before she vanished. She wasn't going to hurt them. She was furious with me, was protecting them from me. She's not altogether sane."

"You're all right?" Logan stayed crouched in front of her. "You're sure?"

She nodded, but she drank more brandy. "It's going to take a little while to come down from it, but yes, I'm okay."

"I've never been so scared." Hayley looked toward the stairs. "Are you sure all the kids are safe?"

"She would never hurt them." Stella laid a reassuring hand on Hayley's. "Something broke her heart, and her mind, I think. But children are her only joy."

"You'll excuse me if I find this absolutely fascinating, and completely crazy." Mitch paced back and forth across the floor. "If I hadn't seen it with my own eyes—" He shook his head. "I'm going to need all the data you can put together, once I'm able to get started on this."

He stopped pacing, stared at Roz. "I can't rationalize it. I saw it, but I can't rationalize it. An . . . I'll call it an entity, for lack of better. An entity was in that room. The room was sealed off." Absently he rubbed his shoulder where he'd rammed against the solid air. "And she was inside it."

"It was more of a show than we expected to give you on

your first visit," Roz said, and poured him another cup of coffee.

"You're very cool about it," he replied.

"Of all of us here, I've lived with her the longest."

"How?" Mitch asked.

"Because this is my house." She looked tired, and pale, but there was a battle light in her eyes. "Her being here doesn't change that. This is my house." She took a little breath and a sip of brandy herself. "Though I'll admit that what happened tonight shook me, shook all of us. I've never seen anything like what happened upstairs."

"I have to finish the project I'm working on, then I'm going to want to know everything you have seen." Mitch's eyes scanned the room. "All of you."

"All right, we'll see about arranging that."

"Stella ought to lie down," Logan said.

"No, I'm fine, really." She glanced toward the monitor, listened to the quiet hum. "I feel like what happened tonight changed something. In her, in me. The dreams, the blue dahlia."

"Blue dahlia?" Mitch interrupted, but Stella shook her head.

"I'll explain when I feel a little steadier. But I don't think I'll be having them anymore. I think she'll let it alone, let it grow there because I got through to her. And I believe, absolutely, it was because I got through mother to mother."

"My children grew up in this house. She never tried to block me from them."

"You hadn't decided to get married when your sons were still children," Stella announced, and watched Logan's eyes narrow.

"Haven't you missed some steps?" he asked.

She managed a weary smile. "Not any important ones, apparently. As for the Bride, maybe her husband left her, or she was pregnant by a lover who deserted her, or . . . I don't know. I can't think very clearly."

"None of us can, and whether or not you think you're

fine, you're still pale." Roz got to her feet. "I'm going to take you upstairs and put you to bed."

She shook her head when Logan started to protest. "You're all welcome to stay as long as you like. Harper?"

"Right." Understanding his cue, and his duty, he got to his feet. "Can I get anyone another drink?"

Because she was still unsteady, Stella let Roz take her upstairs. "I guess I am tired, but you don't have to come up."

"After a trauma like that, you deserve a little pampering. I imagine Logan would like the job, but tonight I think a woman's the better option. Go on, get undressed now," Roz told her as she turned down the bed.

As the shock eased and made room for fatigue, Stella did what she was told, then slipped through the bathroom to take a last look at her children for the night. "I was so afraid. So afraid I wouldn't get to my boys."

"You were stronger than she was. You've always been stronger."

"Nothing's ever ripped at me like that. Not even . . ." Stella moved back to her room, slipped into bed. "The night Kevin died, there was nothing I could do. I couldn't get to him, bring him back, stop what had already happened, no matter how much I wanted to."

"And tonight you could do something, and did. Women, women like us at any rate, we do what has to be done. I want you to rest now. I'll check on you and the boys myself before I go to bed. Do you want me to leave the light on?"

"No, I'll be fine. Thanks."

"We're right downstairs."

In the quiet dark, Stella sighed. She lay still, listening, waiting. But she heard nothing but the sound of her own breathing.

For tonight—at least for tonight—it was over.

When she closed her eyes, she drifted to sleep.

Dreamlessly.

*   *   *

SHE EXPECTED LOGAN TO COME BY THE NURSERY THE next day. But he didn't. She was certain he would come by the house before dinner. But he didn't.

Nor did he call.

She decided that after the night before he'd needed a break. From her, from the house, from any sort of drama. How could she blame him?

He'd pounded his hands, his big, hard hands, bloody from trying to get to her boys, then to her. She knew all she needed to know about him now, about the man she'd grown to love and respect.

Knew enough to trust him with everything that was hers. Loved him enough to wait until he came to her.

And when her children were in bed, and the moon began to rise, his truck rumbled up the drive to Harper House.

This time she didn't hesitate, but dashed to the door to meet him.

"I'm glad you're here." She threw her arms around him first, held tight when his wrapped around her. "So glad. We really need to talk."

"Come on out first. I got something in the truck for you."

"Can't it wait?" She eased back. "If we could just sit down and get some things aired out. I'm not sure I made any sense last night."

"You made plenty of sense." To settle it, he gripped her hand, pulled her outside. "Seeing as after you scared ten years off my life, you said you were going to marry me. Didn't have the opportunity to follow through on that then, the way things were. I've got something to give you before you start talking me to death."

"Maybe you don't want to hear that I love you."

"I can take time for that." Grabbing her, he lifted her off her feet and circled them both to the truck. "You going to organize my life, Red?"

"I'm going to try. Are you going to disorganize mine?"

"No question about it." He lowered her until her lips met his.

"Hell of a storm last night—in every possible sense," she said as she rested her cheek against his. "It's over now."

"This one is. There'll be others." He took her hands, kissed them, then just looked down at her in the dusky light of the moon.

"I love you, Stella. I'm going to make you happy even when I irritate the living hell out of you. And the boys . . . Last night, when I saw her in there with them, when I couldn't get to them—"

"I know." Now she lifted his hands to kiss his raw, swollen knuckles. "One day, when they're older, they'll fully appreciate how lucky they are to have had two such good men for fathers. I know how lucky I am to love and be loved by two such good men."

"I figured that out when I started falling for you."

"When was that?"

"On the way to Graceland."

"You don't waste time."

"That's when you told me about the dream you'd had."

Her heart fluttered. "The garden. The blue dahlia."

"Then later, when you said you'd had another, told me about it, it just got me thinking. So . . ." He reached into the cab of the truck, took out a small pot with a grafted plant. "I asked Harper if he'd work on this."

"A dahlia," she whispered. "A blue dahlia."

"He's pretty sure it'll bloom blue when it matures. Kid's got a knack."

Tears burned into her eyes and smeared her voice. "I was going to dig it up, Logan. She kept pushing me to, and it seemed she was right. It wasn't what I'd put there, wasn't what I'd planned, no matter how beautiful it was. And when I did, when I dug it up, it died. It was so stupid of me."

"We'll dig this one in instead. We can plant this, you and me, and the four of us can plant a garden around it. That suit you?"

She lifted her hands, cupped his face. "It suits me."

"That's good, because Harper worked like a mad scientist on it, shooting for a deep, true blue. I guess we'll wait and see what we get when it blooms."

"You're right." She looked up at him. "We'll see what we get."

"He gave me the go-ahead to name it. So it'll be Stella's Dream."

Now her heart swirled into her eyes. "I was wrong about you, Logan. You're perfect after all."

She cradled the pot in her arm as if it were a child, precious and new. Then taking his hand, she linked fingers so they could walk in the moon-drenched garden together.

In the house, in the air perfumed with flowers, another walked. And wept.

Turn the page for a look at

bLack roSe

the second book in the
IN THE GARDEN TRILOGY.
Coming in June from Jove Books.

chapter one

Harper House
December, 2004

DAWN, THE AWAKENING PROMISE OF IT, WAS HER favorite time to run. The running itself was just something that had to be done, three days a week, like any other chore or responsibility. Rosalind Harper did what had to be done.

She ran for her health. A woman who'd just had—she could hardly say *celebrated* at this stage of her life—her forty-fifth birthday had to mind her health. She ran to keep strong, as she desired and needed strength. And she ran for vanity. Her body would never again be what it had been at twenty, or even thirty, but by God, it would be the best body she could manage at forty-five.

She had no husband, no lover, but she did have an image to uphold. She was a Harper, and Harpers had their pride.

But, Jesus, maintenance was a bitch.

Wearing sweats against the dawn chill, she slipped out of her bedroom by the terrace door. The house was still sleeping. Her house that had been too empty was now occupied again, and rarely completely quiet any longer.

There was David, her surrogate son, who kept her house in order, kept her entertained when she needed entertaining, and stayed out of her way when she needed solitude.

No one knew her moods quite like David.

And there was Stella and her two precious boys. It had been a good day, Roz thought as she limbered up on the terrace, when she'd hired Stella Rothchild to manage her nursery.

Of course, Stella would be moving before much longer and taking those sweet boys with her. Still, once Stella was married to Logan—and wasn't that a fine match—they'd only be a few miles away.

Hayley would still be here, infusing the house with all that youth and energy. It had been another stroke of luck, and a vague and distant family connection, that had Hayley, then six months pregnant, landing on her doorstep. In Hayley she had the daughter she'd secretly longed for, and the bonus of an honorary grandchild with the darling little Lily.

She hadn't realized how lonely she'd been, Stella thought, until those girls had come along to fill the void. With two of her own three sons moved away, the house had become too big, too quiet. And a part of her dreaded the day when Harper, her firstborn, her rock, would leave the guest house a stone's throw from the main.

But that was life. No one knew better than a gardener that life never stayed static. Cycles were necessary, for without them there was no bloom.

She took the stairs down at an easy jog, enjoying the way the early mists shrouded her winter gardens. Look how pretty her lambs ear was with its soft silvery foliage covered in dew. And the birds had yet to bother the bright fruit on her red chokeberry.

Walking to give her muscles time to warm, and to give herself the pleasure of the gardens, she skirted around the side of the house to the front.

She increased to a jog on the way down the drive, a tall, willowy woman with a short, careless cap of black hair. Her eyes, a honeyed whisky brown, scanned the grounds—the towering magnolias, the delicate dogwoods, the placement of ornamental shrubs, the flood of pansies she'd planted only weeks before, and the beds that would wait a bit longer to break into bloom.

To her mind, there were no grounds in western Tennessee that could compete with Harper House. Just as there was no house that could compare with its dignified elegance.

Out of habit, she turned at the end of the drive and jogged in place to study it in the pearly mists.

It stood grandly, she thought, with its melding of Greek Revival and Gothic styles, the warm yellow stone mellow against the clean white trim. Its double staircase rose up to the balcony wrapping the second level, and served as a crown for the covered entryway on the ground level.

She loved the tall windows, the lacy woodwork on the rail of the third floor, the sheer space of it, and the heritage it stood for.

She had prized it, cared for it, and worked for it since it had come into her hands at her parents' death. She had raised her sons there, and when she'd lost her husband, she'd grieved there.

One day she would pass it to Harper as it had passed to her. And she thanked God for the absolute knowledge that he would tend it and love it just as she did.

What it had cost her was nothing compared with what it gave, even in this single moment, standing at the end of the drive, looking back through the morning mists.

But standing there wasn't going to get her three miles done. She headed west, keeping close to the side of the road though there'd be little to no traffic this early.

To take her mind off the annoyance of exercise, she started reviewing her list of things to do that day.

She had some good seedlings going for annuals that should be ready to have their seed leaves removed. She needed to check all the seedlings for signs of damping off. Some of the older stock would be ready for pricking off.

And, she remembered, Stella had asked for more amaryllis, more forced bulb planters, more wreaths and poinsettia for the holiday sales. Hayley could handle the wreaths. The girl had a good hand at crafting.

Then there were the field-grown Christmas trees and hollies to deal with. Thank God she could leave that end to Logan.

She had to check with Harper, to see if he had any more of the Christmas cacti he'd grafted ready to go. She wanted a couple for herself.

She juggled all the nursery business in her mind even as she passed In the Garden. It was tempting—it always was—to veer off the road onto that crushed stone entryway, to take an indulgent solo tour of what she'd built from the ground up.

Stella had gone all out for the holidays, Roz noted with pleasure, grouping green, pink, white, and red poinsettias into a pool of seasonal color in front of the low-slung house that served as the entrance to the retail space. She'd hung yet another wreath on the door, tiny white lights around it, and the small white pine she'd dug from the field stood decorated on the front porch.

White-faced pansies, glossy hollies, and hardy sage added more interest and would help ring up those holiday sales.

Resisting temptation, Roz continued down the road.

She had to carve out some time, if not today then certainly later this week, to finish up her Christmas shopping. Or at least put a bigger dent in it. There were holiday parties to attend, and the one she'd decided to give. It had been awhile since she'd opened the house to entertain in a big way.

The divorce, she admitted, was at least partially to blame for that. She'd hardly felt like hosting parties when she'd felt stupid and stung and more than a bit mortified by her foolish, and mercifully brief, union to a liar and a cheat.

But it was time to put that aside now, she reminded herself, just as she'd put him aside. The fact that Bryce Clerk was back in Memphis made it only more important that she live her life, publically and privately, exactly as she chose.

At the mile-and-a-half mark, a point she judged by an old, lightning-struck hickory, she started back. The thin fog had dampened her hair and sweatshirt, but her muscles felt warm and loose. It was a bitch, she mused, that everything they said about exercise was true.

She spotted a deer meandering across the road, her coat thickened for winter, her eyes on alert at the intrusion of a human.

You're beautiful, Roz thought, puffing a little on the last half mile. Now stay the hell out of my gardens. Another note went in her file to give her gardens another treatment of repellant before the deer and its pals decided to come around for a snack.

She was just making the turn into the drive when she heard muffled footsteps, then saw the figure coming her way. Even with the mists she had no trouble identifying the other early riser.

They both stopped and jogged in place, and she grinned at her son.

"Up with the worms this morning."

"Thought I'd be up and out early enough to catch you." He scooped a hand through his dark hair. "All that celebrating for Thanksgiving, then your birthday, I figured I'd better work off the excess before Christmas hits."

"You never gain an ounce. It's annoying."

"Feel soft." He rolled his shoulders, then his eyes, whiskey brown like hers, and laughed. "Besides, I gotta keep up with my mama."

He looked like her. There was no denying her stamp was on his face. But when he smiled, she saw his father. "That'll be the day, pal of mine. How far you going?"

"How far'd you?"

"Three miles."

He flashed a grin. "Then I'll do four." He gave her a light pat on the cheek as he passed.

"Should've told him five, just to get his goat," she chuckled, and slowing to a cool-down walk, she started down the drive.

The house shimmered out of the mists. She thought, Thank God that's over for another day. And she circled around to go in as she'd left.

The house was still quiet, and lovely. And haunted.

She'd showered and changed for work, and had started down the central stairs that bisected the wings when she heard the first stirrings.

Stella's boys getting ready for school, Lily fussing for her breakfast—good sounds, Roz thought. Busy, family sounds she'd missed.

Of course, she'd had the house full only a couple weeks earlier, with all her boys home for Thanksgiving and her birthday. Austin and Mason would be back for Christmas. A mother of grown sons couldn't ask for better.

God knew there'd been plenty of times when they'd been growing up that she'd yearned for some quiet. Just an hour of absolute peace where she had nothing more exciting to do than soak in a hot tub.

Then she'd had too much time on her hands, hadn't she? Too much quiet, too much empty space. So she'd ended up marrying some slick son of a bitch who'd helped himself to her money so he could impress the bimbos he'd cheated on her with.

Spilled milk, Roz reminded herself. And it wasn't constructive to dwell on it.

She walked into the kitchen where David was already whipping something in a bowl, and the seductive fragrance of fresh coffee filled the air.

"Morning, gorgeous. How's my best girl?"

"Up and at 'em anyway." She went to a cupboard for a mug. "How was the date last night?"

"Promising. He likes Gray Goose martinis and John Waters movies. We'll try for a second round this weekend. Sit yourself down. I'm making French toast."

"French toast?" It was a personal weakness. "Damn it, David, I just ran three miles to keep my ass from falling all the way to the back of my knees, then you hit me with French toast."

"You have a beautiful ass, and it's nowhere near the back of your knees."

"Yet," she muttered, but she sat. "I passed Harper at the end of the drive. He finds out what's on the menu, he'll be sniffing at the back door."

"I'm making plenty."

She sipped her coffee while he heated up the skillet.

He was movie-star handsome, only a year older than her own Harper, and one of the delights of her life. As a boy he'd run tame in her house, and now he all but ran it.

"David . . . I caught myself thinking about Bryce twice this morning. What do you think that means?"

"Means you need this French toast," he said while he soaked thick slices of bread in his magic batter. "And you've probably got yourself a case of the mid-holiday blues."

"I kicked him out right before Christmas. I guess that's it."

"And a merry one it was, with that bastard out in the cold. I wish it *had* been cold," he added. "Raining ice and frogs and pestilence."

"I'm going to ask you something I never did while it was going on. Why didn't you ever tell me how much you disliked him?"

"Probably the same reason you didn't tell me how much you disliked that out-of-work actor with the fake Brit accent I thought I was crazy about a few years back. I love you."

"It's a good reason."

He'd started a fire in the little kitchen hearth, so she angled her body toward it, sipped coffee, felt steady and solid.

"You know if you could just age twenty years and go straight, we could live with each other in sin. I think that would be just fine."

"Sugar-pie." He slid the bread into the skillet. "You're the only girl in the world who'd tempt me."

She smiled, and resting her elbow on the table, set her

chin on her fist. "Sun's breaking through," she stated. "It's going to be a pretty day."

A PRETTY DAY IN EARLY DECEMBER MEANT A BUSY ONE for a garden center. Roz had so much to do she was grateful she hadn't resisted the breakfast David had heaped on her. She missed lunch.

In her propagation house, she had a full table covered with seed trays. She'd already separated out specimens too young for pricking off. And now began the first transplanting with those she deemed ready.

She lined up her containers, the cell packs, the individual pots or peat cubes. It was one of her favorite tasks, even more than sowing, this placing of a strong seedling in the home it would occupy until planting time.

Until planting time, they were all hers.

And this year, she was experimenting with her own potting soil. She'd been trying out recipes for more than two years now, and believed she'd found a winner, both for indoor and outdoor use. The outdoor recipe should serve very well for her greenhouse purposes.

From the bag she'd carefully mixed, she filled her containers, tested the moisture and approved. With care, she lifted out the young plants, holding them by their seed leaves. Transplanting, she made certain the soil line on the stem was at the same level it had been in the seed tray, then firmed the soil around the roots with experienced fingers.

She filled pot after pot, labeling as she went and humming absently to the Enya music playing gently from the portable CD player she considered essential equipment in a greenhouse.

Using a weak fertilizer solution, she watered them.

Pleased with the progress, she moved through the back opening and into the perennial area. She checked the section—plants recently started from cuttings, those started more than a year before that would be ready for sale in a few months. She watered, and tended, then moved to stock plants to take more cuttings. She had a tray of anemones begun when Stella stepped in.

"You've been busy." Stella, with her curling red hair bundled back in a ponytail, scanned the tables. "Really busy."

"And optimistic. We had a banner season, and I'm expecting we'll have another. If Nature doesn't screw around with us."

"I thought you might want to take a look at the new stock of wreaths. Hayley's worked on them all morning. I think she outdid herself."

"I'll take a look before I leave."

"I let her go early, I hope that's all right. She's still getting used to having Lily with a sitter, even if the sitter is a customer and only a half mile away."

"That's fine." She moved on to the catananche. "You know you don't have to check every little thing with me, Stella. You've been managing this ship for nearly a year now."

"They were excuses to come back here."

Roz paused, her knife suspended above the plant roots, primed for cutting. "Is there a problem?"

"No. I've been wanting to ask, and I know this is your domain, but I wondered if when things slow down a bit after the holidays, if I can spend some time with the propagation. I'm missing it."

"All right."

Stella's bright blue eyes twinkled when she laughed. "I can see you're worried I'll try to change your routine, organize everything my way. I promise I won't. And I won't get in your way."

"You try, I'll just boot you out."

"Got that."

"Meanwhile, I've been wanting to talk to you. I need you to find me a supplier for good, inexpensive soil bags. One-, five-, ten-, and twenty-five-pound to start."

"For?" Stella asked as she pulled a notebook out of her back pocket.

"I'm going to start making and selling my own potting soil. I've got mixes I like for indoor and outdoor use, and I want to private label it."

"That's a great idea. Good profit in that. And customers will like having Rosalind Harper's gardening secrets. There are some considerations, though."

"I thought of them. I'm not going to go hog-wild right off. We'll keep it small." With soil on her hands still, she plucked a bottle of water from a shelf. Then, absently wiping her hand on her shirt, twisted the cap. "I want the staff to learn how to bag, but the recipe's my secret. I'll give you and Harper the ingredients and the amounts, but it doesn't go out to the general staff. For right now, we'll set up the procedure in the main storage shed. It takes off, we'll build one for it."

"Government regulations—"

"I've studied on that. We won't be using any pesticides, and I'm keeping the nutrient content to below the regulatory levels." Noting Stella continue to scribble on her pad, Roz took a long drink. "I've applied for the license to manufacture and sell."

"You didn't mention it."

"Don't get your feelings hurt." Roz set the bottle aside, dipped a cutting in rooting medium. "I wasn't sure I'd go on and do the thing, but I wanted the red tape out of the way. It's kind of a pet project of mine I've been playing with for awhile now. But I've grown some specimens in these mixes, and so far I like what I see. I got some more going now, and if I keep liking it, we're going for it. So I want an idea how much the bags are going to run us, and the printing. I want classy. I thought you could fiddle around with some logos and such. You're good at that. In the Garden needs to be prominent."

"No question."

"And you know what I'd really like?" She paused for a minute, seeing it in her head. "I'd like brown bags. Something that looks like burlap. Old-fashioned, if you follow me. So we're saying, This is good, old-fashioned, dirt, southern soil. And I'm thinking I want cottage garden flowers on the bag. Simple flowers."

"That says, This is simple to use, and it'll make your garden simple to grow. I'll get on it."

"I can count on you, can't I, to work out the costs, profits, marketing angles with me?"

"I'm your girl."

"I know you are. I'm going to finish up these cuttings, then take off early myself if nothing's up. I want to get some shopping in."

"Roz, it's already nearly five."

"Five? It can't be five." She held up an arm, turned her wrist and frowned at her watch. "Well, shit. Time got away from me again. Tell you what, I'm going to take off at noon tomorrow. If I don't, you hunt me down and push me out."

"No problem. I'd better get back. See you back at the house."

An all-new bouquet of novels from
#1 *New York Times* bestselling author

Nora Roberts

Don't miss the rest
of the
~IN THE GARDEN~
trilogy:

The official
Nora Roberts
seal guarantees
that these are
new books

~Black Rose~
coming June 2005

~Red Lily~
coming November 2005

Three women at a crossroads in their lives find in
each other the courage to embrace the future.

J989

NORA ROBERTS

NR

NORTHERN LIGHTS

PUTNAM

Now Available in Paperback

NORA ROBERTS

BIRTHRIGHT

JOVE
0-515-13711-1

#1 NEW YORK TIMES BESTSELLING AUTHOR
NORA ROBERTS
Remember When
J.D. ROBB
FIRST TIME IN PAPERBACK